MYSTERIES BY

...NER OF

...SSOCIATION

MUSE MEDALLION

SHIRLEY ROUSSEAU MURPHY

"**M**urphy's surefire plotting makes this more than just another cute cat cozy."

Publishers Weekly

"**W**ith an uncanny understanding of a cat's behavior and personality quirks, Murphy has created a series of suspense yarns that not only capture the feline 'attitude' but offer a satisfying read. Cat lovers, you'll be nodding your head in agreement as you follow the adventures of this threesome!"

The Californian

"**E**xcellent. . . . The combination of interesting human characters and cats with human characteristics ensures that these Joe Grey mysteries will stay popular for many years to come."

Tampa Tribune

"**T**ry the Joe Grey series. . . . It is entertaining to see cat behavior from the inside out."

Houston Chronicle

"**A** must-read for those who en-

By Shirley Rousseau Murphy

CAT STRIKING BACK
CAT PLAYING CUPID
CAT DECK THE HALLS
CAT PAY THE DEVIL
CAT BREAKING FREE
CAT CROSS THEIR GRAVES
CAT FEAR NO EVIL
CAT SEEING DOUBLE
CAT LAUGHING LAST
CAT SPITTING MAD
CAT TO THE DOGS
CAT IN THE DARK
CAT RAISE THE DEAD
CAT UNDER FIRE
CAT ON THE EDGE
THE CATSWORLD PORTAL

CAT PLAYING
CUPID

A JOE GREY MYSTERY

SHIRLEY
ROUSSEAU
MURPHY

AVON
An Imprint of HarperCollinsPublishers

This book is a work of fiction. The characters, incidents, and dialogue are drawn from the author's imagination and are not to be construed as real. Any resemblance to actual events or persons, living or dead, is entirely coincidental.

AVON BOOKS
An Imprint of HarperCollins*Publishers*
10 East 53rd Street
New York, New York 10022-5299

Copyright © 2009 by Shirley Rousseau Murphy
ISBN 978-0-06-112398-6
www.avonmystery.com

First Avon Books paperback printing: January 2010
First William Morrow hardcover printing: February 2009

Avon Trademark Reg. U.S. Pat. Off. and in Other Countries, Marca Registrada, Hecho en U.S.A.
HarperCollins® is a registered trademark of HarperCollins Publishers.

Printed in the U.S.A.

10 9 8 7 6 5 4 3 2 1

Cupid drew from his quiver two arrows of different workmanship—one to excite love, the other to repel it. The former was of gold and sharp pointed, the latter blunt and tipped with lead. With the leaden shaft he struck the nymph Daphne . . . and with the golden one [he pierced] Apollo . . . Forthwith the god was seized with love for the maiden, but she, more than ever, abhorred the thought of loving.

Charles Mills Gayley,
The Classic Myths in English Literature and in Art,
1893, Ginn and Company

ACKNOWLEDGMENTS

I want to thank Dr. Alyce Wolford for her understanding comments. Any errors or deviations are mine.

CAT PLAYING
CUPID

1

THE NEWSPAPER CLIPPING was yellowed and tearing at the folds, though it had been handled carefully over the years by the detectives who worked the case or who, during the preceding decade, had taken a fresh look at the cold file, reading the missing report on Carson Chappell, and making additional inquiries. Unable to come up with any new leads, each had committed the folder once again to limbo among the department's unresolved cases.

BRIDEGROOM VANISHES BEFORE WEDDING

Local resident Carson Chappell, senior partner of the accounting firm of Chappell & Gibbs, did not appear for his wedding on Sunday afternoon at Community Church and has not been heard from for nearly a week. His fiancée, Lindsey Wolf, also of Molena Point, told reporters she last saw Chappell five days earlier, when he set out alone on a camping trip into state park land east of the village . . .

The file contained a dozen such articles clipped from central California papers, as well as the detective's original interview with the would-be bride, his case notes, random notes by the various officers who had later studied the case, and several human-interest pieces published over the intervening years. The fact that a well-known accountant and financial adviser had disappeared, and that any prospective bridegroom would go off camping, alone, a week before his wedding, certainly provided reporters with ample questions around which to weave a story.

The most recent clipping in the file, however, did not mention Carson Chappell. It was dated just this previous week, ten years after Chappell's disappearance, and had been cut from the *San Francisco Chronicle*. This was the article that currently interested Detective Dallas Garza as he sat at his desk talking on the phone with Lindsey Wolf, the clipping lying on the desk before him:

REMAINS OF HIKER FOUND IN SEASIDE TREE HOUSE

The skeleton of a man was discovered last evening in a makeshift tree house shelter on the central Oregon coast by a group of Boy Scouts on a weekend camping trip. The victim had apparently died from gunshot wounds, and two bullets were recovered by sheriff's deputies. The heavily wooded acreage is on private land and is a new campsite for the Scouts' yearly outings. The body had been disturbed by small animals and possibly a bobcat, but enough of the bones remain for possible identification. Neither the Oregon Bureau of Investigation, Oregon sheriffs' departments, nor Oregon police have outstanding missing reports of hikers in that area. "All past missing cases have been resolved," said OBI agent Henley Mills when interviewed at the scene.

This three-pronged congruence of players and events—the sudden availability of someone to work the department's cold files, the discovery of this body though it was not likely related, and the phone call from Lindsey Wolf—held Garza's interest. He sat staring at the article as he spoke with Lindsey; she had faxed it to him just a few moments earlier, and then had followed up with the call.

He knew Lindsey casually, she had dated his brother-in-law several years back, starting some months after Chappell disappeared. That was nearly nine years ago. Now, Dallas wondered if he'd been smart to include her file among the cold cases he'd given Mike to work, wondered if it was wise to stir up that old and painful relationship.

But Mike had seemed okay with it, as if he was completely over Lindsey—and Dallas wondered, for a moment, amused at himself, if he hesitated to put Mike on the case because of his own sudden surge of interest. Lindsey Wolf was the kind of woman who too easily stirred a man's blood, a tall, lovely, creamy-skinned woman in her forties, quiet and self-assured.

He'd already seen the article she'd sent him, he had read it over breakfast a couple of hours before her fax arrived. Now, when he'd asked Lindsey on the phone if she had information on the Oregon body, she'd said, "Not information, no. But I have questions, Detective Garza. Are you familiar with the disappearance of Carson Chappell some ten years ago?"

"I know the case. I wasn't with the department then, but I've read the cold file."

"I'm on my way up to the city on business—I'm an accountant, as you may remember. I worked for Carson until just before he . . . Before our planned wedding. We're into tax season now, and I can't put that off. I'd like to call you as soon as I return, make an appointment to come in. I have no information on the dead man in Oregon. But I think . . . I have such a strong feeling that that body in Oregon could be Carson. I can't get past that idea. I know that seems far-fetched and unlikely, when he was supposed to be up on the state park land, here. That's what he told me, but . . ." She paused, her voice breaking. Then, "I need to talk with you about it, I need to talk with someone."

"Call me when you get back," Dallas said. "You can try me on the weekend if you like, but I may be hard to reach."

"Your niece is getting married this weekend?"

"She is," Dallas said, knowing there had been no announcement in the paper. "I guess you've talked with Ryan?" Ryan and Clyde, wanting a low-key wedding without a lot of village interest, had given no notice to the local paper; they meant to send in a brief mention when they returned from their honeymoon.

"It's a small village," Lindsey said easily. "I think I heard the news at Jolly's Deli. Isn't he doing the catering?"

"I believe he is," Dallas said. "Call me when you get back, I'd like to hear your thoughts on the Oregon case."

Hanging up, he sat quietly, his square face and dark eyes solemn, wondering exactly how Lindsey Wolf had felt when Chappell didn't show for the wedding. Angry. Cheated. Mad enough to . . . What? Then his thoughts turned to his niece's wedding, and he smiled. That would be a far different matter; there was no chance that Ryan or Clyde would back out.

This would be Ryan's second marriage and, he hoped—he knew, damn it—that this would be the right and final one; and Clyde wasn't about to run out on her. Ryan's first husband had been a tyrant, a bully, and Clyde was nothing like that—he was funny, low key, completely honest, and without any social pretension whatever—that in itself was refreshing. And Clyde had sufficient determination to make a good match for Ryan's stubborn nature.

When his thoughts turned back at last to Lindsey Wolf, several questions nagged him. On the phone she had sounded wound tight, her voice sharp and quick, not the way he remembered her—her words now were harsh with raw, untempered emotion that seemed strange considering that she'd had ten years to come to terms with Chappell's disappearance, with his possible injury or death. Or with the possibility that he'd abandoned her. Her distress seemed too fresh, too overwrought after so long a time.

When the department's original investigation had come up with nothing on Chappell's disappearance, Lindsey kept up the search on her own, had kept at it for nearly a year, making contacts, even hiring a private investigator—though at the same time, she'd seemed to get on with her life. After some months of searching and grieving, she'd started dating Mike, apparently needing someone, and they'd grown pretty serious.

But then suddenly something had happened between them that Mike would never afterward talk about. Lindsey had left the village, had moved down to L.A., there'd been no phone calls, no contact that Dallas knew of. She'd started her own accounting service down there, apparently successfully.

And then, almost nine years later, she'd moved back to central California, back to the village, where she wasted no time opening office quarters in a small cottage in the mixed-business area of the casual village, a nice office with living quarters conveniently located above, and she had slipped quickly back into the life of the village.

He'd seen her only from a distance; he wondered if she'd changed much. Was she still as beautiful? His own quickening interest annoyed him. Turning in his swivel chair to face the bookcase behind him, Dallas reached for the other cold files he'd shoved out of the way between copies of the California Civil Code, his hand brushing against the gray tomcat where Joe lay curled up, dozing. Damned cat really had taken up residence, Dallas thought, amused.

Maybe Joe Grey's nose was out of joint, with Clyde about to be married. Maybe home had already changed, probably the house was in an uproar. Knowing Ryan, they might already be rearranging furniture, cleaning out cupboards to accommodate her belongings. If cats were anything like dogs, the gray tom wouldn't like any disturbance in his home and routine. Change, to an animal, translated into threat.

With enough provocation, who knew? *The tomcat*, Dallas thought, *might move into the station full-time.*

"Things bad at home?" he asked the tomcat, scratching Joe's ear. "Ryan won't throw you out, you know. Or," he said, looking into Joe's yellow eyes, "could you be jealous of her?"

Joe glared at him, and Dallas grinned. "You've had your own way around the house for a long time. Maybe you don't like competition from a new roommate and her dog?"

The tomcat studied him almost as if he understood.

"And why aren't you out catching mice instead of schlepping around in here sleeping and cadging treats from the dispatchers? The time you spend in the department, Joe, you might as *well* move in and get yourself on the payroll."

The tomcat turned to lick his paw, and then looked at Dallas sleepily—as if willing him to get on with his own business and leave a cat to nap in peace. Dallas scratched Joe's head until Joe tired of the attention, sat up, licked the other white paw and gray leg, then washed the white strip down his dark nose.

"Strange," Dallas said companionably, "that Lindsey was so uptight. I hope that wasn't guilt talking."

The gray cat, still washing, raised his yellow eyes to Dallas.

"This wouldn't be the first time a guilty party brought

evidence to the attention of the law," Dallas told him, "trying to turn away any new suspicions."

Joe Grey yawned in Dallas's face, lay down again on the bookshelf, and seemed to go back to sleep. Dallas watched him, a grin touching his stern Hispanic face—he found he liked having the cat to talk to.

He'd never cared much for cats until this one, he'd always been a dog man. Pointers, fine gundogs. But this cat, in some ways, seemed more like a dog than a cat. Joe was, for one thing, a pretty good listener, more attentive than Dallas expected cats to be—the gray tom seemed, in fact, nearly as responsive to his moods as were his dogs.

Part of the comfort in talking to an animal—dog, cat, or horse—was that they didn't offer advice, didn't tell you what to do. Animals were sympathetic and willing listeners, but they couldn't repeat what they heard. Couldn't pass on some casual remark, or the contents of a phone conversation or high-security interview—and as Dallas stroked Joe Grey, appreciating the cat's admirably mute ways, he didn't see, when the tomcat ducked his head under the detective's stroking hand, the cat's sly and knowing smile.

JOE GREY HAD already read the faxed newspaper article over the detective's shoulder, and from his position on the shelf just behind Dallas's left ear, he'd clearly heard both sides of Lindsey's phone call, had heard her tension just as Dallas had, and was equally puzzled by her apparent nervousness and stress.

From what Joe had heard around the village, he thought of Lindsey Wolf as a soft-spoken lady always in charge of herself, a fascinating woman nicely reined in, always in command of her emotions. He knew that his tabby lady had cadged occasional tidbits from Lindsey's hand in restaurant patios, and that Dulcie liked her gentle ways—but today, Lindsey sounded harsh and nervous, almost brittle.

Dropping down onto Dallas's desk, Joe watched the detective set the Chappell file aside and dig into his overloaded in-box. "We'll see what Mike can do with the case," Dallas said, half to himself.

Joe thought it interesting that Dallas's brother-in-law, having just retired from Federal Probation, didn't take a sensible rest, as any cat would do. That Mike wanted to get right back to work, didn't want to be idle when he moved down to the village.

Admittedly he'd be working his own hours, though, investigating the department's cold cases.

"Maybe he won't want to work the case," Dallas said, stroking Joe. "Maybe he'll change his mind, decide not to have anything more to do with Lindsey. Whatever blew up between them," he told the tomcat, "left him cranky as hell for a long time."

Joe Grey twitched an ear and rubbed his whiskers against Dallas's hand; Dallas scowled at the stack of paperwork that seemed to grow taller every day. *Cops always had too much paperwork*, Joe thought, curling up on the blotter, directly in Dallas's way, so that the detective had to work around him; when Dallas pushed him gently aside, Joe didn't get up and move, but stretched out, taking up more space and shoving away papers with his hind feet, as he lay thinking about Mike Flannery and Lindsey Wolf.

Maybe when the two had started dating, after Chappell disappeared, it was because Lindsey had needed someone, needed a friend who didn't make cutting remarks about how Chappell had run out on her, as, apparently, most of Lindsey's women friends and her sister liked to do. Joe picked up a lot of information among Clyde's friends, from casual remarks at parties or over poker games. He knew that Mike would come down from San Francisco to spend his summer weekends in the village, and that he'd been pretty serious about her. Joe thought the two must have made a handsome couple—tall, sandy-haired Mike Flannery and willowy Lindsey Wolf.

But then suddenly she'd pulled up stakes and moved to L.A., and the way Joe heard it, Mike had never talked about what happened between them.

"Just our luck," Dallas said, startling the tomcat. "If Mike does take the case, some troublemaker claims that because Mike dated Lindsey, any current investigation is unethical—if it comes to a full investigation," he said, easing a sheaf of papers out from under Joe. "But, hell, what are the odds that that's Chappell, up there in Oregon?

"Anyway," he muttered, as he scanned and then signed a stack of routine forms, "that was nearly ten years ago. And Mike isn't a member of the department, this is contract work." He looked at Joe, his square Latino face thoughtful. "Let Mike run with it. Who knows what he'll find?"

Who knows what'll happen? Joe thought. And then the

tomcat, watching the detective, caught a glimpse of something else besides concern for departmental policy. Did he see a spark of jealousy in those dark Latino eyes? A surge of macho competitiveness over Lindsey Wolf?

"I can't clear up this mess with you on top of it," Dallas said. Lifting Joe, he set him down at the end of the desk, determined to clean up his paperwork. *Free up the coming weekend so he could enjoy Ryan's wedding,* Joe thought, *without a cluttered desk waiting for him.*

"This wedding better go smoothly," Dallas said, almost as if he could read Joe's mind. "We don't need to call in the bomb squad." And that wasn't a joke, the tomcat knew too well. Just a year ago a bomb explosion had created a near disaster at the wedding of the police chief, the church nearly demolished and several people injured minutes before the guests would have filed in.

A lucky, anonymous tip had averted calamity, had probably prevented a mass murder—a tip that Dallas and the chief still wondered about, the tomcat thought, smiling.

"But no one," Dallas said, "has a grudge against Ryan or Clyde, not the way a few scum would like to seriously damage anyone in law enforcement." Ryan and Clyde weren't cops, but still . . . Ryan was like Dallas's daughter, and Clyde was a close friend to many in the department.

Praying that Dallas was right, that nothing ugly *would* happen, Joe looked up at the detective, purring companionably.

"No," Dallas said, pummeling Joe as if he were a dog, until Joe hissed a warning and Dallas withdrew his hand.

"Sorry," he said. Then, "No, nothing bad is going to happen. This will be a quiet, happy wedding—low key, just as Ryan and Clyde want. The department would take apart anyone who tried to make it otherwise, anyone who tried to harm those two."

2

 INDEED, ON THE day of the wedding there was no bomb threat, no threat of any kind, the casual but smoothly planned ceremony proceeded in a sunny manner quite in keeping with the hopes of the edgy bride and nervous groom—though a dead body had been reported.

The information was relayed to Charlie Harper, wife of police chief Max Harper, the day before the wedding.

A hidden grave had been accidentally uncovered not three miles from the Harpers' home, where Clyde and Ryan were to be married.

Charlie got the word from a friend, but she didn't tell Max about it. She had no intention of telling him, not before the wedding and not afterward. On the happy day, long after the wedding cake was demolished, the sentimental tears were all wiped away, and the euphoric couple had been sent off for a two-week honeymoon in California's wine country, still Charlie didn't tell Max that an unidentified body had been found in his jurisdiction.

Not only was it against the law to withhold such information from the police, it was against Charlie's principles to lie, even by omission, to the one man she loved in all the world.

But this one time, she had no choice. She couldn't tell him about the corpse. There was no logical way she could know about the hidden grave. None of their friends would have been up to the ruins that weekend, to discover it and tell her. Certainly she couldn't tell Max she'd learned about the grave through an anonymous phone call, because any anonymous call would point directly to one of Max's three unidentified informants.

She wouldn't put those three in further jeopardy, they already had enough trouble keeping their secret. Anyway, why would one of the department's regular informants be up there in that isolated location? And why would they call Charlie instead of calling the department directly, as they usually did?

Nor could she tell Max she'd stumbled on the grave herself. She had no reason to be wandering up there among those fallen walls where she had, not long ago, shot and killed a man in self-defense. Max knew she avoided the ruins. And it would be way too bizarre to think she'd slipped away to the old estate just before the wedding, in the middle of cleaning house and fixing special dishes for the buffet, or to think that, on the morning of the wedding, she'd saddled her mare and ridden up there when she should have been filling the coffee urn, icing the champagne, and laying out her good linen tablecloths on the extended kitchen and patio tables.

All during the weekend of the wedding and afterward,

while keeping her secret, Charlie tried to work out a scenario that would seem plausible to Max and yet would inform the department of the unknown grave. The wedding was held on the fourteenth day of February, a Sunday, at precisely eleven A.M. The couple had chosen Valentine's Day only after the weather forecaster solemnly promised that it would be clear and fine.

The day turned out exactly so—a bright morning but cool, the sea breeze cool and fresh, the sky spreading a deep blue backdrop to the masses of white clouds that had piled to heavenly heights above the blue Pacific. The bride wore red, not so much in honor of St. Valentine as because she liked red. Her tailored suit, a muted tomato shade as soft as the spring roses she carried, complemented perfectly her high brunette coloring, her short dark hair, and her intense green eyes.

The groom was dressed in the first suit he'd owned in more years than he cared to count; he'd chosen a pale tan gabardine that would dress down easily to their casual lifestyle. Nor was the happy couple married in the Catholic Church as one might expect of Ryan Flannery's Irish-Latino heritage. The ceremony took place not on their own patio, as they had at first imagined, but on the wide hilltop terrace of the Max Harper ranch. Besides twenty-some close civilian friends in attendance were as many of Molena Point's finest as could be absent from the department at one time without encouraging an untoward outbreak of crime in the small village. The couple had chosen a weekend without any local festivals, golf tournaments, or antique-car exhibits, any of which would have put an extra burden on the department.

Chief of Police Max Harper was Clyde's best man. The bride, again breaking tradition, was given away not by one male relative, but by three: her uncle, Police Detective Dallas Garza; her father, retired Chief U. S. Probation Officer Mike Flannery; and her red-bearded uncle Scott Flannery, who was the foreman of her construction firm.

Dallas was in full police uniform, his short, dark hair freshly trimmed. Ryan's dad, tall, sandy-haired Mike Flannery, wore a dark suit, white shirt, and soft paisley tie. Mike's brother, Scotty, had chosen the only thing in his closet that wasn't a work shirt and jeans; he wore beige slacks, a white shirt open at the collar, and a dark green corduroy sport coat that contrasted sharply with his red hair and beard. The three men walked Ryan down the aisle side by side—while Ryan's big, silver, canine companion looked on from the sidelines, so tense with excitement that the three cats, sitting beside him, thought any minute the big Weimaraner would bolt straight into the middle of the procession: That was *his* family marching down the makeshift aisle between the rows of metal chairs, and the big retriever shivered with nervous intensity at this obviously important event involving those he loved.

But Rock, sitting close between Charlie Harper's left knee and Clyde's gray tomcat, with both Charlie and Joe Grey giving him stern looks, managed to remain on his best behavior.

No guest in attendance thought it strange that Ryan's Weimaraner and the groom's tomcat, and their friends' two cats, were in attendance; animals were an important part of their lives. Charlie stood with her fingers touching Rock's silky head, near his collar, to make doubly sure he didn't bolt to his mistress and new master; she could feel him quivering under her gentle strokes.

As for the three cats, Charlie wasn't worried about their behavior. Joe Grey, his tabby lady, and the tortoise-shell kit knew better than many people how to act during such a solemn and important ceremony.

Though, looking down at the cats, Charlie did wonder at Joe Grey's admirable restraint on this particular day—because this marriage would change dramatically all the rest of the gray tomcat's life. The fact that Ryan would now be living with Joe Grey and Clyde presented a whole new set of rules and priorities for the tomcat; Charlie had worried considerably about how he'd settle into the new routine.

Any cat would find the addition of a new family member a threat to his place in the household and to his treasured habits, but for a cat who could speak with humans and who not only read the morning paper but expected first grabs at the front page, such a life change had to be stressful. Even though Ryan knew Joe's secret, had figured out for herself that he was as skilled in the English language as was she, the changes for Joe, as well as for Ryan and Clyde—for all three strong-willed individuals—would be trying. Particularly considering Joe Grey's secret involvement with Molena Point PD as their prime, though anonymous, informant.

Well, it was no good worrying about difficulties in the Damen household. She expected the three of them would work it out. And as the wedding music of soft Irish folk songs drifted through the outdoor speakers, Charlie centered her attention on the beautiful matron of honor as Ryan's sister, Hanni, stepped out onto the crowded patio through the glass doors from the Harper living room, leading the bridal procession.

It seemed fitting to Charlie that the bride herself had designed and constructed this part of the Harper home that was now the site of her wedding. This portion of the house was particularly bright and open, the airy living room anchored by tall, heavy pillars and soaring beams and the tall stone fireplace. The floor-to-ceiling glass walls that looked out to the sea over the Harpers' green pastures, now reflected Hanni as she led the two flower girls, the bride, and her escorts in slow and measured steps across the patio, between the rows of seated guests to the bower of roses where Clyde waited nervously with Captain Harper and the preacher; Charlie had to smile because Hanni had tastefully dressed down for the occasion, with none of her usual flamboyance.

Only Hanni's short, white hair, in a bright tangle around her smooth young face, could not be dimmed, her natural looks not be restrained by the tailored tan suit, somewhat darker than Clyde's; she wore none of her usual wild jewelry, but only a thin gold chain at her throat and tiny gold earrings, demure pieces she must have borrowed for the occasion, as they were nothing like her usual bizarre necklaces and pendants and wild rings for which Hanni Coon was so well known. Today, Hanni did not upstage her sister. The bride looked delicious in her soft red suit, and she looked so happy that Charlie felt tears starting, the foolish tears that weddings always stirred in her for no sensible reason.

The Irish folk music lilted softly, the stringed instruments blending with the sea's rhythmic pounding and with the far cries of the gulls, an earthy-milieu counterpoint to the minister's voice as he intoned the words of the brief ceremony. Only when he asked for the ring was he interrupted—by the nicker of Charlie's sorrel mare, from the pasture, which made everyone chuckle.

Joe Grey, watching Dallas Garza and Mike and Scott Flannery give away the bride, caught again a hint of bridling on Dallas's part as he glanced over at Mike, and wondered again if Dallas's competitive look centered on thoughts of Lindsey Wolf.

But when Joe looked at Dulcie to get her reaction, his tabby lady seemed to have noticed nothing, she seemed lost either in the sentimental ceremony or off in some distant thought, and did not even notice his glance.

WATCHING RYAN and Clyde joined in holy matrimony, the tabby cat, like Charlie, had to swallow back her own tears. What was it that made females weep at weddings?

She watched Clyde kiss the bride, and then the crowd surrounded the happy couple, laughing and congratulating them, and Dulcie had to hide a wild urge to laugh with delight, not only because of the joyous moment but because practical-minded Ryan Flannery—Ryan Flannery Damen, now—was a member of the inner group, because Ryan had guessed, all on her own, that the three cats could talk to her and understand her, because Ryan had guessed their impossible secret.

As the guests milled around them, the three cats, to avoid the surge of crowding feet, leaped to the top of the cold barbecue, out of the way—cops were a raucous crew, and their civilian counterparts were just as enthusiastic. Rock had joined the fray, yipping and dancing around the newlyweds, abandoning any attempt at obeying Ryan's carefully taught manners.

The couple was toasted, and toasted again; they danced the first dance, and posed for pictures, and cut the cake. Max put on a tape of Irish jigs, and everyone danced: eighty-year-old Lucinda and Pedric Greenlaw; Dulcie's housemate Wilma, and Mike Flannery; the four senior ladies dancing with handsome young cops; fourteen-year-old Dillon Thurwell and twelve-year-old Lori dancing with cops, too, their faces flushed, their eyes laughing. Hanni and her husband danced while their three boys inhaled party food. If this was a small, quiet wedding, Dulcie thought, heaven help a cat in the midst of a big, all-out celebration. Atop the barbecue, she pressed close between Joe and Kit, enjoying their human friends' rowdy pleasure.

By three o'clock that afternoon the party was winding down, the cake had been demolished, only scraps remained on the buffet, and the bride and groom had departed for their drive up the coast.

Most of the officers had gone back on duty. The senior ladies had left, as had Dillon and Lori, the two girls clutching their pieces of wedding cake to put under their pillows. "I will marry a cop," said red-haired Dillon, winking at portly Officer Brennan. But Lori, with her dad still in prison, pushed back her long dark hair and was silent. Lori didn't say what kind of man she'd marry.

The party dwindled to a quiet, mellow aftermath, melancholy and sentimental. Why anyone should feel sad after a wedding, Dulcie wasn't sure. This was the start of a new life for Ryan and Clyde—but while everyone was giddily happy, the cats could not ignore the undercurrent of sadness that now turned folks silent and thoughtful.

But of course Dulcie's housemate felt sad. Wilma was the closest thing to an older sister that Clyde had, and as happy as she was for him, surely she felt she was losing a bit of him—it would be Ryan, now, to whom Clyde would tell his secrets and ask for advice, to whom he'd voice his dreams and fears.

But Wilma knew that was as it should be, and Dulcie could see that her silver-haired housemate was more happy than sad. Wilma had said to Dulcie more than once that it was time Clyde settled down with the right woman— and Ryan was surely the right woman. Two mates of equal strength, Dulcie thought. Two people honest enough and with enough crazy humor to sustain the hardest bumps that might lie ahead.

From atop the barbecue the tabby cat watched Mike and Dallas and Scotty fold up the metal chairs from the patio and carry them out to Scotty's truck, to be returned to the furniture rental. All three men looked both well satisfied at this milestone in Ryan's life, and yet quiet and nostalgic. The cats watched Charlie and Hanni clean up the empty plates and platters and lay out the remaining food in a fresh but smaller array on the big round kitchen table, nesting the dishes on trays of ice. And as the sun dropped and the afternoon grew chill, the few remaining friends retired to the living room, where Max lit a fire on the hearth.

Immediately the cats and Rock stretched out before the blaze, taking the best places. Their friends slipped out of their jackets, shoes came off, a few beers were opened. This was the second party this weekend, and for a while, a peaceful silence reigned as each in his or her own mind wished the newlyweds well, wished them a happy and safe journey on their honeymoon and through a long life. Among their small group only Charlie was strung tight.

Only Charlie and the cats were torn, on this memorable day, by a secret that had nothing to do with the wedding and that they had shared with no one, certainly not with the groom and bride.

To share the discovery of a body with Clyde and Ryan, just now, would only send them off on their honeymoon worried about Joe, about all three cats, as Clyde always worried.

Every time a crime was committed, a robbery or a murder, or in this case the discovery of a corpse, every time Molena Point PD had a new investigation, Clyde worried and fussed. When "that little meddler," as he called Joe, leaped into the middle of an investigation, and though Clyde knew there was no way to keep the three cats out, still he nagged them, harangued Joe, and was sure the cats would end up hurt or dead. Joe couldn't convince him otherwise. Arguing with Clyde Damen was as pointless as trying to herd caterpillars.

Charlie had learned about the body yesterday evening as she was getting ready to leave for Mike's retirement party. She'd had no idea, when she went out to do the last-minute stable chores, that she would soon be *sneaking* into the party, avoiding her friends, and would slip out again quickly, Joe Grey and Dulcie and Kit stealthily following her, and the blood of a fourth cat staining her hands.

3

 MIKE FLANNERY'S retirement party, the night before the wedding, had been a casual cookout on Clyde Damen's patio to celebrate Mike's moving from San Francisco to the village. Most of Mike's family had long since removed to Molena Point from the city, Hanni to open her interior design studio, Dallas to sign on as a detective with Molena Point PD, Ryan to escape the husband she was divorcing and to start her own construction firm, and Scotty to work for her.

Mike, having retired the previous week as Chief U.S. Probation Officer for the Northern District of California, had enjoyed an impressive court ceremony before U.S. judge Donald Clymer and then a crowded and congratulatory office party complete with gag gifts, a thick scrapbook of office pictures from past parties and ceremonies, and deeply felt good wishes; Flannery had been a demanding but infinitely fair and well-loved chief. On the day of the ceremony and party, Mike's rented truck waited, ready to leave San Francisco, packed with the few belongings he meant to keep; the security deposit on his vacated apartment had been refunded, he had sold his aging car and had closed his bank accounts—not that he was in a hurry to depart the city. Not much of a hurry.

Early that evening, as the first partygoers assembled, up at the Harper ranch Charlie Harper, dressed in fresh jeans and a clean shirt, was ready to head down the hills to join the celebration; she had just put an insulated carrier full of potato salad in the back of her SUV, and had gone to feed the horses and dogs and put them up for the night when, from deep within the stable, a small voice spoke to her. She pause, startled. "Who's there?"

Earlier, opening the pasture gate, she'd moved the four horses into the barn, followed by the two gamboling half-Danes, the big, fawn-colored mutts had let her know that nothing was amiss in the stable by the way they frolicked around her, carefree and untroubled. But now, as she finished graining and started to fill the water buckets, Hestig gave a huff and Selig growled, staring toward the rear door that she'd left ajar for air circulation.

The Harper barn had two rows of stalls facing each other across a covered alley where she and Max groomed and saddled the horses or doctored them. A wide, sliding door opened at the front, and another similar door at the back. This was open only a few inches, and as Charlie paused, watching the dogs, the soft voice spoke again from the shadows.

"Charlie? Charlie Harper?" A voice barely discernible through Hestig's puzzled rumble.

Charlie took Hestig's collar, though the dog didn't

lunge or bark. He only cocked his head, watching the dark corner.

There was no one standing there, nothing that she could see, and the chill she felt was not of fear but of anticipation.

The miracle of hearing that small, wild voice here in the barn made her shiver. Quietly she approached the back of the barn until, where the shadows were deepest, she made out a little white smudge crouched and watching her. She knelt some distance from the pale cat. "Willow?"

There was no answer.

"Willow? What's wrong? What brings you here?" She knew the lovely feral would never come among humans unless she badly needed help, unless there was terrible trouble for her or her wild band. Fearing that Willow would slip away again, Charlie didn't reach out to the bleached calico, she did nothing to alarm her—though Willow had no reason to fear her, the cat *was* feral, as wild and wary as a forest fox; none of Willow's band of speaking cats trusted humans, and Charlie had indeed been flattered when Willow accepted her.

"What is it?" she said again, softly. "What's happened?"

But then, watching the frightened calico, Charlie smelled the sharp, ironlike scent of fresh blood—and Willow stepped out from the shadows, watching Charlie with huge green eyes. Revealing what lay behind her. Showing Charlie the small, still form that lay amid scattered wisps of straw on the dark barn floor: a young cat, bloodied and limp.

Charlie wanted to reach out to him, but she remained

still. "May I get a light?" she said softly. "I can't see as well as you. He's hurt bad, I need to see. Could I turn on the overhead lights? They're very bright."

"Turn them on," Willow said tremulously. "He's unconscious. Yes, he's hurt bad, Charlie Harper. It took three of us helping him, carrying and supporting him as he tried to hobble. He's used the last of his strength. The others ran as soon as we had him safe here—they wouldn't remain in a human place, and with the big dogs near."

Charlie rose, switched on the lights, and knelt again, catching her breath at the little cat's cruelly twisted and bloodied leg. He lay against the stable wall, so limp and small, a young white tom marked with vague, soft gray splotches like Stone Eye, the clowder leader, marked the same as many of the clowder cats—Stone Eye dominated the females, and most of the kittens were his.

Stone Eye's tyranny was why Willow and a small band of cats had left the clowder, going defiantly off on their own, making every effort to stay clear of him.

"Sage is my cousin," the pale calico said, nosing gently at the young tom's ear. "There was a terrible battle. Stone Eye attacked us; we had no choice," she said ashamedly, "but to run from his warriors."

At the sound of their voices the young, hurt cat had awakened. He was looking at Charlie rigid with fear.

"It's all right," Willow told him. "Charlie's a friend. It's all right, Sage.

"His leg is broken," she said sadly, "and I think the bone might be crushed. Stone Eye did that. I . . . Be still, Sage. Let Charlie look at you. *She's a friend. Do as I say, and be still.*"

The young tom grew still, but remained wary in Charlie's presence. Gently she touched the angled leg, and felt sick. She could see the jagged bone sticking out beneath the blood-soaked fur. She looked at Willow, desolate. "I can't mend such a thing. I'll have to take him to a doctor—a friend. A man we can trust."

"Not a strange human," Willow said.

"I promise we can trust him."

"Can't you help him, can't you do this?"

"I'm not a doctor. I would ruin his leg. If I muddled this, he might never walk again—he might not live. This will take skilled hands. Even then . . . if the bone is crushed . . ." She didn't finish. Sage looked so weak, and surely he'd lost a lot of blood. He must be in terrible pain, and that was what sickened her the most.

Watching Charlie, Willow's eyes were huge with distress. "Please, could you try?" She was so afraid, and didn't know what to do.

"Our veterinarian is a good man," Charlie said. "He needn't know what this young cat is. He treats Joe Grey and Dulcie and Kit, and he doesn't know about them. He's a kind man, Willow. He's honest and caring, and he's very skilled. Please, let me take him there? You could come with us, to calm and reassure him."

Willow dropped her ears; she bent her head to nudge Sage, then looked up at Charlie. "I will come, but I must return quickly and see to the others. Others are wounded, though not so bad as Sage. I must help with them, lick them clean, do what we can."

Did Willow, Charlie wondered, not expect Sage to live? So she was committing herself to those who would live? She wanted badly to ask more about what had happened, she knew that Stone Eye could be brutal. But there was no time to ask. Rising, she fetched clean towels from the tack room, and a large metal tray that she used to lay out doctoring supplies for the horses. She folded a towel on this, to pillow Sage's body. She gathered antiseptic, a bottle of water, and gauze and clean cloths to staunch the blood.

Kneeling again beside Sage, gently she lifted him onto the makeshift stretcher. "Lie still. Oh, please, Sage, lie still." And she began carefully to bathe the wound and try to staunch the bleeding before she moved him very far. His pain seemed to have eased; she didn't know whether that was good or bad. If the young cat was in shock, she knew they must hurry.

Willow crouched close to him, speaking softly. "Listen to me, Sage. We can trust Charlie Harper, we must trust her. We must go with her, and you must do as she tells you. She will take us where you will be safe and cared for, where someone with skill can mend your leg so you can walk again. Do you understand?"

Sage blinked and nudged weakly at Willow, as if meaning to say he would try. But he cut his eyes at Charlie, not daring to speak in her presence.

Charlie, pressing gently with gauze pads, got the blood stopped, for the moment. Looking deep into the young tom's eyes, she tried the same uncompromising tone that Willow used, and that seemed to comfort him. Perhaps such authority seemed secure to Sage, perhaps it translated into safety.

"We'll go in my car," she told him, "and that will be

frightening for you. You will be safe, I promise. I'll do my best for you, and so will Dr. Firetti. He won't know what you are, Sage. You can be sure that I won't tell him. He'll be kind, he'll give you something to stop the hurt, and he'll mend your leg."

Charlie hoped she wasn't promising more than Firetti could deliver; she saw in Willow's eyes the same question. They looked at each other for a long moment. What if the leg could not be mended? What if it must be amputated? Or what if Sage kept his leg, but would be forever lame, unable to hunt properly or to travel fast and far with their wild band, unable to keep up with the clowder?

"Dr. Firetti will do the best he can," she repeated. "No one, *no one*, could do better."

Carefully picking up the makeshift stretcher and heading for her car, she looked down at Willow trotting along beside her, looking warily at the car. Willow stood watching as Charlie tucked the tray safely down on the front seat of her SUV, laid a soft lap blanket gently over Sage, and fastened the seat belt around the tray, securing his rigid little body. He widened his eyes as the belt seemed to imprison him.

"You must lie still. The belt is to protect you, to keep you from falling. The car will seem fast and bumpy. I'll hold on to you, too."

Willow hopped up into the car, seeming to swallow her own fear of the great metal machine as she settled gently next to Sage. Charlie, moving around the SUV, swung in and laid a hand on Sage's shoulder; as she started the engine he went even more rigid, his eyes growing huge with fear.

"It's all right, Sage. That noise is just the engine. Please be still. Please, don't hurt yourself more. I promise I won't let you be harmed—and soon the hurt will ease."

But Willow said simply, "Be still, Sage. You must mind us! It won't be long." It was all Willow *could* say—she, too, was shivering with fear of the noisy vehicle as Charlie set out up the ranch lane, driving slowly. When they went over a bump in the gravel road, Sage whimpered with pain, and Charlie felt her stomach twist.

"Dr. Firetti will ease the hurt," she repeated. "He'll help you rest and heal."

Sage blinked up at her in a terrified yet slowly trusting way that made her heart hurt with tenderness. He was in such pain, yet he was doing as Willow and she told him, the terrified young cat was trusting her, and that innocent trust almost undid her.

Heading out on their long road to the highway, she punched in Dr. Firetti's number on her cell phone. One ring. Two. Firetti answered on the third ring as she turned onto the highway and down the hills toward the village. She thought her call had probably interrupted his dinner. Driving as smoothly as she could on the old, two-lane road, through the heavy dusk, she told Firetti that the cat was a stray she'd been feeding, that she'd been waiting for him to grow a bit tamer before she took him down to be vetted and have his shots.

She told Firetti the cat had been in a fight with another stray. She didn't know how else to handle the matter. She thought about the possibility of rabies, but she didn't think that likely; there was not much rabies in their area except for the occasional rabid skunk or bat—and certainly those two bands of speaking cats were far too wise to get near a rabid beast.

But Firetti wouldn't know that. Under the circumstances, the doctor would probably have to quarantine Sage, and that would complicate matters. Sage was not a cat to be kept in a cage, the speaking cats loved their freedom too well, were too intelligent to tolerate confinement; Willow had had experience with cages, and Charlie knew how stressed she had been.

Well, she'd deal with that problem when Firetti mentioned it.

"When you are healed," Willow told Sage, "Charlie will take you back to the ranch so you can come and find us, so you can rejoin the band on the far hills."

"Not back to Stone Eye's band?" Charlie whispered.

Willow looked up at Charlie, her green eyes flashing with challenge. For a moment their gazes held again, transcending their difference in species; it was a moment that seemed beyond time, where species were no longer separated, where each knew the other intimately; it was an exchange that thrilled Charlie.

"Stone Eye is dead," Willow told her.

Charlie looked at her, startled.

"Last night, Stone Eye's warriors slipped into the ruins, stealthy and swift. Stone Eye wasn't with them, not in the first wave. They attacked brutally. We fought them, but they were fifty or more, and we were only twelve. We couldn't stand against them, it would have been our end. When they killed two of our young strong cats, we ten slipped away and ran.

"Just north of your barn, they surrounded us again.

We dove into a hollow tree that Cotton knew. We left our scent down inside it, for them to follow, and then we climbed. Sage . . . Sage was with Stone Eye's warriors."

Charlie looked down at Sage, shocked.

"Sage ran with Stone Eye," Willow said. "When our band broke away from him, Sage was young and he clung to the security of that tightly ordered life. I think that sometimes he wanted to be away from Stone Eye's brutal rule, but other times he was too afraid to leave. He would not come with those who escaped to join our free band. He wouldn't leave, despite Stone Eye's cruelty," she said sadly.

Charlie shivered, trying to imagine the young cat's indecision and fear.

"But last night," Willow said, "as they gathered around the tree to dig us out, with Stone Eye yowling orders, we leaped down on them, slashing and raking. In the dark, Cotton throttled Stone Eye before he could twist and grab him—and it was then, when Stone Eye screamed with pain, that Sage saw Stone Eye's weakness, and turned on him wildly.

"This so infuriated Stone Eye that he flipped over, threw Cotton off, grabbed Sage by the leg and shook and flung him.

"And then Coyote was there, fighting Stone Eye. I've never seen such a fight, Cotton and Coyote were crazy with rage at Stone Eye's brutality to young Sage, they killed him before his warriors could help him.

"When Stone Eye lay dead, Charlie Harper, the cats began to cheer. What a wild sound, that excited cheering breaking the still night. Now . . ." Willow's green eyes burned at Charlie. "Now we are all free of him. Free of the slave master." And for the first time that evening, Willow smiled, her pale ears sharply erect, her eyes glowing. "The tyrant is dead, Charlie Harper. Now, Cotton and Coyote will rule, now we will all live free again, and there will be no tyranny."

But Charlie, slowing behind a creeping truck, only hoped they could keep their freedom. In the world of humans, it seemed to her, there was always another tyrant ready to destroy the meek and gentle, another dictator burning to enslave those weaker than himself.

Willow lifted a paw, watching her. "There is something more, Charlie Harper."

Charlie passed the truck, then pulled quickly back into the single lane. The evening traffic was growing heavy in both directions on the darkening two-lane.

"We had another death," Willow told her. "A week before we were attacked. An elderly member of our band. We buried her in the ruins." Willow's small clowder had lived in the ruins of the old Pamillon Estate, among its fallen walls and crumbling cellars, ever since they'd left Stone Eye's domination.

"We dug deep to bury her, but we had to abandon the first grave we started. There was a human body there, we uncovered human bones. Old, earth-stained bones. A hand, an arm, part of a shoulder."

Charlie thought they had found one of the Pamillon family graves, that they had been digging in the old family cemetery.

"We covered them over again, and moved to the soft earth of the old rose garden," Willow said.

Charlie glanced at her. "But the rose garden *is* the cemetery. What . . . ?"

Willow looked up at her. "Yes," she said softly. "We buried our dead one beside the graves of the Pamillon family, buried her at the back of the garden where the tall old bushes bloom best."

Charlie pulled over as a speeding driver passed, narrowly missing them. "But where was the human grave?" she said, cursing the hare-brained driver.

"It was in a little courtyard outside a bedchamber, a sheltered garden walled in on three sides by the house, and overgrown with bushes and vines. Through a glass door you can see into a chamber, see a toppled dresser and an old, carved bed with tattered hangings."

Willow flicked her tail. "The strangest thing, Charlie Harper, is that the human skeleton wears a bracelet. The corpse wears a bracelet that bears the picture of a cat. What do you think that could mean?"

"Anyone might wear such jewelry. Millions of humans are fond of cats."

"But that particular cat . . . There is another exactly like it, carved into the stone over the bedchamber door." Willow licked her pale calico shoulder. "Exactly the same cat. Rearing up, with his mouth open and his paw thrust out."

"Maybe the Pamillons kept cats," Charlie said. "Maybe other cats lived there at one time, ordinary cats but so dearly loved that they became a kind of symbol—the way people put bumper stickers of dogs on their cars." But she knew that was a weak explanation.

Beside her, Willow's eyes glowed with unease. "There

is more about cats," Willow said, "there is a book about cats hidden at one side of the grotto. A book about cats like *us*, a book about speaking cats. Could the people who lived there have known about us, Charlie Harper? Did someone in that house know about speaking cats?"

Charlie's pulse had gone cold. Every stranger who knew the cats' secret was a potential threat to Willow's wild band, and to Joe and Dulcie and Kit.

They were nearly to their turn, the evening traffic now bumper to bumper; though she kept her distance, twice she had to brake abruptly, reaching to hold Sage and to try to calm him; he was very nervous, and he seemed almost panicked with pain. She was so anxious for him that she wanted to race ahead on the wrong side of the two-lane; the slow bumper-to-bumper traffic was maddening.

"Near the human grave," Willow said, "is a fissure where the walls have caved into an old cellar; several weeks ago Coyote chased a squirrel down there and found a small wooden box tucked among the stones.

"We pulled the box out with our claws. I don't know what made me fight so hard to free it and get it open. Coyote would have left it, but I had a terrible, urgent feeling that we needed to see inside.

"What clever hands humans have. It took three of us fighting that lid to unhook it. Inside was a piece of folded leather wrapped around something heavy. Inside that was an old book wrapped in frail cloth, a book with a leather cover and gold lettering. We dragged it out of the box and opened it, and in the starlight we read the first pages."

Charlie turned left on Ocean, headed for Firetti's

clinic. Beside her, Sage lay limp and still, his head down on the seat in a way that turned her cold.

Willow put her face to his face. "He sleeps," she said softly. "He is breathing." She was quiet a moment, then, "Some of the tales were the same ancient stories our clowder used to tell before Stone Eye forbade them—he called them the lies of humans, stories about our ancient beginnings. We remembered them from when we were kittens, gathered, of an evening, in the big clowder circle.

"But there were other stories, written by a human who knew about cats of our kind, who had seen them and spoken with them, in another country. Those stories frightened us. We shoved the book back in the box and hid the box again, deep in the crevice. If any cat loyal to Stone Eye had found it, they would have clawed it to shreds."

"Why didn't you destroy it," Charlie said, "when such a record is so dangerous?"

"I don't know," Willow said worriedly. "In that book is our history, our story. It gives away our secret, and yet it is our treasure, too, so rich in our own history. How could we destroy it?

"I don't like that humans would have such a book," the calico said thoughtfully. "But maybe some humans felt as I do. Maybe they meant to keep our secret, hiding the book carefully. As if they could not bring themselves to tear or burn it? It is a precious thing, that book, those words that tell about us."

Charlie couldn't answer; the idea of the book both frightened and excited her, just as it did Willow. But right now . . . She pulled up to the clinic, praying for Sage, her hand on his limp little body.

4

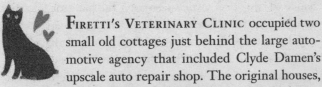 **FIRETTI'S VETERINARY CLINIC** occupied two small old cottages just behind the large automotive agency that included Clyde Damen's upscale auto repair shop. The original houses, one a small frame structure, the newer a one-bedroom cabin constructed of heavy beams and cement blocks, had long ago been joined together by a central kennel and turned into a pleasing professional complex. Dr. and Mrs. Firetti, Mary, lived in the cottage next door. Pulling up in front, Charlie turned to look at Willow. "Do you want to stay in the car, or come in with Sage?"

Willow rose as if to follow her, but then the pale calico, looking out warily at the big building, seemed to lose her nerve. Charlie couldn't fault her, the poor cat was about at the end of her strength. She'd fought two battles this long day, had run for her life from the first violent attack, then had escaped the warriors a second time and helped the wounded young tom to safety—despite her fear of the human world, she had entered the stable, surely terrified.

She seemed, in fact, not only at the end of her strength but of her resolve. Charlie touched her gently.

"Stay here, Willow. If Sage needs you, if he grows nervous again, I'll come and get you. You'll be safe here." Willow looked at her uncertainly.

Charlie reached to the backseat for a soft lap robe to make a bed for her. "I'll be as quick as I can." She opened the windows enough so Willow could escape if she chose, enough so she wouldn't feel trapped. Willow nosed at Sage, and licked the young cat's ear. She gave Charlie another long look, almost of contentment, as if glad of the chance to rest, and settled down on the blanket. Charlie picked up the stretcher and locked the car doors.

John Firetti met her at the front door of the clinic, his light brown hair ruffled, his bright blue eyes turning at once to Sage. Firetti's round face, which seemed perpetually sunburned, was filled with concern. Taking the makeshift stretcher, he led her through the empty waiting room and quickly past the door to the kennel, the large, airy central room that connected the two older buildings; this was a solarium-like structure with a high ceiling brightened by skylights. Its cement floor, which could be hosed down, was warmed by hot water pipes imbedded in the concrete. The dogs were barking so frantically that it was all Charlie could do to reassure Sage as they passed. The hospital itself and the cages for the cats were in smaller rooms, away from the noise.

The examining room to which John Firetti led her was warmer than the rest of the building, a small, cozy cubicle with a metal table and two soft, vinyl-covered easy chairs where clients could sit to talk with the doctor. Firetti spent some time examining Sage, then took him back to be X-rayed, asking Charlie to help him.

"Very likely he won't hold still, Charlie. He's terrified. I'm sorry about the noise." During the day, taped music played in the canine section and an attendant was there to soothe and quiet the patients. But this was after hours, and Firetti was alone. "Mary's off at our daughter's for the week. You'll have to hold him, try to calm him."

"He'll hold still," Charlie said.

"Did you say he's feral?" Firetti said uncertainly.

"He's a stray. I don't know whether he's feral—but ever since I found him hurt, he's been so still. I suppose he's in shock?"

Firetti didn't answer. At the X-ray table, Charlie put on a lead apron and lead gloves, and held Sage the way John Firetti showed her; under her gentle hands, even though they were encased in the thick gloves, Sage remained obediently quiet—but his little body was rigid as he stared up, terrified, at the X-ray machine. Firetti watched him with growing interest as he took the pictures, moving the injured cat into several positions. He had given Sage a shot to ease the pain, and soon, despite the cat's fear of the strange room and strange machinery, he began to relax.

When Firetti was finished with the X-rays, he said, "This will be a long surgery, and I'll need to do more tests before we begin. Natalie is on her way in, to help me." Natalie had been his assistant for many years. He looked intently at Charlie. "I'll need blood."

"Don't you keep a couple of kennel cats for that? The black cats I've seen in here?"

"Their blood won't do."

Charlie frowned. "You mean cats have blood types, like humans? I didn't . . ."

Firetti was silent, watching her. "Cats do have blood types, Charlie. But what I need is not common cat blood."

"What other kind is there? This cat isn't some exotic breed. What . . . ?"

"I think you know what I mean. I will need special blood. I'll need a transfusion from Joe Grey, or from Dulcie or Kit. Maybe from all three. Will you try to round up the cats while I set up for surgery?"

"But . . ." Charlie stared at him feeling her own blood drain to her toes.

"We're wasting time," Firetti said. "I hope they're not up in the hills hunting."

She couldn't speak. She heard the outer door open, heard Natalie call out that she would be right in. Charlie didn't know what to say to Firetti.

"I know about them," he said. "I've known about these amazing cats since I was a boy, since shortly after my father opened the clinic. I knew Dulcie's mother, I knew all about her—Genelle Yardley, with whom she lived, died keeping the cats' secret."

Charlie looked at him for a long time. How could she tell Joe and Dulcie and Kit this? How could she tell the three cats that one more person shared their secret, even if John Firetti was their friend?

But did she have to tell them?

Couldn't she bring Willow in for the transfusion, and never mention this to Joe or Dulcie or Kit?

But Willow was so exhausted. When Charlie thought

how terrified she would be of the clinic, of the metal table, of a strange human handling her—of the needle plunging in—she knew she couldn't do that. Besides, such dishonesty showed only disrespect for the cats. Charlie wouldn't deceive them, that was not how she viewed friendship.

Firetti was saying, "I've never told Wilma or Clyde that I know; I didn't tell the Greenlaws when they took Kit to live with them." He laughed. "It wasn't hard to know what the kit was, with her bright curiosity, the way she listened to every word. Of course I've never spoken of my knowledge to the cats themselves. They'll have to know now," he said quietly.

"They'll understand," Charlie said, hoping she was right. Wondering how the three cats *would* react.

She touched Sage lightly, nodded to John Firetti, and left the clinic, greeting Natalie on her way out, wondering for a moment if Natalie knew, too.

Oh, but Firetti would have told her, if that was the case. Surely he would have.

In the car she told Willow, "He's given him something for the pain, and to rest. He needs blood for transfusions so he can operate on the leg. As soon as I take you back, I'm going to fetch Joe and Dulcie and Kit." She was going to tell Willow that Firetti knew about them, but she couldn't. Willow was already upset, and to Willow, every human who knew their secret represented an additional threat, a worry the feral band must carry with them no matter how far they traveled or how well they hid themselves among the wild, unpopulated slashes of land between the spreading towns and cities.

In the car, as they headed back up the hills, almost as

if Willow had read her thoughts, the calico said, "There's been a human prowling among the ruins. We've seen him—or her?—only from a distance, someone dressed in black—black pants and a long black coat. Always the same figure, we think. But driving different colored cars. Coming up that far little gravel lane, from the houses below."

"Not the larger dirt road?"

"No, never. They drive the car into an old shed down at the end of the property, beyond the dying orchard, then come slipping through the ruins. Searching, always searching. Could they be looking for the book?" she said in a small, miserable voice.

"Where do they search?"

"Inside the house, and in the smaller buildings, too. Whenever we saw them, we stayed away, hid until they were gone. Then we went over their trail, but all we could smell was chemicals. Perfume or something like it, covering all other scents."

They had reached the ranch; before Willow raced away into the hills, Charlie fetched from the house some leftover roast and a bowl of fresh water. Willow drank and ate quickly.

"Must you go back alone? It's nearly dark."

"Our wounded aren't far away, Charlie Harper. And I'll be careful. I can smell danger, I can climb, and leap. And I have these," she said, baring her formidable claws and giving Charlie a little cat smile—and she streaked away past the barn and into the dusky woods, her pale shape vanishing among the thickening shadows.

Worrying because Willow was traveling alone, and puzzling over the prowler at the ruins, Charlie headed down the hills again. *Was* someone looking for the book? Or maybe for that hidden grave? Pulling into Clyde's crowded driveway behind Max's truck, she quickly grabbed her cooler and made for the front door, praying she could find Joe, and maybe Kit and Dulcie, could get them out without argument, and without anyone noticing.

Like the Firetti clinic, the Damen house had been remodeled from a small vacation cottage built during the early years of the last century, when Molena Point was a religion-based summer retreat. Only later had the artists and writers and musicians arrived, to change the persona of the small village from religious to more earthy pleasures. They, too, built cottages, enlarging the village, and now many of the old cottages housed restaurants and shops, or had been connected to become quaint motels. Designer Ryan Flannery had changed Clyde's dumpy little cottage into a handsome dwelling.

First she had transformed the weedy backyard into a beautiful private patio, then had added the second story to provide a new master suite and study, with a deck over the garage and carport. It was here that Charlie found Joe Grey sitting at the edge of the deck washing his paws, looking down at the street, checking out the arriving guests.

"Why the frown?" Joe said softly, turning to look at her. "What's wrong?"

"Why aren't you down in the middle of the party?" she whispered. "In the middle of the *food*?"

Joe gave her a long, cool look. "Since when have I ever been, as you put it, in the middle of the party food? Don't you think—"

"Joe," Charlie said softly, "I need you to come with me quickly, there's been an accident."

Joe's yellow eyes widened with fear.

"No, not Dulcie or Kit—it's a feral." She knelt on the deck, facing him, speaking quietly. "Willow came to me tonight, in the barn. She brought a young, wounded tomcat—there was a battle up at the ruins. Stone Eye attacked them, and Cotton and Coyote killed him."

Joe looked surprised, then smiled with satisfaction. "Good for them! One less tyrant in the world."

"I took the hurt cat to Dr. Firetti." But when she told him what Firetti knew, Joe Grey's yellow eyes narrowed warily, and his sleek body went rigid with apprehension.

"He's always known," Charlie said. "He knew about Dulcie's mother." She reached to touch Joe's muscled gray shoulder. "He's never told anyone. Never! I believe him, Joe."

She couldn't read Joe's expression; it was a mix of cold feline suspicion and yet a flash of confidence, too, as if he wanted to trust John Firetti, as if he knew, deep down, that he could trust him.

"Firetti needs you, Joe. He needs blood for Sage's surgery—it has to be the blood of a talking cat, he told me your blood is different."

Joe looked at Charlie for a long moment, and now his uncertainty had nothing to do with trusting what Firetti had said. *Blood? His* blood? His stomach had gone a bit queasy, and his paws began to sweat.

Joe Grey had never in his life shrunk from a fight. He could whip any tomcat that challenged him, and could send most dogs running. But the drawing out of his life-

blood was another matter. He already felt violated. He envisioned Dr. Firetti shaving away his sleek gray fur to pale,
naked skin, and sticking in a large and painful needle, and
he didn't like the thought.

Seeing the fear in Joe's eyes, Charlie hid her amusement.
"Firetti may need blood from all three of you," she said dip-
lomatically. "But I know you'll be the bravest. I guess we'd
better fetch Dulcie and Kit, though." She was guessing that
the lady cats, like most women, would feel less stricken at do-
nating a few drops of blood, but she couldn't tell Joe that.

"We're here" came a small voice from the roof above
them. Looking up she saw two pairs of bright eyes fixed
on her—green-eyed Dulcie, her dark tabby coat nearly invisible against the evening sky, and Kit's yellow eyes as
round as twin moons, the tortoiseshell's darkly mottled
fluff lost in the falling night.

"He *knows*?" Dulcie hissed at her. "*Firetti knows?*"

"*Blood?*" Kit said. "*Our* blood? Oh my . . ." But whether
the tattercoat was frightened by the thought, or impressed
with such an important mission, Charlie couldn't tell.

"If he needs us now," Dulcie said sensibly, "let's get on
with it." And Charlie watched the two lady cats leave the
roof, backing down the pine tree, their claws scratching
away loose bark, watched them drop to the ground and
race to her red Blazer, where they melted into the bushes,
waiting for her to open the door.

Picking up Joe without ceremony, garnering an irritable growl, Charlie hurried down, taking the stairs two
at a time, hoping she could get through the crowd without anyone stopping her—but from the living room, she
heard Clyde's and Mike Flannery's voices.

Most of the party was crowded into the back patio, and she could hear only a few voices from the kitchen. But there by the fireplace stood Clyde and his soon-to-be father-in-law in deep and serious conversation. She set Joe down, giving him a look that said he'd better follow her. And quickly she slipped into the living room, snatched up her cooler, which she'd left by the front door, and carried it into the kitchen.

"Potato salad and shrimp dip," she told Ryan hastily, setting the carrier on an empty chair. "I forgot to shut the dogs in, I have to go back." And she was gone again out the front door, Joe at her heels, before anyone thought to ask questions.

Holding open the door of her SUV, she pulled out the lap robe and pretended to fold it, hiding the cats as they leaped inside. Backing out of the drive, she hoped Ryan and Clyde were too tightly strung over the wedding to have paid attention to her hasty behavior. They didn't need this added worry just now.

Well, but of course they were nervous, getting married was a big step. Clyde had been a bachelor for a long time, despite numerous involvements. And Ryan, having only last year broken away from an abusive marriage, was still gun-shy. But, *They'll be good together*, Charlie thought. *They'll survive the wedding, get away by themselves, and that's all they need.*

What worried her, as she headed toward Ocean and the clinic, was the changes this marriage would bring to the Damen household. Joe and Clyde had lived together a long time, a bachelor household, the two of them bantering and confrontational, ribbing each other and supremely comfortable in their abrasive relationship. Now, what was in store for the two hardheaded males who were so entrenched in their rough ways? And Ryan . . . though Ryan had grown up in a household run by three strong-willed men and had learned early to hold her own, she'd never lived with a smart-talking tomcat who was as strong willed as any cop.

Parking in front of the clinic, she and the cats headed for the door, the cats pressing close to her legs. Firetti let them in and urged them on through the empty waiting room to the surgery, where he lifted the three cats onto a table.

"Natalie can't hear us," he said softly. "She stopped to tend to another patient; we had a couple of afternoon surgeries, and they're just recovering."

There was a short argument among the cats over who would go first. "I will, of course," Joe said boldly, drawing himself up, his ears sharp, his muscled shoulders gleaming, all macho tomcat and not a sign of fear.

Firetti nodded with approval. "You're bigger and stronger, Joe. And I'll take Kit's blood, too."

Kit looked smug, and lashed her fluffy tail.

"The blood of two cats should be sufficient, unless there are complications," Firetti said. "I'd like Dulcie to stay as a backup—like you to stay the night, Dulcie, to be here when Sage comes out of the anesthetic. He'll need another cat to talk to, he'll be confused, he—"

"*I'll stay!*" Kit interrupted. Charlie put a hand on Kit's head to silence her.

"He'll be disoriented," Firetti continued. "He may not

remember where he is, or why. In that state, the fear of finding himself alone and confined among humans could be very hard on him, and he—"

"*I'll* stay," Kit said again. "Sage and I are friends, we were kittens together, *I* can comfort him."

Joe and Dulcie exchanged a look, a concerned parental kind of glance that amused but puzzled Charlie. And Dulcie said, "Kit, you don't want to miss the party."

"*I want to stay!*" Kit hissed at her, showing formidable teeth.

"Dulcie will stay!" Joe said angrily, and the two older cats glared at Kit until the tortoiseshell backed away from them, round-eyed with surprise. Charlie didn't see what all the fuss was about. She didn't see what difference it made—until she looked again at Kit.

Even cowed by the older cats, the tortoiseshell's yellow eyes hardly left the sleeping patient. Kit watched Sage intently, and as Dr. Firetti prepared Joe to give blood, Kit crept nearer Sage, nosing at him and worrying, the tip of her fluffy tail twitching, her golden eyes filled with emotions that Charlie had never before seen in the young cat.

So, Charlie thought, hiding a smile. *So, is Cupid among us, then?*

But why would Joe and Dulcie be against Kit and Sage's friendship? The tortoiseshell was no longer a kitten, she was a grown cat now.

All through their whispered exchange, Sage lay sleeping on the table, sedated and kept warm. And whatever the problem, in the end Kit and Joe gave the first blood, and Dulcie was left to stay the night.

As the scent of alcohol filled the room, Charlie didn't like to watch John Firetti draw blood from Joe; the tomcat, despite his macho pretense, lay as rigid as if he were about to be field dressed. When Joe flinched, Charlie flinched. When the needle went in, she felt sharply its stinging bite—she was nearly as shaky and unnerved as she knew Joe was. The big, brawny tomcat suddenly seemed very small and frail—Joe seemed, himself, in need of tender protection.

When Dr. Firetti finished taking blood from Joe and Kit, he called Natalie on the intercom to help with the surgery. Kit refused to go home, so he settled Charlie and the three cats comfortably in his adjoining office; he gave Joe and Kit chicken broth to lap, and tucked them up in a blanket to keep warm, and showed Charlie where he kept the coffeepot. As the friends waited during surgery, Kit's eyes never left the connecting door, and silently Charlie and the cats prayed for the young feral.

5

At about the time Charlie entered Dr. Firetti's clinic, Mike Flannery was headed for Molena Point PD to pick up Dallas, to go on to the party at Clyde's place. He was stopped at a crosswalk in the center of the village, waiting for a pair of overdressed tourists to wander past, when he saw her—he caught his breath, felt his heart do a flip even after all these years.

She had started across the street when she paused, studying the car uncertainly, looking at the license plate and then to his driver's-side window; she wouldn't see much in the reflected light from the setting sun. He put down the window, when she saw who was driving she stepped back, looking as uncomfortable as he felt.

"Mike? I thought it was Detective Garza. The tan Blazer, the police license . . . The sun was in my eyes . . ."

"It's his car," Mike said. "Hello, Lindsey. Let me pull around the corner."

He'd dreaded this moment, he hadn't known how he'd

feel when he did see her. He'd considered telling Dallas he didn't want to work this case.

Well, here it was. So what was he going to do?

Take the case and throw himself back into the old feelings? They were still there, he knew that now. Or distance himself, be polite but turn away from her? Hand the case back to Dallas?

Lindsey had called Dallas early in the week concerning what she thought was a new lead, a body found up in Oregon, time of death maybe ten years ago . . . If that wasn't grasping at straws.

She had never gotten over Carson. As far as Mike knew, that was why she'd broken with him and left the village. He'd been pretty shaken when suddenly she'd told him she was moving back to L.A., gave him no reason.

They hadn't fought, they had been getting along fine, or so he'd thought. He had, in fact, been feeling pretty serious, almost to the point of proposing—a commitment he had not once considered since his wife died.

Lindsey's excuse for leaving was that she still felt involved with Chappell, that she'd realized she still cared for him. That not knowing whether he was alive or dead had left her unable to commit herself fully.

That had seemed fair enough—even if, he thought wryly, Chappell *had* run out on her.

Mike had wondered if maybe she hadn't wanted to be saddled with his three daughters, but he couldn't see why, they were all grown up by then and out on their own. Still, though, they were family. Lindsey had not had a pleasant family experience, none of the closeness that had warmed his own life, and maybe she was wary of that involvement.

To Lindsey, having grown up in a dysfunctional family and with an older sister who bullied her, maybe the whole idea of family was abhorrent, was not a relationship she wanted.

But why hadn't she said so? Why the hell did women have to be so devious? He'd never thought of Lindsey as devious.

For a long time after she left, he'd been angry, bitter.

Strange that now, despite his painful memories, he *wanted* to work the ten-year-old case, that this last week he had found himself looking at the case as a challenge.

And so who was devious? So who wanted to get back together again, and was afraid to admit it?

Parking in a green zone in front of the library, he watched her approach on the passenger side; the moment seemed almost in slow motion. She was just as beautiful, slim, willowy, her creamy oval face meant to be touched and kissed, her huge hazel eyes too painfully familiar, her soft brown hair floating around her face, changing in the glow of the dropping sun from chestnut to dark gold. Light, feathery brows, no makeup but a hint of pale lipstick. Her hands gave her age more clearly than her face, smooth hands but the veins standing out, her oval nails colored a soft salmon tone. She was around forty-five, ten years his junior. She wore a pale blue sweater with a V-neck over a white, open-collared shirt, her long slim legs easy in faded jeans. She leaned down, smiling in at him.

He reached over, pushed the door open. "Dallas is at the station," he said almost curtly. "How have you been, Lindsey?"

"I . . . Fine," she said uncertainly. "And you? I talked

with Dallas a few days ago. I had to be out of town, I didn't know when I'd be back, to make an appointment. When I saw the car, I thought . . ." Slipping into the car, she studied his face questioningly, her hazel eyes picking up amber lights. "You've retired, Mike. You're moving down to the village?"

"I'm staying with Dallas at the moment." He didn't tell her he'd be moving into Clyde's house, would be staying there alone while Clyde and Ryan were on their honeymoon, nor that he'd then be moving into Ryan's vacated apartment. Was he afraid he might weaken and ask her over? Afraid she'd ask herself over? His reticence both amused and annoyed him, he felt as awkward as a kid.

He told himself he was just protecting his privacy. It was true that he'd been looking forward to some downtime, to a period of quiet isolation during which he could do a little unhurried work at his own pace, his own hours. His daughter's big, airy studio with its expansive view of the village rooftops and of the sea beyond was just what he wanted, an ideal bachelor pad.

Was that what he was afraid of? That he'd invite her up? Afraid to be alone with her?

So why the hell, then, did he take the case?

Her smile was like the sun coming out. She made him feel too vulnerable; he hadn't meant to be thrown back into this. He'd intended to keep the investigation strictly business—or that's what he'd told himself. He'd thought he'd see her again and it would mean nothing, just old friends who'd moved on. Had told himself that was a long time ago and now they were both different.

But now, suddenly, it was all with him again. Every

detail of their time together seemed like yesterday, their casual dinners at her place, their runs on the beach, nights before the fire, holding her close.

Forget it. Keep your mind on the case. Or step back, tell Dallas you don't want to work this one. He looked at her sternly. "Why, after ten years, have you decided to pursue the case again?"

"You know I spent a year, after he disappeared, trying to find him, Mike. You know how I pushed the police and the California Bureau of Investigation. You know I didn't have any evidence that would put him across state lines, that would make it a case for the FBI. But now, maybe there is something."

He studied her, seeing how tired she looked suddenly, and older.

"When Carson disappeared, I came up with nothing but dead ends. You know I was weary, so scared and worried for him sometimes—not knowing whether something awful had happened to him, whether he was dead or hurt somewhere. And then at other times so angry, feeling totally betrayed. Wishing, if he *had* walked out on me, that he'd just told me, and broken it off." She reached to touch his hand. "Have you forgotten how it was, Mike?"

He hadn't forgotten. But he'd thought that, over the years, she would have come to terms with this, with not knowing—just as he had turned off the memory of her, or thought he had.

"When I felt so down, you helped me to heal. Without you, Mike, I couldn't have gotten through that year."

She was making him uncomfortable. Had she needed him, then, only for the sympathy he supplied?

But she looked at him with sudden fire in her eyes, a look that startled him.

"Now . . . ," she said, "maybe there is something. Maybe Carson has been found. Did Dallas show you the clipping, the body found last week, up in Oregon? A hiker, somewhere deep in the forest, some private land that I guess no one goes into much. The man was a *hiker*, Mike. They have his backpack, what's left of it. I can't get this out of my mind."

"I read the article," he said noncommittally. "But Carson was supposed to have gone camping near the village."

Camping, the week before their wedding, up in the hills south of the village. Lindsey had had no plans to go with him, she'd said there was a lot to do even for the simple wedding they'd planned, reminded him it was tax season and she had too much work to do, and that anyway, she'd never liked camping.

He remembered her saying, "Carson likes to hike alone, he likes those times of solitude—we both believe there are some things each of us can enjoy alone," and she'd laughed softly. "I don't like sleeping and cooking out in the cold, with no hot shower in the morning."

She'd worked for Carson Chappell's accounting firm at the time. She'd said that three of her biggest accounts had sent in very late tax figures and that she'd needed to finish those. Each of Chappell & Gibbs's employees had been solely responsible for their own accounts; she'd said Carson's accounts were all in order and filed.

Now, she looked at him levelly. "I want to know if that hiker in Oregon is Carson. Is that so hard to understand? I know it's unlikely, but . . . If I could put an end to it, to the questions . . .

"When I saw that newspaper article, I had this . . . *certain* feeling. A sudden jolt, as if I *knew*." She looked at him intently, her hazel eyes now as green as the sea. "I felt so sure. And I needed again, desperately, to find out what happened to him. To find out, and to let go of it at last, for good."

They looked at each other for a long time, Lindsey's hands folded quietly in her lap. "I know it's grasping at straws. Carson didn't say anything about going to Oregon, he told me he'd be hiking just above Molena Point. He gave me a map, marked where he planned to go." The betrayal and hurt in her eyes was just as raw as it had been ten years ago.

When she'd reported Carson missing, there'd been searchers all over the open land above the village, crisscrossing the miles of woods and hills that made up the state park land. The county sheriff, then the forestry department, volunteers, tracking dogs . . . They'd found no sign that Chappell had ever been there.

Mike studied her for a moment, then started the engine. "I'm headed for the station to pick up Dallas. We can talk there for a few minutes, maybe set up something for Monday." Pulling out into the slow village traffic, he could feel her watching him and he wondered again if this was smart, taking this case.

Sitting turned away from the door, she glanced into the backseat at the dog-hair-covered blanket, and smiled. "You have a dog? I miss Newton, I finally had to put him down."

"The blanket belongs to Dallas's pointer," Mike said. "The last of many, and he's getting along. Timber's partner died this last year, so Dallas takes Timber with him when he can—no, I have no dog now, it wouldn't have been fair to confine a big dog in the city."

"And little dogs don't appeal," she said, remembering. He didn't mention that he would be babysitting Ryan's Weimaraner this coming week, that he would be running the dog on the beach, as they used to run Newton.

She was quiet for some time, then, "Your girls are doing well?"

When Mike's wife died of cancer, her brother Dallas and Mike's brother Scotty had moved in with him to help raise the girls, to share the time-consuming responsibilities, to fill a little of the emptiness, to offer steadiness and love.

They had lived in San Francisco then; he'd met Lindsey during a family weekend at their Molena Point cottage; she had been the first and only woman he'd dated since his wife's death.

They'd packed a lot into their discreet weekends when he could get away to the village or could meet her somewhere halfway, along the coast. Lindsey had been interested enough in his family, from a distance; she had asked about the girls and enjoyed seeing their pictures, but she'd made it clear she didn't want to be involved.

"The girls are doing well," he said briefly, never having liked her distancing herself.

All three girls had turned out to be strong and resourceful young women. They worked for what was important to them, and they could take care of themselves. Hanni was a bold and original interior designer, Ryan an equally inventive architectural designer and hands-on building contractor. And their older sister, with a degree in economics from Stanford, had married an electrical engineer and moved to the East Coast where they were raising five fine kids. He had eight grandchildren, counting Hanni's three boys.

Maybe now, he thought, Ryan and Clyde would decide to have a family. Or not. Whatever they did, he felt more than sufficiently blessed.

He felt lucky, too, that in the process of raising the girls, he and Dallas and Scotty had grown as close as any brothers ever were. They'd run a tight household, and had taught the girls as many skills as they could.

Turning in through the wide parking area that served the Molena Point courthouse and the PD, moving in between its gardens and oak trees, he parked in a reserved slot in front of the station, then turned to look at her.

"Dallas said you still have Carson's clothes and personal possessions?"

"I've kept everything that was in his apartment—clothes, books, even the kitchen things—everything but the furniture. After the police were finished with the apartment and the office, everything they didn't hold for evidence was given to his mother. When she died, four years ago, she left a simple will that gave those things to me. I put it all in a small storage locker here in the village.

"I had to come up from L.A. to claim it, and I didn't want to ship it down there. Didn't want it handled any more than necessary. I thought that someday the police might want to look at it all again."

Mike swung out of the car, and before he could move around to open her door, she was out and on the sidewalk.

He caught a glimpse of the two of them approaching the glass door to the station, and was startled by the rightness of the reflection, his lean build and her slim, long-waisted figure seeming to cleave together naturally. Watching the reflection, he felt as if they had never broken off their relationship.

He held the door for her, and when he looked up, Dallas stood in the foyer, beside the dispatcher's counter, watching them with that unreadable, dark-eyed gaze that would intimidate the hardest felon. The Latino detective was freshly shaved, his short, dark hair newly cut, and was dressed for the party in jeans, a white turtleneck, and a tweed sport coat. The look on his face, as he studied Lindsey, gave Mike pause. It was a look of interest that Mike seldom saw in his brother-in-law's eyes—Dallas's warm Latin temperament embraced his good hunting dogs in a far more constant manner than it had ever done with any of his short-lived love affairs.

Mike tried not to bristle at Dallas's interest as they moved down the hall to the detective's office where Dallas made Lindsey comfortable in the leather easy chair and offered her coffee, which she refused. There was a brief discussion of what the cold file contained, and they made an appointment with her for late Monday morning, at the station, the morning after the wedding. If not for Dallas's watchful interest, Mike might have asked her to join him for breakfast before they were to meet. Dallas rose first, to escort Lindsay out to the front. Watching the two of them walk down the hall together, Dallas's broad, tweed-covered shoulders and dark hair, Lindsey's slim, graceful walk in the pale, faded jeans and sweater, the two of them looked, he thought, startled, as if *they* had known each other for a long time—maybe it was a trick Lindsey had that he'd never before noticed, maybe her way of bonding with a man.

Or maybe her compliance was totally unconscious. Whatever the case, the effect was charming—or, in this instance, damned annoying.

He didn't want to be at cross purposes with Dallas, certainly not just before Ryan's wedding. He watched Dallas escort Lindsey out, then he and Dallas headed for the party, saying little on the short drive, their silence not their usual easy quiet, but tense—they were, for the first time he could remember, at odds over a woman.

But as they pulled up in front of Clyde's house, he looked at Dallas and grinned, and they put their bristling aside and went in, wisecracking and looking for a beer.

6

AFTER THE BLOODLETTING, as Joe Grey thought of his stress-filled donation of vital bodily fluids, the tomcat lay safely on the couch in Dr. Firetti's private office snuggled among Dulcie, Kit, and Charlie, listening to the doctor's voice from the surgery and the occasional sound of instruments clicking against the metal table—and thanking the great cat god that he was out of there.

"How did it go?" Charlie said, gently stroking him. "You seem a bit pale."

Joe glared up at her. "How can a cat look pale? You can see beneath my fur?"

"Your expression is pale. Wan," she said. "Inside your ears is pale."

In truth, he felt pale. Felt wiped out. His paws were still sweaty, and he could still feel the cold metal table under him, where he'd lain half blinded by the harsh hospital lights reflecting off the table and the bright metal instruments and glass tubes; he could still feel that huge needle going into his little cat vein—he'd tried to be macho when his foreleg was shaved, his sleek gray fur stripped away to pale, naked skin and blue veins and then that huge needle was plunged deep in and his lifeblood drawn from his body into a syringe big enough to bleed a cart horse.

How could a heretofore kind and caring doctor coldheartedly remove all his life-sustaining juices? As Firetti had drawn the plunger back farther and farther, extracting more blood than any cat could *have* inside him, Joe had resisted a terrible urge to claw and tear at the doctor. In fact, though, with the needle in him, he'd been afraid to move at all and cause himself further damage—but then, when he'd glanced across at Kit expecting to see her trembling and cowering, what he saw had shattered him.

There she lay on the next table, calmly purring while she was shaved and the needle was inserted and her blood burbled out into the vial. *Purring.* As mindlessly relaxed as a stuffed teddy bear—her cool nonchalance had left him furious and shamefully embarrassed.

The fact that Firetti had said he'd take less than sixty cc's had no meaning for Joe. And it wasn't Firetti's blood.

At least Dulcie hadn't seen his cowardice, she hadn't been in the operating room; *she'd* been out here with Charlie lounging in Dr. Firetti's office, supplied with catnip, a bowl of turkey tetrazzini gourmet cat food, a cuddle toy, and a soft blanket.

Now, listening to Firetti's and his assistant's voices resonating softly from beyond the closed door against the harsh sounds of metal on metal, he pictured scalpels and other sharp cutting instruments, and he felt sick and hurting for poor Sage—every alarming TV show he'd ever seen featuring veterinary surgery came back to him. Why had he ever watched that stuff? He vowed never to watch again. He was glad Clyde and Ryan's taste in TV ran to turning off the set and snuggling before the fire or opening a good book. Beside him, Charlie was still fussing over him, stroking him way too gently.

"You want more custard, Joe, to get your strength back?"

"I've had three."

"I expect Kit seemed braver," Charlie said, as if reading his mind. "I expect she seemed more stoic in the matter of blood and needles?"

Joe stared coldly up at her.

"Human males are the same," Charlie said. "It's in the genes, that sudden weakness at the sight of blood."

"Cops can handle blood," Joe said irritably, wishing she'd mind her own business.

"Cops get used to it early, they have to. Anyway, you don't shrink from mouse blood."

"Mouse blood is not *my* blood."

Beside him, Kit had begun to squirm, as nervous as a rat on a hot stove, pawing the blanket one minute and deadly still the next. She didn't take her eyes from the inner door to the surgery. Her tortoiseshell ears were sharply forward, picking up every faint sound, her whole being focused on the young tomcat lying in there under the knife. Joe had seldom seen her so distressed; he watched her uneasily.

"You and Sage were kittens together?" he asked.

"Ever since my momma abandoned me where the clowder roamed. I remember her taking me there, carrying me by the nape of my neck swinging and jiggling through the tall grass. She laid me where the clowder would find me then she went away again and I think she was sick. I guess she died," Kit said sadly. "I followed the clowder, but they kept chasing me away. Sage was little, too, but he was Stone Eye's nephew, he belonged with them. I was an outsider, they didn't want me. Stone Eye didn't want me, and they all did as he told them. He didn't want any kittens besides his own. Sage was the only one who liked me, and he would sneak away to be with me. I was terrified of Stone Eye, but I needed to stay with them, I was only small and I needed the safety of that big band of cats. I didn't know how to hunt, and there were foxes and raccoons and coyotes in the hills.

"Sage stood up for me against the other young cats, and then one day Stone Eye mauled him real bad for being my friend. You can feel the scars under his fur."

She pricked up her ears at a new sound from the surgery, as if a table had been rolled across the room. Then all was still except the doctor's voice, too soft to understand.

Charlie said, "What happened after Stone Eye mauled Sage?"

"After that, Sage didn't fight for me anymore, but he still slipped away so we could be together. He helped me hide from the others and sometimes he'd lead the bullies away. And he brought me scraps from a kill or a garbage dump."

Kit frowned, her ears back, her whiskers flattening against her cheeks. "But still he thought Stone Eye was a good leader. He said we needed to be ruled by a strong paw. I never understood that, I never believed it had to be a cruel paw. When I got older, we argued a lot," Kit said, staring worriedly toward the closed door.

"Sage wouldn't run away from the clowder when I did, when I found Lucinda and Pedric up on Hellhag Hill and knew we were meant to be together. He was afraid to leave the clowder, he said only Stone Eye could protect us. He didn't trust Lucinda and Pedric, he had no faith in humans. I'm surprised he let you touch him, Charlie."

"He had no choice," Charlie said. "He was too hurt and weak to run. And Willow was right there, telling him to be still."

Joe looked at Kit for a long time, wondering. Earlier, when Charlie had first carried her into the surgery, when she'd first seen Sage, she had looked sick with fear for him, had let out a wailing mewl of shock and distress at how broken and weak he was. Even after they'd had their legs shaved and blood drawn for Sage, and Dr. Firetti had carried them in here to his office and to Charlie, Kit had been so filled with pain for Sage, it seemed her little cat heart would break—and yet there was this difference between them, which so deeply bothered Kit, Sage bowing to the tyrant's oppression while Kit defied such bullying.

It was more than an hour later when Dr. Firetti came out of the surgery wearing a clean lab coat and smelling of hand soap, and sat down to talk with them. Charlie, having left Joe and Dulcie and Kit in the office for a few minutes, had returned with her aunt Wilma. Dulcie's housemate, dressed in jeans and a red cashmere sweater, her gray hair tied back with a red cloisonné clip, sat now at the other end of the couch, holding Kit on her lap as Kit licked up a bowl of rich chicken soup. Dulcie lay behind Wilma along the back of the couch, her head on Wilma's shoulder.

Knowing the cats would be weak and emotionally wrung out after giving blood, Wilma had brought a thermos of canned soup, quickly warmed in Clyde's kitchen, and an array of party food from the buffet. Joe, at the other end of the couch, was gulping his share of shrimp canapés and little ham rolls stuffed with an assortment of cheeses, all therapeutic, of course.

"Sage did very well," Dr. Firetti said, "and is resting comfortably." Charlie smiled at the reassuring words used by most doctors. "The femur was broken in three places, so I've put in a metal plate, which is our best chance for sound healing. And I've put a pin in the one break in the tibia."

Charlie shivered. "Will he use the leg again?"

"I'm hoping he will, that it will heal as strong as it ever was. All we can do now is keep him quiet, care for him. And pray," Firetti said. "I want to keep him for a few days, to watch him. Then, Wilma, you're taking him home with you? That's closest," he said, "in case you need me at odd hours."

Charlie said, "I'll have to tell the Greenlaws that you know about the cats. And we'll have to tell Clyde and Ryan."

Firetti nodded. "Then Ryan knows, too?"

"She figured it out for herself," Charlie said. "It's a good thing she did."

Dr. Firetti laughed. "That would be an impossible

situation after they're married, if Joe couldn't talk in his own house."

Joe looked at the doctor with more warmth, assessing this man who had, for all these years, known their secret and never said a word. "No one," Joe pointed out, "seems worried that I'll hold my own with those two. Ryan Flannery can be just as stubborn and smart-mouthed as Clyde."

Firetti smiled. "I wasn't worried about you, Joe. I don't think you'll have a problem."

Joe just looked at him.

"You've done all right keeping your investigations secret, holding your own with the law."

All five stared at Firetti. Wilma said, "You knew this, too? The police part?"

Firetti nodded. "It took me a while to figure that out. But I've known about the cats since long before Dulcie was born, Wilma. I was doctor to her mother.

"My father, when I was a boy, years before I grew up and went off to school and then joined the practice . . . he treated several generations of speaking cats. When I was about ten, a Molena Point woman married a Welshman and they resettled in the states, in Molena Point, near her family. They brought with them four pairs of speaking cats.

"They planned to breed and sell them, but of course they didn't tell the cats this. When two grew very ill, they were forced to find medical care, and they came to my dad. The way those cats responded to medication he found very strange—it took him a long time to treat them, they had lymphadenitis, but they didn't respond well to penicillin. He brought them through, but their reactions puzzled him.

"He had read tales of unnatural cats in parts of Wales and Ireland, and now, when he researched the matter, he began to suspect there might be some truth in the stories, as impossible as they seemed.

"And then, when he examined the cats' blood, he found it was not like any known type, not A or B, not AB. And of course it was not like any of the several subtypes, which were discovered more recently. AB is, in itself, extremely rare, but this blood was none of those, it was different. Confronted with this irrefutable fact, he began to believe the tales.

"He could find no medical reference to help him, not even the newest, ongoing studies—no medical research even in the British Isles, where he thought there might be more such cats. Either no other speaking cat had ever been in a veterinarian's office, at least with an illness that would stir curiosity, or any other doctor who had known the truth had kept it secret.

"Of course, his investigations were done quietly, he daren't tell anyone what he suspected. He could ask no doctor or medical facility for any kind of help, he had only the myths and folk tales—and the unrecorded blood type.

"At one point, he was inclined to diagnose himself with mental derangement, was convinced he'd lost his grip on reality. He grew so upset that my mother intervened. In her direct way, she went right to the cats.

"When two cats were brought into the clinic for nail trimming and shots, she insisted they speak to her, and she told them why. She explained how upset the doctor was, and how carefully he had kept their secret. At last one of them did speak."

Firetti smiled. "She was determined the young cat would answer her. But when he did, the experience left her deeply shaken. The cats told her that the Welsh couple, in order to get them to travel willingly, had promised that in America people would treat them like gods, that they would live pampered lives, would enjoy total freedom to come and go as they chose, and would enjoy, as well, all manner of fine foods and luxuries.

"When they arrived in the village, the couple kept them inside the house, saying they must wait until the time was right to announce themselves to the public. The cats were here, and so far were being treated well enough, though nothing like they'd been promised.

"But after many months of being shut in, they grew restless and morose, and determined to leave that place.

"They found the door and window locks a kind impossible for a cat to open. They grew more and more worried, they ceased to trust the couple, and soon they would not speak unless they were tormented and forced to.

"Then the couple sold two pairs. The other four cats were enraged, there had been no talk of selling them like common beasts. The buyers lived in the village, and when one pair of cats had kittens, which is rather rare, the buyers in turn sold them. When the cats in the Welsh house learned this, that they were indeed being treated like livestock, they wanted only to get away.

"They tipped a bookshelf over against a window, breaking the glass, and escaped. They searched for their friends, were at last able to find the four, they freed them.

"One of their descendents was your mother, Dulcie. She remained with Genelle Yardley all her life. You were born on Genelle's bed. You were the only one of the small litter that would grow up to speak." He looked from Dulcie to Wilma, then stroked Dulcie. "Genelle felt certain, when Wilma took you home to be her kitten, that if and when you did speak, Wilma was the kind of person who would guard your secret.

"But years earlier, when the captive cats were all free, they headed up into the open hills, where they soon found the lush acreage of the Pamillon Estate. The property was beautiful then, with vast gardens, flowering bushes and trees among which to hide, and there they took shelter. There were several branches of the Pamillon family living there then, in the mansion and in several guest cottages that have since become uninhabitable.

"The cats lived on the estate through several generations, and they were fed and loved by the Pamillons. My father doubted anyone knew the truth about them, doubted the cats ever spoke to anyone. But there was one daughter, Olivia, who seemed especially fond of her cats, and he wondered sometimes about her.

"I was in my second year at Davis when the Pamillons undertook some repairs and remodeling of the estate. It may have been then that most of the cats moved away, into the farther hills—there were fewer and fewer visits from the Pamillons for shots or to treat an occasional illness.

"And then, at about that time, there was some kind of dissent within the family, and gradually the extended family, aunts and uncles and their children, moved away and seemed to lose interest in the property. Olivia remained, living as a recluse in just a few rooms. She stayed active in the village for a long time, but then as she grew older she fired gardeners and housekeepers and maintenance people, and let the estate fall into disrepair. There were two cats she would bring to me for shots, but I felt sure the rest had moved on."

"Maybe," Kit interrupted softly, "maybe they traveled way south, on the coast, where I guess I was born, the place I first remember."

"Maybe," Firetti said. "I went up to the estate occasionally because I was concerned about Olivia. I didn't see any other than the two cats that stayed with her. I always thought the family held on to the property simply for the increasing land value. It's a big, sprawling family, all scattered now, and apparently at loggerheads with one another. The estate has been divided and redivided, with numerous deeds and trusts and wills drawn in such a way that no one can sell his share without approval from the others. I know one attorney who did some work for the Pamillons, and he said the titles and legal entanglements were almost impossible to sort out and set straight, with so many conflicting restraints and demands.

"It was knowing about the speaking cats," Firetti said, "that started me feeding and trapping the stray cats of the village, as my father had done. He fed and trapped all the feral cats around the wharf and the village, and continued to do so long after he retired. He spayed and neutered them and gave them shots to keep them healthy and then turned them loose again." He laughed. "That might have been the first TNR program.

"He made very sure, of course, that none was a speaking cat. Not much chance, they were too clever to be trapped. He would have sheltered such a cat if it so chose, would have brought a speaking cat here to live, if the cat wanted such a life.

"He was already gone when I met Joe and Dulcie." Firetti looked down at the cats, sitting on the couch listening so attentively. "You were only a tiny thing, Dulcie, when Wilma brought you for your first shots. Though I knew who your mother was, the talent is not passed on to all the kittens in a litter. But from what Wilma told me about you, from your stealing of the neighbors' pretty clothes, for instance, I suspected that you were special and that one day you would discover your talents.

"And then you arrived on the scene, Joe. In the beginning, you and Clyde were just as clueless about who you really were." Firetti smiled, his blue eyes crinkling. "I knew when you and Dulcie discovered the truth. I would see you around the village, see the changes in your relationship, see your looks at each other.

"And then, strange things happened in the village. When the owner of the car dealership was murdered, the way the police captured the killers was odd. I was fascinated by the details of that investigation—and I began to see what you two cats were up to.

"From then on, I paid attention to crime in the village. I listened to the sometimes puzzled remarks of one officer or another about cats showing up near a crime scene. And when you came to live with the Greenlaws, Kit—and I heard Officer Brennan's story about a cat jumping from a roof onto a burglar's head, didn't that make me laugh."

"I kept it all to myself," Firetti said. "All this time, I've just enjoyed the ride."

Charlie studied Firetti's smooth, oval face, his direct

gaze, and was warmed by his quiet kindness. But then she thought, would nothing in the world make him tell what he knew?

There would be huge money in revealing the cats' secret, in bringing speaking cats to the attention of the world—the attention of avaricious promoters and the hungry news media.

But that was insane. John Firetti had been silent for so many years, when he could have sold out the cats at any time. Why wait until now?

No, despite money or power, here was one man who would remain true. John Firetti, like Max and the few other men she most admired, would not suddenly turn corrupt, would not deliberately use the innocent for financial gain. Here was one man who would not reveal this most hurtful of secrets, Charlie was certain of that.

7

FROM THE LIVING ROOM, through the big, open kitchen, and out onto the walled patio, Clyde Damen's house was filled with the beat of Dixieland and the happy voices of Clyde's and Ryan's friends, who had gathered with Ryan's family and with more than half the officers of Molena Point PD. The smell of hickory smoke and barbecued ribs filled the early evening; coolers stood about brimming with iced wine and beer. In the kitchen, where the big round table was loaded with appetizers and deli salads, Ryan stood replenishing a platter of cold cuts. She wore an apron over her jeans and T-shirt, a bridal present from her dad, printed with prim, old-fashioned sayings that made them both laugh . . . PRETTY IS AS PRETTY DOES . . . GENTLE JANE WAS GOOD AS GOLD, SHE ALWAYS DID AS SHE WAS TOLD . . . SUGAR AND SPICE AND EVERYTHING NICE . . . None of the clichés fit her, she was not a woman who valued sugar and spice and coy blushes. She was refilling the bread tray as Clyde came in from the patio.

He put his arm around her. "Where are the cats? Have you seen Joe?"

She gave him a puzzled look. "Charlie went off with them, with all three. She . . . sort of *sneaked* out of the house." Her eyes searched his. "What was that about?"

"I don't know . . . Sneaked?"

"Sneaked. She and Joe, fast and stealthy. Dulcie and Kit were waiting outside. That was over an hour ago. What are they up to?" Ryan was so new to the cats' true nature that she had no idea what might be normal behavior for them or for their human friends.

Clyde stood frowning at her. "Why would she . . . ? What's going on? They *sneaked* out? What the hell . . . ?"

"There . . . ," she said, looking away through the crowded living room where she could just see out the front windows. "She's back, her car is pulling up . . ."

As they waited for Charlie and the cats, she busied herself refilling the bowls of deli salads. Clyde said, "You nervous about tomorrow?"

"Don't talk about it, I'm a basket case."

He grinned, and kissed her. They looked up as the front door opened.

Charlie came in with Kit riding on her shoulder and Joe Grey strolling beside her, rubbing against her ankles. There was no sign of Dulcie. As they crossed the living room, Joe looked up at Charlie and gave her a whiskery smile, then swaggered ahead toward the kitchen, brushing through the crowd against bare legs and sheer stockings and pants legs, his stubby tail erect, his white nose lifted to the rich smells from the buffet and barbecue. The tomcat and Charlie and Kit all looked so patently innocent that

Clyde was afraid to hear what this was about—he wasn't sure he *wanted* to know what they'd been up to.

"Hi," Charlie said, joining them, balancing Kit as she took a piece of bread and reached for a beer.

"Where have you been?" Clyde said. "Where's Dulcie?" He saw how pale she was, her freckles a dark spill across ashen cheeks. "What happened to Dulcie?" he said quickly.

"She's fine," Charlie said, clutching Kit to her. "I have to talk to you. Can we go somewhere? It's . . . Ryan, you come, too."

Clyde picked up Joe, looking deep into the tomcat's yellow eyes but seeing no answers, only that same innocent stare. They headed down the hall to the guest room—this had been Clyde's bedroom before Ryan added the new upstairs master suite. It had now been redone for guests in a far more luxurious manner than Clyde had ever wanted. Ryan's sister, Hanni, forgoing her designer's markup, had chosen golden oak and wicker furniture and three of the bright Oriental rugs that she imported. The bedcover was a puffy patchwork of East Indian prints nearly as rich as the rugs. The white plantation shutters, in the daytime, would reveal the twisted branches of the oak trees outside the window. Mike Flannery's leather bag stood on the floor beside the open closet, where a few of his clothes hung at one end of the otherwise empty rod. His leather briefcase lay open on the wicker desk, revealing half a dozen file folders stamped MOLENA POINT PD.

"Looks like Dad can't wait to get rid of us," Ryan said, laughing, "and have the house to himself." Mike had moved in with Clyde a day early, to get acquainted with the animals and learn their habits.

He would not, of course, learn all their habits. Joe Grey had been lectured several times about his behavior around Mike Flannery, about his tendency to tease and create problems—about what would happen to him if he made trouble.

Shutting the door behind them, Clyde dropped Joe on the bed, and he and Charlie and Ryan sat down at the wicker card table before the window. Kit slipped from Charlie's shoulder to the table, and Joe leaped up to join her. Both cats looked nervous and wrung out.

"Dulcie's fine," Charlie repeated. "She and Wilma are . . . doing a favor for a friend."

"What friend?" Clyde said suspiciously. He hadn't seen Wilma leave the crowded house.

"A cat," Charlie said. "One of the wild band. He came to me tonight at the ranch; I was just ready to leave, and there was Willow hiding at the back of the barn, crouched and frightened. She . . . they . . ." She wiped her eyes on the sleeve of her sweatshirt.

Clyde reached for the box of tissues from the desk, surprised to see Charlie cry. Charlie never cried. She seemed surprised herself.

"They've left the ruins," Kit interrupted, "Willow's clowder . . . They're going back with the wild band, there was a terrible battle and Cotton and Coyote killed Stone Eye, and the whole band is free again, Cotton and Coyote will rule now but Sage was hurt bad . . ." Kit was so worked up she was shifting from paw to paw. ". . . wounded and bleeding and in pain and Willow took him to Charlie and Charlie doctored him and then took him and Willow to Dr. Firetti and he—"

"He had to operate," Charlie cut in. Kit *could* run on. "Firetti needed blood." She looked intently at Clyde. "He said it had to be special blood. From a special kind of cat."

That got Clyde's attention. Beside him, Ryan was silent, her green eyes turning from Charlie, to Clyde, to the cats. Sometimes lately she felt as if she'd been dropped into Neverland.

Charlie put her hand over Ryan's hand. "Dr. Firetti said, 'I think you know what I mean. I will need special blood.'"

"He knows," Clyde said, swallowing. "All this time? Taking Joe in for shots . . . ? Oh, my God."

"He's known since he was a boy," Kit interrupted, "and his father who was the vet before him knew, someone brought speaking cats here from Wales and started to sell them and the cats hadn't agreed to that and they escaped and that was the beginning of our clowder and . . ."

Listening to Kit's high-speed monologue, Ryan felt seriously unbalanced. She was barely used to Joe's acerbic comments, was still startled every time the tomcat spoke to her—was barely used to the fact that the cats *could* talk, and now here was Kit rattling on at a speed that left her giddy.

"And shaved our front legs," Kit was saying, thrusting out her own naked forearm for all to see, "and stuck needles right in under our skin into our veins and drew out so much blood I felt weak and fainty and then Dr. Firetti gave us broth and custard and roast beef that Mrs. Firetti sent over and then Wilma brought us chicken soup and party food and we felt stronger," she said, sucking in a breath, "but our poor fur, Joe's beautiful silver coat and my dear black-and-brown fur that I groom every day all spoiled and our skin all naked and cold and will it ever grow back again?"

"It's only a small shaved spot," Charlie said softly, taking Kit in her arms.

Ryan, with a sense of walking on quicksand, reached to gently examine Kit's shaved forearm, the dark veins showing boldly beneath the paper-thin skin. "I've had dogs shaved like this," she told Kit. "It doesn't take long to grow back. A few days, it will already be bristly. But how is Sage? How is the patient?"

Clyde put his arm around Ryan, hugging her. She was so cool, was fitting right in with this madness.

"He's doing fine," Charlie said. "Wilma's up there with Dulcie, in case they need more blood. She'll call when he's fully awake, when they know how the surgery went. Dulcie will stay there overnight. Dr. Firetti plans to sleep in the surgery, on a cot, but he wants another speaking cat near when Sage wakes, a cat he knows, to reassure and calm him. Being inside a building, in a cage, will terrify him until he's fully conscious—a wild little animal like Sage, with no other cat to talk to . . ."

"We have to tell Lucinda and Pedric," Clyde said. "They—"

"I . . . ," Kit began, crouching on Charlie's shoulder, ready to drop to the floor, ready to race through the house searching for her humans, to be the first to tell them. Hastily Charlie grabbed her and held her securely.

"I'll find them, Kit," Charlie said. "You stay here. You can't talk to them out there." Setting Kit firmly on the table and giving her a threatening look, Charlie went in search of the Greenlaws. Behind her, Kit fidgeted. Clyde and Ryan rose to follow, Clyde promising to bring the cats a plate of party food.

"Heavy on the shrimp," Joe said, "and the ribs."

"And some of those little quiches," Kit said, reluctantly settling down. "Nice and fresh from the oven."

Clyde gave the two a long look, then moved down the hall with Ryan, shutting the door behind them, Ryan pressing her fist to her mouth to keep from collapsing into uncontrolled laughter.

"Am I dreaming?" she asked him softly. "Am I making this up? Have you lured me into some alternate world?"

He paused in the hall, drawing her close and kissing her. "Does that feel made up? If you think you're dreaming, come on upstairs . . ."

She laughed and kissed him back, then slipped out of his arms and headed back to the party, holding his hand. But all the rest of that evening she wasn't really certain they hadn't slipped, together, through Alice's looking glass or through some other innocent-seeming portal into a startling new universe. The kaleidoscopic events, since the morning that Joe Grey had spoken to her for the first time—Christmas morning, the morning Clyde proposed to her—had left her waking suddenly in the night laughing out loud and then seriously questioning her sanity.

But then she thought, trying to steady herself, *To-morrow we'll be married, and* that's *real. How many women marry, for life, into the family of a talking cat?*

8

 CHARLIE FOUND LUCINDA in the kitchen setting out a plate of homemade cookies on one side of the round table that was loaded with party food. The tall, older woman was so thin that when Charlie put her arm around her, she could feel every bone—but bone covered in lean muscle. Even at eighty-some, Lucinda Greenlaw was healthy and strong; she did most of her own housework and walked several miles a day. "I need to talk with you," Charlie said softly.

Lucinda looked at her, startled.

"Nothing bad," Charlie breathed, "only private. Kit will tell it later, but she's—"

Lucinda laughed. "So impetuous you can't get in a word. Come on, Pedric's in the laundry." And Lucinda headed across the kitchen, away from the crowd. Charlie, following her, heard through a tangle of laughter Dallas's raised and angry voice from the living room and Mike's sharp retort.

What was that about? Mike and Dallas never had

words. Glancing across the room, she caught Ryan's eye. Ryan shook her head almost imperceptibly before she turned away.

On the closed laundry door hung a little sign: PLEASE DO NOT OPEN, which Clyde had posted to give the three household cats some semblance of quiet and privacy—none of the three liked loud parties. Two were elderly, and the younger, Snowball, had always been shy. Slipping the door open, they found Pedric sitting hunched on the bottom bunk, his head ducked beneath the upper bunk of the animals' bed, petting the three cats. Snowball lay in his lap, and Scrappy and Fluffy were snuggled in the blankets next to him. The cats had shared the two-bunk bed with the two old dogs until Barney, the golden, and then Rube, the black Lab, had passed away. Snowball was still grieving for Rube.

Against the party noise beyond the closed door, Charlie told the Greenlaws about Willow and Sage, then about John Firetti knowing the cats' secret. Neither of the two tall, thin, eighty-year-olds seemed too surprised; it took a lot to amaze Lucinda and Pedric.

"I always thought," Lucinda said, "that John Firetti acted a bit strange around Kit. When we first took her in for her shots, he looked at her for a long time without saying anything, and then he seemed to *expect* her to lie still and behave herself. He asked if she'd had her kitten shots, and when I told him we didn't know, that she was a stray, he asked where we'd found her," Lucinda recalled. "When we said Hellhag Hill, there was a sudden light in his eyes, a gleam of excitement, then he quickly looked down."

"But," Pedric said, "mostly it was his assuming Kit

would lie still. Why would he think he could just look at her and tell her it would hurt more if she wiggled, and she would hold stone still for him? I thought at the time that it was his tone, that he had a unique understanding of a cat's nature, that his voice and inflection somehow told his patients he expected them to behave.

"But later," Pedric said, "we wondered."

"Apparently he *does* have a unique understanding," Lucinda said, smiling. "More understanding than *I* ever guessed. We did think it strange, though, that he never suggested spaying her. He never brought up the subject. And of course we didn't."

"Well," Charlie said, stroking Snowball, "looks like I'm more shaken by this than you two. I never imagined . . ."

But when she looked at the older couple, who had recently been through a frightening kidnapping that could have cost them their lives, who had escaped unharmed with great resourcefulness, she knew there wasn't much that would shock the Greenlaws—until she mentioned the hidden book.

When she told them more about the battle at the ruins, and described the old volume the ferals had found, Lucinda's eyes brightened with excitement. "Where is it, Charlie? What did they do with it?"

And Pedric was burning with even more excitement. "More tales of speaking cats! Do you think . . . Are there stories we've never heard?" Charlie could imagine the old man avidly reading those tales, and memorizing every word.

• • •

BEYOND THE LAUNDRY room's closed door, as the three discussed the mysterious volume, Mike Flannery and his daughter had left the crowd, heading up the open stairs to the new second floor, to the construction project that had marked the beginning of Ryan's romance with Clyde. On earlier visits Mike had seen the impressive addition Ryan had built for Clyde when they'd first met; now Ryan wanted to show him how she would add her own studio. Carrying fresh cans of beer, leaving behind the sounds of the party, neither father nor daughter glanced back to see the gray tomcat pad watchfully out of the kitchen to follow them, they didn't see him slink up the stairs behind them to the master suite and into the shadows beneath the king-size bed.

Joe ignored a twinge of guilt at spying on his friends. At breaching father and daughter's privacy. Dulcie would have said, "Can't they have a few minutes alone, the evening before Ryan's to be married? Do you have to be so nosy?"

But of course he was nosy, he was a cat. Cats were driven by nosiness, they were masters of curiosity. The investigative instinct was their finest mark of uniqueness, and who was he to go against basic feline nature? He followed. He hid under the bed. And he listened. And if the stab of guilt continued to accompany the tomcat's eavesdropping on his about-to-be housemate, Joe thought Ryan wouldn't really mind, that he could talk his way around her annoyance.

• • •

THE NEW ADDITION had a high ceiling of open rafters, where Ryan had raised the hip roof of the old one-story cottage to form two walls of the new second floor, then added new window walls. Mike admired again the stone fireplace she had built in the master bedroom, the compartmented bath and dressing rooms, and Clyde's cozy study. When Ryan was little, she'd loved to draw floor plans and elevations. Every minute she wasn't riding or working with the dogs, or going out on construction sites with her uncle Scotty, she was inventing her own house designs. Mike had only smiled when her teachers complained that all her school papers and notebooks had little floor plans or architectural details in the margins, sketches quickly made to record some fleeting idea.

Passion, he thought. The child had had a passion for what she loved, for what she knew she wanted to do with her life.

She had never abandoned that drive; she had learned her carpentry skills from Scotty, had studied structural design, had never wavered from the intensity of her goal. Now, having gotten where she wanted to be, she relished the work she did.

So many kids, Mike thought, didn't seem to feel strongly about anything, didn't have any kind of ongoing passion, any dream to follow and fight for. Did today's schools take it all out of them? Or was it the canned culture they grew up in? He thought sometimes that an entire generation had morphed into mind-numbed spectators, that their passion had so badly turned in on itself that they were able to hunger only for the quick, immediate sensation with no meaning.

Well hell, wasn't he getting jaded. He guessed he'd worked too long among criminal types—maybe it was time to turn his back on law enforcement before he grew really bitter.

Shaking his head, both amused and annoyed with himself, he put his arm around Ryan. "You did a great job with this house," he said, studying the details of the master suite, the deep window seat beside the stone fireplace, the Mexican-tile floor and carved doors. "And it's a perfect arrangement for a couple. Almost," he said, laughing down at her, "as if you *expected* to move in."

Ryan laughed, and blushed a little. "I expected someone would. I didn't think Clyde would remain a bachelor forever, he didn't seem the type—despite his philandering ways."

"That's in the past for Clyde," he said reassuringly. "Where will you put the new studio? You plan to enclose the deck over the carport?"

"No, the studio will go just behind it." She crossed Clyde's study to the glass doors that led to the upstairs deck. "We'll leave the deck, put the studio back there, over the dining end of the kitchen—if we can get the permit."

She turned, pushing back her short, dark hair. "After the battle I had on the last job, I'm not looking forward to another hassle with city planning—to a fight that has nothing to do with standard building codes. I should be used to it, it goes with the territory. But I never will be." She looked up at him, her green eyes angry. "I understand sensible restrictions to protect the lovely setting of the village, but—"

"But what you can't abide," Mike said, "is high-handed

authoritarianism for no reason but personal power."

She laughed. "Those people don't own the world," she said. "But they sure like to think they do." Molena Point's building codes and the patronizing attitude of its building inspectors were a sore point among most of the village contractors, except for those few who passed sufficient sums under the table.

"What if they won't okay the studio?"

She studied him. "We're not buying them off, if that's what you're thinking. I can take over the downstairs guest room, though I'd rather not. Clyde likes having a guest room, and so do I. And I really want a studio with a view, I like to look down on the rooftops when I'm working. That's why I like the apartment.

"If they flat-out refuse the permit," she said, "if I get tired of fighting them, and if you've found a place of your own by then, I'll keep the apartment as my studio. Not as convenient for late-night fits of inspiration, but I can have a small setup here, in a corner of the study. I really do need the apartment's downstairs garage for equipment storage. If I don't have that, I'll have to rent space somewhere."

She pulled a blueprint from a stack of papers on Clyde's bookshelf and unrolled it on the desk; as Mike looked over the studio's floor plan, she studied her dad. "You had a little tiff with Dallas?"

He looked at her and shrugged. "A small difference of opinion, nothing important."

She waited.

"Something about the Carson Chappell cold case," he said.

Ryan hid a smile. "Lindsey Wolf is lovely."

Ignoring that, he studied the blueprint intently, look-ing over the interior elevations, nodding with approval at the high, slanted ceiling with its long skylights and the small, raised fireplace in the far corner between the glass walls, its stone matching that in the bedroom.

"Plenty of room for my drafting table," she said, amused by her dad, "for file cabinets, computer, and a deep storage closet here for drawings and blueprints." Was he getting serious again about Lindsey? Ryan thought Lindsey was the only woman he had ever really cared about since her mother died.

"The plan's perfect," Mike said, "and it would be nice to be able to work at home. Not to mention my being able to keep the apartment," he teased. "I'll think good thoughts."

"Maybe the construction gods will smile. Maybe, by the time Clyde and I get back from our honeymoon, the permit will be waiting for us. But I'm not holding my breath." Her green eyes searched his. "Are you okay with staying here while we're gone, taking care of Rock and the cats? I could take Rock up to the Harpers'."

"I'm looking forward to having a dog again, even if he is only on loan. Looking forward to long runs on the beach, walks around the village, taking our meals at the patio restaurants. With that handsome fellow at my side, I can pick up any good-looking woman I choose."

"You're an old rounder, you know that? Tell me more about the cold case." Watching him, she curled up com-fortably on the leather couch, sipping her beer.

Mike stretched out in the club chair, his long, lanky frame easy in his worn jeans and faded T-shirt. "You're pumping me, but okay."

He felt uncomfortable telling her about meeting Lindsey on the street earlier that evening. "I'd already read the file," he said. "I wasn't sure I wanted to work this case, but it has the best contacts. Not only Lindsey, but her sister and some of the crowd they ran with when Chappell disappeared, quite a few of their friends still in the village."

"I always thought that was a strange thing to do," she said, "to go off camping just before his wedding." Glancing down at her engagement ring, she frowned.

"That won't happen to you and Clyde—you couldn't drive Clyde away with a club."

"I know," she said, smiling smugly. But still a coldness held her, a sudden sense of misfortune, and she saw again the day of Charlie and Max's wedding. The explosion in the church, debris suddenly hanging in the sky then starting to fall in slow motion, and a split second later the deafening boom of the blast. Parts of the church walls flying everywhere, mixed with white flower petals floating down and bits of silver fluttering all around her, silver foil that forensics would later identify as the elegant wrapping paper in which a "wedding gift" had been detonated remotely.

She thought, shivering, about her own wedding day tomorrow, about the gathering at the Harpers' house—so many law enforcement people in the wedding party, so many prime targets. And for a long moment, an unreasonable wave of dread held Ryan cold and still.

9

DON'T LET THE EXPLOSION at the Harpers' wedding eat at you," Mike said. "Things like that don't happen twice. Or . . ." He looked at her more closely. "Is there something else bothering you?" Sounds of the party drifted upstairs to them, and to the tomcat listening from the adjoining room beneath the king-size bed. "You don't have second thoughts about marrying Clyde?" Mike asked. "You're not regretting this new step in your life?"

"Oh, it isn't anything like that. It's just . . . Maybe I'm a bit tired."

There *was* something else, of course, something she couldn't share with her dad, ever. "It's . . . someone else's secret," she said inadequately, "that I'm committed to keep."

"Well, that's okay, then," he said easily. Then, "You care if I take Rock in to the station now and then? He'll be bored out of his mind if I leave him here all day, this breed was never meant to be idle."

"Take him, if Max doesn't mind. Rock loves a crowd, it would be good for him." She studied her dad. "Dallas and I've talked about training him to track. He tracked Charlie when she was kidnapped, he figured it out on his own, and showed a fine natural skill. But then, he loves Charlie."

"No question he's smart and eager," Mike said. "He's how old? Three? It's easier to start a puppy. But Rock . . . the way he watches a person, wanting to be part of the action, wanting to *do* something. He needs some kind of work."

She knew that too well. A dog like Rock, with so much desire and drive—he was too fine an animal to be lying around doing nothing, or looking for trouble. But she never seemed to have the time to give him what he needed, there weren't enough hours in the day.

From the shadows beneath the bed, Joe Grey listened first with amusement, then with rising interest at the idea of training Rock to track, to find felons or lost children. This, the tomcat realized, might solve the problem that had been eating at him. The dilemma for which, until this moment, he'd had no solution.

Rock could find the body that neither Charlie nor the secret snitches dared report. *I can teach Rock to track! I can train a tracking dog in ways no human ever dreamed! And then . . .*

The more he thought about the idea, the better he liked it. He lay working out the details, deciding which humans to enlist, to do the legwork, as it were, and by the time Ryan and her dad headed back downstairs, the gray tomcat was grinning with anticipation.

Quietly he followed father and daughter down to the living room where Clyde was changing discs in the CD player, putting on some old ragtime from early in the last century—how many cat lifetimes ago? Hiding his grin, he sauntered past Ryan and Mike and Clyde, leaped to the back of the love seat and to the top of the six-foot bookcase, startling Mike, who stared up at Joe as he stretched out with his paws hanging over the edge.

"That cat sneaks around like an undercover agent."

"Nature of the cat," Clyde said easily, setting aside some discs. "It's the sneaky cat that catches the mice." And he turned away to sort through the remaining CDs.

Ryan had turned away, too, hiding a grin as she brushed lint from her jeans. Behind Mike's back she glanced up to the bookshelf where Joe was washing his paws. She winked at him, then turned back to Clyde. "We were talking about Lindsey Wolf," she said. "She's lived in the village off and on. Do you know her?"

"I used to see her in the vet's office," Clyde said. "She had a golden retriever, and we'd swap anecdotes." He glanced at Mike. "Didn't you date her for a while? Is that the cold case you're working, her fiancé? What was his name? Chappell? Some people said he got cold feet, bailed out because he really didn't want to get married."

Mike nodded. "Carson Chappell. Lindsey came to Dallas because of an article in the paper, the skeleton of a hiker found up in Oregon. Apparently died about the time Chappell disappeared." Mike stepped to the bookcase to stroke Joe, wanting to know the tomcat he'd be caring for. "Not likely it's Chappell, but Lindsey's fixed on the idea."

"I heard Lindsey moved back," Clyde said, "moved her accounting practice up here. I've seen her sister around the village lately, too. That should be interesting, the two of them in the same small town again; I think they were both dating Chappell, and Lindsey was pretty angry about it."

Mike smiled. "I guess there's no love lost." He stroked Joe for a few moments, studying the tomcat a bit too keenly, then turned away and stretched out in a leather chair, eyeing Joe's clawed and furry easy chair with such obvious amusement that Joe bristled.

What's wrong with that chair? That chair is a masterpiece of feline creativity, it's a rare art form. Some people have no taste.

Clyde was saying, "Lindsey told me once that she and Ryder have been crosswise since they were kids. I guess, when Chappell started seeing Ryder on the sly, that didn't go down too well. Then Chappell and Lindsey announced their engagement, and then Chappell disappeared. About the same time, his partner's wife moved away, and of course village gossip had it that Nina Gibbs and Chappell ran off together."

"It isn't rumor," Mike said, "that after Lindsey moved back to L.A., her sister showed up with Ray Gibbs, Chappell's partner. He and Ryder are still together, they have a place in the city, and they're buying a condo in the village."

"You've been busy," Ryan said. "And Gibbs never found his wife? Never heard from her?"

"Not that anyone knows," Mike said. "I haven't talked with Gibbs yet."

Above, on the bookcase, Joe Grey might have added

his own take to the scenario. His thoughts might be off the wall, but he couldn't leave it alone. That hiker up in Oregon died some ten years ago. And what about the skeleton Willow had found among the Pamillon ruins? How old was that body? Two unidentified skeletons, discovered within the same week. Nothing at all to indicate a connection. And yet . . .

The tomcat didn't believe in coincidence. Too often, in the world of criminal investigation, if one looked deeply enough one would come up with some oblique and overlooked relationship between seemingly unconnected incidents. While the assumption didn't hold true in every case, the general concept had served Joe well.

This time, am I way off base? When Dallas and Harper get a look at that body in the ruins—as soon as we set them up to find it without involving the secret snitches—and when the coroner establishes a time of death on it, what will we have then?

Only forensics could date the Pamillon body. And first, the law had to find it among those isolated ruins where no one ever went, not picnickers, not even many lovers wanting privacy, the Pamillon ruins being too eerie for most lovers.

In short, it wasn't likely anyone was going to accidentally stumble on that lost grave, not without help. And, for sure, the report daren't come from the cops' favorite but unidentified snitch.

The cops get a tip that something's dug up a body there—and how else would it get uncovered? And they wonder about the feral cats around the ruins. He could just hear Dallas: "Something dug it up. And there are cats all over that old estate. Would a band of cats dig up a body? But even if they did, who the hell found it? Who was up there to call in the report? That voice—sure as hell, that was our phantom snitch. What was he doing up there?"

Right. The cops start asking questions, that's way risky. A cop's as nosy as any cat. A cop starts wondering about cats and dead bodies and that could be the end of feline investigative work for the rest of recorded time.

No, fate needed a little help here to keep the snitch out of the picture. And excitement filled Joe as, crouched atop the bookcase, shutting out the conversation around him, he laid out his scenario.

How long, he wondered, once the coroner had dug up the Pamillon bones, would it take to get them dated? Sometimes the lab came through right away, sometimes forensics could be backed up and maddeningly slow. And how long until the department had a more definitive date on the Oregon body? All across the country, law enforcement was shorthanded, short of money, backed up for months and sometimes years, pushing court cases into gridlock and even forcing the court to let a suspect walk—while the government spent billions of dollars, Joe thought, on programs that benefited no one but the paper pushers.

Bottom line: he had no notion how long, after the body at the ruins was "found," until the department would have a comparative age on the two sets of bones and there was any real basis for his gut feeling. For a cold case, there could be a long wait. This was not a killer awaiting trial.

Not yet, it isn't, Joe thought. *But with luck, it will come to that.* Joe Grey was not a patient tomcat.

Nor did he ordinarily indulge in the kind of presumption that now held his attention. His attempt to connect the two bodies was squirrely, but he couldn't shake his feeling that there *was* a connection—and the more he thought about his plan to anonymously report the body, the more he liked the scenario.

To pull it off, the body would have to remain buried in the earth of the Pamillon ruins for another week, given the fact that tomorrow was the wedding. Well, that couldn't be helped, he'd just have to live with that.

IT WAS EARLY the next morning, three hours before the wedding, when Wilma and Kit went to visit Sage and pick up Dulcie; the clinic was closed on Sundays. Dr. Firetti let them in the side door. He was smiling but looked like he could use a night's sleep; there were smudges under his eyes and his usually ruddy color was pale. In the recovery room, they found Sage and Dulcie in a big cage with its door open, Dulcie lying close to the patient, yawning. Sage was awake and licking up a little warm broth. He looked very small and frail wrapped in the heavy white bandages and with the cast on his leg.

"He's done very well," Firetti said. "I think he's out of danger, barring something unforeseen. Dulcie helped a great deal to reassure him when he came out of the anesthetic. She didn't have to give blood," he said, smiling, "though I used most of what I had.

"With the metal plate and pins in, the leg should heal just fine. The thing now is to avoid infection." Firetti lifted Kit into the open cage beside the patient, so she could visit. "I'd like to keep him another day, to watch him. Isn't the wedding today?"

"Yes, it is," Wilma said. "I can pick him up tomorrow morning, early. Shall I call first?"

Firetti nodded. "Please. When you come for him, I'll give you instructions and show you how to change the dressings."

Wilma was a stranger to Sage, and the young, bleached calico looked up at her warily; but Dulcie and Kit were obviously comfortable with her, and soon he relaxed.

"Was it very bad?" Kit asked him, glancing around uneasily at the wire cage. She did not like to be inside a cage, even with the door open, and she didn't like to see her friend there. Didn't like to see him all bundled up in those heavy bandages, either.

"The doctor is very kind," Sage said sleepily. "Very kind and good." And he laid his head down beside his empty bowl. "I don't hurt anymore . . . ," he said, and he was asleep again, still groggy and worn out.

Wilma gave Dr. Firetti the custards she had brought, and she and the two cats left, Kit looking back at Sage until the office door closed and she could no longer see him; and in the car the tortoiseshell hunched down miserably, thinking only of her friend. "I just wish . . . ," Kit said forlornly, "I wish . . . I wish Stone Eye could die all over again, slowly and painfully!"

"This is Clyde and Ryan's wedding day," Wilma said. "Are you going to feel all sour and grumpy and make *them* feel bad, and spoil their happy day?"

"I'm not," said Kit. "I mean to smile and purr. But right now I mean to feel bad just for a little while." And she turned over on the seat with her back to Wilma and Dulcie and said not another word as Wilma headed home to dress for the wedding.

FROM THE CRACK of dawn, Clyde and Joe's house was a turmoil of prewedding excitement that made the tomcat laugh, but that he wouldn't have missed. Mike left early to help Max pick up the folding chairs. Max called later to see if Clyde needed any assistance, and Clyde snapped that he could still dress himself, thank you. Max told him, "Don't forget the rings," and Clyde and Joe argued fiercely about which pocket to put the rings in, which was arguing stupidly about nothing. And then at last they were in the sleek Cadillac Escalade that Clyde had borrowed for the honeymoon trip—borrowed because Ryan had said that, if they were going to be tooling around the wine country with all those great antiques stores, they'd better take her pickup. And Clyde said he wasn't going on their honeymoon in a pickup. "So," Ryan had said, "if you're such a snob, borrow an SUV," and Clyde had gotten a two-year-old, top-of-the-line loaner from the dealership where he had his automotive shop.

Dulcie had come over the rooftops to ride to the wedding with Joe and Clyde. She had, after her long night at the vet's, a great need to be close to Joe. Waiting for Clyde, the two cats leaped into the front seat of the pearl-colored Escalade hoping the groom wasn't going to be late. "I never want to see you in the hospital," Dulcie said, snuggling against Joe. She didn't say, Please take care. But

Joe winced because that was what she was thinking. He hated being told to be careful, that kind of female meddling made him feel totally caged. But then he looked at her, saw how tired she was, and tenderly licked her ear.

The luxurious SUV had creamy leather upholstery, an OnStar GPS system, and, best of all according to Ryan's assessment, it had a good strong trailer hitch—if she found some irresistible architectural pieces that wouldn't fit inside, they could haul them home in a rental trailer. Clyde had scowled at that. This was a borrowed and like-new vehicle, as pristine as the day it came off the floor. Now, in the back of the vehicle, besides the couple's two suitcases, were half a dozen thick blankets, presumably to protect the interior, and two coils of rope.

"Some honeymoon," Joe said, "hunting for dusty old stained-glass windows and distressed paneling with spiders in the cracks."

"They're happy," Dulcie said. "Who knows, maybe they'll come home with some ancient car Clyde can't resist."

"Just what he needs, another deteriorating Packard or Maxwell. Some pitiful wreck just crying out for loving attention."

Dulcie laughed. "They're a couple of nutcases. They're not planning a honeymoon, they're off on a treasure hunt." But, watching the groom lock the front door and head for the car, looking very nice in his new tan suit, white shirt, and the first tie he'd worn in months, the cats smiled with tolerance for their crazy human friends.

10

WHAT A JOYOUS wedding it had been, with all the friends gathered on the Harpers' bright patio, the sun glinting off the far sea, the smell of spring in the air, and the lilting Irish music reflecting the bride and groom's shy excitement. Joe and Dulcie and Kit had crowded among their human friends at the edge of the makeshift aisle, watching Ryan slowly approach the minister, looking radiant in her soft red suit; the joyous ceremony stirred tears among the guests, and then stirred happy laughter. But now the wedding toasts and good-natured ribbing were over, the bride and groom had long ago departed to drive up the coast in their borrowed chariot, and the bright day was slipping toward evening.

Most of the guests had left, many of Harper's officers reporting to the station for second watch. Dulcie had left with Wilma, and Kit with her elderly couple. By eight o'clock, only Ryan's dad and her two uncles remained with Charlie and Max—and of course Joe Grey and Rock, dozing before the fire, waiting for Mike to take them home.

Joe, full of buffet treats, watched Dallas and Scotty shrug on their jackets, both men quiet and reflective, heavy with fatherly nostalgia. As if each wished, for a moment, that they could go back in time, that Ryan was small again, still their feisty little girl learning all over again to ride, to train the hunting dogs, to cook and keep house and to use properly Scotty's carpenter's tools. As the two men swung out the door, Scotty's red beard catching the light, behind them Mike Flannery, muttering that he'd have to buy a car soon, pulled on his coat and fished out the keys to Clyde's antique yellow roadster, in which Ryan had driven to her wedding, Rock sitting tall and dignified beside her.

Charlie picked up Joe, holding him against her shoulder, and she and Max walked out to the car with Mike, where she set Joe on the front seat. As the silver Weimaraner leaped obediently into the backseat, Mike looked at Joe and then at Charlie. "Where's the cat carrier?"

"Doesn't have one. He'll be all right," Charlie told him.

"A cat can't ride loose like that. This is an open car. I don't—"

"He'll ride just fine," Charlie said, stroking Joe. "He likes cars. He'll mind you just as well as Rock will. Watch," she said, turning a sly green-eyed look on Joe.

"Get in the backseat, Joe," she said, tapping the backseat beside Rock. "Backseat! Now!"

Joe gave her a *Just-you-wait, you'll-get-yours look*, but hopped obediently into the back.

"Lie down, Joe."

Joe lay down beside Rock's front paws, glaring at Charlie.

"Stay, Joe. Stay until you get home."

Mike stared at Joe and stared at her. He shook his head and had nothing to say. Both cat and dog turned the same expectant expression on him, as if willing their human chauffeur to get a move on, making the tall, sandy-haired Scots Irishman swallow a laugh. "That," Mike said, "is a pretty unusual cat."

Max looked impressed, too—but as much with Charlie's expertise as with the behavior of the gray tomcat. Ever since Charlie had published her book about the journey of a little lost cat, he had seemed almost to hold in reverence his redheaded wife's uncanny knowledge in matters feline—and now that *Tattercoat* was selling so well, Charlie's e-mail was filled with fan letters saying the same: *How did you learn so much about cats? It's almost like you can speak with them and understand them . . . I've had cats all my life, but there's so much in your book that I've never known . . . I'm convinced the cat herself wrote this book . . .*

And that, of course, was the case. This was Charlie and Kit's secret, the tortoiseshell was, indeed, Charlie's collaborator. Kit had told Charlie her own story, from the time she was a small kitten—though Max would never know the truth, Charlie thought, smiling to herself.

Joe, curled down between Rock's front paws, glimpsed Charlie's secret amusement in the flash of her green eyes, a quick sharing that neither Max nor Mike would correctly read; then the tomcat turned away, pretending to doze as Mike started the engine and headed the yellow roadster for home.

• • •

AT HOME, IN the Damen kitchen, Mike fed Rock and the household cats. He fed Joe, too, reluctantly. "How can you eat again? You'll be sick after all the party food." He stood scowling down at Joe. "Did Clyde mean it when he said you could have anything you want, and as much as you want?"

The tomcat looked back at him, wide eyed and innocent. He loved this, loved when people talked to him not knowing he could have answered them. Such earnest, one-sided conversations were so amusing that he often had to turn away and pretend to wash, so as not to laugh in their faces.

Mike went into the laundry to tuck the other three cats in for the night in their cozy quarters, fluffing their blankets and pillows, and petting and talking to them. Snowball was the needful one; Scrappy and Fluffy were quite content with each other. Mike gave the little white cat a long time of extra attention, moving away only when she dozed off under his stroking hand.

Back in the kitchen, he picked up Rock's leash. As the silver hound pranced and huffed, Mike stood regarding Joe, uncertain whether he should keep the tomcat in for the night, or let him roam as Clyde had instructed.

Clyde said Joe could come and go as he pleased, night or day, that the tomcat was to have free access to both cat doors, 24/7—to the cat door that opened to the front porch, and the one high among the upstairs rafters, which led out to Joe's tower and to the roofs of the village.

Mike didn't approve of cats out at night to wander the streets, unseen by hurrying drivers, but he did as he'd been told. He headed out with Rock, locking the front door and leaving Joe on his own. Telling Rock to heel, he headed through the village and toward the shore.

• • •

THE WEIMARANER HEELED nicely on a loose leash. Mike looked back several times, half expecting to see the tomcat following them or see him racing above them across the rooftops—though with the party food that cat had gulped down, he was probably curled up on the couch belching and sleeping it off. He hoped, when he got home, Joe hadn't upchucked all over the living room. He'd never seen any animal eat that amount of food, all of it rich, without coughing his cookies and blowing his liver. But Clyde swore the cat was in perfect health.

The waxing moon brightened the rolling breakers, silvering the skein of wet sand where he and Rock jogged close to the water. Rock wanted to pull, wanted to race to work off steam. Mike ran with him but wouldn't let Rock loose until he knew the dog better. He wished Lindsey were with them, running on the beach with her golden retriever as they used to do, wished she would appear suddenly out of the dark, running beside him—a fanciful dream. He put it aside, and thought instead about his coming years of retirement.

Starting a new life. Not with Lindsey, as he'd once thought, but that was all right. He was free of heavy demands. His time was his own to do with as he pleased. Free of his long and often vexing commitment to the increasingly frustrating workload of the U.S. court.

The fact that he wasn't chained to a desk anymore, that he didn't have to hit the office Monday morning, should have left him feeling like a kid at the beginning of summer vacation.

But already he was beginning to see that retirement might have its downside, already he felt himself missing the security of a set routine—with that steady, longtime support suddenly withdrawn, he felt for a moment as if he had no anchor.

How juvenile was that!

He guessed everyone, when they retired, felt that way for a while. But the fact that he did deeply annoyed him, as if he had no more inner resources than a wind-up mannequin.

He knew he'd miss some of his coworkers, but they'd be in touch, the city wasn't that far away. He'd miss his two favorite judges, but he sure wouldn't miss some of the other federal judges. The deterioration of the judicial system, on all levels, was one thing he was not ambivalent about, he was damn glad to be away from that breakdown.

His only regret was that he hadn't been able to do more to hold the line, to maintain the principles on which the federal courts had traditionally been based. The change in the quality of judges and their misuse of the law, both at local and federal levels, were hard to live with. Very hard, when the results of that disintegration were too many felons walking the streets committing more crimes, robbing and raping and killing law-abiding folk.

Bitter, he thought. *Getting old and bitter.*

But he hadn't been old when he'd started that battle, he'd fought it for twenty-five years. He had to admit, he was tired. Tired of locking horns with elected officials who didn't have a clue as to the damage they were doing or didn't give a damn.

Around him the night was very still, the only sounds the

crashing of the breakers and Rock's excited panting. Where the bright waves rose and fell, a seal surfaced suddenly and it was all he could do to hold Rock, to stop the big silver dog from plunging in and swimming after the animal—when the ninety-pound Weimaraner abandoned his manners and set his mind to something, he was a powerhouse.

A hardheaded powerhouse, Mike thought, *the kind of dog, if he's well trained and well directed, will work his heart out for you.* The obedience simply had to be on Rock's terms, on terms of mutual respect.

To settle Rock down Mike did a two-mile run with him. Turning back at last, winded, they stopped at the foot of Ocean, where Mike brushed the wet sand off Rock's belly and legs before they headed home.

Now Rock walked easily at heel, just tired enough to wag and laugh up at him, his panting expression filled with happiness.

"You don't miss your mistress and your new master?" Mike asked him. "You don't miss Ryan?"

At the mention of Ryan, Rock came to full attention, tensed to leap away again, and looking all around into the night searching for her, sniffing for her scent.

"She isn't here," Mike said contritely. "I just meant . . . It's okay, boy," he said, patting Rock's shoulder with a hard and reassuring hand and then rubbing his ears. "It's okay, she'll be home soon."

At his steadying voice and at no further mention of Ryan, and when the silver dog could not pick her scent from the wind, he at last settled down, looking up at Mike as if almost trusting him, as if hoping he could trust his new friend.

"You're a fine fellow," Mike told him as they walked up through the moonlit village and past the open small and charming shops and restaurants, past couples and four-somes leaving the cafés or looking in boutique windows at the elegant wares. Leaving Ocean, turning down Clyde's street and entering through the back gate into the patio, he toweled the big Weimaraner dry, and then in the kitchen gave him fresh water. As he made himself a cup of coffee, the gray tomcat wandered in, yawning, staring up at him.

"You can't be hungry. It's a wonder you're still alive. I hope Clyde doesn't start feeding Rock like that, sneaking him rich snacks." Strange, he thought, that the tomcat was in such good shape, his sleek silver body muscled and lean. He gave Joe a small snack of cold steak that Clyde had left, watched Joe gobble it, then carried his coffee down the hall to the guest room, the cat and dog crowded at his heels.

Opening his briefcase he flipped through the files and laid the Carson Chappell folder on the night table. As per Clyde's instructions, he told Joe and Rock they could sleep on the bed—a useless gesture, considering that the two were already tucked up together hogging most of the king-size mattress, Joe Grey stretched out across the big dog's front legs. At Mike's voice, the cat looked up at him with bold yellow eyes, keenly assessing him, then closed his eyes and tucked his head under.

Ready for sleep, Mike thought, watching the tomcat. And he pulled off his shoes and shirt, preparing for bed, looking forward to a cozy evening tucked up by the fire accompanied by the sleeping dog and cat as he went over the Carson Chappell file.

11

THE MOMENT MIKE went into the bathroom to brush his teeth, Joe Grey's eyes were wide open again, his attention fixed on the Chappell cold file as keenly as if he'd spotted a rat lumbering across the white sheets. Hungering to get at the information, he debated whether to try for a look while Mike was out of the room.

Right. Mike comes out and catches him pawing through the file, and then what? Could he pretend to be sniffing the scent of mouse in the department's archived papers? Well, sure, that would explain a cat's interest.

He waited impatiently until Mike returned, wearing navy pajama bottoms and a short robe; he watched the tall, lanky Scots Irishman light the gas logs in the stone fireplace, set the glass screen in place, and then slide into bed, propping the pillows behind him. Then Joe, making a show of stretching and yawning, sauntered up the bed to Mike's pillow. Yawning again, he curled up beside Mike purring with such sudden affection that Flannery did a double take, frowning down at him.

"What's with you? You miss Clyde already? Is that why you're not out roaming the streets? You're lonesome? Well, dogs get lonely, so I guess cats do, too." And Mike spent a few moments scratching Joe's ears.

But soon, still absently stroking Joe, he was scanning the Chappell file—and Joe, sprawled among the pillows near Mike's left ear, was just as eagerly soaking up additional details of Carson Chappell's disappearance and of Lindsey's search for him.

But as Joe read, he watched Mike, too, and was slyly amused.

Where the original report discussed Lindsey and Carson's relationship, Mike's expression changed from interest to what surely resembled jealousy. In the ten-year-old report, Lindsey had assured the interviewing detective that she and Chappell were very much in love and that he would never have left her. They had planned a honeymoon in the Bahamas, they'd had their plane tickets and hotel reservations and had intended to go directly from the church to the airport. They had planned, on their return, to move into a cottage in the village, on which Carson had made a sizable down payment—they had intended to move their furniture and other belongings in two days before the wedding, the day that Chappell was due home from camping. Lindsey said they had wanted, when they arrived back, to be already comfortably settled in their new home.

In the short quotations that had been included among

the dry sentences of the case file, it wasn't hard to read Lindsey's shock when Carson didn't return; Joe could detect nothing contrived or uneasy in her recorded answers, though without the sound of her voice, the intonations, and the facial expressions, it was difficult to make such an assessment. It wasn't hard, though, to imagine a bride-to-be's growing despair when there was no word from the intended bridegroom.

At that time, neither Lindsey nor the police had found the plane tickets, not in Chappell's apartment nor in his office, these had disappeared as surely as had his passport.

Halfway through, Mike set aside the file and sat quietly staring into the fire, a deep and preoccupied look, almost a dreaming look, that Joe studied with interest. Was Flannery keener on finding Chappell? Or on rekindling his relationship with Lindsey?

But that was unfair. Maybe Mike wasn't sure, himself, where his conflicted emotions wanted to lead him.

Only when Rock stirred in his sleep and turned over did Mike come back to the present, reach for the steno pad, and begin making notes. Joe, easing higher up on the pillow, positioned himself where he could read them clearly. Mike glanced at him, frowning, but didn't push him away.

Most of Mike's notations were questions, or lines of investigation that he meant to pursue, and many were the same questions Joe had. When at last he put down the pen and sat staring at the fire again, Joe wished he could read this guy's mind, wished he could follow Mike's thoughts and not just the words on the paper.

But soon the tomcat's own thoughts turned back to

that one perplexing connection, to the unlikely coincidence of the two bodies coming to light in the same week. Why did he keep imagining a relationship between them? There was nothing to hint at that, except the timing of the two discoveries.

Or was there some clue in the file, or in something he'd overheard, that he didn't know he was aware of? Some minute detail, caught in his memory, that kept him returning to that improbable conjecture?

No one knew, yet, even if that *was* Chappell up there in Oregon. Only Lindsey Wolf seemed convinced. And, the tomcat thought, why was she so sure? Did Lindsey know something that was not in the report, and that she might not have told the law?

But why would she hold back information, when she seemed so committed to finding Chappell?

Was she, in some way, covering up her own guilt? Certain that Oregon would identify Chappell, and trying to establish her own innocence?

Dulcie would tell him he was chasing smoke, batting at shadows, that he was way off, on this one—but he couldn't leave it alone. His gut feeling was that there *was* a relationship between the bodies, and that maybe Lindsey knew that.

Or was he as batty as if he'd been bingeing on catnip?

He watched Mike open the file again and flip to several handwritten pages tucked at the back: three pages of notes on plain white paper, and a yellow, lined sheet with different handwriting. Having to shift against Mike's shoulder again to see around his arm, Joe pretended to scratch his ear.

"You better not have fleas," Mike said absently, knowing that Clyde had the animals on medication against such small, unwanted passengers. The white pages were dated six years ago, the yellow one three years later. That one was signed by Officer Kathleen Ray. That would be about the time Kathleen had come to work at Molena Point PD, Joe thought, not long after he, himself, started hanging around the department when he'd first discovered he could talk and could read and, most alarming, that he was thinking like a human—and, more alarming still, was thinking like a cop.

Mike shifted position again. And again Joe craned to see the file, wondering what Lindsey might have told Kathleen, who was a kind, sympathetic person, that she wouldn't share with a male officer. But as he read Kathleen's notes, he had to remind himself that Lindsey wasn't under suspicion here, that she was the one who had filed the missing-person report.

Lindsey had repeated to Kathleen the gossip about Carson having had several women on the side while Lindsey and he were engaged, including Lindsey's sister, Ryder. Kathleen's interviews with Lindsey's friends had produced the same comments. When Kathleen asked Lindsey about the wife of Carson's partner having left her husband, Lindsey said she doubted there was any connection.

Partner Ray Gibbs, when he had originally been questioned about Carson's disappearance, had seemed open and cooperative. He had been straightforward about Nina leaving him, and had produced a letter from her saying that she would not be back. She did not mention divorce, and Gibbs had speculated that she might not want a divorce, hoping one day to inherit his share of the firm. He said she didn't know that wasn't possible, he was sure she didn't know the terms of the incorporation agreement. A photocopy of her letter was in the file, and the original had been booked in as evidence.

The plane tickets for Lindsey and Carson's honeymoon turned up several months after Carson disappeared; they had been used for a reservation in the name of Mr. and Mrs. Carson Chappell. Neither the flight attendants or airport personnel had been able to describe the boarding couple. Officers had, a week after Chappell disappeared, found Nina Gibbs's car in short-term parking at the San Jose airport, but had turned up no flight ticket issued in her name.

Joe thought the simple solution, that Chappell and Nina Gibbs had run off together, should have resolved the case for Lindsey. But not so. She had kept after the department to search for him, and then later had continued the search on her own. It was during this time that Lindsey and Mike began to date.

Joe thought she must not have involved Mike in trying to find Carson or he would have gone into the department and read the file then. Maybe because Mike worked for the federal courts, his reading of the file might have presented a conflict of interest somewhere down the line? So Mike had deliberately kept his distance from the ongoing investigation? He watched Mike turn back to Kathleen's notes.

Lindsey told Kathleen that she'd known Nina Gibbs only casually, that because of Gibbs's and Chappell's partnership, they had attended the same functions, that Nina had been friendly on some occasions but withdrawn on others; in short, that they'd not been close. Joe was so intent on the notes about the Chappell & Gibbs partnership agreement that he didn't notice he was digging his claws into Mike's shoulder until Mike swore and pushed him away.

It took him a few minutes to get positioned on the pillow again, drawing a stern look from Flannery. According to the partnership agreement, if either partner became incapacitated, could not or would not participate as a working member of the firm, the court was to dissolve the company after a year, and the assets were to be sold. When Chappell didn't show in the allotted time, the firm was sold, Ray Gibbs received half the proceeds, and Chappell's mother the other half. Chappell & Gibbs had had a sound business, showing healthy annual profits, and there seemed to be no reason for either partner to have wanted out.

A recent notation at the bottom of the yellow sheet, written by Max Harper just a few months ago, said that Ray Gibbs had divorced Nina, who, as far as the department knew, had not reappeared, and that Gibbs and Ryder Wolf were living together, dividing their time between a San Francisco condo and an apartment on Dolores, in the village.

Finished with reading the memos, Mike set the file aside and leaned back among the pillows, lost in thought. From the look on his thin face, Joe guessed he was thinking not about Carson Chappell but about Lindsey; he sat stroking Joe so sensuously that Joe twitched and stared at him and backed away, his retreat jerking Mike from his reverie.

But it was some time before Mike rose to extinguish the fire. Joe, yawning, padded down to curl up against Rock, receiving a long, wet lick across his ears and nose. He'd grown almost used to dog spit, but soon his wet fur began to feel chilly. As he burrowed deeper against Rock to get warm, he wondered how long it would be before they had an ID on the Oregon body, wondered whether the Oregon investigators were thorough enough to come up with a sample of the DNA.

But DNA to match *what*?

Was there, among the evidence the department had retained on Chappell, any item belonging to the killer that would produce the needed match to DNA found in Oregon? And, he wondered, when forensics began work on the body from the Pamillon ruins, could they get a match on that DNA? Would the lab find anything that might link that body to the Oregon corpse?

But why was he chasing after phantoms? Why was he so fixated on some relationship between two bodies that had lain, for so many years, some five hundred miles apart?

Well, he'd have his first look at the Pamillon grave in the morning, Joe thought, drifting off to sleep. And who knew what he and Dulcie and Kit would find?

He'd barely closed his eyes when he blinked suddenly awake, staring into the first light of dawn filtering in through the accordion shades. Rolling over, he looked at the clock—and came wide awake. Six bells. Dulcie would pitch a fit. He'd said he'd meet her and Kit before daylight—it was a long run up the hills to the Pamillon estate. Padding lightly across the bed, trying not to wake

Mike, and only momentarily waking Rock, who sighed and rolled over, Joe fled down the hall, up the stairs to Clyde's study, and onto the desk. Leaping to a rafter, he was through his cat door and into his tower—and smack into the stern faces of two scowling lady cats.

There they sat, chill and austere, coolly assessing him, their paws together, their ears at half-mast, regarding him as they would a rude and misbehaving kitten.

"Overslept?" Dulcie said. Her sleek, brown-striped tabby coat was immaculately groomed, every hair in place, her green eyes piercing him. Beside her, Kit's long tortoiseshell fur was every which way, as if she'd had no time to groom. Kit looked at him just as impatiently as Dulcie had, lashing her fluffy tail.

He thought of all kinds of excuses: that he'd overslept because he wasn't used to sleeping in the guest room, wasn't used to sleeping with a stranger whose snores were different from Clyde's. But neither lady looked patient enough to listen to the shortest explanation, their twin stares said, *We've been waiting an hour. The sun's nearly up! Come on, Joe. Move it!*

Sheepishly he slipped past them and out through the tower window to the shingled roof and took off fast across the rooftops, Dulcie and Kit running beside him.

At Ocean Avenue they scrambled down a honeysuckle vine, crossed the empty eastbound lane, and turned to race up Ocean's wide, grassy median beneath the dark shelter of its eucalyptus and cypress trees, heading for the open hills, heading for the unidentified grave.

12

ABOVE THE RACING CATS, the Molena Point hills rose green with new grass, their emerald curves bright against heavy gray clouds; the damp grass soaked the cats' paws and fur as they raced ever higher above the village. *If a cat had wings,* Dulcie thought, running beside Joe and Kit, *we'd fly over the hills, we'd see all our haunts below us, see all our world laid out . . . The scattered gardens and the dark oak woods, the red roofs of Casa Capri where those helpless old people were murdered. Janet Jeannot's studio, burned down when she was killed. We'd see Mama's house where I played lost kitty to spy on her crooked son, we'd see all the houses we've tossed, finding evidence. And just up there,* she thought, pausing and rearing up to look, *I'd see the broom bushes where Joe and I first met, where the moment we stood so close, face-to-face, after I'd watched him in the village, the moment he was so close to me, I knew that I loved him. And there above us,* she thought, swerving closer to Joe through the fresh, damp grass, *there where the ruins rise up like broken towers, there's where Charlie shot the man who kidnapped her.*

Soon their paws pounded through the rubble of broken stone walls where they'd once seen a cougar, the beautiful prowling cougar that might have eaten them. *The cougar*, Dulcie thought, glancing at Kit, *who so enchanted the tattercoat that she touched him while he slept—and then ran like hell.*

Up the last steep incline, racing up, they stopped at the foot of the first garden wall, broken and rough, a relic of jagged stone, beyond which the old house rose up among its tangles of half-dead oak trees. All three cats were thinking of what they would find, of the human body, lost and forgotten, a forgotten soul all alone among the decaying buildings.

Weeds grew tangled among old and dying bushes, crowding against the sides of the rambling, two-story mansion. At the front of the great house, where walls had crumbled away, the rooms stood open to the world like a stage, revealing peeling wallpaper and broken, moldering furniture: the hoary set of a macabre theatrical production that seemed about to begin, that waited for them, chill and silent—then the off-key blather of a house finch broke the spell, and from the fields beyond, the bright crystal song of a meadowlark. Then the lark's song was rudely hushed by the harsh cawing of a crow that perched ahead of them on the mossy roof, staring belligerently, his bright glare keenly accusing, his raucous voice scolding indignantly the presence of invading cats.

Rearing up, Joe eyed the big black bird. "You thought all the cats left here? You're telling us to go, too? Too bad, buddy. Come on down if you don't like the drill. We'll put an end to your misery."

Dulcie smiled. "Count me out. I'd as soon eat vulture." The crow cawed rudely. Kit studied him, lashing her fluffy tail as if *she* would surely eat him. But then, forgetting the nervy bird, she raced away toward the back of the mansion, toward the kitchen and the old cellars and the grotto that was their destination. Joe and Dulcie followed.

Paying attention to Willow's directions as Charlie had repeated them, moving past the kitchen and around the house among tangles of broken walls and overgrown bushes, they trotted under tall, dirty windows that had once sparkled with candlelight and with flickering flames from the hearth.

Rounding a jutting wall, they came to the small terrace sheltered between two wings of the house, a space just large enough for a bit of garden, a moss-covered stone bench, and, perhaps at one time, an outdoor tea table and chairs, furniture that would long since have rusted away or been destroyed by storms. The terrace bricks were dark with decades of dirt and overgrown with moss. On two sides of the sheltered terrace were raised planting beds but on the third, against the house, a sinkhole opened into a crumbled cellar.

Nearer them, flanking the terrace, a weedy garden plot had been freshly dug into, the disturbed earth crisscrossed with paw prints.

As Joe and Dulcie stood looking, and scenting the earth, at the side of the terrace Kit looked into the house through cracked French doors, pressing her nose to the grimy glass. Within lay an old-fashioned bedchamber that had once been elegant. She could see a smooth stone fireplace, a cream-colored Victorian bed, a toppled dresser, a matching dressing table and little chair, and a carved dressing screen that lay fallen against the rotting silk bed-spread. The bed's silk canopy hung in shreds as delicate as spiderwebs. Kit imagined an elegant woman wrapped in a diaphanous dressing gown, coming out into the garden to sip tea among the ferns and flowers where, now, the planter beds held only weeds, dead leaves, and an over-grown jasmine that had tangled itself over dead bushes.

Dulcie joined her, and the lady cats were still a moment, filled with dreams of being human ladies, Dulcie dreaming of silk and velvet garments and cashmere wraps, as she had dreamed all her life. Not until Joe huffed softly did the two give up their fantasies, and the cats began to dig in the flower bed where the earth had already been dug, Joe and Dulcie carefully pawing away the rotted leaves and earth so as not to disturb the frail bones that surely lay beneath—but Kit, in her enthusiasm, kicked out earth like a dog.

Joe stopped her. "You're destroying evidence. You know better."

She hung her head.

It was Dulcie, going slowly, with gentle paws, who soon stroked something small and rigid. She stopped dig-ging, and delicately brushed away the earth until, at their feet, lay little dark bones clean of flesh and stained brown by the earth, seeming as frail as the bones of a long-dead bird.

The sight of a human hand so diminished and helpless sickened Dulcie. She turned away and sat down, her head down, her ears down, her heart feeling empty.

This was not the first human grave they'd ever found, and the other graves had upset her even more, for they had held the bones of little children. That memory had stayed with her in nightmares, and now it returned again, to leave her shivering.

Why does this upset me so? The bones of animals don't bother me, the bones of rats and mice or of a dead deer in the forest, they are just natural bones.

But a dead human is nothing like a dead animal. The remains of a dead human should be treated with respect, should not be hidden and abandoned. A human body without proper burial, a proper marker, without ceremony and closure, is a tragedy of disrespect. As if that's all there is to a human, these moldering bones, and nothing more at all.

Seeing her distress, Joe pressed close to her and licked her ear, his silver coat gleaming in the slant of early morning sun. Dulcie's green eyes were filled with mystery. "Were cats *meant* to find this grave?" she whispered. "First the ferals found it. And then we came . . . Were we meant to come here?"

Joe just looked at her. He didn't like that kind of question. He began to dig again, carefully but steadily, until he had uncovered the side of the skull and then a line of spine defining the throat. He tried to work as carefully as he knew the coroner would; and soon his digging paw revealed the outer rim of the shoulder. Joe had begun to uncover the arm when suddenly he stopped.

Dulcie and Kit moved closer and the three cats stood transfixed, their eyes on the frail wrist—on the bracelet that circled the wrist, still half buried in earth. It was a wide gold band embossed with the image of a cat. A rearing cat, just as Willow had described, a cat holding out its front paw as if beseeching, or perhaps commanding.

"Where is the other cat?" Dulcie whispered. "Willow said—"

"On the lintel," Kit said. "There, over the French doors to the bedchamber. Same cat, with its paw out."

Who was this woman, so fond of cats that she wore a feline signet? That she had the same cat carved over her bedchamber? If that *was* her bedchamber, if this wasn't a stranger buried here.

But a stranger whose bracelet showed the same cat as on the lintel? Not likely.

At last they covered up the poor, vulnerable body, and with careful strokes they roughed up the loose earth until they had destroyed all the paw prints—their own, and those of the ferals.

"One thing for sure," Dulcie said, "we can't report the body—the department knows there are cats up here. Those guys are already too curious since seeing the ferals attack Charlie's kidnappers."

"Why do we *have* to report it?" Kit said. "Who knows how long that body's been here? What difference . . . ?"

Joe and Dulcie turned to look at her. "Someone," Dulcie said sternly, "wants to know what happened to this woman."

"But what about the book?" Kit said. "The book Willow found? Maybe that will tell us." And the tattercoat leaped across the garden toward the dark fissure where the wall had caved into the cellar.

"Don't, Kit!" Dulcie cried. "Don't go down—" But Kit had already disappeared into the dark hole among the fallen stones—and before Joe could snatch Dulcie back she had leaped after her, disappearing in the blackness. Joe was poised at the brink, ready to go down, or haul them out, when with considerable thrashing they emerged again dragging a small, heavy-looking box between them.

It was made of dark wood, and when they had pawed open the lid to reveal a leather packet, then had clawed open the packet, they found inside a package wrapped in frail and yellowed cloth. They could see where Willow had unwrapped the thin linen and then rewrapped it, where the cloth was folded differently, revealing darker creases. Several white cat hairs were caught in the folds. There were no markings on the box, or on the leather packet.

Lifting out the wrapped book, they laid it on paper, which they had spread on the bricks. The leather cover was old and dry, and was embossed in gold: *Folktales of Speaking Cats and a History of Certain Rare Encounters.*

"No one," Dulcie hissed angrily, "*no one* should write about speaking cats." The author's name was Thomas Bewick. What cruel impulse had made this man reveal their secret? Why had he done such a thing?

But despite its content, the book was frail and beautiful, and Dulcie's touch was feather soft as she turned the dry, yellowed pages.

At the beginning of each chapter was the color etching of a cat, each with a motto or homily.

She speaks of a world beneath the meadow, where the sky is greener.

They prowl the night, listening. And to whom will they tell their secrets?

The cats read in silence, scanning the passages, and soon Dulcie's tension eased and she began to purr: These stories were only myths and folktales, all were innocent enough, folktales about magical cats written in a fairy-tale manner that no human would take for fact. That was all the book would be to the uninitiated, a collection of fairy tales, stories about cats who spoke to kings, cats who vanished into cavernous worlds beneath the earth, cats who led lost children from war-torn medieval cities. Indeed, their own ancient heritage lay between these pages, but so well disguised that few humans would dream there was truth to the stories.

Dulcie and Kit were transfixed, but the tales made Joe edgy, turned him increasingly irritable; he didn't have the temperament for this, his yellow eyes burned with impatience.

It was enough for Joe to live in the here and now, he didn't need fairy tales to explain himself. The world could take him or not, as it chose, and to hell with the past, he preferred to leave all foolish conjecture to dreamers—and Dulcie preferred Joe just as he was. A tough, practical tomcat who faced the world straight on. A four-legged cop who hid very well the tender streak deep within.

"And what," the tomcat said, staring at the gold-embossed volume, "what do we do with this? There's nothing safe *to* do with it, Dulcie. Except bury it again. It's too heavy to carry, and we can't let someone find it."

Dulcie looked dismayed. "We can't leave it here, it will rot."

"It hasn't rotted yet."

"It's old and frail, Joe. I don't think—"

"If we carry and drag it down the hills, we'll rip the leather, tear the pages. And if we haul it in the box, we'll need our little cat spines adjusted."

She sat down and washed a front paw.

She wanted this book, she wanted to read the rest of it. Wanted to look into the back pages, wanted . . .

Joe Grey sat down beside her and licked her whiskers. "I guess if you want it that bad," he said softly, "Charlie can get it for us."

Dulcie looked at him uncertainly. "Charlie hasn't been up here since she was kidnapped. She doesn't come here anymore."

"She will for this. She will if we nudge her. She *has* to be wondering about the book. She has to be as curious as we were. Do you think, after Willow told her there was a book about speaking cats, that she isn't wild to see it?"

Dulcie looked at him bleakly. "Maybe she won't *want* to come up here, where she shot that man. She's already worried about how to report this grave. Maybe—"

"Leave it to me," Joe said, smiling a sly, tomcat smile. "I have a trade for Charlie. A trade that will make her happy to do what we ask. She'll fetch the book, and she'll do it gladly."

13

CHARLIE STOOD at the top of the cliff watching the sea, thinking about little Sage. It was nearly noon and the tide was coming in, the waves crashing and foaming against the rocks far below, turning them glistening black; the surf's wild and gigantic power, the vastness of the sea and of the earth itself, made a creature as small and hurt as Sage seem to her all the more helpless.

The fear and confusion that that little wild cat must have felt coming out of the anesthetic, waking in a strange world inside a building, not remembering how he got there, finding himself in a cage, hurting and sick and afraid. Even with Dulcie there to calm him, he must have been terrified.

Well, but he was being gently cared for now, with a special understanding that the young cat would find in no other doctor. She was still amazed that for all these years, John Firetti had looked upon the speaking cats as a natural part of his life.

It was strange, too, that she, when she first discovered

the truth about the cats, had felt that such cats should have been a part of her life all along, that not knowing about them had left something incomplete in her world, left it flat and dull. She'd not been surprised that, once she shared the cats' secret, a buoyant feeling of richness had filled so many of her life's empty spaces.

She thought about the day she and Ryan and Hanni had been returning from their weeklong pack trip, riding home across the open hills, the day that Willow and her wild band first appeared to her, slipping out of the pine forest.

Glimpsing the little phantom beings secretly following her, wonder had gripped her, the same thrill that had touched her the night Willow had come to her, needing her, trusting her enough to seek her out.

Now, turning away from the cliff's edge, she stepped back into the Blazer and headed down the hills to Dr. Firetti's clinic, down Highway 1, a left at Ocean and a left again at Beckwhite's Fine Cars, where she glanced absently at Clyde's automotive garage.

Clyde and Ryan on their honeymoon, she thought, amused. She'd never thought it would happen. No little beforehand hints, no asking for help picking out rings, no sharing of plans and secrets, though the three of them were close friends. The two had been dating for a while, but Clyde had dated a long string of women, including Charlie herself.

But then, Christmas Day, Clyde had started calling all their friends with the big announcement. Wilma said Dulcie had been so surprised she nearly did flips. The little tabby had just clawed the wrapping off her Christmas gift, which turned out to be Charlie's portrait of Joe Grey, so she was already giddy, wired with excitement when they heard Clyde's news. To learn that he had actually proposed, that he and Ryan meant to take the big step . . . no one had thought it would happen.

Parking at the side of the clinic, she paused to retie her red hair with its ragged ribbon, then grabbed her package off the seat, got out, and locked the car. She had brought half a rare filet for Sage, from last night's dinner. Through the clinic's front window, she could see Wilma inside the crowded waiting room.

The door was blocked by a man in shorts and sandals trying to pull his basset hound away from a pair of fluffy "designer" mutts, while a black cat in a carrier hissed angrily. At the other side of the cheerful room, with its wicker chairs and hanging plants, Wilma was chatting with the receptionist, dark-haired Audrey Cane, about Audrey's young German shepherd; Audrey was radiant with pride in the dog's talents, was sharing her plans for his training when John Firetti came out and led Wilma and Charlie back to the small, quiet recovery room.

Sage lay in his large cage, the wire door propped open, looking helpless in his bandages. When he saw Charlie and Wilma, his eyes brightened and he got clumsily to his feet, wobbling in his cast; the doctor reached to steady him.

"Get him to drink all he can," Dr. Firetti told them as he lifted Sage into Wilma's carrier, onto a soft blanket. "You shouldn't have a problem getting him to eat, he's hungry as a wolf. Aren't you, Sage?" He looked seriously at Charlie. "Max doesn't know about the cats?"

"He doesn't need to know," Charlie said. "Later, when Sage comes up to us, we'll be careful only to talk when we're sure Max is gone. Sage will have a nice bed in my studio, and another in our bedroom at night. I'll tell Max he's a stray I've seen hanging around, that I found him hurt."

"And how will you explain that you didn't ever tell him about this stray, when you tell Max about every animal that comes around the ranch, the wild fox you like to draw, the skunk . . . You've drawn them all, and Max has seen them all."

"I'll think of something. Preoccupation with the wedding . . . Mind on a new book . . ."

Firetti nodded but looked unconvinced. Cops didn't buy easily into even the most reasonable alibis.

"I have Sage on antibiotics," he said. "He doesn't mind taking pills if you put a dab of butter on them; he's a good patient." He glanced toward the closed door. "Of course the staff doesn't know. They say he's an amazing patient, that he does just what they want." He winked at Sage, and doctor and patient exchanged a long and trusting look. Then Firetti laid out the medicines they were to take home, and went over the times and doses.

"I want to see him every day for a while. I'll stop by the house, Wilma, if that's all right—Sage can tell me how he feels, and I'll change the bandages." That was more than all right with Wilma. They set a time for his visits, and within half an hour the three were headed for Wilma's house, Sage's carrier strapped into Wilma's car, Charlie following in her red Blazer.

WILMA HAD SET up a bed for Sage near her desk in the living room where she and Dulcie liked to sit by the fire at night;

she had covered the blue velvet chair with a puffy comforter, and had taped several sturdy boxes together to form a wide, shallow set of steps from the rug to the chair. Behind an end table was a sandbox, and on the floor beside Sage's chair was a plastic tray big enough to hold his water and kibble bowls. They entered the house through the back door, into Wilma's bright blue-and-white kitchen. A welcoming committee awaited them—Joe and Dulcie and Kit looked up from a plastic bowl where they had been enjoying leftovers from last night's dinner, and the three followed Wilma through to the living room where she set down the carrier.

As she and Charlie settled Sage in his new bed, Kit leaped up and curled carefully beside him on the soft comforter, staying away from his cast. Wilma headed for the kitchen, and soon the house smelled of fresh coffee, warm milk, and warming cinnamon buns, soon Charlie carried a tray through to the living room, setting it on the coffee table. "You're taking the week off?" she asked her aunt as Wilma poured the coffee.

Wilma nodded. "I plan to do my taxes—last minute, as usual, with Sage to keep me company. We'll have a cozy fire in the hearth, and I have the CD set up with Dulcie's favorite music, which maybe Sage will like."

"And my bandages off soon?" Sage asked shyly.

"As soon as the doctor allows," Wilma told him. "Meanwhile, all the steak and custard you can eat." She pushed back her long silver hair where it had escaped its ponytail. "You're our guest, Sage. You mustn't be shy about asking for what you want."

"Or shy about getting spoiled," Dulcie said. "A few days with Wilma and you won't want to go back to the clowder."

Sage looked uncertainly at Dulcie. The young cat was still trying to get used to the idea of feline/human conversations, was still trying to decide just how one behaved among humans.

And he was still trying to get used to being shut within solid walls. Confined in a man-made structure, it seemed to Sage that a part of him must have gone missing. The open hills, the wind, the shadowed woods had all been taken from him, had left him feeling incomplete and small.

Kit, lying close to him, watched him intently, her round yellow eyes just inches from his, gazing at him as if trying to see into his very soul, as if trying to know the young tom's deepest thoughts. That unnerved Sage, but excited him.

"You'll stay here with me," Wilma told Sage, "until I go back to work, then you'll go to Charlie's house, at the ranch, and that's nearer your own hills and woods." She looked at Charlie. "First day I get back, I start training the new reference librarian."

Charlie looked so alarmed that the cats came alert, watching her. "You're not planning to quit? The new librarian isn't taking your job?"

Dulcie looked at her housemate in amazement. She'd heard nothing of this. If Wilma quit her job as a reference librarian, she'd have to give up her library office where the cat door opened from among the bushes outside, the door that let Dulcie into the closed library at night.

No more midnight prowling among the books? No more pulling books from the shelves, dragging them up onto a table where she could read alone and unseen? No more nighttime adventures into exotic lands and distant times?

"I'm not quitting," Wilma said quickly. "Only cutting

back. And we do need more help. The new librarian will be full-time, and that will give us more actual hours, even with the reduced schedule I've set for myself." Wilma didn't have to work, she had an adequate federal retirement pension from her first career as a probation officer.

Still, Charlie looked uneasy. "You're not . . . You're feeling all right?"

"I'm feeling fine. Don't fuss," Wilma scolded. "I'm not sick, there's nothing wrong with me, there are simply some other things I'd like to do. How could I quit? How could I give up my library key?" Wilma said, mirroring Dulcie's thoughts. "How could I give up my office, and Dulcie's cat door? Who knows, I might even start riding again."

"Are you serious? You can ride Redwing all you want, she really needs the exercise. If . . ."

Charlie paused, watching Joe. On the desk, the tomcat sat at rigid attention, studying Wilma and then turning his gaze on Charlie, watching the two of them so fixedly that Charlie shivered. Joe's yellow eyes were far too intent and calculating. Whatever he had in mind, he made Charlie feel like a cornered mouse.

"This is perfect," Joe said softly, turning to watch Wilma. "Are you serious about riding again?"

Wilma looked at him warily.

"This couldn't be better," Joe purred. "This fits right in with our plans."

"What plans?" Charlie and Wilma said together.

A slow smile spread over the tomcat's face, sending both women into a paroxysm of suspicion. "What?" Wilma said. "What's in that sneaky cat mind, that you think you can get me to do?"

14

 At least Charlie's acting sensibly, Joe thought as he leaped from a pine tree to the tiles of the courthouse roof—*a lot more sensibly than Dulcie.*

Dropping down onto the lower roof of Molena Point PD and then into the branches of the ancient oak that sheltered its front door, he stretched out along a branch, thinking about his plan.

"You're a fair poker player," Charlie had said when he'd told her what he had in mind. "Wilma and I get the book, which is too heavy for you to carry down the hills without tearing the pages, and you see that the department finds the body without involving me or involving you cats."

"That's it," Joe had said, smoothing his whiskers with a white-tipped paw. "I can talk with Ryan myself if you'd like, to put things in motion. But I'd have to wait until they get back, I don't think she's up to talking with me on the phone yet—she's still getting used to face-to-face discussion." Joe and Dulcie had been sitting on Wilma's desk as, on the blue velvet couch, Charlie and Wilma finished their coffee and cinnamon buns and, in the easy chair, Kit napped, curled up on the comforter with Sage.

"I'll call the honeymooners tonight," Charlie said. "I'm sure they can't wait for people to disturb them."

"It's a good deal for Ryan, too," Joe had pointed out. "She'll love the plan, she'll be happy you called."

Charlie sighed. "A honeymoon, Joe, by its very nature, is—"

"What kind of honeymoon? Those two are up there scrounging through junk shops and wrecking yards. How romantic is that?"

"I'll call her," Charlie said, looking helplessly at the tomcat.

Joe gave her a satisfied smile, leaped down from the desk, and headed for the kitchen, pausing only to scowl pointedly at Dulcie. He was nosing through Dulcie's cat door when Dulcie, following him, pushed him aside, cornering him against the washing machine. Her green eyes blazed. "What are you angry at me about? What did I do?"

"You're matchmaking, that's what you're doing."

"Matchmaking?"

"You needn't smile so fatuously over them, you needn't encourage them."

"Shhh, keep you voice down. I can't make her *ignore* him, he's her friend. And why would I? He's weak and hurting, the poor cat needs sympathy. Kit grew up with Sage, they were kittens together, she—"

"They're not kittens anymore. She's smitten with him. And you're not doing a thing to discourage her."

"Why would I discourage her? Why would I want to?"

"You're just like every other female! So damned romantic you lose all perspective. No more common sense than a chicken."

Dulcie stared at him, her paw lifted to slap him. "You're *jealous*!" she hissed. "You're . . . You . . . Oh!" And she spun away, her ears down, her tail tucked under.

"I'm not *jealous*!" he snapped, snatching her back with a hasty paw, his claws locked in her fur, his eyes blazing with amazement. "How could I be *jealous*! I think of her as a kitten! She's like our kitten! I feel like we raised her together."

She simply stared at him.

"Listen to me," he said angrily. "Remember how hard it was for Kit to leave the wild? What she went through when she felt pulled both ways, half of her wanting to go feral again, running wild, half of her wanting to be a part of human lives in her very special way? Do you remember how hard that was?

"But she did decide," he said, "and she was so happy and proud of herself. She's doing more here than in the wild. Think of the crimes she's helped solve. She's so full of life, so clever and inventive . . . But now, with Sage pulling on her, she'll soon be torn apart again! If they become a couple, when Sage is ready to return to the wild, what do you think Kit will do? You *want* her to follow him? You *want* her to leave the village forever? You want never to see her again?"

"She wouldn't do that. This is her home. Maybe Sage won't return to the clowder. Maybe—"

"What else would he do? He doesn't like the human world. The minute he's healed, he's out of here, headed for the hills. And Kit with him, just as sure as mice have tails. Is that what you want?" And he shoved out the cat door, scorched up a pine tree and across the roofs, heading fast for Molena Point PD.

Now, dropping from the oak branch down into a bed of cyclamens near the front door of the station, he stalked between the bright red and pink blooms and up the steps, and peered in through the bulletproof glass.

The reception area, with its electronic control center and its one holding cell, was empty except for the cats' favorite dispatcher. Watching blond, middle-aged Mabel Farthy busy at her computer, he reared up to claw at the glass, demanding her attention.

Mabel looked up, saw him, and frowned with exasperation. But she rose, hurried out from behind the counter, and swung the heavy door open.

"Come on, Joe. How do you know when I'm right in the middle of something urgent? And how did you know I have carrot cake? Come on, up on the counter, if you want some. Where are your pals?"

Heavily Joe jumped to the counter, his belly so full of Wilma's cinnamon rolls that even his favorite carrot cake didn't appeal. But he wouldn't hurt Mabel's feelings— couldn't afford to hurt her feelings and sour their relationship, Mabel Farthy was their entrée into the building. And Mabel's electronic realm, her ability to reach every law enforcement agency in the U.S. and beyond, gathering information from them, was the cats' entrée into the department's most sensitive intelligence.

Besides, he liked Mabel. He would never hurt her feelings by rejecting her lovingly made offerings.

Mabel spoiled her own cats, and she loved bringing treats for "her three freeloaders" and petting and talking to them. Now, although Joe thought he'd burst, he ate the carrot cake slowly, choking down each delicious bite and purring extravagantly for Mabel—while praying he wouldn't upchuck on her clean counter. He could hear, down the hall, the chief's voice from his office, in a tense discussion with a woman.

Would that be Lindsey Wolf? But it was still early, not yet eleven—and her appointment wasn't with Max Harper but with Mike and Dallas. Keen with curiosity, he finished the cake, rubbed his face against Mabel's arm by way of thanks, and dropped heavily to the floor, belching delicately as he headed down the hall.

Lights spilled from the office doors he passed, from the conference room that smelled of overcooked coffee, and from the report room where the faint click of computer keys told him several officers were catching up on their reports. Only the interrogation room was dark; Joe was passing that small windowless space with its little table and two straight chairs when, from Harper's office ahead, the woman's voice grew sharp and authoritative.

"This is most important, Captain Harper, or I would not have disturbed you."

Slipping in through the chief's open door, Joe vanished beneath the credenza.

Max and the woman stood in the center of the room, as if she had just entered, and as if he didn't mean for her to stay long. *This* was Lindsey Wolf? This showy, sleekly made-up woman? This was not what he'd expected. She was some looker, all right, but she sure wasn't the soft, tastefully clad, restrained beauty he'd pictured from Mike's remarks and from Clyde's description.

She was maybe in her forties, though it was hard to tell with humans, particularly women. Her sleek, brown, shoulder-length hair shone with red highlights as perfectly shaded as the color in a cosmetics commercial. Her makeup was artful, too, but not the subtle glow that Joe had envisioned. Her brown eyes, gazing up at the chief from beneath mascara-thick lashes, were way too friendly for a meeting that should be businesslike; she stood too close to Max, looking up at him in a way that was far too familiar.

Harper stood his ground, watching her with that closed cop look in which Joe read sharp dislike, a look that sometimes alarmed the tomcat but usually amused him. Max was holding a clear plastic bag; inside, Joe could see a small sheet of letter paper, carefully hand-printed with a blue pen.

"Why did you wait until now to bring us this, Ms. Wolf?"

So this glamorous creature *was* Lindsey. Joe tried to put this new view of her into perspective, but this certainly changed his opinion of Mike Flannery's taste in women.

"I didn't bring the letter to you at the time I found it," she said more equitably, "because I was afraid for my sister."

"Afraid for her?" Harper said coolly.

Beneath the credenza, Joe frowned.

"Please, Captain, call me Ryder."

Joe did a double take—but of course he should have

guessed, that this was Ryder Wolf, and the belated revelation left the tomcat highly irritated at his own miscalculation.

"As you can see," she said, "the letter is dated three days after Carson disappeared, the same week Nina Gibbs vanished. I found it only a couple of years ago, in my sister's dresser, when I was looking for a sweater I'd loaned her. When . . . when I read it, I was afraid to bring it in."

"Why were you afraid?" Harper looked increasingly uncomfortable with her standing so close, but he refused to back off and give ground.

"If anything terrible had happened to Carson, I was afraid this letter would make Lindsey appear to be a suspect."

"Why is that?" Harper was having trouble keeping his temper. A nerve had started to twitch at the side of his face, matching the spark of impatience deep in his brown eyes.

"When you read the whole letter, you'll see. Nina told Lindsey she feared that her husband meant to kill her and Carson, that Ray would come after them, and that Ray had a gun. She begged Lindsey's forgiveness for going away with Carson, and asked Lindsey to take the letter to the police, said there was no one else she could trust to do it.

"Apparently, Lindsey didn't do that," Ryder said. "She must have received this right after they left. If she had brought it to you then, you might have extended the search for Carson. And I don't think I'd have found the letter. Wouldn't you have kept it as evidence?

"After Lindsey reported Carson missing, I was interviewed by one of your detectives. I didn't know about the letter then, of course. The detective mentioned nothing about Nina, didn't question me about her. Wouldn't he have, if he'd seen this?"

Harper remained silent.

"Then, when I found the letter, I was certain she'd never shown it to you. That upset me because if she'd brought it to you right away, you might have stopped whatever happened. I thought that because she didn't, that would make her look guilty, like some kind of accessory."

"So you thought all along," Harper said, "that something had happened to Carson?"

"I thought it might have. And then yesterday when I saw that newspaper article, the hiker's body up in Oregon . . . You said you had a copy of that?"

Harper nodded.

"I thought . . . I wondered if that could be Carson. That's why I came now, because of that hiker, because maybe this letter is right, maybe Ray did follow him and kill him. "

"Why come to me at all if you're afraid Lindsey will be implicated?"

"I . . . I guess my conscience," she said demurely. "Though certainly Lindsey would never kill anyone, certainly *she* wouldn't follow Carson, no matter what he'd done. That's not in her nature.

"I'm sure she never owned a gun," Ryder said. "Like me, she's afraid of guns."

"Do you have the envelope this came in?"

"I didn't find it. Just the letter, tucked among her sweaters."

Harper was silent, his thin, leathered face as expressionless as stone.

"I know Lindsey would never deliberately withhold information. I think she was so upset, she just didn't think about what she *should* do. But . . ." She stepped so close to Max that Joe expected her to reach up and touch his face with those long, well-manicured fingers. Ryder Wolf's cherry nail polish exactly matched her red lipstick; when she looked up at Max, all Joe could see was lipstick and mascara—and all he could think was that he wanted a look at the letter.

Max tucked the plastic-wrapped letter into a file on his desk and moved toward the door, effectively herding Ryder Wolf out; she was moving reluctantly when Joe heard Mike Flannery's voice up at the dispatcher's counter, and a softer female voice—and immediately Ryder stepped back into the office, slipping around Max, putting herself out of sight of the hall.

But at this little maneuver, Max took Ryder's elbow and moved her firmly into the hall—where she came face-to-face with her sister.

Joe, slipping out from under the credenza, crouched behind Max in the doorway, watching.

Yes, this was the way he'd imagined Lindsey Wolf. Peaches and cream subtle, a treasure of cleanliness and soft tones that contrasted with her sister's bright, attention-demanding packaging.

Lindsey Wolf was a woman to turn heads, a woman any man would want to follow. Soft brown shoulder-length hair that changed color with the light. Hazel eyes lighter than Ryder's, with no harsh makeup, kind eyes touched with a smile. Her oval face was creamy smooth, and she wore only pale lipstick.

There was a strong resemblance in height and build, in the shape of their faces, and in their fine bone structure, but there the likeness ended in the two sisters. They looked at each other for a long moment, Lindsey's expression puzzled and questioning, Ryder's look stony. She drew herself up stubbornly, as if expecting Lindsey to scold or attack her.

"Why are you here?" Lindsey asked her.

"To inquire about that article in the paper." Ryder looked at her archly. "To see if there could be some connection with Carson Chappell. You have seen the article? A lost hiker, a man who was never found . . ."

"I saw it," Lindsey said. "Carson wasn't hiking in Oregon, he was here in California."

"That's what he told you."

"And you know differently? What do you know, Ryder?"

"I just thought I'd ask. See what the police might know. I didn't mean to step on any toes—or get you in trouble."

"Why would you get me in trouble? And why, after all this time, would you care?"

Captain Harper took in the exchange without expression, but Mike Flannery clearly showed his annoyance. Lindsey stepped back as Ryder edged past her up the hall toward the front door.

But when Max had seen her out, and Mike was escorting Lindsey down the hall toward Dallas's lighted office, Max called Mike back. "Why don't you buy Lindsey a cup of coffee?" Max said, nodding toward the conference room. "Take a little break, give me a few minutes with Dallas on several matters."

Mike took Lindsey's arm, his eyes meeting Max's with a question that received only a level look, then guided her back up the hall toward the conference room, toward the smell of overcooked coffee.

15

 IN CHARLIE'S BIG family kitchen, the coffee was freshly brewed; Wilma and Charlie had finished their pastrami sandwiches and were feasting on the first strawberries of the season, gleaming in a glass bowl on the table and liberally dusted with powdered sugar.

"This is a *good* time for you to start riding again," Charlie said. "Of course you don't forget. All your childhood years on a farm before you moved here, how could your body forget? Come on, finish your lunch and let's head out."

Wilma was not a timid person. And how often in the past years had she toyed with the idea of having a horse again? Now that Charlie had offered a place to keep a mount, how could she do otherwise than return to that freedom she'd known in childhood?

"The two of us together," Charlie said, "going up to the ruins, really would look less suspicious if Max finds out. Not that I mean to tell him, but . . ."

"It's been hard," Wilma said, "keeping secrets."

"As if I had a choice." Charlie rose to carry their dishes to the sink. "When Max proposed, you know that was my one concern, that I'd have to lie to keep the cats' secret." She looked desolately at Wilma. "I didn't know, then, half how hard that would be."

She put the remaining strawberries in the refrigerator and unplugged the coffeepot. "I'd always believed that in a good marriage you wouldn't ever have secrets, would never have to lie, that a solid marriage is based on trust.

"I still know that's true. But here I am lying to him nearly every day, or holding back information, which is the same thing."

"Most marriages," Wilma said wryly, "don't involve this kind of secret." She put their dishes in the dishwasher, they grabbed their jackets, locked the door behind them, and headed for the barn.

In the fenced-in pasture, the two big, half-breed Great Danes raced to the gate, anticipating a run, but Charlie, rubbing their ears, told them they had to stay home. They watched longingly as their master disappeared into the stable—she didn't want them following, nosing around the ruins and sniffing out the buried corpse. While that would be a natural way to "discover" the body, those two would tear up the grave, scatter the bones before she could stop them.

And, worse, their discovery would destroy Joe Grey's plan, which, she had to admit, was very close to brilliant— though it would be a few more days before Ryan and Clyde got home and Joe could put his scenario into action. It was a crazy plan, but one that would accomplish a mission near to Ryan's heart, a project that Ryan had put off for some time.

Bridling Bucky, and watching Wilma, Charlie knew that her aunt had forgotten nothing. Wilma already had the mare brushed and saddled, had checked her feet, and was leading her out into the yard to mount up. And the look on Wilma's face as they headed their horses around behind the barn and up the little trail through the woods was enough to keep Charlie smiling for days. This was what Wilma needed to balance the depression and perhaps fear that could bedevil a person as he or she grew older, even her cheerful and courageous aunt—fear of becoming ill and incapacitated, and, for many, an innate sadness at leaving this world, though she'd seen none of that in Wilma.

Now, if Charlie knew her aunt, she'd soon be shopping for a horse of her own. Wilma was, after all, only in her sixties, way too young to stop doing the things she loved best.

They rode side by side as long as the trail permitted, then Wilma let Redwing take the lead, as the mare wanted to do. Max's big buckskin gelding always deferred to Redwing, usually with a twitch of his ears that Charlie knew was tolerant male humor. They talked only intermittently, enjoying the silence of the woods, the call of a squirrel, the hush of wind in the trees. Redwing snorted at the skittering of small animals racing to hide from them, and once she shied away, but Wilma sat her easily. The birds were busy building nests, calling out their mating songs. They were up on the open hills, above the woods and above the Pamillon ruins, when Wilma turned in the saddle, looking back at her.

"That body, Charlie . . . isn't there a family cemetery on the property? Could that simply be one of the family graves? Could the cats . . . ?"

"There is a cemetery, but it's in the rose garden at the far north end. Willow said this grave is right beside the house, in a sheltered patio adjoining a bedroom. Who would bury a dead relative outside a bedroom? Where, every time you stepped out the door or wanted to have tea on the terrace, you were walking on them?"

Wilma laughed. "The Pamillons might. They were a strange bunch. I guess they still are. The way they divided up the property, all entangled in trusts and wills that have never gotten sorted out, refusing to get together, leaving this valuable land to fall to ruin."

"I didn't think there were any Pamillons left, at least not around here."

"Nina Gibbs was the last I know of to live nearby, the others are scattered who knows where. Olivia Pamillon was Nina's aunt."

Charlie moved Bucky up beside Redwing, looking with amazement at Wilma. "Nina Gibbs? Ray Gibbs's wife? The woman people said ran off with Carson Chappell?"

"Yes. Why?"

"Mike's working the Chappell case, it's one of the cold files Max and Dallas gave him."

"I wish him luck," Wilma said. "Some people think Carson's still alive, that he and Nina are living somewhere romantic like Trinidad or the Bahamas."

"You didn't hear about the body, the one in Oregon? It was in the paper."

Wilma looked at her, waiting.

"A hiker's body, apparently. Been in the woods for years. Lindsey Wolf thinks it's Chappell."

Wilma was silent, frowning, thinking about that. Moving down the hill and into the ruins, approaching the front of the mansion, the horses began to snort at the specter of ragged, fallen walls tangled among the fallen oaks, at the open caves of the mansion's front rooms. Bowing their necks, backing and snorting, they wanted to wheel away. Urging them on, the riders moved around the far side of the rambling structure, where the rear walls stood intact.

Dismounting, they haltered the horses and tied them to a healthy young oak, one of a new generation of saplings striving to reclaim the land. They made their way on foot over the rougher ground, over the rubble of fallen garden walls, skirting the back of the mansion, seeking the small sheltered grotto that Willow had described among the jutting wings and unexpected terraces.

They found the sheltered garden with its overgrown bushes and weeds, tall grass pushing up between the brick paving. Past a central flower bed, at the back of the grotto, a short wall had collapsed into a cellar, just as Willow had described. Was this damage perhaps from an earthquake? The adjoining walls of the bedchamber looked solid enough.

"Looks like this was a closet jutting out," Charlie said. "Maybe one that had been added on?"

"Perhaps," Wilma said. "I've been told the cellars run all under the house—wine cellars, root cellars, who knows what? Old Frederick Pamillon believed in building to last, and I guess that included basement-deep foundations. He was a civil engineer, you know. Highways, bridges, big projects."

"Maybe he built solidly," Charlie said, kneeling down to look into the cellar, "but the closet itself has only a slab under it, no foundation. The slab is tilted into the cellar. You've been researching Frederick Pamillon?"

"For library patrons, but not recently. It's all there in the local history department. Olivia Pamillon was a well-known figure in the village, and during her time there was a lot of interest in the estate. When the property began deteriorating, the historical society kept after her to repair it. Olivia may have had reasons for not doing so, perhaps because of the tangle of multiple owners. Or maybe she was just interested in other things. She had a busy social life, lots of charity projects, though she no longer entertained at the mansion. That was some fifty years ago."

Charlie lay down on her stomach, looking deeper into the black hole beneath the fallen wall, then reaching in. She hoped there weren't spiders. She could tolerate common spiders, but the brown recluse, with its flesh-eating bite, frightened her, and she'd forgotten to bring gloves.

She could feel what remained of the closet floor, several inches above the tilting slab. There was a space between the two. Reaching in, her fingers stroked something smoother than the slab or the floor. Yes, something wedged there, she could feel a smooth corner of what might be the small wooden box.

Sliding in on her stomach, hoping that more of the wall wouldn't fall, or the box drop out of reach, she worked it free and drew it out. Rising, she spread her jacket on a mossy bench, and opened the miniature chest.

Carefully she lifted out the leather wrapping, stirring

a fine powdering of disintegrating leather. Leather dust came away on her fingers.

Within lay the cloth-wrapped book. Lifting it out, she laid it on her jacket. The linen wrapping was dry and frail, the folds stained brown, with paler lines where it had been refolded. And it was marked with faint, dusty paw smudges that made her smile.

The book was old and looked handmade; the leather covers seemed to be hand tooled and were embossed in gold, the pages a thick, rich paper yellowed with age. The long title of the little volume startled both women: *Folktales of Speaking Cats and a History of Certain Rare Encounters.*

Gently Wilma turned to the title page. "Thomas Bewick," she mused. "He lived over a century ago." The date of publication was 1820. "He was a typographer and engraver . . ."

"I remember his wood engravings," Charlie said, "from art history."

Wilma nodded. "I studied him in my library courses, and I've done several research questions on him." She frowned. "He's well represented in histories of that era, but I don't remember this title. He didn't produce that many books that I'd forget this. Certainly if I'd seen it in recent years, since I learned the truth about the cats, I would have been terribly upset."

She looked at Charlie, puzzled. "He would have been in his midsixties when he published this—after he published Aesop's Fables, some years after he did *Land Birds*, and *Water Birds*, and *A History of Quadrupeds*. If this is a genuine Thomas Bewick, Charlie, and if it's as rare as I think, it could be worth a fortune."

The two women knelt side by side as Wilma carefully turned the dry pages. The text was deeply embossed in a handsome, old-fashioned typeface—they could see where Willow had turned pages, too, could see the little, faint smudges.

Wilma had read all the old stories and history she could find about ancient and unusual cats, and had listened to many medieval tales and earlier folklore recited by Pedric Greenlaw. But she had never come across these stories. Still, the book seemed harmless enough, there was nothing to indicate that speaking cats were anything but fiction, ancient and entertaining myth—until they turned to the last third of the volume.

The last chapters were given over to Bewick's personal observations, which he presented as being true. The author's encounters with cats that spoke to him, his experiences while on a walking trek across the Scottish highlands, left Wilma and Charlie deeply shaken.

Closing the book at last, Wilma looked at her niece. "Bewick knew about the cats, and whoever buried the book knew." Turning to the front, to the flyleaf, she read aloud from a child's round, neat script. *This book belongs to Olivia Pamillon. Christmas 1922.*

Charlie rose to look above the French doors, staring up at the rearing cat. "If there are cats embossed on the building, then did the whole family know?"

"Maybe Olivia added the carving," Wilma said, "when she lived here alone, maybe contracted to have the carving done then?"

"Dr. Firetti said some of the cats who escaped from the Welsh couple came here, he said that was at the time the mansion was falling into disrepair." Charlie pushed back a lock of red hair. "Olivia could have overheard the cats whispering among themselves, could have discovered their talents, then. She would have been terribly excited to find out that what she already believed, from this book, was indeed real."

"Or maybe she *knew*, all her life?" Wilma said. "Remember, when Olivia was small, many of the Pamillons traveled in Europe and Great Britain. The grand tour, it was called then. Maybe they learned about the cats on those journeys? Maybe even brought a pair back with them, years before the Welsh couple brought more?"

"Imagine, if there were speaking cats here on the estate during Olivia's last years," Charlie said, "when she was alone. Maybe they were her only friends. She could have become obsessed with them. People think she turned strange and reclusive, but maybe that was simply her preoccupation with the cats."

The two women looked at each other, both wishing they could see into the past. "Whatever happened," Wilma said, "I find it strange that she didn't destroy the book, to keep safe the cats' secret."

Charlie rewrapped the book and placed it in the box, and slipped the box into the little backpack she'd brought, where it would ride safely; she rose, wondering where the book would lead them now that it was unearthed again. And knowing that, above all else, in the end it must be destroyed, and feeling sad about that.

16

THAT EARLY AFTERNOON while Charlie and Wilma examined the rare old book, their horses waiting patiently among the fallen walls, down at Molena Point PD, Joe Grey paused uncertainly in the hallway. Crouching on the cold floor, he wondered whether to follow Mike and Lindsey into the coffee room, or stick with the chief as he headed for Dallas's office carrying the plastic-wrapped letter.

The letter won. Quickly he slipped inside behind Max's heels and ducked beneath Dallas's credenza. Crouching in the shadows, he watched as the detective ended his phone conversation and looked up at the chief. "That was Oregon. You won't believe this."

"They've ID'd the body?"

Dallas grinned. "From the dental records. It's Chappell."

"I'll be damned," Max said. "Had to be Greg Emerson, he's the only dentist I know who keeps records that far back. Keeps everything, that storeroom over his office is crammed with files. Ever since that cold case where records had been destroyed and he tried to do it from memory."

"He went right down to the office last night," Dallas said. "Found the file—called me around midnight. I met him here and we called Oregon. Palmer, at OBI. They compared the details over the phone, got a perfect match. Emerson's overnighting them a copy of his film."

Max shook his head. "So Lindsey Wolf was right. What kind of odds are those?"

"Or what does she know?" Dallas said, frowning.

"Looks like this isn't a cold case anymore," said the chief. "You want to take it? Here's something you'll need. Ryder Wolf brought it in. Here are the notes I made." He laid the bagged letter and a notepad on the desk, and turned toward the door. "Have to be in court," he said shortly.

Dallas watched him disappear up the hall. After he'd read the letter and Max's careful notations, he buzzed the coffee room, told Mike to bring Lindsey back.

As their footsteps approached along the hall, Joe sauntered out from beneath the credenza, hopped up on the couch, and stretched out full length, in plain sight. He wanted to get a better line on Lindsey Wolf. You could tell a lot about a person by the way they reacted to animals, particularly to cats. Cat lover, probably okay. Cat hater, beware.

He knew this theory was an oversimplification, he'd met a few ailurophobes who were decent, honest folk. And he'd met a number of cat lovers who'd rob a person blind, including one full-blown psychopath who was a real pushover for cute kitties.

But still, the premise had merit; one didn't have to abide by it completely, it was just one more guidepost in the feline roster of clues to the human mind. He wanted a line on Lindsey Wolf, wanted to know what made her tick.

Well, he thought, she *had* had a dog, a golden retriever. He understood she'd treated the animal well, and that was in her favor. He watched her intently as she entered, Mike walking close behind her looking very possessive.

She seemed at ease in the office, had none of the telltale signs of nervousness. She exchanged pleasantries with Dallas, then sat down on the couch near Joe and reached to stroke him as if it was the natural thing to do. She smelled good, like soap and water.

"What a beautiful cat." She looked up at Dallas. "Is he yours? Hello, tomcat," she said softly. "You run the shop around here?"

Dallas grinned, and Joe had to hide his own smile. Even the fact that she realized, right off, he was a tomcat was in her favor. Most people, on first meeting, didn't care or bother to check things out. Her hazel eyes were kind as she looked deep into Joe's eyes. "Are you the department mascot? What's your name, big fellow?"

Mike stood by the desk watching her, both men assessing Lindsey just as keenly as was the tomcat. Was her animal-friendly gentleness an act, to gain favor? Of course she knew she was being judged, though if that made her nervous, it didn't show.

"That's Joe Grey," Dallas said, leaning back in his desk chair. "He has another home; he hangs around here because the dispatcher brings him fried chicken." He glanced at Mike, then looked back at Lindsey. "We have an ID on the body in Oregon."

Lindsey's stroking hand went still. She searched the detective's face. "It's Carson," she said softly.

Dallas nodded. "OBI got a match on the dental records. Your theory was a long shot, but it turned out to be right."

Joe could feel the sudden tension in Lindsey's touch, but then she began to stroke him again. Mike sat down at the other end of the couch. "He didn't abandon me, then," she said softly, her voice catching. "He didn't run out on me, on our wedding."

Dallas said, "Why *were* you so sure that was Chappell? Is there more, something you haven't told us?"

"Nothing," she said, searching his face. "I've told Mike everything I can remember, or it's in the file." She studied Dallas. "The paper said the sheriff found bullets." She leaned forward a little, her hand still. "*Did* someone shoot him? Did they find a gun? Can they identify who did it?" She slumped back, and started stroking again. "Why would someone shoot Carson? I didn't think he had any enemies, nothing he ever mentioned. Is there anything to lead to the killer? Or was this a random thing?" Her hand on Joe's shoulder was suddenly too tight, and he thought she was doing more talking than was needed. "Do they know what he was doing up there?"

"He said nothing to you about going to Oregon?" Dallas asked. "No last-minute change in plans?"

"Nothing. That wasn't at all what he planned . . . what he told me he meant to do," she said, faltering.

At the other end of the couch, Mike sat watching her.

She looked pleadingly at him. "Why did he go there?" she said almost inaudibly. "What *was* that tree house? Was that something Carson put together for shelter? Or was it something he found or knew about? Did other people use it?"

"It was there before he died," Dallas said. "It's old, rotting away now. A crude shelter made of log slabs—discards from the lumber mills—nailed together for a floor between the branches of a large oak, with two slab sides to cut the wind and a shed roof of the same material. It must have leaked, even then. Chappell had pitched a pup tent on the platform, under the roof.

"When the sheriff's department located him, the owner of the property said the structure had been there as long as he'd owned the land, some thirty years. He has fifty acres up there, running back from the coast, most of it overgrown forest. He told the deputies he seldom went there, seldom goes into those woods."

"Would *he* have shot Carson?" Lindsey asked. "Because he was trespassing? But if he never went there . . . Or could someone . . ." She went very still, her body rigid, but she was still holding on to Joe.

"Did they find Carson's backpack?" she said. "I guess there was no billfold, or they could have identified him. Did it look like he was robbed?"

"The backpack had been torn into," Dallas said, "the contents scattered, but apparently by animals."

"The paper said a bobcat."

Mike looked at her as if he wanted to hold and comfort her. Lindsey remained still, except for her left hand, where she was kneading Joe's shoulder too hard. He felt her shiver but then she seemed to take herself in hand and relaxed, watchful and waiting.

"Now that we have an ID on Carson," Dallas said, "this is no longer a cold case. Our department will be handling it in cooperation with Oregon."

She nodded, gripping Joe harder.

"There's something else," Dallas said. "The deputies found a second backpack."

Again her hand clutched Joe so tightly he had to stop himself from slashing out at her.

"A backpack," Dallas told her as gently as he could, "containing a woman's clothing and makeup kit."

"I see," she said softly. "Then if he was shot . . . did a *woman* shoot him?" She gripped Joe so hard that he wondered if a cat could record these reactions as accurately as a lie detector. There were cat therapists for the ill and lonely. Why not cat interrogation assistants?

"Can they identify the gun?" she asked hesitantly.

"They haven't found a gun," Dallas said patiently. "They've sent the bullets to ballistics, to record the rifling, but they have no gun to match them to. Did Carson own a gun?"

"He never mentioned one. He never talked about guns, and I never saw one."

"Would you have any idea of a gun that might have been used?"

She shook her head.

"Do you have a gun? Have you ever owned one?" Dallas asked.

"I've never . . . I guess I'm a little afraid of guns."

Dallas was quiet for a long time. Mike sat, watching them, his expression unreadable.

"One other thing," Dallas said, rising and coming around the desk. He handed her the plastic-wrapped letter. "Do you recognize this? Have you ever seen this?"

She turned the plastic over and back again, examining the letter within; it was addressed to her. As she read the handwriting through the clear plastic, so did Joe Grey.

"It's written to me, to my name, but I never received this. This is dated just after Carson disappeared. Have you had it all this time? Do you have the envelope? Why would . . ." She looked up angrily at Dallas. "Why didn't someone do something about this? This might have saved his life!"

Her left hand was trembling against Joe. "Who sent this? Why did no one show me this?" She studied the printing with rising anger. "Why wasn't I shown this when Carson disappeared?"

"We didn't know about it," Dallas said. "It was brought to us today."

She looked again at the date. "But where has it been? For nearly ten years! My God. If I'd received this and brought it to you, Carson might still be alive. If you didn't have it, where was it?" She withdrew her hand from Joe, balling it into a fist, pressing her fist to her mouth. She was silent for a very long time. Neither Mike nor Dallas showed any expression.

At last she seemed to gather herself. When she looked up again at Mike and Dallas, her voice was uncharacteristically harsh. "Ryder?" she said. "Did Ryder give you this?" She looked from Mike to Dallas. "Ryder gave you this. But why? Why didn't she bring it to you then? Why would she keep it all these years? She knew? Ryder knew where he was? All this time?"

Dallas shook his head. "Ryder said she'd just found it. You're sure you've never seen it?"

"No," she said, her voice catching again. "No, never."

"This is a fresh investigation now," Dallas said more gently. "And very likely a murder case. You'll need to expect this kind of questioning, and more, until it's resolved."

She nodded and sat quietly.

"Would you feel like going over the file now?" he said. "Over the things we need to clarify?"

"Yes." She swallowed. "That's fine."

Easing back into the leather cushions and pulling Joe gently up into her lap as if for support and comfort, she glanced at Mike and reached to take his hand. Behind the desk, Dallas leaned forward.

"Carson Chappell and Ray Gibbs were equal partners in Chappell and Gibbs?" he said, taking a new and different tack.

"Yes, equal partners."

"And you worked for them?"

"Yes, until Carson disappeared. Afterward, I couldn't stay there, it was too painful. After a few months, I left the firm. Later that year I started my own accounting business."

"When Chappell didn't return, what happened to the firm?"

"After twelve months the court put Carson's half into a trust for Irene, his mother, in case he should reappear.

Irene Chappell became the silent partner, and Ray Gibbs ran the firm."

The detective knew all this, as did Mike. Joe had seen it all in the file. Was Dallas giving her a breather from the more painful questions? Or did he think that even these straightforward questions might trip her up? Was he checking her story from ten years ago against what she'd choose to tell him now? This was not only Dallas's case, now, but an interdepartmental, interstate investigation.

"And Ray Gibbs seemed to manage the firm in a professional way?"

"No," she said quietly. "After Carson disappeared, Ray didn't run the business well. That was another reason I left, I didn't like to see that. He let things go, little details that soon multiplied into problems. I heard much of that from employees with whom I stayed in touch.

"Finally," she said, "Irene's trustees forced Ray to sell his share. Under the trust agreement, she had the right of first refusal. She bought the business and created a new trust to manage it, using the same three trustees. Her health wasn't good, she had diabetes with several complications, and her trustees hired someone new to run the firm."

"And the trustees were?"

"George Walker, who was a local bank president; Alan Seamus, who managed one of the golf courses; and her attorney, Marvin Wells."

Dallas nodded, scanning the notes in the file. "And the manager they hired? How did he do?"

"Apparently, only passably well. About a year later, the trustees liquidated the business. I was in L.A. by then."

"And you had no share in the business at that time?"

"I never did, I'd been only an employee."

"How much did Irene get for the business?" Dallas said. "And where is she now?"

"She died last year, you must know that, Detective. She was an old, sick woman. I don't know how much she got, I was in L.A."

"The original interview says she was very fond of you. When she died, how much did she leave you?"

"She didn't leave me anything," Lindsey said, stiffening. "Except for Carson's personal belongings, which I don't think are of any monetary value. I was fond of her, and when I lived in the village we had lunch now and then. But we didn't talk about personal business, certainly not about money. She was a very private person."

Joe supposed that, after Carson disappeared, the department had checked Lindsey's bank accounts and net worth. He knew Dallas would now do that again.

Soon Dallas finished with his questions, checked his watch, and rose. Shoving some papers in his briefcase, he told Lindsey he had an appointment, thanked her for coming in, nodded to Mike, and left the office.

Mike and Lindsey remained only a few minutes, idly talking, and then followed Dallas out. Joe thought Mike should be more relaxed with her now, since he wasn't running an investigation, but instead he seemed ill at ease.

But then, as Joe followed them up the hall, Mike said, "You want to have dinner tonight? Maybe Lupe's Playa—if you still like Mexican?" And Joe didn't know whether to read romance into the question, or whether Mike wanted to pursue more questions on his own, or whether he had doubts, maybe new ones, that kept him operating in cop mode.

"I'd love to have dinner," she said. "Of course I still like Mexican, and I love Lupe's."

And that was fine with Joe Grey. At Lupe's he could settle comfortably atop the patio wall above Mike and Lindsey's table, get their attention, pour on the charm until they'd fixed a plate for him, and then comfortably eavesdrop while enjoying an appealing selection of his favorite Mexican delicacies.

17

DINNER AT LUPE'S PLAYA didn't turn out as the tomcat had planned. While Mike and Lindsey enjoyed an array of delectable Mexican dishes, Joe left the restaurant with a hollow belly, feeling grossly neglected. Heading hungrily home over the rooftops, followed by the aroma of enchiladas and chiles, he prayed fervently that Clyde and Ryan would be home soon so he could once more indulge freely in the delicacies to which he was accustomed.

The minute Mike had left the house, tonight, in Clyde's yellow roadster to pick up Lindsey, Joe had high-tailed it over the rooftops to Lupe's, to crouch on the patio wall, concealed among the branches of a bottlebrush tree, waiting for them to arrive and be seated. At Lupe's he couldn't drop down to the patio's brick floor and wind charmingly under the tables mooching handouts. Unlike other village cafés with outdoor dining, Lupe's frowned on cats among the guests' ankles. At Lupe's he had to wait atop the wall for Clyde to hand him up his supper—and tonight he'd expected to do the same. Expected to yowl at Mike and make up to Lindsey until the two shared their orders with him, passing up a bit of tamale, or enchilada, or chile relleno.

But not so. When the couple entered, they were seated not against the wall, as Clyde always requested, but near the center of the patio, next to a table of loud folks in a partying mood.

There was no way he could cadge a treat. Worse, with the surrounding talk and laughter pounding at him from dozens of tables, he had to strain to hear even snatches of their conversation; he could barely make out Mike's questions, or Lindsey's soft answers.

He heard Lindsey say, "It's a shock, but . . . ," then something more, then ". . . know where she got . . ." Then again something the tomcat couldn't hear. And then during a lull in the surrounding noise Mike said, "If not Nina, do you have any idea what other woman might have gone with him?"

Loud laughter from the four couples at the next table drowned out Lindsey's answer. They were celebrating the skinny brunette's birthday, and her laughter was the loudest. When at last they quieted, Lindsey was saying, ". . . but did the sheriff *look* for a second body?"

Mike said something Joe couldn't hear, then during another short silence he caught snatches of Lindsey's words. "If that woman . . . her clothes in his pack?" Another loud burst from the happy diners, then Mike said something that made Lindsey look the way she had in Dallas's office as she read the plastic-wrapped letter, made her go pale and still and rigid. Joe was watching her so intently, pushing out from among the bottlebrush leaves, that he almost fell off the wall. There was more laughter from the party table, then two waiters appeared with loaded trays and began serving the revelers—and soon all was still there, as the diners concentrated on their sizzling platters, and Lindsey was saying, ". . . didn't know her that well, she would never have confided something like that. If she'd had a gun, with California's strict gun laws, surely she wouldn't tell anyone."

"Was she coming on to Carson, back then," Mike asked, "despite the fact that her husband and Carson were partners?"

"That could have been," she said, looking down, twisting her hands in her lap. "I didn't see much of her, she was my boss's wife, but I didn't like her much, and I guess she felt the same." At the next table several people were talking at once. Mike leaned closer to her, lowering his voice. He looked at her for a long moment, then put his arm around her, his words soft and private. Joe crouched on the wall for a few moments more, but when the large party of diners had demolished their dinners enough to start talking again, even louder, he gave it up, abandoned his supperless vigil, and headed home ravenously hungry, royally out of sorts, and having learned very little of interest.

He was in the kitchen morosely eating dry, tasteless kibble when the two came in, the heady scent of Mexican food wafting in with them to further enrage the tomcat. At the sound of the front door opening, a commotion of barking rose from the patio where Mike had left Rock for the short time he'd been absent. Joe sat in the center of the linoleum floor listening to Rock scratch at the locked doggy door. He scowled up at Mike and Lindsey as they came through to the kitchen smelling unkindly of Lupe's Playa—scowled until he saw that Lindsey was carrying a small, white Styrofoam box.

Abandoning the kibble, he rubbed against Lindsey's ankles, purring loudly.

She stood holding the box, looking uncertainly down at him. "You *sure* this won't hurt him? It's awfully spicy."

Mike shrugged. "Clyde says to give him anything he wants. Chinese, curry, Mexican. Says the cat's never sick." But Mike, too, regarded Joe with misgiving.

Joe, leaping atop the counter, yowled demandingly in their faces. He wished he had a tail to lash. Having lost his tail when he was a kitten, he missed it only when a wildly switching appendage could augment a repertoire limited, temporarily, to imprecise yowls and hisses.

"He's so hungry," Lindsey said. "The poor thing. If you're sure it's all right . . ."

"It's what Clyde said to do. If he gets sick," he said, grinning, "you get to clean it up."

She opened the box. Joe rubbed against her arm, purring louder than ever. When she set the container on the counter before him, he shoved his face into the still warm enchilada, lapping and slurping. Heaven couldn't be better than this.

But did the two have to watch him? Did they have to laugh? Didn't it occur to them to give a cat a little privacy?

Joe didn't emerge from the Styrofoam carton until he'd licked the plastic clean, until he was replete and purring with enchilada, chile relleno, and beans. Outside the back door, Rock was still pawing and yipping impatiently. Mike had sensibly left him there until Joe finished his supper—Rock's digestive system, unlike Joe's, couldn't handle such rich treats. Joe remained on the counter washing his paws and whiskers as Mike let Rock in, gave him some kibble, then fixed cappuccinos for himself and Lindsey. When the couple retired to the living room, where Mike lit a fire, Joe sauntered in past Rock, who had stretched out on the rug, and leaped into his own clawed and fur-covered easy chair, where he curled up pretending to doze as the couple settled cozily on the couch. Mike was saying, "You and Ryder have always been at such odds? Even when you were children?"

"We never got along, it was always war."

"That had to be stressful. Is that why you never told me much about your childhood?"

"It's painful to talk about, painful for me to go back to that time. Even when we were little, Ryder always demanded to be boss. She'd pitch a fit to get her way, and it was easier to let her have it."

She sipped her cappuccino, her hazel eyes sad. "She'd get me into trouble for something she did, and Mama never believed me. I guess that's a common enough scenario, the world over. But even so, it hurts."

"And you didn't fight back, didn't stand up for yourself?"

She shrugged. "Ryder was two years older, and she was the beautiful one, she was Mama's girl. Our father died in a highway accident when I was five, he was a trucker. After he died, I had no one to stand up for me, no one who really cared. I was the throwaway child.

"Later, the few men Mama dated, none of them made friends with me. It's strange—they were all weak men, nothing like my dad. Almost as if Mama didn't want them to compete with him? I never knew the answer.

"But then George came along," she said, the sadness leaving her face. "She started dating George Afton. They were married when I was twelve. He was older than she, a coach at a private academy in Sacramento, and we moved there. It was a coeducational academy, but boys and girls had separate classes. Ryder didn't like that, she didn't like any of the rules. She didn't like wearing a uniform, didn't like being separated from the boys. I liked it all—the rules made me feel safe, as if someone cared about me."

Tears glistened in her eyes. "George was the first person who ever stood up for me after Dad died." She found a tissue in her pocket, was silent a moment, shook her head with embarrassment. "He defended me against Ryder and against Mama. He made Ryder back off, and he showed me how to stand up for myself." Joe could see this wasn't easy for her. "He taught me how to get back at Ryder, to give as good as I got. He showed me how to do that quietly if I could, or," she said, grinning, "sometimes, not so quietly."

She sipped her drink, leaning comfortably against Mike when he put his arm around her. "When George entered our lives, Ryder started treating me with some respect. It didn't make her like me more, but it got her off my back."

She gave him a wry smile. "She's never forgiven George for that change in me. She's never forgiven me.

"George tried to help Ryder, too, tried to get her interested in something that would deserve all her abundant energy. But it never happened. All she cared about were boys, clothes, movie magazines—she had a terrible hunger for surface pleasures, a voracious hunger for glitz and glamour."

Lindsey looked down again at her hands, as if only they were neutral, offering a calm focus. "It's a waste. Ryder's beautiful, but what's come of it? She's not happy, far from it. And I'm not happy when I'm around her. I wish she hadn't come back here, I wish she'd stayed in L.A."

"She came because of Ray Gibbs?"

Lindsey nodded.

"And your opinion of Gibbs?"

"Oh, that he's . . . an opportunist." She looked at Mike intently, then burst out laughing. "The guy's a sleaze. What else could you call him?"

Mike laughed, and touched her cheek. "That wasn't a pleasant childhood. After your father died, you were lucky to have a second chance, lucky that George came along."

She looked grateful for his understanding. "George's friendship meant everything to me, he showed me the strength to grow up without losing myself. Without going off the deep end and getting into trouble."

Mike looked at her for a long moment. She had tears glistening again, and she leaned into him. "It's silly to be so emotional," she said, "after so many years. I just . . . I guess I'm easily undone, just now."

He kissed her and held her. Embarrassed, Joe Grey dropped off the chair and padded silently out of the room, heading upstairs to his tower, to the cool, empty, impersonal winds of the roof. Private was private, he was not a voyeur.

But even so, he spent the next week listening to Mike's side of their increasingly romantic phone calls, watching Mike dress to take Lindsey out, or watching the two of them cook dinner together in Clyde's comfortable family kitchen, laughing and easy with each other. Who knew a romance could progress—or be rekindled—so quickly?

But they had been very close once. And he had to wonder if this reawakened romance was indeed mutual. Or if Lindsey, despite what seemed to be her genuine and honest caring for Mike, despite her quiet charm and the touching account of her childhood, was only putting Mike on, winning him over again after their long separation—winning the law to her side.

No one could be sure, yet, that Lindsey Wolf wasn't simply a very good actor. No one could be certain that she hadn't killed Chappell.

The most obvious scenario was that she'd found out he'd taken another woman with him to Oregon, had followed them in a rage and shot him. Or shot them both.

If so, where was the woman's body? Or had she not been shot, but escaped, seen the shooting and run?

And where did Lindsey dispose of the gun? He thought she wasn't bold and arrogant enough to have kept a murder weapon that could easily lead back to her.

Had she buried it in that Oregon forest, thinking it would never be discovered? And then, ten years later when she read that the body had been found, she'd panicked? Afraid of what the cops might find, had she, with practiced innocence, contacted Detective Garza wanting to learn what the department knew or guessed? Wanting to know if Oregon had any evidence pointing to her? Wanting to know if she should run, but at the same time hoping to charm and distract the law? But that would be foolish, and would take more brassy nerve than Joe saw in Lindsey. If, indeed, he was seeing her clearly.

And what if Lindsey *hadn't* killed Chappell, but *had* received that letter? What if she'd suspected Chappell was in danger but hadn't gone to the law, if she'd simply let the murder happen? If so, then wasn't she as guilty as the killer, when that letter, in the hands of law enforcement, might have saved Chappell's life?

One minute the tomcat had the gut feeling that Lindsey, despite her gentle charm, was lying, that she'd known for ten years that Chappell was dead. And the next minute he wanted badly to trust her and thought it more likely that Ryder had forged the letter, that maybe Ryder, or Ray Gibbs, had killed Chappell.

And, sprawled among the cushions in his rooftop tower, Joe thought the quickest way to find out was to move in with Ray and Ryder. Play lost kitty. Move in as a homeless stray, get cozy with them, listen to their conversations, toss their condo, see what he could learn.

Right. Get cozy with Ray Gibbs and Ryder Wolf. Play up to Gibbs, and Gibbs snatches him up and rings his little cat neck, or tries to. And for all he knew, Ryder could be just as vicious.

But what the hell, he was a big, strong tomcat. Those two sleazeballs couldn't intimidate him. And it might be interesting, doing the lost kitty act.

He had soon talked himself into it, soon felt okay with the deception. "A piece of cake," he said later when he told Dulcie his plan.

"Are you out of your furry mind? Move in with Ryder Wolf and Ray Gibbs? That Gibbs is a creep, Joe! He was Chappell's business partner. He could be the killer, he might have had plenty of reason to kill Chappell." They were crouched on Dulcie's roof, watching for wood rats on the hill behind the house, speaking softly so as not to draw the attention of Wilma's neighbors.

"He could have had something crooked going with the business," Dulcie said, "and Chappell found out." Her green eyes narrowed. "Do you know what went on in the firm, back then? Have you bothered to research that?"

"If Gibbs had anything to do with Chappell's disappearance, Dulcie, the cops would have found out ten years ago. I read the file. Gibbs was the first one they looked at, the business partner, the possibility of embezzlement. Don't you think they looked? A detective *and* Chappell's trust officers went over all the books and found nothing."

"But—"

"And Gibbs wouldn't have killed him to inherit Chappell's half of the firm," Joe added, licking his paw. "That all went to Chappell's mother, Gibbs didn't get a cent."

"But maybe Gibbs didn't know that."

"He had to know, it was all in the corporate papers. And two years before Carson disappeared, when Chappell and Gibbs caught one of their accountants embezzling funds, Gibbs went right to the law and to the newspaper. Laid it all out, furnished the DA with enough evidence to convict the employee, cooperated in every way."

"Maybe that was a setup, to make Gibbs and the firm look good."

Joe sighed. "Harper investigated it himself. In Harper's report, they were squeaky clean."

Dulcie flicked her tail. "I still don't like you moving in with them, pretending to be a helpless stray."

Tenderly Joe licked her ear. "You played lost kitty after Janet Jeannot's murder."

"This feels a lot more threatening than moving in with that nice old woman and her crooked son, spending a week among her collection of China figurines trying not to knock them over. She was right there in the house, he wouldn't have dared hurt me—though I did worry about being trapped in there. It's too easy to get shut in, Joe. If those two suspect you—"

"I'm a *cat*, Dulcie. *A stray cat*. What would they suspect? That I'm a cop in cat skin, working undercover?" He nuzzled her whiskers. "Their purchase of the condo closed this morning. They're moving in this afternoon. I'll give them the day to get settled, then join them. If you want to help, you can play lookout, run surveillance for me."

Dulcie was silent.

"Are you up for this?" Joe said impatiently. "Or do you mean to let me get skinned all alone?"

Dulcie looked him over, and sighed. "If you plan to play starving kitty, you'd better start fasting. Try to drop some of the fat off your ribs." And she stalked away, her ears back, her striped tail lashing, her green eyes dark with unease.

18

DESPITE DULCIE'S DISAPPROVAL of the plan she was there the next evening waiting for Joe, crouched on the roof above the Wolf/Gibbs second-floor condo as the tomcat, sucking in his belly in a forlorn charade of starving stray, of dejected homelessness, prepared to charm his way into enemy territory.

The small, five-condo complex was tucked atop a row of village shops, the apartments surrounding a small roof garden that could be reached from the street below or from the underground parking garage by elevator, or by a stairway whose narrow steps were faced with bright, hand-decorated tiles. The views from the condos were of the village rooftops, of the small shops and cafés below and the sea beyond. The Wolf/Gibbs unit faced Ocean Avenue with a private balcony overlooking that wide, divided street and its tree-shaded median.

This evening the sliding glass doors to the balcony stood open to catch the breeze, and through them drifted the voice of a national anchor, treating pedestrians on the street below to the early evening news. Joe, padding silently across the condo roof, left Dulcie beneath the branches of an overhanging oak and dropped down to the balcony where he peered in through the sliding screen.

Ray and Ryder had made short work of moving in. The living room furniture was already in place, and the happy couple sat on the couch having a drink and watching the overwrought commentator. The entire room looked as if it had been decorated by Rent-A-Center, Ray and Ryder taking advantage of a discount for the shopworn condition of the oversize off-white upholstered pieces and the matching white coffee and end tables flamboyant in design and scarred from frequent use. A vase of artificial mauve roses graced the ornate coffee table.

The couple seemed entranced by the news, with the latest lurid details of the latest high-profile murder, this one a multibillionaire widow found dead in her Rio de Janeiro penthouse. They were drinking something pink and tall with little flowered umbrellas tilting to the sides of their glasses, a drink that was highly amusing in the big hand of sweaty Ray Gibbs with his two-day growth of beard, his black jeans, and his black T-shirt emblazoned with a skull. Holding the delicate glass in meaty fingers, he laughed at the news shots of the murdered woman's bloody body. Joe watched him with disgust and an unwelcome fear as he decided how to play this hand; crouching even this close to Gibbs made his paws sweat.

Should he finesse the sliding screen open and stroll on in, boldly treating the couple to his macho charm? He'd known several ordinary cats to handily open a screen door.

Or should he push his nose at the screen and give out with the pitiful mewls, cringe, and play frightened kitty? See if a gentle stroke and a kind word were forthcoming—or a thrown shoe? He paused, debating, looking Gibbs over.

Ray Gibbs was a handsome man fast going to seed; he looked to Joe like a heavy drinker, with his cheeks starting to puff and his eyes baggy. He was maybe forty-five, about six two, well set up, but soft around the middle. His dark hair, though not excessively long, was ragged and could stand a good trim. What did young, well-turned-out, glamour-conscious Ryder Wolf see in the creep?

Money? Or maybe Gibbs was really good in bed? Whatever the case, the longer Joe watched him, the more he disliked the man—and the more certain he was that he didn't want to barge brazenly in and lock heads with that hulk.

Maybe better to win Ryder over first, try to get her on his side, though he didn't think she'd be a pushover. He glanced up at the roof, at Dulcie's dark silhouette in the shadows of the oak branches. Her green eyes were intent on him. Taking heart from her claw-quick backup, knowing his lady was a tiger in a fight, he moved into the path of light that fell through the living room sliders, dropped his ears and sucked in his gut again, and let out a weak and tremulous mewl. A faint and frightened cry that neither Gibbs nor Ryder heard, apparently, over the loud deodorant commercial that now demanded their attention.

He tried again, louder, a plea so pitiful that Joe almost felt sorry for himself.

This time Ryder heard him. She half-rose, staring toward the door. "What's that? What the hell is that?"

Gibbs turned to look. "A squirrel or something. What the hell's it doing at the door?"

When Joe mewled again, Gibbs grabbed a folded newspaper. "A damn cat!" he said and headed fast for the screen.

"Mewwwooooooww," Joe cried pitifully, crouched and subservient but tensed to run like hell. In one move Ray shoved the sliding screen back and swung the paper—but Ryder was behind him. She grabbed his arm. "Wait, Ray. Look at it, it's starving."

"It ain't starving, look at that gut."

Look at your own gut, Joe thought, primed to run as Gibbs towered over him.

"Oh, the pitiful thing." Ryder knelt and reached out to him. Which only went to prove, after all, that you couldn't always judge human character by a person's response to an animal in distress.

"Come on, kitty," Ryder said in a high, fake voice. Joe cringed and shivered. "Oh, look at him, Ray, he's pitiful. And you've scared the poor thing."

Hiding a smile, Joe rubbed against Ryder's ankles, followed her into the living room and, at her baby talk and beckoning, followed her straight through to the kitchen. Ray stood watching them, scowling and fidgeting as if he'd like to get his hands on the damned cat.

In the kitchen Ryder poured milk into a bowl and set it on the floor. Joe was not a big fan of milk, and this milk was fat free, thin, blue, and disgusting. He lapped it up as heartily as he could, trying to look grateful, making a mighty effort to purr as he choked it down.

He cleaned the bowl as a starving cat should, wanting to upchuck the disgusting liquid, then followed her back to the living room and jumped on the couch close to her, prepared to snuggle down and treat her to a session of grateful purrs.

Ray, with one hard swat, slapped him to the floor.

Ryder looked angrily at Ray, but she made no objection. "Cats on the floor," she told Joe sternly, shaking her finger at him—one minute kitty's best friend, the next minute to hell with the cat as she submissively knuckled under to her lover. Joe looked at her narrowly but, remembering his mission, switched on the pitiful again, rolled over on the carpet looking up at her—and putting himself farther away from Gibbs.

Ryder leaned down, stroked him, and gave him the baby talk. "Leave him alone, Ray, he's not hurting anything." But she didn't invite Joe back on the couch.

For the next hour Ryder was all sugar to the stray kitty, leaning down every few minutes between sips of her fresh drink to pet him as if to apologize for Ray's rude treatment. Ray looked so annoyed that Joe wondered just how much information he'd be able to collect before this guy tried to strangle him.

But then, as darkness drew down and the glow of shop lights shone up from the street, Ray started talking about dinner and soon the couple left the couch, to dress. Joe, waiting impatiently for them to get out of there and leave him to search the place, could see into the bedroom and could hear them talking about an evening on the town, and that suited the tomcat just fine.

He watched Ryder shimmy into a short black dress, pulling it down over black panties and bra. Ray seemed to think that straightening his black T-shirt and brushing off his jeans was all the cleaning up necessary—that, and pulling on a pair of lethal-looking black boots with metal toes that could kill a cat with one kick.

Just before they left the condo, Ryder called the kitty into the kitchen again, where she unwrapped half a cold hamburger, scraped off the mustard and onions, broke it up, and put it on a paper towel on the floor next to a stack of packed moving boxes. "You be a good kitty, okay?"

"You're not leaving that cat inside. Put it out, Ryder, before it makes a mess and stinks up the place."

"He has no home, Ray, or he wouldn't be here. It's getting cold out. Look at how beautiful he is, just the color of that silver satin dress you bought me." She looked up at Ray, batting her mascaraed lashes. "Someone's dumped the poor thing, or has moved away and abandoned him."

"The way Nina left me," Ray said. His laugh made Joe shiver.

"We can leave the balcony door open," Ryder said, "so he can go out if he needs to. No one's going to climb in here over the roofs. And what would they take?"

Ray glanced toward the bedroom, scowled at her as if she'd lost her mind. But he left the sliding screen cracked open, turning once to stare at the apparently sleeping tomcat, a hate-filled look that made Joe's fur crawl. The moment they were gone out the front door Joe was up again, ready to toss the place.

Padding out the open slider to the edge of the terrace, he peered down between the decorative wrought-iron rails watching them cross Ocean and turn in at the first restaurant that had a bar. When they'd disappeared he reentered the apartment, heading first for the bedroom where he could see several stacks of movers' boxes jammed in the corners and around the door, all apparently sealed tight.

He didn't much want to shred the tape and rip the boxes open, leaving awkward evidence. First, he tossed the room, clawing open the drawers in the nightstand and dresser looking for letters, for anything with hand printing like the letter Ryder had brought to the station. They hadn't unpacked much. He found a wadded-up grocery list in a neat, cursive handwriting; he prowled the closet and its high shelf, searched under the bed and behind the pillows, and under and between the mattress and box spring as deep as he could reach. He left the sealed cartons for the moment and headed for the kitchen, where the boxes were already open.

Yes, five cartons stood on the floor by the dinette table, their flaps loose but still filled with dishes and pots and pans jumbled together with cans of food and a few articles of clothing that had been used as packing, and that smelled of Ryder's musky perfume and of Ray's sweat. Did Ryder intend to put all this directly in the cupboards, or did she mean to wash them first? No *cat* would eat food smelling of human sweat, to say nothing of human feet.

Burrowing down into the nearest box, he knew this venture was a real long shot. And yet . . . What if he did find the same hand printing—or found a gun?

The odds were great against finding a gun in this tangle—and greater still that it would be the murder weapon after all these years. Ridiculous odds. And yet . . . That twitching sense of needing to do this kept the tomcat digging.

He was tunneling between bottles of cleaning liquids, trying not to spill any on himself, when he found, tucked among a stack of Ryder's hastily folded sweaters, a small box of linen stationery, its lid embossed with a logo and with BARTON'S FINEST LINEN-WEAVE LETTER PAPER, SINGLE FOLD. Pawing off the lid, excitement making his fur twitch, he inspected the envelopes and felt his heart pound. This looked like the same kind of paper as Ryder's letter, and when he eased the envelopes aside, the pages with their rough edges looked to be an exact match. Same color, same weave, same feathered borders. So good a match that he wanted to yowl with success—fate had smiled on him, big time.

Or he hoped it had.

With velveted paws, trying not to leave claw marks or paw prints, he worked the lid back onto the box then eased the box into one of Ray's T-shirts, wishing, as he so often did, that he had opposing thumbs for these complicated maneuvers.

But with agile claws, and using his teeth, he managed to twist the ends of the shirt into a crude knot. Dragging his smelly package through the condo and out onto the balcony, he crouched beneath the overhanging oak. And, with the knot of the T-shirt clenched tight between his teeth, he leaped up the trunk, dragging his burden between his forelegs. He climbed awkwardly, the bundle scraping along under his belly. One last leap, from the tree to the roof, the package swinging precariously over empty space, and Dulcie reached out with fast claws and snatched it—and snatched Joe, too, to safety. He landed in her face, the package between them.

She nosed at the T-shirt, grimacing at the smell, but clawing with curiosity at the knot Joe had tied. "It stinks, Joe. Stinks of Ray Gibbs."

"Couldn't help it. Look what's inside—it's the stationery. At least, it looks the same as what Ryder said she found."

"Oh, my. If it is, we have proof she was lying."

"But it isn't enough," Joe said.

"But if it's the same, if it can prove that Ryder wrote the letter—"

"Forgery, if that's what the letter turns out to be, isn't evidence of murder." He looked at her intently. There was a sample of Nina's handwriting in the cold file, but could that help identify hand printing? "I want to find the gun, Dulcie. I'm going back in. There are open boxes I can get through in a hurry, and then a whole stack of unopened ones." Dragging the dark package beneath the oak's overhanging limbs and out of sight, he said, "If I can open those boxes from underneath and crawl up into them, maybe they won't notice for a while."

She peered over the edge of the roof to the patio's open door. "I'll come, it'll be faster." And she crouched to leap down.

Joe stopped her with his teeth in her shoulder.

"Come on, Joe, before they get back."

"If you come, we won't have a lookout," Joe said reasonably. "If Kit were here instead of—"

"Well, she isn't," Dulcie said shortly. "Come *on*. We can listen for them." And as they leaped down to the balcony, she said, "How *could* that slob Gibbs be an accountant? That's a respectable profession, or supposed to be."

Joe padded to the rail again, scanning the village for any sign of the absent couple.

"Gibbs owned half the firm," Dulcie said, pausing by the open screen, "but he looks and talks like he just wandered in off skid row."

"Whatever Gibbs is, Chappell *is* up there in Oregon, apparently shot twice, and if we can find the gun . . ."

"If he has a gun, won't he be carrying it?"

"You don't think he'd carry the same gun, do you? If he gets caught with that one on him . . . If he has that gun, Dulcie, it'll be hidden somewhere."

Dulcie looked at his determined scowl, refrained from pointing out that the murder had been nearly ten years ago, that a lot of gun trading could occur in ten years, and slipped beside him into the condo, through the open screen.

19

 It took all of Joe's and Dulcie's strength to tip over a box, at an angle against the dresser, slice the tape with rigid claws, and rip open the bottom of the carton. Tunneling up inside, they dug among layers of clothes and sheets and towels and through a tangle of dog-eared paperback novels. They found no gun. They had reached the top, nearly smothered, when they heard footsteps on the outside stairs, then Ray's enraged voice just outside the front door, Ryder's angry retort, and a key turn in the lock.

Backing out of the box fast and pushing it upright, they fled for the living room just as the couple entered. Like a shadow Dulcie slid under the couch. Joe leaped into the white upholstered chair and curled up, pretending to be asleep. Why were they back so early? The two had hardly had time for a drink, much less dinner.

Ray barged in ahead of Ryder and stomped through to the kitchen; they heard him open the refrigerator and pop a beer. Ryder stood in the living room, her fists clenched as if trying to collect her temper. Joe heard Ray open a cupboard and slam what sounded like a jar onto the counter, heard him unscrew the lid and soon smelled peanut butter.

When Ryder seemed calmer, she crossed the living room and stood in the kitchen doorway, watching him.

"That tears it!" Ray snapped at her. "Your sister snooping around. What the hell was she doing in there?"

"She was having a drink. What else would she be doing? Don't be so suspicious."

"Why would she drink with a cop? He's *some* kind of cop, I've seen him around the station. What's she up to? Why's she nosing around, hanging out with cops? What did she say about the letter?"

"I don't know what she said. I gave it to that Max Harper, the chief, and I left. How would I know what she said?"

Ray was silent; Joe could hear him scraping a spoon or a knife into the peanut butter jar.

"I still don't understand why you wanted me to write that letter," Ryder said, "when it lays the blame squarely on you."

"I was already a suspect. Even if I didn't kill him. Ten years ago, when he disappeared, they grilled me like I was Mafia or something. I *told* you, if the case is being looked at again, that letter'll throw them off. Can't you understand that? If that *is* Carson up there, and your sister had that letter all the time, then that throws the guilt on her. And why would you care? Better her than you."

"Why would they suspect me?"

Ray's laugh was sarcastic. "Think about it. If that body

turns out to be Carson, and if the cops think that letter is for real, Lindsey will look guilty as hell. But if they find out it's a fake, you're the one in the hot seat. Either way, they'll quit suspecting me, I'll be off the hook."

There was a long silence.

Ray scraped more peanut butter, most likely eating it from the jar.

"You don't *think* that's Carson up there," Ryder said coldly. "You *know* it is! You said Carson took off for Europe with your wife, you said you had proof. *You* said if I wrote that letter it would take the heat off you and wouldn't hurt anyone. You said that couldn't be Carson because he was out of the country, but now you're saying . . ." The floor shook as she moved fast across the kitchen. There was the sound of a slap and scuffling and a jar fell to the floor, bouncing.

"They never flew to Europe," she screamed at him. "You've known all along he's up there. *You* killed him! *You* made me write that letter laying the blame on my sister!"

"What difference! You hate your sister. Hell, they don't even have an ID on that body. How would they get an ID?"

"That's what DNA is for."

"Those police labs are backed up for years. You think they're going to waste time on a ten-year-old corpse?"

Gibbs, Joe thought, would freak out when he learned Oregon had already ID'd Chappell. The tomcat smiled, wondering how many felons had been taken down by their own blind stupidity.

"They'll ID him," Ryder snapped, "one way or another, and now I've set Lindsey up. You said—"

"I just want her to quit snooping around. Stop her from

messing around with those cops. Why's she running with that cop, following us tonight?"

"How could they follow us? They were already in there, their drinks were half finished. *You* killed Carson, and now you're worried about my *sister* snooping on *you*?"

"*You* talk about snooping! *You* went through Nina's things after she left."

"I thought I might find something to show where she went, something a woman might notice that you wouldn't."

"That's a crock," Ray snapped. "By then, you were glad she was gone . . . But earlier, before she started seeing Carson, you and Nina got pretty close. What secrets did she tell you, Ryder? Did she tell you where she went when she used to go off by herself? I followed her once, up in them hills," he said. "She was looking for something. Poking around those old ruins. Did she tell you what she was looking for? She damn well never told me!"

"If *she* wouldn't tell you, why should I! It was personal, it was about her aunt, nothing to concern you!"

"Money? Was that it?" he scoffed. "What, her crazy old aunt left buried money?"

"It was a keepsake, something of sentimental—"

"Oh, right! Nina was real sentimental!"

"Leave it alone, Ray. It was nothing that concerns you."

"Everything concerns me!" The scuffling started again. A thud shook the floor, as if someone fell or was slammed hard against the wall. Joe and Dulcie left their cover, creeping closer to look, peering into the kitchen.

"Bastard!" Ryder shouted. "*You* followed him up there! You killed Carson!"

"I didn't kill him! How could I when he was in Europe? I just don't like cops nosing around." There was a long silence, then, "You were crazy with jealousy when Lindsey told you she and Carson were getting married. *You* wanted Carson, you were hot as hell for him. You followed him up there and—"

"How could I shoot him when I'm scared of guns?"

"How did you know Carson was *shot*?"

"Lindsey told me. It was in the paper, for Pete's sake."

"I didn't see that in the paper. And you and Lindsey hardly speak. Why would she tell *you* anything?" Ray hit her again, and she came storming out of the kitchen. The cats vanished under the couch. Peering out, they saw her grab her purse and slam out of the apartment banging the front door so hard Joe was thankful they hadn't tried racing through.

"*Out*," Dulcie whispered the moment the room was empty, "Out of here, now!" But even as they fled for the sliding screen, Ray emerged from the kitchen. He saw them and lunged for them, burning to take out his rage on anything that moved—as he grabbed for Dulcie, Joe leaped in his face, digging his claws deep, raking Gibbs's whiskery flesh. He leaped free before Ray could grab him and was out the door beside Dulcie, across the balcony, and up the oak tree. As Ray burst out, they streaked higher among the concealing branches. Ray stood on the balcony swearing, staring up into the tree. At last he turned back inside, slamming the glass slider and pulling the draperies.

• • •

HALF AN HOUR EARLIER, in the sunken patio of the Running Boar, at the table closest to the stone fireplace, Lindsey Wolf and Mike Flannery sat talking softly as they sipped their hot spiced rum. In the early twilight, the patio was darker than the streets above. The fire on the hearth cast a ruddy, dancing glow across the small tables and onto the faces of the half dozen couples who sat enjoying early cocktails.

"It was only a little one-story cottage," Lindsey was saying, "built during the days when the village was a religious retreat. In the old photos I have of it, the roof was really low, mossy, and sagging. Whoever renovated it and added the upstairs made a great attic living space."

"You were lucky," Mike said, "to find a combination office and apartment."

"I *was*," she said. "Perfect location, two blocks from Ocean. And the office is just right, with its open beams and fireplace—a far cry from the generic office I rented in L.A. And this one is all mine," she said, her eyes crinkling with pleasure, "bought and nearly half paid for."

She looked into the fire, sipping her toddy, then looked back at him, her hazel eyes dark in the dusky light. "It's good to be back, Mike. Despite all that's happened, despite having to face this pain and ugliness again."

"Why *did* you leave, Lindsey? You've given me excuses. But why, really?"

She looked at him for a long time. The waiter appeared, then turned away again as if loath to interrupt their intimate exchange.

"To simply say you were all mixed up," Mike said, "that left me pretty uncertain. Mad as hell one minute, ready to fly down there the next minute and demand some straight answers—and then the next minute resolving to put it behind me, to forget you and move on."

"And you did move on," she said softly. "Why did you, Mike, why did you let me go?"

His jaw hardened. "What the hell? You were doing no more than playing hard to get?"

"No, I . . . I didn't mean . . ."

"I didn't think you were that childish, Lindsey. I didn't think . . ." He stopped and turned to look behind him, where she was staring, watching the couple who had come down the five steps from the street. A big, scruffy-haired man in black jeans and black leather jacket, and Ryder, wearing a short, low-cut black dress, her tawny hair fluffed around her shoulders; Mike noticed again how closely Lindsey resembled her sister.

Seeing Lindsey, they paused at the bottom of the short stairs, and the man's voice rose. "What the hell is this, Ryder!" He clutched her shoulder, spun her around, and dragged her back up the short flight. "Christ! Sitting there waiting for us! What did you do, *tell* her you were coming here?"

"I didn't tell her anything, I didn't know where we were going! I hardly speak to her!" Ryder hissed. She mumbled something more that Mike and Lindsey couldn't make out as Gibbs hurried her away.

Behind them, Lindsey had gone pale. Mike put his arm around her, and she leaned into him. He searched her face sharply.

She shrugged. "Ray never liked me."

"He was your boss, one of your bosses."

"He . . . came on to me once, pretty roughly. In the file room. I told him if he did that again, I'd tell Carson—and that I'd file charges against him.

"He pretty much left me alone after that."

Mike took her hands to warm them, they were cold and shaking—but whether from distress or from a harsher anger, he couldn't be sure.

BACKING DOWN the oak tree to the roof of Gibbs's condo, the cats licked bits of oak bark from between their claws, but Joe couldn't wash away the sour taste of Ray Gibbs's stubbly face.

"I wish," Dulcie said, "you'd slashed his throat, down to the jugular."

Joe smiled, wishing he had, too.

"Gibbs shot Carson Chappell," Dulcie said. "He accused Ryder to make himself look innocent. *Is* there a gun hidden in there? Or is it buried in that Oregon forest? I guess," she said with distaste, "I guess we'll have to go back and toss the rest of the place."

"Not tonight," Joe said. He wasn't going in again with Gibbs there. And more important was to deliver the box of stationery. He tried to decide where was best to leave it. At the back door of the station? Haul it through the window of Dallas's Blazer and drop it on the seat?

How many pieces of evidence, over the years, had they dragged across the village to deliver to Molena Point

PD—each time increasing the unease of Max and his officers over the identity of the unknown snitch? How many times had they made that delivery just hours after someone in the department expressed a need for such evidence? Or after some development that cried out for additional information?

It wasn't half a day, now, since Ryder had brought in the letter—in front of Joe Grey. Then an anonymous someone provides the detectives with a lead to the source of the letter. The cats looked at each other, thinking about that. And they left the condo hauling the black T-shirt over the dark rooftops, taking turns dragging it, moving directly away from Molena Point PD.

Carrying it perilously between them across spreading oak branches above the narrow streets, taking a circuitous route above the dimmest streets to avoid being seen from below, they at last backed down a pine tree in Wilma Getz's garden and, with difficulty, were just able to force the package through Dulcie's cat door, into the laundry.

They could hear Wilma in the kitchen, at the sink, could hear the water running. Dragging their prize through, they dropped it by the kitchen table.

"What?" Wilma said, turning from the sink where she was washing salad greens. She eyed with suspicion the wad of black T-shirt, lying like something dead on her clean blue linoleum. "What?" she repeated.

The cats looked up at her innocently.

"*What?*" she said a third time, not liking their wide-eyed stares.

"Evidence," Joe said. "We need to leave it here for a while."

"What evidence? Evidence to what? What have you two stolen now? Who's going to break in here looking for it?"

Joe said, "You can't *steal* evidence. Evidence, by its very nature, is—"

Wilma wiped her hands on her apron, her look stern, her eyes never leaving Joe. Dulcie was silent, watching the two of them, thinking that over the years Wilma had grown as acerbic as Clyde—though she knew very well that, in the end, Wilma would join them in hiding the box of stationery.

The upshot was that Wilma put the black package in a shoe box and hid it at the back of her closet until the cats chose a more opportune time to deliver it to the law. Then, returning to the kitchen, she fixed them a snack of crackers, Havarti cheese, and deli turkey. "I have," she said as she added a plate for herself and poured a cup of tea, "I have something to tell you."

It was now that Sage woke and came hobbling out to the kitchen, encumbered by his cast and bandages. Kit padded sedately beside him, quiet and responsible, quite unlike herself. When Wilma lifted Sage into a chair, Kit leaped up beside him.

Wilma set the cats' plates on their chairs. "While Charlie sat with Sage and Kit this afternoon, I did some research in the library." She looked very pleased with herself.

"I looked first in the computer index of local history, and then went to the microfilm reader. My arm's sore from cranking through back issues of the *Gazette*. I thought I'd find it in the society pages, hoped I would . . ."

She paused to sip her tea. "And there it was," she said with excitement.

"There what was?" Dulcie and Kit said together, lashing their tails with impatience.

"A picture of the same rearing cat."

"In the society pages?" Dulcie said.

"The society pages. I thought I remembered it. I had an idea about what year it was from helping a patron research Molena Point in the 1920s. And there was the picture, just as I remembered. A photograph of Olivia Pamillon, a close-up of four women dressed for a charity ball."

"And?" Dulcie said, fidgeting. She hated it when Wilma dragged things out, and she knew Wilma did it on purpose.

"She was wearing the bracelet," Wilma said. "The rearing cat was quite clear."

"Then that *is* Olivia's body," Dulcie said. "But why would they bury her in that little courtyard and not in the family cemetery?"

"That I haven't found out," Wilma said. "I did find her obituary, and it says she's buried in the family plot."

"Did her family change their minds at the last minute?" Kit said. "Why would they?"

"Or," Joe said, "did someone move the body?" The tomcat looked around at their unlikely little group, four cats in chairs and one human with her silver hair looping out of its ponytail. "Or," Joe said, "is that *not* Olivia, in the grotto? Is that not Olivia, wearing her bracelet?"

20

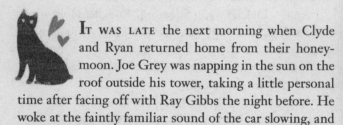It was late the next morning when Clyde and Ryan returned home from their honeymoon. Joe Grey was napping in the sun on the roof outside his tower, taking a little personal time after facing off with Ray Gibbs the night before. He woke at the faintly familiar sound of the car slowing, and looked over the edge of the shingles.

The sight of the Damen entourage pulling up the street was so amazing that he nearly rolled off the roof. Standing with his front paws in the gutter, taking in the scene, he wished Mike were there to observe the newlyweds' spectacular homecoming—talk about a pair of nutcases!

Early that morning Mike had gone off to the station, having cooked breakfast for Joe, a more than adequate omelet—though he had offered no imported sardines, a condiment the tomcat considered essential with his breakfast eggs. Joe couldn't talk to Mike, couldn't demand sardines. Sometimes he didn't know how he'd survived before he discovered he could speak. All that incessant meowing just to get his message across and half the time people would stare blankly down at him with no clue at all, looking incredibly mindless.

Though he had to admit, despite their communication problems, Mike was fairly responsive—and he did make a pretty good omelet. This one was with sausage and goat cheese, a combination that Joe intended to bring to Clyde's attention.

He wondered if Ryan would be making the omelets from now on. Not likely—she'd made it clear she'd rather repair the plumbing than cook a meal. But now . . .

The SUV had pulled into the drive, his family was home, and what a laugh. He couldn't see much through the vehicle's tinted windows, but it was so heavily loaded that it rode way low on its axel, and the tangle of cast-offs tied to the top of that shining, cream-colored Escalade was enough to make a whole gaggle of cats crack up laughing. There was a carved mantel undoubtedly ripped from some decrepit house before the wrecking ball hit it. Five lengths of carved stair rail, ornate and dirty. A pair of heavy carved doors and various other odd-looking building parts Joe couldn't identify. Further insulting the nice Cadillac SUV was the orange rental trailer hitched behind it, riding equally low, loaded with two more bulky mantels, five big cartons sealed with tape, and a dozen stained-glass windows carefully stacked, with folded blankets tucked between them.

Where was Ryan planning to put that stuff?

Clyde swung out of the Escalade, but Joe couldn't see Ryan—then a big orange rental truck came up the street and turned into the drive, beside the Cadillac. Ryan, at the wheel, looked jaunty in a Windbreaker and baseball cap. This was the blushing bride's demure return from a romantic honeymoon? As Clyde crossed the yard, Ryan stepped out of the rental truck flinging her cap on the seat. Both were dressed in worn old jeans and T-shirts, Ryan's short, dark hair more than usually mussed and a streak of dirt across her nose, and Clyde with a big purple bruise on his arm. The newlyweds looked, not like a couple glowing from a week of romantic indulgences, but like a pair of traveling junk dealers.

If this was how they'd started their marriage, who knew where it was headed. Who knew where this pack-rat insanity would lead? As Joe hung over the roof peering down, Ryan, heading for the front door, seemed to sense him there above her. She paused to look up.

"Come on, Joe, come on down and greet the bride and groom—greet your new housemate." Then she halted, listening for the sound of barking from the patio but hearing only silence. "Where's Rock?"

Joe slipped across the roof and into his tower, then in through his cat door to a rafter above Clyde's study. Dropping down to Clyde's desk, then to the floor, he bolted down the stairs and into the living room—he couldn't hold back his laughter as Clyde carried his dirty-faced bride across the threshold, he laughed so hard he thought he'd choke himself.

"Is this how you're starting your new life? Looking like a pair of itinerant trash peddlers? Where have you two been?"

"When you've finished laughing," Clyde said coldly, "would you like to welcome us home? Would you like to welcome your new housemate?"

Ryan had her fist to her mouth to keep from laughing, too, her green eyes merry, her cheeks flushed.

"You'll get used to him," Clyde said. "I hope you will."

"Where's Rock?" Ryan repeated suddenly, looking worried.

"At the station with Mike," Joe said. "Making nice to Mabel, begging cookies."

Ryan smiled. "Scoffing up *your* treats," she said with perfect understanding.

Joe grinned at her. "Where," he said, "are you going to put all that stuff?"

"Not stuff," Ryan told him. "These are treasures, Joe! Architectural gems. I'll put them over at the apartment, in the garage. You didn't think we were bringing it all in here?"

Joe looked at her in silence, the kind of unblinking cat stare that made people begin to fidget.

"Well," she said, "there *are* one or two pieces that I'll slip into the carport until I'm ready for them upstairs. You want to see?"

He really didn't want to look at the torn-out parts of old buildings that Ryan insanely coveted, but she was so thrilled with her discoveries. He couldn't refuse, couldn't hurt her feelings.

"I want you to see the mantel," she said. "I'll be saving that for some really special job. Beautiful hand-painted tiles, Joe, and it's in wonderful shape."

So, tiles. Joe yawned. *So, okay.*

"Tiles," she said, "painted with cats. It came from Los Gatos, the city of cats, from a big old house that was torn down. It's charming, please come and see."

Cats? Curious, Joe trotted beside her out to the rental truck, leaping in when she opened the back doors—at once he saw the mantel and felt his fur bristle.

The face of the mantel was set with blue and white tiles, each six inches square, each painted with a cat: cats hunting, cats sleeping, cats rolling over, everything a cat could think to do. But it was the cat on the center tile that held his attention. This was exactly the same cat that appeared at the Pamillon mansion, the rearing cat carved over the doors to the bedchamber. The same cat that was embossed on the dead woman's bracelet, rearing up with its paw thrust out in an attitude of austere command.

Joe stared at it for a long time, then he leaped to the top of a wooden crate, face-to-face with Ryan. "What did the dealer tell you about this?"

"Not a lot," she said, frowning. "What's wrong? I thought you'd be pleased."

"What did he tell you?"

"That the house was built by a cousin of the Pamillon family, the family that built the mansion," she said, gesturing in the direction of the hills and the old ruins. "What is it, Joe? What's wrong?"

"Charlie told you about the body up at the mansion?" Joe said.

"Yes, she called us." Ryan glanced out through the open tailgate at the neighbors' houses. "Let's go inside where it's private." She picked Joe up from atop the crate and slung him over her shoulder with a familiarity that both amused and pleased the tomcat. She smelled of cinnamon and of seasoned lumber. Heading inside, she set him on the couch and sat down beside him.

"What?" she said again, her green eyes searching his, wide with curiosity. "What *about* the mantel?"

"The cat in the center," Joe said. "The rearing cat.

The body that the ferals found . . . It's wearing a bracelet with the same cat."

Ryan was silent, thinking about this. Clyde had sat down beside her and was holding her hand; he watched the two of them, saying nothing.

"And that cat is carved on a lintel, too, over a door of the mansion. The same cat as on the bracelet and on that tile."

Ryan looked at him for a long time. "I don't know what it means," she said, "but maybe we can find out. Charlie told me your plan—if that works, maybe we'll be closer to knowing what all this means."

"And?" Joe said nervously. "*You* think the plan will work?" Was she going to buy his idea? Or was she going to start hedging, saying it might not work, might be nothing more than an off-the-wall cat dream?

Ryan was silent a moment, then laughed and reached to pet him. "It's a great idea, Joe! It's inspired!"

Joe looked up at her and purred, and was glad Clyde had chosen, so well, their new housemate.

"I tell Dad I want to test Rock," she said, "to see if he has tracking potential. He'll say I'm crazy, that there's no point testing him until he's had some training, no matter how naturally talented he is, that I would never be able to teach Rock anything in one day, that it doesn't work that way." She sat very still, looking at Joe so deeply that he began to shiver. Then, "He'd be right, you know. It's absolutely nuts, no human could train a dog that way. But," she said softly, "I think maybe you can," and she grinned at him. "Let's do it. Let's go for it, Joe."

21

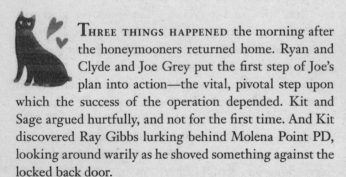THREE THINGS HAPPENED the morning after the honeymooners returned home. Ryan and Clyde and Joe Grey put the first step of Joe's plan into action—the vital, pivotal step upon which the success of the operation depended. Kit and Sage argued hurtfully, and not for the first time. And Kit discovered Ray Gibbs lurking behind Molena Point PD, looking around warily as he shoved something against the locked back door.

The cats' argument had begun the evening before at the Greenlaw home as Kit and her two humans, and Wilma and Dulcie and Sage, gathered for an early supper and a reading of the Bewick tales; it was that reading that sparked Sage's sullen response and Kit's anger.

The Greenlaw house was one story at the front but two at the back; the daylight basement had been converted to a separate apartment, which still stood empty, waiting for the right tenant. The view from both floors was of the village rooftops and the hills beyond.

Surrounding the house, Lucinda's garden shone bright with early spring flowers, but the evening was chill, and within the cozy rooms a cheerful fire burned on the hearth. As the Greenlaws and Wilma settled down for supper in the corner dining room, they looked out over hills awash in golden light as early evening tucked itself down around the village. Wilma had brought a salad to complement Lucinda's shrimp Creole, and for desert Pedric had baked a key lime pie. The three cats ate on the kitchen floor where they could splatter Creole sauce without regard for the rugs and furniture; already Sage's pale fur and white bandages were splattered with tomato sauce as if he'd just endured a second bloody encounter. Whoever said cats ate tidily hadn't seen these three, particularly when shrimp was on the menu. Only Joe Grey was missing; the tomcat was not a big fan of the ancient Celtic tales—and after supper, as everyone settled before the fire, it became apparent that Sage felt the same. As the humans sipped their coffee, and the cats licked the last splashes of Creole sauce from their paws, and Pedric read about doors that led beneath the green Celtic hills into under-earth worlds where lived cats that spoke like men, Sage grew increasingly uncomfortable.

The stories made Dulcie and Kit shiver with wonderful dreams, but Sage turned his back and curled up tight, his face hidden, not wanting to listen. Kit watched him, frowning.

Pedric read of cats appearing suddenly in ancient villages then disappearing, and the villages filling as suddenly with human strangers. His scratchy voice told of how an orphan child followed music from within a hill, and entered through a door carved with a rearing cat. "'And there,'" Pedric read, "'lay an ancient world, its sky as green as emerald, a world all peopled with cats who spoke like men.'"

But if Bewick's retold folktales made Sage uneasy, it was the author's own experiences with speaking cats as he rambled on a walking journey across Scotland that startled everyone, his encounters at crofts and farmhouses where the country families gave him lodging.

"'I had been, in this short tramp, particularly charmed with the border scenery; the roads, in places, twined about the bottoms of the hills, which were beautifully green, like velvet, spotted over with white sheep, which grazed on their sides, watched by the peaceful shepherd and his dog.

"'But it was the cats I met in that part of the country, the strange and unnatural cats that gave shocking credence to the folklore of the region. These were the speaking cats of legend,'" Bewick wrote, "'and one cat in particular, who lived in a small thatched cottage with an old grandmother, entertained me with the gossip of that region, telling stories of the weddings and births, and, purring slyly, telling me the misdeeds of his human neighbors; and he related heartrending tales, too, of the ferocious battles among the region's forbearers, where wars seemed a way of life.

"'But no war, no atrocity, nor wonder of the land itself, could match the amazing existence of that cat and of those four like him whom I met on my Scottish journey. Even the folktales which I have published herein cannot begin to match that wonder. And surely those stories were based far more on fact than most men could ever guess.'"

Wilma recognized passages that were the same as in the

more common edition of Bewick's memoir, where the folk-tales and encounters with speaking cats did not appear at all. She'd never seen this rare composite, she hoped that perhaps Bewick had printed only very few copies. When Pedric closed the book, they were all wondering how many people over the years had read these same pages, how many well-meaning folk had shared Bewick's discoveries, not thinking how dangerously cruel such knowledge could be when passed on to others, how it could inflame human greed.

Sage, by this time, was fidgeting and scowling. Everyone watched him, but Kit most of all, her dark ears back, her tail twitching with irritation. When Pedric had finished reading, she crouched for a long time looking at Sage, then she rose to prowl the house, her tail lashing, her yellow eyes blazing; and soon she slipped out of the dining room window and across the oak branch to her tree house where she could be alone.

Quietly Dulcie followed her, concerned for the young tortoiseshell. She found Kit curled up on a cushion in the far corner of the tree house, still scowling, her fluffy tail tucked morosely beneath her. Dulcie approached, sniffed at her, and curled up beside her.

"What, Kit? What's wrong? Sage doesn't like the old tales, but why does that bother you so? Joe doesn't like them either."

"That's different," Kit said, hissing at her.

"Can't Sage have his own likes and dislikes? You're his friend, you should understand that. Or maybe more than his friend?"

"It's the way he . . . ," Kit began miserably. "He so hates the old tales where there are heroes, where there are brave cats saving the weak. He calls those stories foolish." She looked crossly at Dulcie. "That's what Stone Eye told him, and he always believed Stone Eye, he thought Stone Eye knew everything—when all he really knew was how to bully us."

"But Sage turned on Stone Eye," Dulcie said, puzzled. "Sage fought him, and helped kill him." This was more complicated than she'd imagined—and more important to Kit.

"Yes," Kit said, "I thought he'd changed. Maybe he did for a little while. I thought after the battle, with Stone Eye dead and the clowder free again to run and live as they choose, I thought Sage *saw* what a tyrant Stone Eye was.

"But he hasn't changed," she said sadly, tucking her nose under her paw.

"But you love him, Kit?"

Kit looked up pitifully at Dulcie. "I love what he could have been. What *we* could be, running free together on the hills and no one to beat us down and fill us with ugliness . . .

"But I can't love that he still worships Stone Eye's cruel ways. I don't want to be with him if those ways are still part of him." And miserably Kit closed her eyes and ducked her head again, shivering.

Dulcie lay beside her for a long time puzzling over Sage and hurting for Kit, and the evening ended, for all of them, not filled with the joy Dulcie and Wilma had expected from hearing the old tales, but with unease all around.

●　●　●

THE NEXT MORNING Kit didn't appear at Dulcie and Wilma's house to share breakfast with Sage, as she had every morning since he'd arrived. When they had finished their pancakes and she still hadn't come, Wilma phoned Lucinda.

"She slipped out at first light," the older woman said. "She isn't there?" she said worriedly. "I saw her padding away over the farthest roofs, her head down and her tail dragging, and I thought . . . She was like that all night, would hardly talk to us. I'm frightened for her, Wilma. I'm frightened that she's sick; she says not, but . . ."

Dulcie lifted her nose from her syrupy plate. "Tell Lucinda she's not sick. I know what's wrong, I'll go and look for her," and, licking syrup from her whiskers, she took off though her cat door, raced through Wilma's garden, and up a tree to the neighbors' roofs. There she paused a moment, then headed for the library—this morning was story hour. Sometimes when Kit felt blue, she would join the children while they were read to, wanting the warmth and love of the children petting her and the joy of a good story for comfort.

Across the rooftops to the library's red tile roof Dulcie raced, and down a bougainvillea vine to the front garden, where she reared up, looking in the big bay window of the children's reading room.

Yes, there was Kit crowded among the children on the long window seat. Dulcie could hear the librarian's story voice, and the kids were laughing.

Waiting for the story to end, Dulcie padded in through the open front door as if to make her official library rounds, preening and purring while the patrons and librarians petted and spoiled her. She was, after all, the official library cat. When she didn't appear on a regular basis, Wilma was deluged with questions: Was Dulcie all right? Was she sick? Did she not like the library anymore?

It was nearly an hour later when Kit came padding out of the children's room. When she saw Dulcie, she followed her out into the garden and up to the roof, but when they were alone, she said nothing. She paced irritably, as fidgety, now, as she had been dark and morose the night before.

"What?" Dulcie said. She was grateful for the change in Kit, that she no longer seemed to be grieving. But what was wrong now? The curved roof tiles felt cold under her paws, the shade of the overhanging cypress tree damp and chill as she watched the pacing tortoiseshell.

Kit paused in a patch of sunshine. "I saw that man this morning on my way to the library. That Ray Gibbs. I saw him at the PD, he sneaked in through the back gate to the police parking lot and up to the back door looking all around not wanting to be seen and he left a note there with a rock on it to hold it down and then he sneaked away again, fast." Now, though she seemed as eager as ever in telling what she'd seen, just beneath that paws-over-tail earnestness was the same flat pall that had subdued Kit last night, her eyes not quite as flashing, her enthusiasm not bursting out like rockets, as was her way. That saddened Dulcie, that made her feel flat and grim, too.

"Maybe the note's still there," Dulcie said, hoping to distract and cheer Kit, and she crouched to run, to head for the PD.

"No," Kit said. "Officer Brennan saw it, coming to work. He picked it up. What would . . . ?"

Dulcie imagined hefty Officer Brennan bending down in his tight uniform and picking up the note. "If Brennan found it, then it's inside, on someone's desk. Come on." And she took off across the roofs, glancing back to make sure Kit was with her.

They arrived on the courthouse roof just before the change of watch. Backing down the oak tree, they waited, crouched in a bed of Icelandic poppies, for someone to open the heavy glass door so they could slip inside.

"You feel better this morning?" Dulcie said softly. "You want to talk about it?"

"No. Yes . . . No."

"He's still your friend."

"I suppose." The joyous young tortoiseshell seemed to have slipped away again, leaving only a morose shadow of what she should be, and Dulcie hurt for her.

They were quiet for a while, waiting to get inside, the morning brightening around them, cars pulling into the parking lot beneath the big oak trees as folk went to their jobs in the courthouse. Most of the officers were going in and out of the back this morning, they could hear car doors slam behind the building. But then a uniform approached the door. "Come on, Kit, here's Wendell." And the cats slipped out from among the poppies and skinned inside on the heels of the young officer.

LEAPING TO THE dispatcher's counter, waving their tails, they smiled at Mabel Farthy then wandered down to the end where Detective Davis was talking on the phone. Kit looked at the note Davis held and cut her eyes at Dulcie, hiding a little smile, as if she recognized the look of it, and that was the first smile Dulcie had seen all morning. Davis was saying, "Brennan brought it in, it was tucked under a rock at the back door."

The note was typewritten, and unsigned. When Dulcie reared up, rubbing against Davis's shoulder and her face brushing against the phone, she could hear Harper's voice clearly. "Typewritten or computer?"

Davis petted Dulcie absently, glancing down to see if the tabby was depositing cat hairs on her dark uniform. "It's a printout." Beside her, Dulcie read it quickly.

Police Chief Max Harper:
Regarding the reopened investigation of Carson Chappell's disappearance: When Lindsey Wolf reported Chappell missing, she lied to the detective about where she was. She was not in the village. She rented a car from Avis and was gone all week. Here is a photocopy of the dated rental receipt in her name. I do not know where she went. Good luck in this investigation.

Had Ray Gibbs written this? Dulcie wondered. Or Ryder? She hadn't seen a computer in the condo. Maybe Ray had a laptop tucked away somewhere. Or he could have used a library computer. But were these Gibbs's words? Was his English that good? Well, he *had* held an executive position as half owner of Chappell & Gibbs, no matter how unfit he seemed for that kind of work.

Davis said, "Who the hell drops these things? Is this one of our snitches?"

The phone crackled as Harper said, "Whoever dropped it, why wait until now?"

"My gut feeling is that Lindsey Wolf isn't the kind to follow Carson up into the forest and shoot him," Davis said.

But, Dulcie thought, could anyone say for sure what another person would do? Could anyone be positive that another person wouldn't commit a crime completely out of character, given sufficient cause and the right conditions? And she could see that despite what Davis said, the officer knew that was so.

Had Lindsey killed him, despite how nice she seemed? Did Lindsey have the missing gun that they hadn't yet found in Gibbs's condo? And the romantic little tabby thought, *Oh, if Lindsey turns out to be a killer, that will break Mike Flannery's heart.*

"I'll see if I can lift latents from the letter," Davis was saying, "or get it off to the lab." And as Davis hung up, Dulcie dropped down to the counter.

Now, with this new piece to the puzzle, with two anonymous notes in the mix, Dulcie burned to bring the box of stationery to the detectives. And she burned to slip into the condo again, look in the remaining boxes for a laptop and maybe a small printer, for a gun, and for samples of hand printing. And she left the station beside Kit thinking, with sweating paws, about another break-and-enter within those confining walls.

22

IT WAS JUST dawn when Ryan's red pickup headed up the hills on the narrow dirt road that led to the Pamillon estate. Sunrise stained the green slopes and sent a rosy glow into the cab. Ryan drove, her dad sitting in the front beside her. Behind them Rock rode restlessly in the backseat of the king cab, his short tail wagging madly: Adventure lay ahead, he sensed Ryan's intensity, and the big dog quivered with anticipation.

Mike sat turned, watching him but thinking about Lindsey, who had gone on an errand with Dallas this morning, and the Scots Irishman was as restless as the Weimaraner. Ryan watched her dad with amusement, knowing that he was jealous, jealous that Lindsey was with Dallas, and she turned away to hide a smile.

Dallas, now that he had an ID on Carson Chappell, had wanted a look at Chappell's belongings, which Lindsey had stored in a locker up the valley. A perfectly straightforward errand, but it had Mike fidgeting. *Dad, you're getting serious*, she thought, grinning.

The day before yesterday, when Ryan and Clyde had gotten home from the wine country, her dad had swung by the house to bring Rock home, to drop off Clyde's roadster, and to pick up his clothes; Lindsey had followed him in her Mercedes. He'd said they were off to the dealerships, that it was time he bought a car, that they'd have an early dinner up the coast. In Ryan's opinion, when a guy took his date with him car shopping, he was hooked—and now this morning Lindsey was off with Dallas on a perfectly innocent errand and he was as jealous as a kid.

But as Ryan came up over the last hill below the Pamillon estate, she thought she'd have her dad's full attention very soon. That for the next hour, Lindsey would take a backseat to what was about to happen.

Mike thought this venture to "test" Rock's tracking skills was foolish, he'd made it clear it could do more harm than good, could create problems with Rock's future training—but early this morning, in the dark hour before dawn, Clyde and Joe Grey had left home in the roadster, heading up here to the ruins to execute their part of the plan.

Mike didn't have a clue to what he was about to witness. He knew Clyde had laid a trail, but he thought he was going to see a confused, uncertain dog or a dog running crazily off after squirrels or deer, that he was going to see a very embarrassed handler. But in a few minutes, her good dog was going to prove Mike Flannery way wrong. Was going to show Mike the impossible—and was going to win her a hundred-dollar bet. She could already feel that crisp bill lining her pocket.

Mike didn't often gamble. When he did, his bets were

penny ante, never for a hundred bucks, but this morning he knew he couldn't lose.

He believed he couldn't lose, Ryan thought smugly. Yesterday she and Clyde, and Joe Grey, had worked with Rock up at the Harper ranch, with only Charlie to witness their bizarre training session as, quickly and efficiently, the gray tomcat had instilled in Rock a hunger for tracking, an intent focus, that would have taken a human trainer months to accomplish.

Joe's tutoring was inspired. The tomcat employed a brilliant show-and-tell method that no human trainer could ever duplicate.

Rock already knew the word "Find" that Clyde and Ryan used around the house: "Find Clyde," or "Find Ryan." Before Joe's first training session, Rock had considered the command a word to be obeyed, or not, depending on his mood.

Now, after Joe's training, that word brought the big dog to full attention. The command was no longer arbitrary.

Now, they must never again use "Find" in a casual or unthinking way. Now, "Find" must be reserved only for Rock's serious work.

Yesterday afternoon, before Ryan and Rock arrived at the ranch, Clyde had walked a complicated trail through the Harpers' pastures, leaving his scent in the air and on the low grass and earth, a trail that only an animal could detect, then he had vanished into the woods.

When Ryan and Rock arrived, her command to "Find Clyde" had garnered only a happy, doggy smile. Not seeing Clyde nearby, Rock had laughed up at her and was about to race away to the pasture to play with the two Harper dogs when Joe Grey took command.

The tomcat moved in front of Rock, fixing him with a bold gaze. *"Find Clyde! Find Clyde now!"*

Rock had always paid attention to Joe. The phenomenon of a talking cat had never quite lost its shock value. Now, when Joe commanded, Rock cocked his head, staring down at Joe, his ears up, his short tail wagging. Of course he had caught Clyde's scent, but Clyde wasn't in sight, so what was all the fuss?

Joe put his nose to the ground, sniffing up Clyde's scent, and again he told Rock to *"Find! Find Clyde now!"* and he set off on the trail in a passion of excitement, the tomcat's every move meaning business—and Rock came to full alert. Touched with doggy awe of the tomcat, the Weimaraner put his own nose to the ground and fell in beside Joe, drinking up the scent, huffing with Joe's challenge: This strange tomcat was, suddenly, keenly fixed on matters of mysterious importance.

Following Joe's lead, Rock stayed intently on Clyde's trail back and forth along every turn and backtrack that Clyde had made. Joe's intense concentration was the key. This predatory pursuit of the trail by another animal awakened in the Weimaraner's blood all the skills he was bred to. Soon he was racing ahead of Joe, nose to the trail, caught in the deep animal thrill of tracking, experiencing an explosive epiphany in his doggy soul—this pursuit spoke to the Weimaraner's deepest needs, to a genetic hunger older than the breed itself, to an imperative as ancient as Rock's wolf ancestors. He knew nothing but the scent he tracked, he flew after it, he wheeled and doubled back and plunged ahead through the woods, cutting sharply around the oaks and pines. He never wavered onto a rabbit or deer track, though Joe said later that those smells had been fresh and enticing.

When at last Rock found Clyde hiding in the woods, he keened a sharp, quick series of barks and plowed into Clyde, leaping on him, yipping and whining. The two of them tussled roughly, Clyde laughing and Rock barking with pleasure. The word "Find" had become a red flag of fierce excitement, the lesson imprinted so sharply on his keen Weimaraner mind that it would never be forgotten.

That same afternoon, under Joe's direction, Rock had tracked Ryan with equal focus and joy. And just before supper he'd tracked Charlie. When he found her hiding in the hay barn, he was all over her—manners were on hold when it came to tracking, manners would be considered later, under different circumstances. Right now the key was enthusiasm and joy, and the team let Rock know he was the most wonderful dog the world had ever seen.

Ryan had been so thrilled with the performance that she had hugged Joe Grey, nearly smothering him, hardly knowing what to say to him. "If you weren't so valuable to the department, you could be a professional dog trainer. Except Detective Davis, for one, would rather you stayed on as snitch, forever."

"What?" he said, shocked. "She doesn't know! What did she say?"

"She doesn't know," Ryan said, laughing, teasing him. "But after Christmas, after you three helped nail the man who killed that little girl's father, Juana said she didn't care who the phantom detectives were, she just hoped they'd be on the job until hell froze over."

Joe smiled hugely, couldn't stop smiling. He watched Ryan stroke Rock as the big dog leaned happily against her. "He's ready for tomorrow," he'd told her. "More than ready."

She'd hugged him again, and kissed his ear. "This is a miracle, Joe. And Dad thinks our test is going to bomb." And she and Joe Grey grinned at each other. This time, this one time, Mike Flannery would have egg on his face.

So it was that early this morning, before daylight, before Mike and Ryan set out, Clyde and Joe had driven up to the ruins where Clyde walked a circuitous, wandering path that ended at last within the grotto beside the unknown grave. There, with a stick, Clyde had uncovered one bony hand so that Rock, and then Mike, couldn't miss the body.

Joe, losing himself among the fallen walls, had stayed well away from Clyde's trail so as not to lay his own scent and divert Rock. As the sky began to lighten, stained by the brilliant sunrise, Clyde could just see the tomcat atop a far wall, a gray shadow, rearing up for a moment to watch Ryan's red truck make its way up the narrow dirt road.

Quickly Clyde scattered a few leaves over the skeletal hand, then settled down on the mossy bench with a book, waiting for Rock to find him.

But he didn't read much, he was too interested in the

drama about to unfold. In the cool little grotto surrounded by overgrown jasmine vines and camellia bushes entangled with the weeds, he listened to the truck pull in among the fallen walls. Standing concealed among the shadows, he watched Ryan and Mike swing out, Ryan holding Rock on a short lead. They were perhaps a third of a mile away. Clyde watched Ryan open a plastic bag containing one of his own dirty socks and present it to the Weimaraner. She would be saying, *"Find Clyde. Find Clyde now."*

He watched Rock sniff the sock, then sniff the ground, then stare up at Ryan. Rock circled, and circled wider, pulling her along—and suddenly, his short tail wagging madly, he took off fast, his nose to the ground, forcing Ryan to run; as the big dog sped along the scent, Clyde could hear Ryan's occasional encouragement, hear Rock's faint huffing, and hear pebbles being dislodged as Rock scrambled among the fallen walls.

He'd catch it tonight, he thought, grinning, for the rough route he'd laid, for every one of Ryan's scratches and bruises. He watched the two disappear and reappear beyond tangled walls and fallen trees and then among the sheltering wings of the house itself, watched Mike following at some distance, an incredulous frown on his face, a hard look of disbelief—as if sure that his daughter was scamming him.

Clyde could still see Joe among the far rubble, observing the unfolding drama from atop a pile of broken concrete, his gray coat barely visible as he watched Rock's sure and steady progress. Clyde found it hard to believe that that lovely woman leaning back on the lead, that beautiful, lithe woman with the short, dark hair, her lovely green eyes lifting up to him once, that beautiful woman in the faded jeans curving so enticingly over her tight little butt was his wife. That tough, gentle woman speaking so softly to Rock and with such contained excitement as the big dog pulled her along between the fallen walls and dead trees.

He watched the Weimaraner make a sharp turn around the broken gate just as he, himself, had done earlier, then circle the remains of a collapsed toolshed, then wind twice through the tangled, half-dead fruit orchard—and head straight for the grotto. Rock's nose was up now, air scenting Clyde, as sure and skilled as any seasoned tracker— then suddenly Rock saw him. Jerking the lead from Ryan's willing hand, he streaked for the grotto, leaped on Clyde, barking and roughhousing. Ryan hurried in, Mike behind her, saying exactly what they'd expected.

"You've been training him! This is no test, you two! This is a seasoned tracker. This is a scam! The bet's off, my girl."

"How could I train him?" Ryan said indignantly. "When have I had the time? We've been on our honeymoon, in case you hadn't noticed. *You've* had the dog all week." She sat down beside Clyde on the bench, hugging and praising Rock, then looked up at her dad again. "The bet's not off. I've had no time to train him."

Mike looked at his daughter patiently. He knew he'd been scammed but he didn't know how.

Ryan smiled and shrugged, looking blank. She daren't look at Clyde, she knew they'd both laugh and they couldn't afford to do that. This was not a joke that could be told later, this was a secret they must keep forever, that they could never share.

And it was then, as she pummeled Rock and looked up secretly at Clyde, that the dog swung suddenly away from her, scenting eagerly toward the bushes. She grabbed his collar.

"What?" she said softly. "What is it?"

Rock was at full alert, huffing in deep breaths.

Snapping on his lead again, keeping the big dog close, she let him pull her. Rock was on perfect point, steady and intent, his attention focused on a few small, frail bones barely visible beneath the rotting leaves.

23

 Ryan knelt beside Rock, holding him while Mike pulled aside the overgrown bushes. "What do you have, boy?" she said softly, trying to sound puzzled. "What's there?"

But when Mike, parting the overgrown camellia branches, saw the small dark bones of the fleshless hand he grabbed Ryan's shoulder, pulled her and Rock back so they would disturb nothing more.

"What the hell?" Clyde said, moving up beside them, looking down at the frail hand then looking up at Mike as if his father-in-law could explain this. "He's found . . . Someone's buried here?"

"Apparently," Mike said, frowning at Clyde. He looked at Ryan for a long moment without expression, and she felt her heart sink. He knew something was going on, her dad could smell a scam a mile away. Why had she thought they could pull this off?

But they had to make him believe this was an innocent discovery, they had no choice. "Could this be a family grave?" she said, looking beneath the branches as if for a grave marker or tombstone. But again Mike pulled her back. "Let the department look, Ryan."

"I didn't think . . . ," she said, and stood with her fist to her mouth, as if embarrassed that she might have disturbed evidence, and distressed by the grisly discovery. She watched Mike flip open his cell phone to call the department, listened to his short discussion with Dallas when Mabel had patched him through.

"Dallas is still up the valley," Mike said. "He and Lindsey—headed this way."

The three of them stood in the silence of the ruins staring at the dark, frail bones and at the gold bracelet half covered with earth. The only sounds were an occasional birdcall, and the scrambling of a squirrel among the crumbling walls. At last Mike turned, studying Ryan again. "Rock did great. But that was no test, he's had training."

"I swear. We just got home! I haven't had time to do any training. This was the test! To see if we *want* to train him."

Mike was silent.

"I *know* he did great. I'm so proud of him," she said, kneeling to hug Rock again. "But he's bred to this, and he's so bright and eager—and he did track Charlie when she was kidnapped. Maybe that's all it took, that one time of being really committed, and he settled right in."

Mike looked at her coolly, knowing as well as she that her explanation wouldn't wash. "Whatever you've been doing," he said quietly, "it's working just fine." And he turned away from them as if listening for the sound of tires on the dirt and gravel road, though Dallas should be another fifteen minutes or more.

"I'll have a look around," he said, "meet Dallas around front, show him where we are." And he moved off toward the building, walking slowly and studying the ground. Behind him, Clyde gave Ryan an uneasy look, and she shook her head with concern. Not only did he not believe her, he was hurt that she would lie to him, and that in turn hurt Ryan.

From the roof above, Joe Grey watched and listened uneasily, his paws kneading with distress because Flannery wasn't quite buying this. The tomcat, having made his way up a dead oak to the roof of the two-story mansion, was crouched, now, on the lower roof of the bedchamber wing concealed by overhanging branches, as worried as Ryan and Clyde by Mike's skepticism.

Earlier, watching Rock find Clyde, he'd wanted to cheer, had felt wild with the thrill of the big dog's eager skill and of his own training technique. He'd watched Rock find the grave, then listened as Mike called Dallas to report the body. Now, listening to Mike tramp away over the fallen rocks, he watched Clyde cuddle Ryan close.

"Did he buy it?" Ryan was saying softly, trying to reassure herself.

"He'd better have," Clyde said. "Why wouldn't he? Rock was sensational. He might argue that you've been training him, but he'll never guess the truth."

Rock, at the sound of his name, pressed close against their legs. Both Clyde and Ryan were quiet, petting him and staring down at the dirt-stained bones, wondering what, exactly, Mike Flannery did think. And above them Joe crouched, wondering the same, then wondering about what he'd heard earlier at the far end of the grounds where a stand of eucalyptus trees sheltered an old, half-fallen garden shed.

Twice he'd thought he heard noises among the rubble, but when he galloped across the broken walls to look he'd seen nothing move, and had smelled nothing unusual among the sharp, nose-tingling scent of the eucalyptus trees. Deciding it had been only a squirrel scrabbling about, he hadn't gone on to the decrepit shed, he'd hurried back to the wall, not wanting to miss the moment when Rock found the body.

Below him, Clyde and Ryan sat down close together on the moss-covered concrete bench, Rock leaning against their knees, the three of them happy just to be together, content in the peaceful surround. For a moment, watching them, Joe felt a sharp pang of loneliness—or was it a stab of jealousy?

It was at this moment that Ryan looked up at him. She wasn't surprised to find him there. She grinned at him, and winked. Clyde looked up, the three of them shared a long look filled with pride in Rock, and in what they had accomplished. The little family remained so, Joe on the roof, the three below quietly snuggling, until they heard from down the hill, beyond the mansion, tires on the gravel road.

They listened to the vehicle approach and then pause, its engine idling, and they could hear another car behind it. They heard men's voices, then the crunch of tires again. And in a moment Dallas's tan Blazer came into view around the far end of the mansion, careening over the rough ground, followed by the coroner's white Ford van and then Detective Davis's car. They could see Mike in the backseat of the Blazer, showing Dallas the way.

As they parked near the grotto, Lindsey got out, too. She was wearing a white tank top and jeans, a Levi's jacket thrown over her shoulders. She paused as if asking Dallas a question. He nodded, and they headed for the grotto while Davis backed her car around, for easy access to her trunk, to the evidence chest and her several cameras. The coroner pulled up beside her as Juana stepped out; the detective was in uniform as usual, dark skirt and jacket, dark hose and black Oxfords. Dr. Bern wore an old pair of jeans and a sweatshirt.

The darkly clad, square Latino woman and the younger, bald-headed coroner made several trips carrying their equipment into the grotto, setting it down on the brick paving, away from the grave. As Dallas asked questions of Ryan and Clyde and Mike, Lindsey stood some distance away, staring across at the grave. Joe could read nothing in her expression.

Was she imagining those other weathered bones, up in Oregon, thinking about Carson Chappell's skeleton, lying alone in that remote forest? Thinking about Chappell dying there, alone?

As Joe watched, the abandoned grotto that had lain peacefully for so long with little intrusion was suddenly alive with activity, with the bustle that always seemed out of place as the living intruded on the silent and helpless dead.

Yet only this controlled invasion by police investigators could help the dead now. Only this obsessive examination of the remains, and the accompanying prodding into their personal lives, could vindicate the dead.

But suddenly Joe's attention centered again on Lindsey.

What was wrong? She had taken a step forward to see better, was pressing her hand to her mouth, staring down into the grave.

Dallas, looking across at her, shook his head slightly. Their glance held for only an instant. Neither spoke. What was this, what was happening? Surely something about the scene engendered a shock of recognition.

Why did the hand of a skeleton evoke that alarmed response? Was it something about the bracelet? What did Lindsey and Dallas know that seemed to be secret? And, watching them, Joe realized he'd been making some huge assumptions.

He'd been thinking of the body as a victim, but they didn't even know if this was a body, it might be only a buried hand. If a body was there, no one knew yet if it was a murder victim or a natural death, only John Bern could determine that. This woman might, indeed, be a peacefully demised member of the Pamillon family, duly laid to rest in her own private garden.

Joe watched Davis shoot several rolls of black-and-white film and then some color, and then record the scene again with the video camera. Then, kneeling, Davis helped the coroner with the slow process of uncovering the frail bones.

They bagged and labeled the fragments of rotting garments, too, gently brushing away the dirt with a small, soft brush in order to discover minute debris, though after this length of time, given rain, wind, and small animals, perhaps nothing useful remained. Watching their tedious work, Joe glanced at Clyde and saw that he didn't look well. He was pale and seemed ill. Leaning out over the edge of the roof, Joe studied his housemate with alarm. A dead body shouldn't upset Clyde, he was used to crime scenes.

Unaware of Joe's scrutiny from above, Clyde was totally fixed on the body that was slowly being revealed. And suddenly he didn't like watching.

He had, indeed, in his lifetime witnessed any number of crime scenes and considered himself an unemotional observer. But now, as John Bern worked the earth and rotted cloth away from the skeleton's frail leg bones, a shock turned Clyde's stomach queasy: The thin femur bones encased in a pair of heavy hiking boots seemed as surreal as a scene from some science fiction movie.

The leather laces were still tied, and he thought crazily, how could a skeleton untie its own boots? Fragments of dirty hiking socks were stuck to the thin bones, and the incongruity, the sense of the unreal, turned him cold. He glanced at Ryan, expecting her to respond with equal unease. But his bride just stood looking, quiet and unruffled.

"Did Olivia hike?" she asked Dallas. "How strange. I imagined her . . . She was so into social functions. Fundraisers, high tea, charity bazaars. I didn't picture her tramping the hills. The photos I've seen of her . . . they were all in elegant dresses."

"The Pamillons had horses," Bern said. "Haven't you seen pictures from the thirties, of riders wearing laced-up boots over those flaring pants?"

"I guess I have," Ryan said. "But why would they bury her in riding clothes?"

During this exchange, Lindsey had moved out of the

way of the coroner and detectives, and stood pressing close to Mike. He had his arm around her, but she was so rigid that Joe thought she must be trembling. The tomcat was so interested in her reaction that he nearly lost his footing on the roof's rotting edge—hastily he backed away.

Wouldn't that be a crock, Clyde's tomcat falls off the roof smack in the middle of the crime scene—a cat who should be down in the village hunting mice, doing cat things. Clyde would have to explain why he had brought his cat up here, and Mike would want to know if Clyde had needed his cat for Rock's tracking test, would want to know if Clyde had used cat scent to lay the trail, and wouldn't that blow it!

John Bern was numbering and labeling the bones, while Dallas examined the space around the grave in widening circles, collecting samples of earth and debris, his square face serious and intent. He was reaching beneath the overgrown camellia, carefully sorting through dead leaves, when he froze, his hand in midair.

"Something's here," he said softly, lifting away dead leaves. John Bern turned to look, then knelt beside him.

Carefully the two men cleared away leaves and earth until they had revealed a slab of pale marble, rectangular and precisely cut.

"'Olivia Pamillon,'" Dallas read, "'1880 to 1962.'"

Ryan looked at Clyde, stricken. Above, on the roof, Joe Grey crouched low, his ears down. This was a legitimate grave? A proper internment into which they had no business digging? The three of them had fabricated their complicated ruse, had brought Bern and the detectives up here for this? Had brought the law up here for nothing?

And now they must watch, hiding their shame, as the frail bones were covered again—must hope, Joe thought crazily, that Olivia Pamillon's spirit could still rest in peace and wouldn't haunt them for the rest of their living days.

"Why," Davis said, "would they bury a family member here, and not in the family plot? And why without a casket?"

"These bones—" Bern began.

It was then that Lindsey stepped forward, touching John Bern's arm. "That is not Olivia Pamillon," she said softly. "That body is not Olivia."

"No," Dallas said, "it doesn't appear to be Olivia. Unless . . ." He looked at Lindsey. "Unless there were two bracelets."

24

IT HAD BEEN two hours earlier that morning when Dallas picked up Lindsey at her apartment and they headed up the valley to her storage locker, to go through Carson Chappell's belongings. Across the green hills, fog drifted in a pale scarf that feathered and vanished as they moved inland up the two-lane road between pastures and small farms; in the yards of the scattered houses, yellow acacia trees bloomed, their honey-scented flowers bright against the pink blossoms of plum and cherry trees; daffodils buttered the meadows in wild clumps; and new colts played and rolled in the wet grass. Lindsey drank in the freshness of the valley, trying not to think about facing Carson's belongings again, not to think about opening those musty cartons that had been untouched for nearly ten years, about handling those small possessions that would stir her painful memories.

"The things we shared," she said, looking over at Dallas. "So sentimental and silly, you'll wonder why I kept them. Old theater tickets when we'd had a lovely evening. A sweater I knitted for him that he tore on a fencepost. And the photograph albums from our trips together, and from office parties."

"How many albums?"

"Maybe a dozen, but most are from before we met."

"How long did you work for Chappell and Gibbs?"

"Four years. We dated for about two years before he . . . disappeared."

She didn't want to look at the pictures again, she didn't want to stir it all up. Didn't want the weight, again, of the memories she had managed to put away. Why had she kept everything? Right now, she wished she'd tossed it all. Wished she'd never seen that newspaper clipping, wished she hadn't started this. What compulsion had made her come to the police with that clipping?

Dallas watched her with interest. She was more reluctant than she should be, considering that she was responsible for this investigation, that *she* had come to him. If not for her intense curiosity, Oregon might never have made the connection, might never have ID'd Chappell.

Probably he and Mike, seeing the article and looking over the cold cases, would have followed up. Or not, he thought. There'd been no indication that Carson had ever gone up there, that he'd ever left the state.

"Still looks new," Lindsey said as they approached the storage locker complex. "It was built the year I rented the smallest locker." The building was well maintained and still looked fresh. It had been designed with the charm of the area in mind, white plastered front, red tile roof, handsome plantings, so that it was not an eyesore in the community. The narrow gardens skirting the outside walls had grown lush now, with tall yellow *Euryops*, and lavender and early daylilies.

Dallas pulled the Blazer in through the wrought-iron gate, past the white stucco office, and on in between the rows of freshly painted metal buildings. The driveways had been swept clean. Her locker was in the center of the third row, a small, six-by-eight cubicle with her padlock on the door. Inside, it was half full of stacked, sealed boxes, and one filing cabinet that held her own back tax receipts, which she had seen no need to cart with her to L.A.

After the police had gone over his apartment, Carson's mother had sold his furniture but had kept his clothes and personal papers and all the other small detritus of Carson's life. Much of that life Lindsey had never known, had never been shared with her. Carson had kept the years after college to himself, didn't talk much about them though he'd been free enough with stories from his earlier years at Cal, and with stories of his childhood growing up along the Oregon coast.

Was that why he'd slipped away to Oregon? A sudden longing for the places he'd known as a boy? A sudden urge to be among the woods of his childhood, a last look back before he settled down to their new life? A need in some way so private that he hadn't wanted to discuss it?

Dallas had brought with him a lightweight folding table to make their work easier, and a small box cutter, and as he pulled out the marked cartons that he wanted and set them on the table, she slit them open and carefully laid out the contents, starting with the boxes of household linens and pots and pans and dishes—the black skillet crusted on the outside with years of buildup that Carson hadn't bothered to remove, the ugly set of yellow-and-brown dishes he'd promised to take to Goodwill, the espresso machine she'd given him for Christmas a few months before they were to be married.

Opening a box marked "Miscellaneous," examining coasters, an ashtray, a handful of keys, Dallas said, "This was all Carson's? None of it was yours?"

"The vases," she said, unwrapping the last of the three. "He never had cut flowers in the apartment, so I brought these—two of them. I don't remember this one," she said, holding up the more garish one with distaste. "It doesn't look like anything Carson would choose."

Wearing gloves, as he'd asked her to do, she set the vases aside and opened a small leather box containing four old watches, three pairs of dark glasses, and two tie tacks.

"I've wondered why Carson's mother kept all this. And why I keep it. Irene said in case the police might want it later. Sometimes I've thought that was sensible, sometimes that it was foolish, that his mother just couldn't bear to throw it all away—and that maybe I felt the same. What *do* you expect to find?"

"I don't know. That's why we're looking. As I said, anything strange or out of place—like the vase. Anything that makes you curious or uneasy."

Opening the box marked "Papers and Files," she laid out the musty folders. There were a few letters in one file, none that seemed very personal.

"And all that we've looked at, so far," Dallas said, "was Carson's? None of it's yours? What about the linens and clothes?" he said, indicating several boxes they hadn't yet opened.

"I don't remember anything of mine. There *were* some women's clothes when his mother packed up." She reached for a box labeled only with a question mark. "None of this was mine," she said softly. "I've never known whose they were."

"You never lived in that apartment?"

"I never lived with him. I've never been in favor of that. It seems so . . ." She frowned, trying not to sound stuffy or say too much, but wanting to put into words what she felt. "An affair, yes, if you're serious. But to live together unmarried seems—so indecisive," she said lamely. "So . . . uncommitted." She felt her face burning. "That sounds prudish and old-fashioned. But living together seems such an easy way out. A casual stop at a fork in the road, knowing that later you can easily change your mind and go another way. I don't like that—I hate the idea that such a relationship isn't important, that tearing it apart doesn't matter."

Embarrassed and uneasy, she busied herself emptying a box of tapes and books. Dallas was silent, watching her.

"I consider your view refreshing," he said quietly. "That kind of relationship should not be incidental and ephemeral."

She still felt uneasy. "Makes me sound like I should be wearing laced corsets and twelve petticoats."

"When Carson disappeared," he said, "apparently there was a good deal of gossip about other women. That had to have upset you, to wonder if he *had* been so casual and secretive after making a serious commitment."

She looked down, nodded. "My friends kept saying, what else should he be? All men expect to play the field, to get away with whatever they can."

Dallas busied himself going through the small boxes of old belt buckles, pocketknives, an old camera, a couple of camping knives. He checked the camera for film and found it empty. "That's what some people want our society to be. Easy sex. Easy drugs. Easy crime. The more that people promote those ideas, the more infectious, and destructive, they become."

Lindsey looked at him directly. "*That* is very refreshing. How . . . how does Mike feel about that?"

Dallas smiled. "Ask his daughters. I lived with Mike and his brother while the girls were growing up. Those girls never bought into the glitzy popular trends, they knew too much. They understood how such views weaken and destroy a culture. They knew the details of many of the cases we worked, they were too well informed to get sucked in."

Turning away, he set the resealed box on the stack they had sorted through, and picked up the one marked "Albums." She felt a chill watching him open it. This one would be painful. All the photos of her and Carson, sometimes with friends, or pictures they'd taken of each other on day trips hiking south of the village.

They spent the next hour going through album pages, Dallas asking people's names and where certain pictures had been taken, Lindsey recalling all she could while trying to numb herself to the memories.

There were pictures from the office, taken at office parties, Ray and Nina Gibbs hamming it up, looking so happy together. Nina overdressed in her too bright outfits and too much jewelry. Lindsey could see, in every shot, the gold bracelet Nina always wore.

"The bracelet was an heirloom," Lindsey said. "It was the only thing about which I ever heard her make a sentimental remark, ever show any warmth regarding her family."

She studied the last page, a party shot of herself with Carson and her sister, Ryder. "One of our clients' homes, the Richard Daltons'. That was when Ryder still lived in the village." She lifted the album, looking closer. In the picture, the glance between Carson and Ryder had always made her uneasy. She looked a long time, then closed the album.

He said, "That picture disturbs you. Why?"

She felt herself blushing. "I . . . She was always a flirt, my sister."

Dallas nodded, and began to pack up the boxes. "I'd like to take some of the albums and the box of women's clothes back to the station. As the investigation progresses, maybe something will strike a note, make a connection."

"Take anything that might help. And you can always come back later, I'll have a key made for you." She taped up the last box, they stacked them neatly, folded up the table, locked the door, and headed out. They were halfway back to Molena Point when Dallas took a call on his cell phone. When it buzzed, Lindsey automatically touched her pocket, then remembered she'd left her phone at home, on the dresser—as she often did when she thought she wouldn't need it. Calls from clients could go on message, she didn't like being tied to the office once she'd locked the door behind her.

"*How* old a grave?" Dallas was saying. "How much of the body did you . . . ?" He paused, listening, talked for only a minute more, then pulled over to the shoulder of the two-lane, where he could park.

"I need to make a stop, up in the hills. There's a turn-off just ahead. You have time to ride up with me? It's the old Pamillon place. It would save me half an hour."

"Of course," she said, interested in his sudden tension. "I have time."

Pulling onto the road again, he said, "You needn't look at the grave, you can stay in the car if you like."

"I know it's silly, but I guess I don't want to look." Yes, she would just stay in the car, sit quietly, take time to steady herself after this morning, after opening wounds that were still raw, that she very much wished she hadn't been foolish enough to stir into new life.

25

As Dallas and Lindsey headed for the Pamillon ruins, down in the village, in Wilma's garden, the tortoiseshell cat crouched beneath the Icelandic poppies, scowling angrily at Sage, who, impeded by his bandages and cast, had backed, hissing, into a pink geranium bush. From beyond the blooms Dulcie watched with dismay the two young cats whose argument had turned hurtful and rude.

They had come out to wait for Charlie to arrive in her SUV, to take Sage up to the ranch for the remainder of his recovery. Kit had meant to go with him, had longed to stay close to him, but after three bad-tempered confrontations this week, and then this angry bout this morning that had nearly come to teeth and claws, Kit didn't know what she wanted.

The argument had started during breakfast, which Kit hurried across the rooftops to share with Sage and Dulcie. As the three cats crouched on their cushioned chairs enjoying scrambled eggs and bacon, Sage told Wilma with amazing boldness that Thomas Bewick's book should be destroyed at once, that the pages must be ripped out and torn to shreds before they were seen by another human.

Wilma, despite her revulsion at destroying the rare volume, meant to do just that, once she and Charlie and the Greenlaws had enjoyed the small volume for just a little while—but she didn't have a chance to say anything, she'd barely opened her mouth when Kit lit into Sage.

"That book's too valuable to burn," the tortoiseshell hissed. "It's old and handmade and rare!" Wilma didn't know whether Kit had absorbed that biblio-friendly attitude from enjoying the library with Dulcie or from her two human housemates who would find it impossible to mutilate a book.

"A beautiful book was never meant to be *burned*!" Kit said, growling at Sage. "What do you know! You're feral, you know nothing, you don't understand!"

Wilma and Dulcie had watched her, shocked that she would be so hurtful. Sage stared at her then turned silently away, hiding his face. Though Dulcie had held her tongue for the moment, Wilma wouldn't stay out of the matter. Hastily she had fetched the Bewick book from her locked desk and shown the cats what else she'd found, during the small hours of the previous night.

Because the book's binding had puzzled her, she had examined it several times. The front cover was the traditional board with embossed leather glued to it, but the back one seemed slightly padded between the leather and the board. The edges of the leather were fixed in the traditional way beneath the gold-decorated endpapers, which were richly printed with a pattern of tiny paw prints among delicate ferns and leaves. But there was one place that seemed a little loose, as if perhaps it had been gently lifted, at some time, and then glued down again.

Late last night, while Dulcie and Sage slept, Wilma had risen from her bed, her curiosity fixed on that one small portion of the back endpaper. Slipping barefoot into the dark living room, turning on the desk lamp, she had examined the book again. As curious as any cat, she had carefully worked at the old, dry paper until she'd loosened it enough to peer beneath. This was a difficult thing for a librarian to do. Guilt had filled her because she was devaluing Bewick's work. But she was sure someone had already tampered with the endpaper, and she wanted to know why.

She had wondered, ever since she and Charlie retrieved the book, if Olivia had hidden it because, though unwilling to let anyone else see it, she couldn't bring herself to destroy it. She still had no real idea of the book's value, though she had researched Thomas Bewick on the Web and in bound catalogs in the library. The highest price for any edition had been a little over a thousand dollars. But this title had not been listed among those auctioned or for sale, had not appeared in any source she could find.

From the writing style, the typeface, and the style of bookmaking, she was certain this was truly Bewick's work. And last night, when she'd peeked with infinite care beneath the loose endpaper and discovered a thin sheaf of papers hidden there, she'd felt a sharp wave of terrible excitement.

Carefully she'd drawn out the handwritten pages. She'd thought at first these were Bewick's letters, and wouldn't that be a find. The papers were yellowed and dry, the ink faded.

But though the letters were old, they were not by the author. She had read them through, then put the frail missives in a heavy envelope and tucked it into her lower desk drawer along with Bewick's book, and had carefully locked the drawer.

Now this morning, because of the cats' angry confrontation, she'd retrieved the letters and read them aloud. They chronicled the experiences by three generations of Pamillons with a succession of speaking cats. She wanted to show Sage that others had known about them yet had been careful to keep their secret. But she also wanted to show Kit that secrets *did* get passed on, that Sage was right to be wary—she'd shared the letters hoping to foster a better understanding between the two cats.

Once she read them aloud, she'd locked up the envelope and the book again and had gone off to work, leaving the three cats to wait for Charlie and praying they'd settle their differences.

But immediately the argument began. Sage wanted to try the lock, get at the book, and destroy it at once. Dropping awkwardly down from his kitchen chair, he'd hobbled through to the living room and attacked the drawer, clawing at the lock until Dulcie drove him back.

"This is my house! Wilma will take care of the book in her own time, in her own way."

"How can you be sure?" Sage hissed.

"I *am* sure. I trust her with my life—every day I trust her to keep our secret."

"Even if she means well," Sage had growled, "even if

she means to destroy it sometime, if she doesn't do it *now*, someone could find it. If it's so valuable, someone could steal it, to sell. Maybe someone's already looking for it—Willow *said* there was someone searching among the ruins.

"If they find it and read it," he hissed, "they'll come looking for us, too, looking for speaking cats!" He'd glared at Dulcie, his ears flat, his eyes blazing, and he'd attacked the desk again.

Together Dulcie and Kit drove him through the house and out the cat door into the garden, both lady cats hissing and clawing at him. There he'd waited alone, crouched miserably among the poppies, watching for Charlie's car, waiting to be taken away from this place.

But then at last Kit had slipped out again among the flowers to make up and be with him; Sage was her lifetime friend, her dear companion, and Kit did not want to see him hurting.

Dulcie had followed her, but then drew back as Sage told Kit how Stone Eye would have destroyed the book. "*That* was why we attacked Willow's band," he said angrily. "Because *they* knew where the book was hidden. Stone Eye had known about the book for a long time, and he wanted it gone. *He* would have clawed it to shreds."

Dulcie listened, shocked. She had watched Kit race back into the house lashing her fluffy tail, and when Charlie came to pick up Sage and Kit, only Sage was there, alone among the poppies.

"Where are Dulcie and Kit?" Charlie asked, glancing toward the house and then kneeling among the flowers, lifting his calico-smudged white face to look at him more clearly. "What's wrong?"

"Dulcie's in the house," he growled.

"And Kit?"

Sage shrugged. "With her, I guess."

Charlie looked at him for a long time, then picked him up and settled him in the car. "Stay here, Sage. Be still and stay here." Her voice said she would brook no nonsense. And she went in to find the lady cats.

She found Dulcie sitting on the desk, but Kit was huddled behind the couch. When Charlie hauled her out, and got to the cause of the argument, she insisted Kit come up to the ranch with the young tom.

"I mean to show Sage my book, Kit, with the drawings of you. I'm thinking of doing some drawings of Sage, and of you two together." This was what Charlie called a white lie, but it forced Kit's attention, bristling with jealousy.

"You wouldn't draw him," the tortoiseshell whispered.

"Why wouldn't I? He's a very handsome young cat."

"Because . . . Because he's all in bandages. You don't want—"

"That might be quite interesting," Charlie said. "I might even do a book about Sage and how he was attacked."

"You wouldn't!" Kit hissed, flattening her ears, glaring up at Charlie. "You wrote a book about me. Why would you want to write one about Sage!"

"Well, of course if you don't want me to take him up to the ranch and take care of him . . . Don't want me to fix him a big bed and special treats, if you don't want to come up and share the nice shrimp I bought, and the roast beef and rum custard, and make sure I change his bandages the way Wilma does—if you want Sage to be all alone, to go back alone to the clowder and never see him again . . ."

Glowering at Charlie's blackmail, Kit stalked through the house and out the cat door to the car, her ears flat, her tail low. When Charlie opened the door, she leaped in past Sage like a streak, over the back of the seat and down onto the shadowed floor among a tangle of bridle parts and sketch pads. There, crawling under a strong-smelling saddle blanket, she rode in sulking silence.

Kit didn't know how she felt. She cared for Sage, but he enraged her. She wanted to be with him, but she didn't. She felt a terrible disappointment in him for wanting to destroy the beautiful book. And why did he have to admire and try to be like Stone Eye? Wasn't there more to Sage than that hard and narrow view? Hunched in the dark under the horse blanket, Kit put her chin down on her paws and tried not to think about Sage, and could think of nothing else.

And when they got to the ranch, the moment Charlie parked and opened the door, Kit leaped out and raced straight to the barn and burrowed in a pile of straw. There she spent the rest of the morning, wishing Sage would come out and apologize, and ready to tear him apart if he tried.

26

CORONER JOHN BERN's bald head and glasses caught the light as he turned to look at Lindsey. "Who did you say this is?"

She stood at the edge of the freshly turned earth looking down at the grave, at the frail dark bones, at the thin legs in their heavy boots, at the skeletal arm and gold bracelet. "I said I don't think this is Olivia Pamillon."

She was surprised when Bern nodded as if agreeing with her. "This is a far younger woman. The incomplete fusion of the skull, the lack of degenerative changes . . . We'll do some studies in the lab, but this can't be Olivia. She was active in the village well into her seventies." He looked at her questioningly. "Do you know who this might be?"

Everyone was still, watching Lindsey. She glanced across the grotto to Dallas. "Nina Gibbs?" she said hesitantly, looking back at Bern. "Could this be Ray Gibbs's wife, who went missing?"

Above, on the roof, Joe watched her with interest.

Despite the hesitancy of her response, he thought she was very sure.

"But that has to be Olivia," Ryan said. "The bracelet . . . I remember now, I read about it when I was doing research for the Stanhope studio renovation. She always wore it, didn't she? A gold bracelet with a cat on it, a one-of-a kind piece that was designed for her." She'd started to say, that seemed to have some special meaning, then realized what she would be saying, and became silent.

Dr. Bern shook his head. "I don't know about the bracelet, but this isn't Olivia. These are the bones of a woman half her age, maybe thirty to forty."

"And," Lindsey said, "*Nina* has . . . had the bracelet. She wore it long after Olivia died. She told me there was only one, that her aunt had left it to her." She looked at Dallas, and glanced toward the Blazer.

"We have pictures," Dallas said. "From Lindsey's locker, shots of Nina wearing it."

"Nina told me once," Lindsey said, ". . . it was at a party, when she'd been drinking . . . that the bracelet held the key to great wealth. I have no idea what she meant. She said it as a sort of drunken bragging, but of course she didn't explain."

John Bern looked away toward the distant rose garden, where its overgrown bushes crowded among the Pamillon family headstones. Saying nothing, he moved toward the old, neglected cemetery. Everyone followed him but Dallas, who remained with the grave—and Joe Grey on the roof above.

The tomcat watched across the far rubble as Bern eased in among the tangled rosebushes, carefully pulling aside thorny branches to examine the old headstones and marble slabs. Three ornate marble angels stood up among the sprawling bushes and the figure of a little winged child. Bern moved among the Pamillon dead slowly until at last he paused, not beside a headstone but at an unmarked patch of earth that, Joe could see, had settled into a shallow concavity. The tomcat, dropping down a honeysuckle vine, out of sight, fled through the morning shadows between the fallen walls and up onto a pile of stones where he could see better—could see that at one end of the unmarked, sunken grave the soil had been disturbed. As if a marker had been removed?

Both Bern and Davis photographed the area from many angles, capturing shadows and indentations. Then they both dropped to their knees as if praying for the souls of the surrounding dead, and carefully searched the hard earth around the unidentified concavity for fragments, for minute shreds of cloth or a lost button, for footprints or any foreign debris.

Watching from among the tumbled stones, Joe grew increasingly impatient because he couldn't examine the grave site himself to sniff out scents that no human would discover. He waited, fidgeting, for nearly an hour before Bern and Davis returned to the grotto and the body to finish labeling and boxing up the bones.

Only when everyone had left the family cemetery did Joe conduct his own investigation. Sniffing every inch of the unmarked grave and its surround, he found very little. Once he caught a whiff of an unfamiliar perfume or shaving lotion, but it was so faint and so entwined with fresh human scents now, and with the smell of the few roses that still bloomed, that even a cat couldn't sort it out; he returned at last to the roof above the grotto, having learned nothing.

Bern and Davis were packing up their equipment, preparing to leave. Joe watched Dallas cross the grotto, dropping into his pocket a small paper evidence bag containing the last item Dr. Bern had found: two minuscule lumps Bern had unearthed beneath the body, at the bottom of the grave.

If these were what Joe thought, they must have settled during the preceding years, possibly falling as the flesh decayed around them. He'd gotten a clear look as Bern bagged them, and he was sure they were bullets crusted with detritus and earth.

Joe found it interesting that as Ryan and Clyde helped carry the coroner's cases to his car, the newlyweds moved close together, as if, in the face of death, they needed to touch, to reassure each other of their own well-being and safety. And when Joe looked at Mike and Lindsey, they were behaving the same, Lindsey leaning into the tall, lanky Scots Irishman, his arm protectively around her. They glanced up when Detective Davis looked in their direction, then turned away as Davis headed for Detective Garza.

Joe watched Davis slip a small plastic bag from the pocket of her dark uniform. He could see a half sheet of paper inside. Was that the note Ryder had brought in earlier? But why bring it here? It was already logged in, and Lindsey had already seen it. The look on Davis's face was one of half annoyance, half amusement. As she handed Dallas the small evidence bag, Joe slipped silently along the edge of the roof until he was just above them.

Whatever this was, it wasn't the letter Ryder had

brought, this wasn't hand printed, but typewritten on smooth white paper.

"Brennan found this at the back door this morning," Davis said. "Just after change of watch. No one saw who left it, and there are no latents." The look between the two detectives was one the tomcat knew well, that wry glance of frustration that heralded another anonymous tip, both welcome and highly frustrating.

But this wasn't Joe's tip. Nor, surely, anything Dulcie or Kit would have taken to the station. Edging farther over the lip of the roof, Joe read the letter over Dallas's shoulder, watched Dallas glance across the grotto at Lindsey, much as Davis had done.

Lindsey was watching them, the end of her scarf thrown back over her shoulder, her tan very appealing against the white tank top. At that moment, Joe would have given a brace of fat mice to know her thoughts.

But he would give a lot more to know them if the detectives shared the letter with her.

Police Chief Max Harper:
Regarding the reopened investigation of Carson Chappell's disappearance: When Lindsey Wolf reported Chappell missing, she lied to the detective about where she was. She was not in the village. She rented a car from Avis and was gone all week. Here is a photocopy of the dated rental receipt in her name. I do not know where she went. Good luck in this investigation.

The letter was indeed like something the real snitches might have discovered and stolen and taken to the detectives, and that angered Joe. He wanted to know who had left this, wanted to know if the message was true or if the killer had written it to lay the blame on Lindsey.

He didn't want to think she'd killed Carson. Despite his uneasy questions about her, he wanted to believe her. *Wanted* her to be telling the truth. Below him, Dallas was saying, "I'd like Lindsey to read this."

Davis said, "You think that's wise?"

"In this case, yes."

She nodded, and he motioned Lindsey and Mike over. They read the printout together. Lindsey stood a moment staring at it, then looked up at the detectives, flushed and scowling.

"Who gave you this? Where did you get this?"

"It was left at the station this morning," Davis said. "We don't know who left it."

"Can you fingerprint it?"

"I tried," Davis said. "There's nothing—we'll see what the lab can pick up."

"It's not typed," Lindsey said, examining the paper through the plastic. "It's too even. Looks like a printout. Is there some way you can trace a printer?"

"We'd have to have something to go on," Davis said. "Another example from the same printer, and even then . . . *Were* you out of town the week Carson disappeared?"

"No. That was the week of the wedding. May I see the receipt?"

Davis turned the plastic over, to show the Visa receipt. Lindsey looked at it, and nodded. "That's my credit card number. But there've never been any forged charges against it, I check carefully. I've never had any theft."

"Would you still have that Visa bill?" Davis said, clearly not expecting that she would.

"I would if there were any business expenses on that one," Lindsey said. "And there usually are. It would be in my tax returns for that year." She looked at Dallas. "They're in the locker, in the file cabinet." Her hazel eyes were still angry, her cheeks flaming. "This is . . . What's he trying to do?"

"Who?" Davis said.

"Ray Gibbs," Lindsey said, looking at Davis. "If that body is Nina, then this note has to be from Gibbs. Or . . ." After a moment, she said, more quietly, "Or . . . Oh, not my sister?"

"What makes you think it was Gibbs?" Davis said. "Or your sister? This could have nothing to do with them."

"It has to do with Carson's death, and maybe with Gibbs's wife, with Nina," Lindsey said, glancing away, toward the grave.

Davis said, "Why are you so certain the body is Nina?" Davis had taken over the interview, and Dallas seemed content to let her run with it.

"She always wore that bracelet, I don't think I ever saw her without it. Wore it all the time, just as her aunt did, before her. Unless . . . ," she said, "unless the story about there being only one bracelet wasn't true, unless there was another."

"Or," Davis said, "unless Nina gave it to someone."

Lindsey frowned at the detective. "That doesn't seem likely. Nina seemed to place some special, almost mystical value on it."

"Can you explain?" Davis said.

"I don't really know. Maybe sentimental value. I think she was truly fond of her aunt. She said once that the bracelet was the one thing that Olivia Pamillon treasured." She looked toward the now empty grave. "Olivia's bracelet, circling that bare bone." She shivered. "Like a manacle holding Nina there." And she turned away, into the shelter of Mike's arms.

Above, on the roof, Joe watched her intently. What a strange thing to say, to read into a simple bracelet with an innocent cat embossed on the band. Below him, both detectives watched Lindsey without expression. And Joe thought, *A bracelet embossed with the emblem of a secret that Olivia Pamillon carried all her life?* And as Clyde and Mike and Ryan turned to leave, the tomcat, staying out of sight, headed fast across the roofs toward Clyde's roadster, Lindsey's words repeating in his head, *Like a manacle holding Nina there . . . like a manacle . . .*

But, galloping across the roofs trying to put Lindsey's comment in perspective, he stopped suddenly and crouched, very still, watching the jutting wing of the mansion beyond the grotto, where he'd glimpsed a figure slipping away. Darkly dressed, visible only for a second, moving fast. Someone near the grotto, listening, and watching.

There! He saw the figure again moving swiftly to vanish beyond the broken walls, moving toward the old shed, and then gone.

27

ALONE IN THE BARN, wishing Sage would hobble out and apologize to her and say he'd been wrong, say that Stone Eye *had* been an evil tyrant and the clowder *was* better off without him, and knowing Sage would never do that, Kit began to smell a lovely aroma from the kitchen. Charlie's delicious shrimp casserole. Crouching in the straw feeling lonely and neglected and sniffing that heady scent, growing hungrier and hungrier but unwilling to go in the house and face Sage and make up—he'd have to apologize first—she waited. Maybe Charlie would come out and would understand and would maybe bring her some nice shrimp to eat and tell her she was right and Sage was wrong. Listening across the yard to little sounds from the kitchen, she longed to hear the door open and Charlie's footsteps approach. She felt sure Charlie could make everything all right.

But Kit waited a long time before Charlie appeared in the barn, calling out to her. Then she waited a long time more, letting Charlie call and call, before she came out from her hiding place in the pile of straw.

Immediately Charlie picked her up, scowling down crossly but gently stroking her. Charlie did not apologize for Sage's behavior. Nor did she sympathize with Kit. She simply headed for the house.

But before they went inside, into the big kitchen, Charlie sat down on the steps, holding Kit tenderly. "You're hurting, Kit. You feel all alone, and Sage doesn't understand."

Kit sniffed.

"Do you think Sage feels alone, too?"

Kit didn't care.

Charlie took Kit's wild little black-and-brown face in her hands, looked into her angry yellow eyes. "Do you think he understands why you're angry? Really understands?"

Kit didn't care about that either. If Sage didn't understand now, he never would. She'd said it plainly enough.

Hadn't she?

"Do you think," Charlie said, "that you might have been thinking like a kitten who expects to be understood but never *really* explains what's wrong?"

Kit glared at her.

"Do you think, if you explained to him that the way *he* sees life is a threat to the freedom *you* see in life, that he would understand?"

Kit was quiet, thinking. Charlie said nothing more. She rose, carrying Kit, and in the kitchen she set her down on the window seat, at the far end, as far as possible from where Sage was tucked up among the cushions. His head was down, his eyes closed in misery.

Charlie served each of the cats a plate of warm shrimp casserole, each in their own corner, then set her own plate beside a green salad and sat down at the table. She didn't talk as she ate, didn't seem to notice them. She sat enjoying her early lunch and reading some manuscript pages from the book she was working on. The cats ate in grim silence—though anger didn't seem to spoil their appetites. They ate fiercely, as if tearing at fresh kill, glancing at each other only occasionally.

After a long while, as Charlie ignored them, their glances grew more frequent and then gentler. And as the soothing effect of the warm shrimp eased and cheered them, they looked at each other more kindly. Charlie gave no sign that she noticed. When she'd finished, and rinsed her plate, she left them alone and headed back to her studio. But in truth, she was so upset by the cats' battle that she wasn't sure she could work, not sure she could put herself back into the fictional world that she built around her as she wrote.

Oh, Kit, she thought, *do you love Sage? Love him enough to follow him back into the wild despite your differences? To follow him even when you can't agree on what's important in life?* Indeed, two sets of their deepest beliefs were at cross purposes here, just as could happen with humans, one set of values deeply threatening the other. *Oh, Kit, don't go if you can't be happy. Don't go if you can't believe alike, don't go and leave us, only to be miserable . . .*

But now all Charlie could do was leave them alone, so her interference didn't muddle their relationship, and hope they'd sort it out.

Getting back to work on the new book, soon immersed

in the tangle of the story, still Charlie was aware of the cats' softer voices, as if they were making up. Later, when she heard only silence she rose and went to look.

They were napping, curled peacefully together. She turned away, smiling, and soon she was deep in the book again, deeply relieved that silence reigned from the kitchen. Later, if she was aware of a soft metallic sound, she ignored it.

It was late that afternoon when, finishing her work for the day, she went into the kitchen and found the window seat empty and a glass panel above it open six inches. Alarmed, afraid the cats were gone, she had turned away to search the house when Kit came bolting in through the window behind her, her claws scrabbling on the sill, and raced to her, smearing dirty paw prints across the cushions.

"He's gone, Charlie. I woke up and he was gone, we were asleep and I was dreaming and then I woke up and the window was open and Sage was gone and I followed his scent that leads into the woods and I'm going back after him but I came to tell you so you wouldn't worry . . ."

Charlie grabbed her before she could leap away. "He's hurt, Kit. I'll come with you! He's awkward and clumsy in his bandages and cast, and it'll be dark soon. He mustn't be out there alone, he can't defend himself!" Carrying Kit, Charlie snatched up her jacket, shrugged it on while juggling the tortoiseshell, and they were out the door and heading for the woods.

"Now, Kit," she said, setting her down. "Now you can track him."

And Kit was off, following Sage's scent around the barn and straight into the heavy woods, tracking the crippled cat while already the shadows of evening were running together toward night.

JOE WAS IN a dither to leave the ruins and get back to the village. Having seen the shadowed figure slip away among the broken walls, he paced the mansion's roof beneath overhanging limbs willing Clyde to hurry, willing the detectives and coroner and everyone to get back in their cars and leave so he and Clyde could search for the guy or follow him.

The dark intruder had been spying close enough to the grotto to know they had exhumed a body. If that mysterious presence was the killer, he'd surely run.

Had he known they'd be there looking for the grave? Joe wanted to alert the two detectives, but he could not.

And he couldn't alert Clyde or Ryan; they stood in a huddle by the cars with John Bern, Mike, Lindsey, Dallas, and Juana Davis. Joe couldn't even go up to them and yowl, couldn't make his presence known. He could just hear Mike: *You brought your cat up here, Damen? Rock was following cat scent! You laid a trail of cat scent! No wonder he tracked like a pro.*

And he couldn't alert the dispatcher, Clyde had the phone on his belt. Even if he had a phone, how could he tell the dispatcher that Davis and Dallas had just missed a fleeing eavesdropper? It would look like the snitch was right up there in the ruins with them, that's how it would look.

And once he got Dallas and Davis wondering why the

snitch was here and how he'd known they were coming here, got them looking for him, combing the ruins to find him, that could be trouble, big time. For one thing, he hadn't covered his paw prints, he'd assured himself that after they left, the wind that softly blew across the hills would wipe away those telltale marks, would destroy his recent trail through the cemetery.

No, the only option he had was to slip through the rubble and into the open roadster without being seen, hunch down on the floor under the lap robe, and pray for Clyde to hurry. He was crouched to leap off the roof when he heard a car start from the direction of the old wooden shed, a soft, smoothly running engine. He reared up, staring through the falling dusk.

There! There it went, a small, dark car sliding away between the dead oaks, over the thick carpet of rotting leaves that covered the narrow back path—and it was gone, down the narrow back road, hardly more than a trail, that would lead out, north of the village. Faintly, he could hear rocks crunching under its tires where the leaves were thin.

When he turned to see if anyone else had heard, they hadn't, no one was looking in that direction. They were too far away, that faint hushing only a cat would hear.

He hoped the rough lane would tear out the underpinnings of the sleek, navy blue coupe, prayed the driver would get stranded in plain sight.

But no such luck. Already the car was gone, dropping down the hills where it would be lost among the narrow streets and small crowded cottages. Racing through the roof's shadows where trees overhung, he slicked down a dead oak and galloped across the rubble to the old shed.

It was half falling down, evening light shining in through the cracks. Investigating the dry earth within, he found tire marks, then sniffed in and around the rough walls for human scent over the stink of lingering exhaust. He detected a trace of shaving lotion or perfume, but it was so mingled with car smells and the stink of lantana vines growing in through the roof that he couldn't make much of it. He wasn't sure he could recognize the same smell in another setting, or even on the human source.

The tire tracks were equally disappointing. Rows of chevrons that he committed to memory, but that were so common they didn't mean much. He could detect no nick or scar to further identify the tread. When he heard the faraway voices change and fade and engines start, he sped for Clyde's roadster.

Leaping in, he waited on the floor, suffocating under the lap robe as he tried to lay out a plan.

If he told Clyde what he'd seen, would Clyde try to find the vanished car? Or would he only demand that Joe leave this alone? Ryan wasn't riding back with them, she wouldn't be there to defend him. At last Clyde swung into the roadster, flipped the blanket aside, and looked down at him, smug and satisfied.

"That did go well. I have to admit, Joe, your scam was a stroke of genius. The coroner has the body, and Rock is now a trained tracker! I guess you know Ryan's way proud of you."

Joe smiled. He decided not to mention the darkly clad eavesdropper and spoil the moment with a fresh argument. He did his best to look both modest and innocent.

Ahead, the line of cars pulled around the side of the

forlorn old mansion between the dead trees and broken walls, to the wider dirt and gravel road that led to the village. The coroner's white van, Juana Davis's blue sedan, then Dallas's Blazer. Then Ryan's big red king cab. Clyde's yellow roadster joined the end of the line, the tomcat crouched out of sight on the seat.

IN THE KING CAB, Rock rode on the front passenger seat beside Ryan, his head out the open window, drinking in the wind. Ryan didn't usually let the big dog put his head out where grit and stones could injure his eyes, but just this once he deserved a treat.

In the backseat beside Mike, Lindsey was silent, deep in thought, looking so solemn that Mike wondered what she'd do once they'd dropped her off at the station to pick up her car. Her expression of hard determination made him uneasy, he preferred the smiling, soft-spoken Lindsey Wolf he'd grown to care about all over again—if he'd ever stopped caring. This angry, alert side of her was worrisome. Her whole take on the morning's events was worrisome.

She seemed so certain that the corpse was that of Nina Gibbs. Seemed just as certain that Ray Gibbs had killed Nina, as sure as if the coroner had already determined identity and time of death, or as if Oregon had found trace evidence of Nina in Carson's tree house. Mike had never known Lindsey to let her imagination run so wild. He didn't try to convince her otherwise, didn't argue with her, he only wondered how prone she might be, given the mood she was in, to doing something foolish.

No one could be that sure what she might be thinking. Did her stubborn certainty have some basis? Were there facts about the case she wasn't telling them?

As Ryan turned down Ocean and into the village, driving slowly, stopping for a group of tourists headed through the gathering dusk for the lighted shops and restaurants, Mike took Lindsey's hand. "You're going home when you've picked up your car?"

She nodded, glancing out the window. "I think I'll rest a little, then I have some work to finish up that I promised for tomorrow. I'll have a sandwich for supper, at my desk."

Not until they pulled into the courthouse parking lot, when Lindsey was fishing her keys from her pocket, did she really look at him. She squeezed his hand, and smiled.

He looked at her levelly. "You'll be in the office, then?" he said uneasily. "You don't mean to do something foolish?"

She looked surprised and laughed, and swung out of the truck, turning to talk through the open window. "Because I said that was Nina, in that grave? Because I said . . ." She shook her head. "Even if that is Nina, what could I do?" She touched his cheek with gentle fingers. "I wouldn't know how to run some kind of investigation, if that's what you're imagining. And I know better than to interfere in cops' work."

Her words eased him, made him think his own imagination had gone astray. And yet as Lindsey leaned in to brush a kiss across his cheek, then headed away toward her car, Mike watched her not with his usual lusty interest but with questions.

He had a strong urge to follow her, at least swing by

her office in a little while, see if her car was still there in the little parking alcove.

But he immediately chucked that. He wouldn't breach her trust and privacy. He didn't want to smother her any more than he'd want to be smothered. And, determining to do the honorable thing even while his instinct told him he was wrong, he settled back, riding home with Ryan to pick up his car.

28

In the courthouse parking lot, Lindsey waited in her car until Ryan's red truck pulled away and disappeared up the street, and Dallas, who had turned in just behind them, had gone into the station. When she could no longer see the detective's shadow inside the door, she started her car and left the courthouse, heading across the village to Ray Gibbs's condo.

The more she saw of Gibbs, the more frightening he became. The longer Ryder was with him, the more her sister seemed to take on his crude style, and this distressed Lindsey. Ryder didn't need Gibbs's trashy influence on her behavior and her future.

Nearing the condo and slowing, she wasn't sure what she meant to do. Having convinced herself that the body in the ruins was Nina, she wanted to confront Gibbs, confront the two of them.

And . . . what?

Accuse them? See how they reacted?

Yes, she could do that. Put herself in danger, and force Gibbs to run. Destroy whatever procedure Detectives Garza and Davis meant to follow.

Yet the anger and hurt that seethed inside her, the sense of injustice, made her burn to take action, to do something positive.

Two blocks before she reached the condo she rummaged in her purse for her cell phone, for a bit of added security—and remembered that she didn't have it. Had left it on the dresser. Had thought she wouldn't need it at the locker, left it collecting her clients' messages to play back later.

She thought of going back to get it, but that would take time. For no reason, a sense of urgency filled her. Instead of going back, she looked for a parking place where she wouldn't be seen from the upper windows.

She had no proof that the body was Nina's or that she'd died about the same time as Carson. Or that Ray Gibbs had killed either of them. She was following her own line of reasoning, which could be way off base. But she felt so sure that jealousy had been the motive. Ray jealous because he knew Nina was with Carson. Or Nina jealous because Carson was getting married. Maybe she'd followed him up there. And maybe Ray followed her, to kill them both.

All conjecture. But jealousy was among the most ancient reasons for murder, along with hatred and greed. Basic emotions dating back to the time of the caveman—and that thought brought a bitter smile, because the more she saw of Ray Gibbs the more she saw in him exactly that caveman mentality, an uncaring creature who hadn't quite made the grade to full humanity.

• • •

WHEN CLYDE PULLED into their drive behind Ryan's truck, Joe slid out of the roadster on the far side where Mike wouldn't see him and dove into the bushes, his mind filled with Lindsey's determined look as she'd gotten into Ryan's truck with Mike to return to the village—but determined to do what? Had she told Mike she was going straight home, to get to work? After all, it was tax season. From the look on her face, Joe thought she meant to do otherwise.

Mike had left his new Lexus van parked in front of the Damen house early this morning, and now he and Ryan stood beside it talking as Clyde made a show of calling Joe.

Waiting a few moments to make it look good, Joe sauntered out from the bushes as if he'd been there all the while, sleeping or hunting gophers. He glanced at Ryan, a sly and conspiratorial exchange. He rubbed against Clyde's ankles in loving greeting, a nice touch that didn't escape Mike. Then he trotted off across the little front lawn, skinned up the oak tree, and disappeared from their view in acceptable feline style. And he took off across the roofs, heading fast for Gibbs's condo. Clyde had no time to call him back, and couldn't have argued with him anyway in front of his father-in-law.

AT MOLENA POINT PD, Dulcie knew neither that Sage had run away and Charlie and Kit were following him, nor that at that moment Joe was bolting across the roofs above her, heading straight into trouble. She sat on the dispatcher's counter sharing Mabel's roast beef sandwich, waiting for an update on what had happened at the ruins, waiting impatiently for Joe.

Looking out the glass door, she saw Ryan and Mike drop Lindsey off, saw Rock in the king cab happily hanging his head out the window. She'd heard enough from Mabel's conversation with Dallas to know that Rock had found the grave, and that both detectives and the coroner had been called. She was excited for and proud of Rock. And she was proud, indeed, of Joe, that he had pulled this off. She was licking roast beef from her whiskers when Ryan's pickup moved away and Dallas's Blazer pulled into the red zone.

Hurrying in, Dallas stopped at the desk to speak to Mabel. A moment later, down the hall, Detective Davis came in from the back parking lot, heading for the front desk.

"You want to bring Gibbs in?" Dallas asked her. "As a person of interest?" That brought Dulcie to full attention. Ray Gibbs? Why would . . . ?

"If he's innocent," Davis was saying, "he should be eager to find out if that's Nina, to help us ID her—relieved to know what happened to her."

Oh my, Dulcie thought. *Was that Nina Gibbs, in that grave?*

"Maybe he can come up with the name of her dentist," Dallas said. "We'll bring him in."

"And set up a watch on their condo?" Davis said. Dallas nodded. They glanced up as Mike Flannery pulled up out front in his new van, which he'd left at Clyde's early this morning. He came in frowning, stood absently petting Dulcie.

"What?" Dallas said, watching him.

Mike frowned. "Lindsey worries me. When I let her out to get her car, when she thought we were gone, she took off like a scalded cat." He glanced at Dulcie and grinned as if he'd made a politically incorrect blunder. Dulcie had to wash her paws to hide her amusement.

"It's tax season," Dallas said, and headed down the hall. "She'll be covered up with work." He turned into the conference/coffee room, where Dulcie could hear him giving orders to one of the officers to get into civilian clothes, take a civilian car, and start a watch on Gibbs's condo. The tabby sat staring out through the glass door, watching impatiently for Joe, to tell her exactly what had happened. With everyone back from the ruins, from exhuming the body and photographing and taking evidence, Clyde and Joe should be home, and the first place Joe would head would be the station, not to miss any follow-up on the unidentified body. Eagerly Dulcie waited—she waited a long time, but Joe Grey did not appear.

JOE, HAVING DESCENDED from the roofs to Fourth Street, was crossing a busy side street, padding impatiently along in the wake of a pair of dawdling tourists to avoid being squashed by oncoming cars, when he saw Lindsey's car a block ahead, moving slowly toward the condo. Reaching the curb, he ran, brushing against a woman's bare ankles, startling a scream from her, ran dodging other legs, keeping the tan Mercedes in sight. When Lindsey pulled over, parking beneath a small oak that would shelter her car from the view above, Joe dived into the shadows of a shop door. Watching her swing out fast and hurry into an antiques shop, the tomcat smiled—she was in such a rush that she'd left the driver's door ajar. Or maybe had left it so on purpose, for a quick reentry?

She stood within the shadows of the shop looking out, watching the condo. Why would she think she'd have to move fast? She must really believe that was Nina in that grave, and that Gibbs or Ryder had killed her. That was a lot of conjecture. And even so, why was she in such a hurry?

Had she seen the spying figure, seen it slip quickly away? Had she *seen* Ryder or Gibbs watching them? Or was she only guessing?

Crouching behind a redwood planter near where she'd parked, Joe settled in to wait. He'd barely fixed on the condo again when Ray and Ryder came hurrying down the outside stairs, Ray carrying a duffel bag, Ryder dressed in jeans and a sweatshirt, Levi's jacket, and old jogging shoes—he'd never seen her when she wasn't dressed to the teeth. Racing down into the condo's garage, they disappeared. At the same moment Lindsey left the shop, moving fast, heading for her car.

Joe moved faster. Under the cover of the planter and a pair of tourists, he reached the car before her, slipped in through the cracked-open door, was inside and over the backseat, crouching on the floor, when Lindsey swung in.

Quietly she closed the door and started the engine. Behind her, Joe took a chance and reared up—just as a dark blue Honda Accord came nosing up out of the parking garage. He dropped down again, fast. Was that the car he'd seen at the ruins? Sure looked like it, small navy blue coupe. Ray was at the wheel and Ryder beside him.

Lindsey waited for three cars to pass, putting them between herself and the Honda. Then she took off slowly, following Gibbs and Ryder through the tangle of cars that crept along the narrow streets.

From the floor of the backseat, Joe had no view of the street, only of the shingled, angled rooftops. She turned left, which would send her back toward Ocean. There she turned east, in the direction of Highway 1.

When she stopped for the light at the top of the hill, Joe, staring up through the window, could see the signal change to the green arrow. She turned left, up 1, heading north. Watching the tops of the cypress and pine trees swing by, he had no idea where this ride would take him. He was alone, at the mercy of Lindsey's judgment. And she was alone, possibly following a killer.

She did *have a phone?* he thought. She must have, she ran her own business, surely she carried a phone. Had she already called the station to tell them what she was doing? Would there soon be officers behind them, to take over this unprofessional surveillance before it turned into a chase?

Or would she think Dallas wouldn't pay any attention to her if she called? Would tell her not to mess in police business, to lay off and go home?

She had her windows cracked, and the smell of pine trees filled the car, soon accompanied by the salty iodine smell of the bay where Highway 1 would be near the shore. Now, on the left, he could see only sky through the windows above him, and once in a while a gull sailing over. He knew they were moving north.

Was Gibbs only heading up the coast to one of the small beach towns? Or *was* he running, making for a connecting freeway, for some distant destination where, if they stopped, a cat might find himself forced out of Lindsey's car for any number of reasons? Where a cat had no backup, where a cat could find himself abandoned in a strange town, alone and on his own?

29

RIDING CROUCHED on the floor of the back-seat, Joe couldn't see anything but sky, and, despite the fact that this was a nearly new, upscale car, the noise and vibration on the floor were singularly unpleasant, and he was breathing gas vapors that humans apparently didn't notice. But more frustrating, he couldn't see the road signs. Couldn't see where they were headed, he only knew they were still going north.

Also, unable to see the traffic and see what the driver was doing, he worried about Lindsey's driving skills or the lack thereof. With the way she was changing lanes, he felt sure she was still on Ray's tail, trying to stay out of sight but not lose them.

What was she thinking as she followed them? Wondering if she'd alerted them so they'd drive farther and longer, trying to ditch her? He wasn't proud of himself that, apparently, either Ray or Ryder had been lurking among the ruins all morning and he nearly hadn't seen them at all from his broad vantage point on the roof.

Well, but Rock had missed them, too, even with his tracker's nose. Weimaraners were adept at both sight and scent, bred to both kinds of hunting. But this morning, honed in on his all-consuming objective to track Clyde, the good dog had apparently not seen or smelled their stealthy presence.

Careening up the freeway on the floor of the car, unable to see much but sky, Joe thought that right then, he would sell his kitty soul for a phone to call the station, a chance to whisper into the speaker and hear a cop's friendly voice.

Getting soft, Joe thought crossly. *Relying too much on human technology.* On the electronic conveniences that had become so much a part of his life. But he liked the luxuries of the human world, no denying it. Liked using the phone both to call in tips to the department and to spy on and harass the perps—to say nothing of calling his favorite deli.

Clyde had once suggested a collar with a tiny, voice-controlled cell phone attached. But despite any excuse they could think of for a cat wearing a phone, such an encumbrance would generate too many prying questions. Besides, he hated the thought of a collar, which seemed to Joe nearly as bad as a straitjacket.

THE WOODS WERE growing dark, but the sky was still silver beyond the dark branches that laced above Charlie and Kit; hurrying ever deeper through the black woods, they had tracked Sage for over a mile. Charlie couldn't believe he'd come this far, hindered by the cast and bandages, yet stayed ahead of them. But Kit still followed his fresh scent, and Charlie, following Kit, stared into every shadow, watching for the young tom's pale coat and the white gleam of bandages.

She had, shortly after starting out, made Kit wait for her, safe in the branches of a pine, while she hurried back for a flashlight and a bottle of water and, feeling silly but thinking better safe than sorry, had strapped on her holstered .38. The woods would soon be pitch-dark, and there were coyotes and sometimes a bobcat that would be a danger to Sage and Kit. Even an occasional cougar visited these wild hills, and cougars living so close to humans had grown bolder than Charlie liked; several dogs had been killed, as well as a neighbor's nice yearling colt; that had truly sickened her.

Kit stopped suddenly, staring back at her. "Did you hear that?" she whispered. "A twig breaking, something moving . . ." Then Kit leaped ahead so fast that Charlie had to run to keep up and made too much noise, stepping on twigs. Unlike Kit, she couldn't run in silence; blackberry vines clawed at her, tripping and slowing her. The next time Kit spun around, Charlie stopped dead still. This time they'd both heard it. A scream. Loud and blood chilling. A cat's scream of rage and challenge—answered by the high, yip-yipping of coyotes.

Hastily Charlie scooped up Kit to keep her safe, tucking her flashlight under her arm and releasing her holstered .38. Another series of yips and another scream of rage, and the dry scrambling of claws on a tree trunk. Kit clung to Charlie's shoulder with claws deep in her jacket.

The enraged scream could only be Sage, and as she swung the light around, snarls greeted them. Two big coyotes were leaping up the trunk of an oak tree. Above them Sage clung barely out of reach, barely keeping his balance on the thin branch, his bandaged leg hanging down as the beasts scrabbled and leaped at him.

Kit tensed on her shoulder, ready to leap at them but Charlie dropped the light and grabbed her. Kit fought to get free. Charlie held her tight, the beam from her fallen flashlight canting off uselessly into the treetops, barely showing the beasts—until suddenly the larger coyote spun around and faced her, his eyes caught in the light. He was nearly on her, Kit clawing into her shoulder to leap at him, he was inches from her, he seemed right in her face when she fired.

He dropped, twisting, then came at her again. She ran backward away from him, fired again, two shots. He dropped and lay still. His companion, who had paused among the trees, suddenly charged her. This was behavior she would not have expected from coyotes. She fired twice more and he dropped. Only one shot left. Feeling in her pocket for her reloader, she stood staring down, sickened, at the two dead coyotes lying at her feet, hoping there were no more. On her shoulder, Kit was shivering.

"Could you ease up a little, Kit? Before you claw me to death?"

Kit eased back her claws and lay more gently across Charlie's shoulder. Above them, Sage still clung to the branch, his eyes huge, his injured leg dangling. Charlie holstered her gun and reached up to him. She got one hand on the pale little cat but was afraid to drag him off, afraid to injure him even more.

IT GREW HOTTER on the floor of the car. Traffic was heavy and fast. Lindsey did a couple of uncomfortable swerves that made Joe wonder if he'd get out of this in one piece, with his sleek silver hide intact. He had no idea whether she'd lost the navy blue Honda or was still on its tail, but from the way she was changing lanes, ducking in and out of traffic, he was convinced she still had them. Twice he heard her rummaging in her purse. Looking for her phone? Trying to find it down among the incredible debris women carried in their purses? Or . . . ? Oh, hell! She hadn't left it at home?

She didn't have her phone? She hadn't called the station? No help was on the way? He remembered Mike laughing once, because she so often left her phone at home.

"What good is a phone, Lindsey, if you don't carry it?" They'd been cozied up after dinner, on the couch, Joe and Rock stretched out on the rug before the fire.

"I carry a phone when something's urgent," Lindsey had said, "which isn't often. You think that's weird?"

"I guess not. Maybe that's sensible," Mike said, frowning and drawing her close. Sometimes this budding romance made Joe feel warm and safe, at other times he'd wondered where it was headed, and had wished both he and Mike knew Lindsey better. Had she scammed Mike once, then left him? And now was deceiving him again?

They were approaching Watsonville, he could tell by the smell of green vegetable crops and strawberries. If he could see out the window, there would be miles and miles of strawberries. She changed lanes again suddenly and sped off the freeway, slowing as she curved up the ramp. Above him through the window loomed a sign announcing FOOD/GAS/LODGING. She changed lanes fast again, and swung into a gas station; gas fumes were sucked into the car. She made several turns, as if pulling around back. Moving out of sight of Ray and Ryder? If, indeed, she was still with them.

When she left the car, when Joe heard her walking away, he peered up through the back window, ready to dive down again. She moved away fast, glanced once at the gas station's phone booth, which stood in plain sight, but didn't pause.

Across the side street was a Burger King, and there was the navy blue Honda, parked at the far side. Through the reflections of the restaurant window, he could just see Ray and Ryder standing at the counter.

Lindsey, keeping several parked cars between herself and the Burger King, hurried inside the gas station's little convenience store.

Now it was hard to keep her in sight through the sign-cluttered glass. Slipping up onto the back of the front seat where he could see better, Joe lay along it watching her speaking with the clerk behind the counter, an overweight grandmotherly type. The way the signs were placed, the clerk was more visible. Grandmother or not, she looked surly and rude. Soon they were arguing. Joe guessed that was a pretty stressful job, behind a gas station cash register, never knowing when some innocent-looking customer would pull a knife or a gun and you'd be cleaning out the till, praying he wouldn't kill you after you'd handed over the cash.

The clerk shook her head again, scowling at Lindsey. Lindsey seemed to be pleading with her while at the same time turning to look out the front window, across to the Burger King. Joe could still see Ray inside, watched him step down a short hall, maybe toward the restrooms. Or maybe there was a phone back there? Who would he be calling? Had they made Lindsey? Had he some plan to get her off his tail?

When Joe peered into the convenience store again, Lindsey was doling out money to the clerk. The next minute she was dialing the phone on the counter, making Joe wish he could read lips. Her eyes hardly left the Burger King. Was she calling the station? Had she dialed Mike? His ears pricked up when she got someone on the line. She was talking fast, using her free hand to gesture across the street as if the listener could see her. She hung up quickly as Ryder and Ray came out of the Burger King carrying two white paper bags.

Slipping out the door, she double-timed it behind the gas pumps and slid into her car. Joe was on the floor again, crouched behind the seat, tucking his white paws under, keeping his white nose down. As Lindsey slammed the door and started the engine, he would have given one of his nine lives to know if she'd reached the department. To know if they could expect some backup before things got dicey.

30

THEY WERE ON the highway again, still moving north. Joe was getting used to the vibration on the floor of the Mercedes, which seemed to have turned into a rumbling purr and was making him sleepy. Was he actually going to drift off while roaring down the highway not knowing where he was headed or what would happen to him?

He had no idea who Lindsey had reached on the phone, but certainly she must have called the department. Had she talked with Harper? Dallas? Had they put out an alert on the navy blue Honda? Or did they not have enough on Gibbs to do that? So far, Ray Gibbs was really only a "person of interest."

They were still on Highway 1, he could smell the sea. He kept wondering why, if Ray and Ryder were trying to avoid arrest, they'd chosen this slower route. Why hadn't they taken the busier, multilane 101? After they seemed to be in a hell of a hurry to get out of the village, here they were tooling along by the narrow, scenic route like a couple of tourists.

Did they think they'd be expected to go the other way? Think that with more cops on the 101, maybe watching for them, they'd be spotted more quickly?

Or were they not running? Had that not been Ray's Honda leaving the ruins? Was this some big fat coincidence, could both he and Lindsey be wrong despite the couple's hurried departure? Were those two simply driving up the coast for the weekend, with no notion that Ray's dead wife might have been found? Were they maybe headed innocently to visit friends in Santa Cruz or Half-Moon Bay?

If this *was* a wild goose chase, and if Clyde learned about it, he'd never hear the last, Clyde would rag him for the rest of his nine lives.

Which, given his present situation and Lindsey's erratic driving, might not be too long.

But what if that dark figure slipping through the ruins had not been Ray or Ryder searching for the possibly valuable old book?

He wondered what Nina might have told Ryder about her aunt Olivia at the time the two were friendly, before they both set their caps for Carson. Would Nina have bragged about some rare old book in the family, a book that had vanished when Olivia died?

He wondered if Olivia, finding herself very ill, had hidden the book, not wanting Nina to have it and sell it. Not wanting to destroy it, but vowing to keep the cats' secret, she'd have no other choice but to hide it.

Olivia dies, but Nina knows about the book and has a nice little drama to recount. She tells Ryder, and then after Nina disappears, Ryder thinks about the story, and starts going up to the old estate looking for Olivia's treasure. Starts looking again after she returns from L.A., maybe venturing down into that labyrinth of old, crumbling cellars and up into the unsafe rooms among the mansion's fallen walls?

But she didn't find it, did she! he thought, smiling.

DULCIE WAITED AROUND the station for nearly an hour, fidgeting and biting at nonexistent fleas, but Joe didn't come bolting in. She was burning to know what had gone down this morning. Dallas was back in his office, very likely filing his report. She wanted to go back there and read it. Or should she join Mike in the conference room where he, too, was recording the morning's events while stoking up on stale coffee?

She was about to head for the conference room when a sleazy little woman in pink tights came in the front door to complain about a traffic ticket. And then, at the desk, Mabel routed a call through to Dallas that, in seconds, brought the detective double-timing up the hall shouting at Mike. "It's Lindsey, she's following them!"

Both men raced out the front door, piled into the Blazer, and spun out of the parking lot, their red light whirling. At the radio, Mabel put out an APB on Lindsey Wolf's tan Mercedes and on Ray's Honda Accord. The little woman in her pink tights had backed up against the holding cell, out of the way. Dulcie felt cold clear to her paws—*now* she knew where Joe was.

Call it instinct, call it feline perception. She felt certain that, somehow, Joe had hitched a ride with Lindsey.

Everyone else was back from the ruins but Joe. Dulcie didn't know the details, but instinct told he'd slipped into Lindsey's car. Or, worse, had managed to crawl into Gibbs's car. Either way, Dulcie's paws were icy with dread.

She sat thinking for only a moment, weighing her options. And as a trio of uniforms hurried in, she slid out the front door, past their ankles, skinned up the oak tree, and took off across the roofs, speeding for Joe's house and Clyde.

DESPITE HIS NERVOUS state and the fast and careening ride, Joe dozed; he woke to the rumble of heavier traffic, as if they were now on a busy freeway. And soon, peering up through the windows at a sky turned hazy with smog, he glimpsed a dark airport sign flash by overhead: SAN JOSE INTERNATIONAL. Lindsey had turned inland, he could hear the big planes taking off, one coming right over them, nearly deafening him. Was she still with the Honda? She had the air-conditioning on, and he could see by the flat, smoggy sky that it was hot here, a haze-filled scorcher.

If Ryder and Ray were headed to the airport to catch a plane, would Lindsey try to get a ticket, maybe on standby, and follow them? Right. And leave her locked car in short-term parking among acres of empty cars, leave him shut in a sweltering vehicle. He stared up at the door lock, wondering if he could open it. Every make and model was different, and this one didn't look easy.

If he couldn't slip out before she slammed the door, he'd be imprisoned alone with no phone and no one to hear his yowls for help. Trapped in the hot car as the heat built and kept building . . . How long could he live in heat that would peak at far over a hundred? How long before he keeled over from dehydration, turned up his claws, and breathed his last?

Shaken by the thought of increasing thirst and a slow and agonizing bodily shutdown, he prayed fervently to the great cat god that he could open that lock—yet even hidden by the back of the seat he was reluctant to reach up an exploring paw and try it, afraid he'd make some little noise or that she'd glimpse his paw in the space between the seat and the door. Tempted as he was, he remained crouched in a frightened funk as more airport signs flipped by overhead on their tall poles. She slowed at the sign for short-term parking.

They sat idling, as if there were cars lined up ahead. Was the Honda up there in front of them? He heard the gate arm rise five times, as the drivers ahead stepped on the gas and pulled through.

Was Ray leading her into a trap? Wanted her to park inside that cavernous, covered, fenced lot, where he could get at her?

As wild as that seemed, if Ray or Ryder *had* killed Carson, and maybe Nina, what difference was one more murder? Had Lindsey thought of that? Did she realize how foolish she might be to follow them?

He kept puzzling over why, after their argument in

the condo, the couple was fleeing together. It had sounded as if each was conning the other, as if either one could be the killer. Now, the only conclusion was that whoever was the killer had at last confided in the other, that they had fled together, partners to the end.

Unless he was reading this all wrong. Unless, despite Ray's hatred of cops, both were in fact innocent.

Could Lindsey be following them knowing full well they were innocent? Following them because *she* needed a scapegoat and was somehow setting them up?

He heard the parking machine whir as Lindsey punched the button for her ticket, heard the gate rise again. She'd turned the air-conditioning down, and already it was getting hot on the floor. He wondered if, at the last minute, he *could* leap out before she slammed the door. Or if he'd lose his nerve, break his solemn commitment to silence, even forget that all he need do was meow, and find himself shouting in fear for her to let him out, to save him? If, in panic, he'd spill his and Dulcie's and Kit's secret to save his own scrawny neck?

They moved through the gate at a crawl. As they crept beneath the concrete roof, the interior of the car darkened to a murky half-light. She stopped several times, apparently as cars paused ahead of her, then she swerved abruptly into a parking space, pulling in beside a tall SUV that blocked his view on the right. He poised to leap as she got out. But she was too quick, she flipped the master lock, slammed the door nearly in his face, and slipped along beside the car, looking across the lot. Watching Ray and Ryder?

Locked in the car, should he make his presence known?

Mewl and yowl like an ordinary cat and paw at the window? One more second and she'd be gone, it would be too late.

Cautiously rearing up, he saw Ray and Ryder crossing the street, heading for the terminal. When Lindsey moved as if to follow them, Joe remained silent, his paws sweating—then it *was* too late, she was gone between the parked cars.

He tried the back door handle and the lock. He couldn't budge either, nor the lock on the other back door. Had she activated some kind of safety lock, some child-proof mechanism? When he rose to look out, she was nearly to the terminal. He paused before jumping into the front seat.

Alone, he began to feel very small. The parking cavern spread over him vast and grim into its own horizons, as if there was nothing else in all the world. Could she mean to follow them onto a plane, find out where they were going, and then scramble to buy a ticket? The car was growing uncomfortably warm.

Maybe she meant only to see what flight they boarded, then use a phone in the airport to call the station?

If one of them *was* the killer, wouldn't they try for an international flight, skip the country, go where they'd be hard to locate? Not likely that Lindsey would have a passport with her. Would Ray and Ryder board using assumed names, carrying false IDs? Who knew what other crimes those two might have committed that would require a fake ID as a tool of the trade. Leaping to the front seat to try those locks, he heard footsteps.

She was coming back. He ducked down fast, didn't

dare jump over into the backseat again, she was too close and he was in plain sight. He crouched on the seat waiting for her to open the door, determined to fly through.

Nothing happened. Her footsteps stopped.

When he rose to sneak a fast look, she was standing in front of the car shielded by a pillar, looking across the vast sea of cars toward the terminal. He could see Ray and Ryder in front of an entry, they seemed to be arguing. Lindsey watched for a moment, but when they turned away, moving inside through the swinging door, she took off running.

31

 Pawing at the driver's-door handle of the Mercedes, Joe was surprised that it pulled down easily. No safety lock here. But he'd set off the alarm! Its whoop deafened him.

Shouldering the door open fast, he was out of there. He remembered only then that if a car was locked from outside, then opened from the inside, this would inevitably happen. Leaping to the top of the car trying to ignore its shrill scream, and watching for security, he stared frantically across the rows of parked vehicles for Lindsey.

He saw where Ray had parked the Honda. Looked like he'd been in such a hurry he'd left the windows down. Even rearing up, Joe couldn't see much on the street beyond. Leaping to the top of a tall RV, wondering how long that siren would keep pulsating, he looked over the tops of the other parked cars, past the gray concrete expanse to the terminal.

There she was, running through the crowd of hurrying passengers. She seemed to be headed for a cop car parked a block away in front of the Delta entrance. As she dodged behind a bus, he saw Ray Gibbs.

Gibbs had spotted her. He spun around, ran straight for her. She didn't see him. The alarm of the Mercedes was still blaring. Another second and Ray would grab her. Joe, speeding over the roofs of parked cars, heading for the unlocked Honda, prayed for luck, prayed they'd been in such a hurry they'd left belongings behind. Had maybe left . . . Leaping up clawing at the partly open glass, he hung there for an instant then bellied over into the seat praying to find . . .

A jacket lay crumpled on the seat, half a dozen empty paper cups and wadded paper bags were on the floor, and, beside the jacket, Ryder's open purse. Then they *were* coming back, he thought frantically.

Rooting in the purse, he found what he wanted. Stuffed down among lipstick, nail polish, wadded tissues, and a packet of broken crackers nestled Ryder's cell phone, either abandoned or forgotten. Pawing open the phone, he was studying it, hoping he could figure this one out, when he heard a scream.

He never knew later how he got up onto the Honda's roof so fast, clawing himself up over the edge and then rearing high . . . Surprised himself that he had the cell phone clutched in his teeth, probably soaking it with cat spit. They were closer, just outside the parking area. Ray had Lindsey, pulling her arm behind her. She elbowed him and kicked at him. People were staring, but no one ran to help. Pedestrians moved back, scattered. Had the cop seen? Joe stared at the unit a block away. It looked empty.

"What the hell do you want?" Ray was shouting. "Why did you follow us?" Joe forgot about the phone as Lindsey fought, hitting useless blows, twisting around trying to strike at his face; Ray ducked, grabbing both her arms. Lindsey kneed him hard. As he doubled over, Joe turned frantically to the phone. Where was the security vehicle that should have come to the Mercedes's siren blast? *Dial 911*, Joe thought frantically, *dial it now—there it is, the Send button.*

But then he stopped.

Ryder's cell phone would be on the Molena Point prefix. If he dialed 911, he'd get Molena Point PD. What he wanted, fast, was San Jose PD or the local sheriff or a nearby CHP unit—and he didn't know the prefix for those. Ray shouted again and hit Lindsey hard, sending her reeling. At the same moment, the Mercedes's alarm went quiet. Lindsey spun around and came at Ray, enraged. "*You* killed him!" she screamed. "*You* shot Carson!"

Dropping down again through the Honda's window, Joe laid on the horn, blasting away in a wild and uneven rhythm that should get someone's attention.

When he stopped for a minute, he heard Lindsey shout, "Who was with him when you killed him? Who was she?" This was not the soft-spoken Lindsey Wolf Joe knew, this woman was wired. "Was that Nina with him? You killed Nina, too!" she shouted, and hit him hard in the face.

Joe gave the horn another long, ear-splitting blast then three short ones. Three more, in the signal for *Need help*. Then he grabbed the cell phone in his mouth, crawled out the open window, dropped to the concrete, and slid under the car. And he took off running beneath the parked cars, listening for footsteps or for some engine starting up, for a car ready to back out. He tried his best not to drool on the phone. Who knew what cat spit would do to that delicate tangle of microchips and electronic mysteries? He was looking for a place to hide, to try to get through to the local cops, when Lindsey screamed in pain. Her voice was closer, and he could hear scraping footsteps as if Ray was dragging her.

Joe leaped to the hood of a pickup in time to see Ray hit her again, so hard she reeled against a car and fell. It was then he saw Ryder, slipping up behind Ray. Joe stiffened as she jammed a pistol in his ribs. He could just see the small automatic in the palm of her hand. "Back off, Ray! Leave her! We're getting out of here!"

Ray spun around and in one swift move slammed Ryder's arm away and grabbed the gun. A shot rang out, echoing beneath the concrete roof. A second shot came as Joe dove for cover behind some crates in the bed of the pickup, wondering if wooden crates would stop a stray bullet.

There was a long silence. He slipped up to look.

He couldn't see anyone. Not Ray, not Lindsey, not Ryder. Leaping to the top of the pickup, he saw a car pulling out of a parking place and another, a black Audi, pulling in hurriedly, as if the driver might be late for a flight.

Apparently the new arrival hadn't heard the shots or had thought they were backfires. As the portly, dark-suited man stepped out of the Audi, Ray appeared behind him, spun him around with a hard punch to the side of the neck. The guy went down in a heap. Ray snatched his keys, fished in the guy's pockets as if looking for a parking ticket, then jumped in the car and burned rubber as he backed out and took off. Over the stink of exhaust, Joe caught a whiff of blood.

Rearing up, he saw Lindsey rise slowly, clutching her side, pulling Ryder up with her. Ryder leaned against her as they stumbled toward Lindsey's Mercedes. Joe lost sight of them as he frantically punched in 911, for Molena Point PD. He thought he should have done that in the first place—but on the first ring, the black Audi came wheeling back, screeching into the same parking spot.

Ray leaped out, gun in hand.

At the same moment, a figure jumped out of the Mercedes and took off running, doubled over. Joe couldn't see if it was Lindsey or Ryder. Brown hair, a glimpse of jeans—both had brown hair, both were wearing jeans. The phone made three rings, then Officer Hendricks picked up.

"Get Garza on your radio," Joe told Hendricks, wanting to shout but keeping his voice low. "Ray Gibbs. At San Jose airport. He just shot either Ryder Wolf or her sister. Short-term parking."

Looking up, he saw Ray standing at the open door of Lindsey's car, looking in. Saw Gibbs fire another shot into the front seat, and then take off running after the escaping figure. As he disappeared among the cars, a police car pulled in, moving slowly, the lone officer scanning the area as he cruised behind the parked cars in the direction of the shots.

Joe could hear Hendricks talking, presumably on the radio, as he'd instructed. The cop car had turned into the lane that would put him behind Lindsey's Mercedes, which stood with its door open. The smell of blood was strong. Stepping out, gun drawn, the officer approached the driver's side, where he could see in. "Hands on top of your head. Get out slowly."

Inside, no one moved.

"Get out *now*!"

A dozen cars away the black Audi slid quietly out of its parking place and headed at a sedate pace for the exit. With the light glancing against its closed windows, Joe couldn't see if Ray was alone or if he had Lindsey or Ryder.

"He's in a stolen black Audi," Joe said softly. "He's leaving, he—"

He could see the cop on his radio calling for assistance—he looked up in Joe's direction, as if he'd heard the tomcat's whisper. Silently Joe laid down the phone in the bed of the pickup, pawed it behind the crates, leaped over the side of the truck bed, and hit the ground running.

32

 DALLAS'S BLAZER had just passed the Soquel exit on Highway 1. From this juncture they had three choices: Stay on 1 up the coast, take 9 toward Saratoga, or take 17 toward 280 and San Jose. They hadn't seen a sign of the navy blue Honda, nor had they had any response to their "Be on the lookout." Moving into the right lane, Dallas pulled off the highway and into a gas station. He was reaching for the radio when Harper came on.

"Where are you?"

"Just pulled over at Soquel. Not a sign of him, don't know which—"

"Cut over to San Jose. His car's at the airport, short-term parking. Wait a minute," Max said. "He just pulled out in a black Audi, no plate number."

Dallas swerved out of the gas station and hit the road again. "Who do you have up there? Why didn't they get the plate? Are they on his tail?"

"No one," Max said stiffly. "No law enforcement."

"What do you mean, *no one*? Who called in?" Dallas stared at the microphone in his hand, then back at the road.

"Mike's with you?" Max said.

"Affirmative," Dallas said, scowling.

"Lindsey's car is there. San Jose is at the scene. There's a woman in the front seat, wounded."

Mike grabbed the radio from Dallas. Max was saying, "A second woman ran, no sign of her."

"Is it Lindsey?" Mike shouted. "How bad is she? What happened?"

"No ID yet. We don't know who, or how bad. Medics are on the way."

"Step on it," Mike yelled at Dallas.

Dallas had already switched on the red light, heading fast for the 17 turnoff that would take them inland to San Jose; as he peeled up the ramp onto the freeway, Mike shouted, "Are they sure it's Lindsey's car? Can't the informant ID her?"

"Informant didn't stay on the line," Max said. "We're talking to uniforms at the scene. Car's registered to Lindsey Wolf but no ID on the woman, no purse."

"Description?"

"Brown hair. Hazel eyes. About five seven. Wearing jeans. A Levi's jacket on the seat under her. Informant said there were two women, thought both might have been shot."

Dallas hit the siren and gave it the gas. "Watch for the Audi coming this way."

Mike leaned forward nervously, watching traffic. "There must be a million black Audis." But he did the best he could, as fast as they were moving. "Why would he come back this way? Why not head north, on the 101? If he hurt Lindsey . . .," he said with cold threat.

"Settle down, you don't know that's Lindsey. You can't do her any good if you're all worked up. Settle down and watch for the Audi."

IN THE FALSE twilight of the parking complex, police and sheriff's cars were crowded around an EMT van, blocking Lindsey's tan Mercedes and four parking lanes. San Jose officers stood redirecting traffic as a pair of medics slid a stretcher bearing a blanket-covered figure into the emergency vehicle, and climbed in behind it. Beyond the tangle of law enforcement, down on the concrete at the level of tires and hubcaps, Joe Grey crouched beneath an old brown Jeep. He hadn't been able to glimpse the figure in the Mercedes. Couldn't see whether it was Ryder or Lindsey. And now all he could see were cops' legs, the place was wall-to-wall cops.

But there had been only one person in the Mercedes, he knew that much. As the medics had put her on the stretcher, he'd gotten a glimpse of slim, Levi's-clad legs, dull-colored jogging shoes such as Lindsey had worn—but so had Ryder. He'd been mildly surprised that she wasn't dressed fancy when he first saw her leaving the condo. And now, with uniforms all around him, he could hardly leap atop a car and peer into the medics' van trying to see more.

Sure as hell, an unattended animal in this setting would

encourage some overzealous rookie to call the pound. And later, what joking comment would these guys, talking with MPPD, make about a weird gray tomcat sitting atop a car, watching the crime scene. And wouldn't that tear it, after his anonymous phone call.

Plus, Joe thought, *I talked with Hendricks on the phone, and Hendricks knows the snitch's voice.* Hearing jokes about a nosy gray tomcat, would Hendricks get curious enough to put two and two together? Put the gray tomcat and the voice together, thinking outside the box? No matter how far out that scenario seemed, it might get others in the department thinking, and watching him too closely, even if, at first, only in a joking way.

The EMT van started its engine, ready to head for the hospital, and Joe still didn't know who was in there. He was moving forward beneath the parked cars, hoping to hear someone mention a name, when the van driver killed his engine. Something was happening.

Joe could see the van rocking, as if, inside, the medics were moving fast. He crept closer, his paws sweating.

He felt certain that after his call, Mike and probably Dallas were on their way. He felt sick for Mike, racing to get here, imagining the worst—as Joe, right now, was trying not to do.

He knew how he'd feel if he thought Dulcie had been shot, he'd race to the scene wanting to eviscerate whoever had attacked his lady. Right now, Mike would be feeling the same.

Whatever was going on in the medics' van seemed to take forever; the van continued to rock, while outside, officers continued to protect the area, turning cars and pedestrians away from the scene. Creeping ever closer, he was only a few feet from the van when the back doors opened and a young, sandy-haired medic stepped down, stood talking with the San Jose sergeant who seemed to be in charge; the sergeant was a tall stringbeany, bald-headed guy. His few brief words chilled Joe.

"Go on out and help work traffic," the medic said. "I'll call for the medical examiner."

Whoever was in the van was with them no longer. Either Lindsey or Ryder had died as the medics fought to save her. Joe had to have a closer look, he had to know.

He was now only two cars away. Crouching against a front tire, he could see inside the van, see the body on the stretcher, covered by a length of sheet, the face also covered. His heart felt as heavy as lead. Despite the danger of being seen, he slipped out from under the car on its far side, leaped to its hood, and crouched in the shadows of a pillar from where he could see in through the van's open door.

A hank of wavy brown hair hung from beneath the sheet, over the side of the stretcher. He was trying to remember the exact shade of each woman's hair, trying to determine which sister lay there, when the whoop of a siren and the screech of tires sent him dropping under the car again, out of sight.

From beneath the greasy underpinnings of the older car, he looked out across the concrete that was reddened now by reflections of a whirling light. He had crept out far enough to see that the light was spinning atop Dallas's tan Blazer when the vehicle screeched to a halt and Mike bailed out, running for the ambulance.

33

 IN THE NIGHT-DARK woods, Charlie headed back toward home carrying Sage in her arms, Kit riding on her shoulder. Her flashlight was nearly dead, just the weakest wash of fading beam as she tried to pick out hindering branches blocking her path. She felt sick that she'd had to shoot the two coyotes. Coyotes were in no way evil, they were only hunting as they'd been born to do, they were only what God had made them. Not evil in the way a human could be evil.

But she'd had no choice. She was just thankful that Sage and Kit were safe.

"More to the right!" Kit said. "You're drifting off again, Charlie." Nothing was the same at night. All that was familiar by day was, in the blackness, a jagged world of hungry branches grabbing and poking at her.

"The barn's just there," Kit hissed. "Five more minutes, straight ahead. Can't you feel it? Can't you sense it there?"

Charlie couldn't. "But of course you can't," Kit said,

placing a soft paw against Charlie's cheek, making her feel grossly inadequate. But then in Charlie's arms Sage looked up at her, and though she couldn't see his face clearly, the trusting feel of him, so relaxed against her, the trust of this wild and shy little feral touched her and made her feel needed.

She was stepping carefully through a tangle of vines when her cell phone played its short tune. Hastily she answered, not liking that electronic sound here in the silent woods; her crackling, clumsy progress through dry leaves and twigs and fallen branches was quite enough intrusion in this wild place—and quite enough to stir other predators.

"Where are you?" Max said. "The house is dark, the door unlocked. Are you all right? I'm at the barn. You haven't fed. The horses and dogs are still out. What is it, what's wrong?"

"I'm in the woods. I'm fine, I'm almost home. Sage ran off, but I found him. He seemed disoriented this afternoon, maybe his medication. When he ran out, Kit followed him, the way cats will." She had no idea whether an ordinary cat would do that, but what could she say? "I ran after her. It wasn't quite dark. I have a flashlight. I found them both, but there were . . . I could hear coyotes . . ."

Was he buying her rambling explanation? He said, "I'll saddle Bucky. I'll whistle to find you. Keep your light on."

"I . . . The battery's about dead."

Max said nothing. He hated it when she forgot to keep the batteries fresh. Cops, she thought. So damned careful about their equipment. But she was glad he was—and she wished she had been.

In a very short time she heard his whistle and the far sound of a horse approaching, stepping on twigs, the rustling sound as Bucky pushed through the dense foliage. He was there so quickly that she knew Max had hardly brushed Bucky's back, had just thrown the saddle on, jerked up the cinch, and headed out.

She'd have to tell him that she'd killed the coyotes. She wasn't looking forward to that. He must have still been on the highway when she fired, or he would have heard the shots. They'd have to send wildlife management to collect the bodies and test for rabies, and Max would question her to see if she or the cats had been bitten. She answered his whistle, and in a moment Bucky came looming out of the night between two stands of pine, nearly in her face, his pale shoulders catching her fading light, his nose pushing at her. She'd never been so glad to see anyone, she wanted to hug both Bucky and Max at once.

Leaning down from the saddle, Max took Sage gently from her.

"Watch his leg," she said. "He may have torn the splint loose."

Max got Sage settled in his arms, and took his foot out of the stirrup so she could swing up behind him. Kit clung to her shoulder, trying not to draw blood. The tortoiseshell was so careful that Charlie hardly felt a claw.

Quietly she settled behind Max on the saddle skirt, leaning against his warmth.

"Why did the cat run?" Max said, looking down at Sage. "Well, you couldn't leave him out here all trussed up. Damn cat. How did you find them in these tangles?"

"I could hear coyotes, that's what drew me. The cats

were on a branch and two coyotes were leaping up at them."

"Lucky the coyotes didn't climb. They will, you know. Then what happened? "

She laid her head against his back. "I killed them."

And Max said nothing more as good Bucky made his way home through the night-black woods.

AS MIKE AND Dallas careened into the San Jose airport, their siren screaming and red light spinning, Dallas glanced at Mike with concern. His brother-in-law, not the type to come apart, was pale and sweating.

During his professional life, Mike Flannery had handled easily the most out-of-control parolees and the most temperamental judges, soothing both with the greatest diplomacy, but now he was a basket case, the detective had never seen him this way, not since the death of his wife, Dallas's sister. Pulling into the airport, navigating between drivers too preoccupied with finding their terminal to pull out of the way, between pedestrians too busy hauling luggage and racing for connections, he said, "You're not helping Lindsey. Get it together, take it easy!"

"What the hell was Lindsey doing, chasing them!"

Dallas slowed for a woman pushing a baby stroller. "Say Gibbs did kill the woman at the ruins. How would Lindsey know that? And how did Gibbs know we found the body? For that matter, why put his car in short-term if he meant to catch a flight and skip?"

Stopping to snatch a ticket to open the gate, Dallas

maneuvered through the covered parking area toward the flashing lights, approaching the cordoned-off crime scene. "Why the hell haven't they cleared a larger area, cleared the whole parking garage?" But most of the area would already be contaminated by the movement of officers and their vehicles. Dallas moved on through, pulling up behind the medics' van. The Blazer hadn't come to a stop when Mike jumped out and ran.

Two officers behind the van grabbed him. He shoved them away, his rage surging, jerked open the van doors and leaped inside, his mind a cold blank, not wanting to think what he would find.

The body was covered with a sheet. The face covered, a hank of brown hair hanging down. A sheet pulled over her face as if . . . as if . . . Kneeling beside the stretcher, he reached over, ignoring the medic's hand on his shoulder. When the medic held him back, he straightened up and spun around swinging.

The medic grabbed his arm. Tall, skinny, no more than a kid, he didn't back off, but looked at him steadily. All he said was "Can you identify her?" Then Dallas was there beside him, too, gripping his shoulder. Mike shrugged him off, wanting to be alone with her, not wanting anyone near them. The two men backed off. He reached out to her, reached to lift the sheet, steeling himself. Needing to touch her, to hold her. Not wanting to see her like this. Wanting to turn away, not really knowing what he wanted.

He folded the sheet back. Didn't want to look, and was drawn to look, to touch her face . . .

He went limp. Felt Dallas supporting him.

Ryder. It was *Ryder.* Ryder Wolf lay there, not Lindsey. Ryder, blood congealing on her face, blood gluing her shirt to her chest. He stared at her, shocked with relief.

She'd apparently taken a glancing shot to her cheek and jaw, the flesh and bone were torn, clotted with drying blood. There was a second, close shot to her chest. Her blouse was torn open where the medics had staunched the wound with gauze. He looked at her for a long time. Thanking God that this was Ryder. Wondering if he'd burn in hell for his joy and gratitude at someone's death. But Lindsey was safe, Lindsey was alive.

Wasn't she? Where was she?

Stepping down out of the van, he realized Dallas was still holding his arm. He looked around, past the cops and security people, past the tangle of vehicles, scanning the covered parking.

"Where is she? Where's her car?"

Dallas pointed. The tan Mercedes, circled by yellow crime scene tape. A man was coming toward him carrying a black satchel, a stoop-shouldered man wearing a mussed suit, his tie loose over the open collar of a rumpled white shirt, a man who held out his hand to Dallas.

He watched and listened to Dallas greet Emmett Brassen, the San Jose medical examiner. None of their conversation seemed to make sense, they could have been speaking in Swahili. Brassen complained about the contamination of the crime scene, then headed for the Mercedes. Mike, behind him, approached Lindsey's car, where cops and a plainclothes detective were working, and now he was afraid again.

But if Lindsey were hurt, they'd have her in the medics' van. Was she in the car, at an angle where he couldn't see? Approaching the Mercedes, his stomach twisted.

He stopped where he could see in through the car's open door. No one in the driver's seat. It was covered with blood. Bloody Levi's jacket bunched up on the passenger seat, a plain Levi's jacket like the one Lindsey had worn this morning. He could not see a purse. Had she carried a purse this morning? He looked into the backseat, saw that it was empty. Moving away, he scanned the rows of parked civilian cars, looking for her, cold with the feeling that he'd see her lying on the concrete. Three officers were walking the scene, not collecting trace evidence but looking for Lindsey, looking in and under cars. Mike was both annoyed by their interference and annoyed by his illogical reaction, and thankful for their help.

He had no notion that someone else had already scanned the scene, far more efficiently, crouched on the concrete where he could see nearly the whole floor of the parking complex except behind the cement pillars.

SEEING NO BODY, Joe had returned to the shadows beneath the Mercedes, where he at last picked up Lindsey's scent trail, carefully sorting it out from Ryder's and Ray's scents and from the aromas of the many officers. Ducking behind wheels and pillars, he had tracked Lindsey until he lost her at the curb, where her trail vanished abruptly. He sniffed the curb and sidewalk for a long time, trying to find her again among the scents of hundreds of pedestrians, and sidestepping those caring folk who were sure he had escaped from his cat carrier and should be bound for the hold of some unknown flight, who wanted to pick him up and take him to security.

Had he simply lost her scent? Had she made it to another level of the parking complex, or maybe inside the terminal? Or had she gotten into a car at the curb? Had Ray Gibbs doubled back after shooting Ryder, found Lindsey trying to get away, and forced her in at gunpoint? And had taken her where in the stolen Audi?

From behind a pillar, Joe watched Mike and Dallas and the other officers searching for Lindsey, watched Dallas place a number of calls and talk with various officers and airport personnel, trying to get a line on what might have happened to her. The two men joined a search of the airport, which, in Joe's opinion, was like trying to catch a fly in a whirlwind. He could see them inside talking with airline and airport employees. They were gone a long time, the tomcat was growing hungry and sleepy again, feeling lost again, when they returned, Mike looking pale and despondent. They were talking with the SJPD sergeant once more when Mike's cell phone rang.

"Flannery." Mike listened, looked up only to signal Dallas. As Dallas joined him, Mike found a slip of paper in his pocket and hastily jotted something.

"We're on our way," he said. "Be careful, stay out of sight. Get out of there, now. Out the back, there has to be a back entrance. Stay out of his way until the law gets there."

Clicking off, Mike stood grinning at Dallas, looking so relieved that Joe's own heart pumped harder. "She's in the city, at the wharf. Gibbs just checked into the Argonaut, or seems to have. Unless he made her and has given her the slip. She called the PD. You better call them."

"How did she . . . ?"

"She followed him in a cab," Mike said. "The fare took most of her cash. She's convinced he didn't see her. Said there were several yellow cabs on the freeway, and her driver kept well back.

"Said that when Gibbs drove around to Fisherman's Wharf, her driver followed on the next street. Said Gibbs was driving really carefully, taking his time. Saw him go in the hotel. She's across the street in a restaurant, thinks he took a room at the front, saw a curtain pulled back and said it looked like Gibbs at the window."

Dallas accessed his phone list, hit the number for SFPD, and made sure there were officers on the way. Then he called San Francisco's detective division and got a detective he knew. As he laid out the scenario, setting in place some backup to the street patrol, Joe Grey moved fast for Dallas's Blazer. He wasn't going to be left behind on this one. Not in this godforsaken airport, forty miles from home.

34

As Dallas and Mike ran for the Blazer, Joe raced to its far side and leaped at the door handle, pawing awkwardly, trying to flip it up and open. Blazer handles were not made for cat paws. Had Dallas locked the vehicle? In his frantic assault, would he set off the alarm? He'd had enough of that. As he flew at the latch, the two men came pounding—and just as he'd feared, the horn blasted suddenly in a heart-stopping cacophony that sent him flying for cover under the adjacent cars.

Dallas halted and circled the car, ready to move on a foolish burglar. Finding no one, he shoved his key in the door, swung in, and started the engine, silencing the din. As Mike opened the passenger door, Joe slipped behind him, crouching to bolt inside.

Mike was too fast, slamming the door as the tomcat leaped clear. Better left behind than crushed like an insect. Slinking away defeated, under the line of concealing vehicles, he watched the Blazer back out and move away through the parking lot, heading for San Francisco.

He was alone. In the vast, unfriendly airport. Alone in a strange city. Crouched on the cold, hard concrete trying to think what to do.

MOST OF THE San Jose officers had left. Two forensics officers were working the scene, photographing Lindsey's car inside and out, lifting prints. They had already walked a large grid through the parking area, and despite the contamination of other officers, had looked for anything dropped, had photographed visible footprints, and, around the car, had used a spray chemical to pick up unseen shoe marks. Now, working the inside of the Mercedes, Joe watched them vacuum, then use a sticky roller to pick up trace evidence. Slipping away behind the officers, Joe steered clear of the few law enforcement cars that were still heading out. None of them was from MPPD, they were all strangers. Taking shelter in the shadows beneath a red Honda Civic, he tried not to panic.

Clyde didn't know where he was. Nor did Dulcie. And Kit was too involved with mooning and sulking over Sage to think of much else. He was alone. Stuck in an unfamiliar and unfriendly airport. He didn't know whether he was more scared or more angry.

How do I get out of this one? How the hell do I get home? He was almost tempted to slip into one of the remaining patrol units, hitch a ride to San Jose PD.

Oh, right. Just his luck to link up with a cop who, finding a presumably stray cat crouched in the back of his unit, would take him straight to the pound.

He listened to the casual exchanges between the two forensics officers. He licked his sweating paws. He tried to ignore the chill in his belly that was fast turning into panic. This was the way an abandoned pet would feel when it was coldly dropped on some unfamiliar street miles from home. Torn away from home and hearth, from its humans and its blanket and food bowl. Set adrift, expected to survive among strangers in a heartless world. And he was filled with the same panic he'd known as a homeless, starving kitten in San Francisco alleys.

Except, now he was far more familiar with the cruelties a cat could encounter in the human world.

But only for a few moments did the tomcat indulge himself in his dramatic bout of self-pity before he remembered the old, horse-scented pickup truck with Ryder's cell phone hidden behind the crates.

He took off running under the rows of parked cars, almost forgetting to listen and look for moving vehicles, praying the pickup with the cell phone was still there, that some disembarking passenger hadn't thrown his bag in the back and taken off for a far-flung farm.

He smelled the truck before he saw it. The sweet scent of horses that made him nostalgic for the Harper ranch. The truck was still there, and the driver wasn't, and he leaped into the metal bed scrabbling for the phone. Half expecting it to be gone, half expecting that Ray had somehow found and retrieved it. He hadn't seen him do that, Ray hadn't had time; but for a moment Joe let his imagination run wild, he envisioned Ray finding another phone hidden in the Audi, imagined Ray slipping back to cruise the parking lot, windows down, calling Ryder's phone and following the familiar ring tone to its source in the pickup.

But of course nothing like that had happened. The phone was where he'd left it. He pawed it free of the crates and dialed Clyde's cell number.

He listened to it ringing. Tried not to think about what would happen later if the cops investigated Ryder's phone bills, checked out the numbers called on this date and wanted to know why Ryder had called Clyde.

One ring. Two . . . If it got to the fifth ring, it would go on message. Did Clyde have the phone off? Joe waited, growing cross. *Turn your phone on! Turn it on, Clyde!*

Or was Clyde looking at the incoming number and, not recognizing it, wondering with his usual annoyance if this was some unwelcome sales pitch?

Three rings, four. Desolation drowned Joe. Maybe he should ride home to the farm with the driver of the pickup. Better that than the city pound, than a cage, dry cat kibble, and forced adoption or the gas chamber.

"Damen," Clyde said gruffly, just before the fifth ring.

"I'm in San Jose," Joe said. "I need a little help here. No money for a cab, or a bus ticket," he said, hoping to get a laugh out of Clyde.

No laugh. Only a long silence. A heavy, demoralizing silence.

"Clyde? I'm at the San Jose airport. I need a ride. Do you think—"

"We're on our way," Clyde said before Joe could grovel and beg. "We just passed Gilroy."

"How did you . . . ? What're you doing in Gilroy?"

"Hold on," Clyde said none too sweetly. There was

some muttering, then Ryan came on. "Joe, are you all right? Where are you, exactly? Where at the airport? How do we find you?"

"How did you . . . ?"

"Dulcie figured it out. How will we find you?"

He gave her directions from the A tunnel entry. "I am, at the moment, in the bed of a 1999 Honda pickup. Green, with three wooden crates tied in the back, and smelling of horses. If the pickup's gone, I'll be . . ." Rearing up, he looked around short-term parking for a likely retreat. "I'll be near the shuttle stop, under a bench. Did this number show on your screen?"

"It did," she said. "We'll call you when we get there. It's nearly supper time. We brought you a little something. Wait, Clyde wants to talk."

Another silence while she handed the phone back. Joe heard her whisper, "Be nice. The poor cat's scared, all alone in that place. I'd be scared silly." And Joe thought, *My God, I love this woman.*

Clyde came on. "I wish, Joe, when these things happen, you would use a little judgment. That you would at least call me. What did you do, stow away in Lindsey's car?"

"Ryder Wolf is dead," Joe told him. "Gibbs shot her. Dallas and Mike are on their way to San Francisco to meet Lindsey—she followed Ray. Hopefully SFPD will find him first."

There was another long silence that made Joe wish he hadn't tried to sort it out on the phone. "Sometimes . . . ," Clyde began, then, "Where did you find a phone?"

"It's Ryder's phone."

Clyde sighed and didn't ask any more questions. "If we

can't find you, we'll call that number. That's a big airport. Stay put if you can. Hold on." There was another pause as Ryan took the phone.

"Fast-food burger okay? With fries?"

"Sounds like heaven," Joe said, licking his whiskers. If Clyde had ever shown good sense, it was when he asked Ryan Flannery to be his wife. He hung up thinking fondly of a hot, greasy hamburger and greasy fries.

Pushing the phone back among the crates, he curled down on the hard metal floor of the pickup, yawned, and closed his eyes. He'd be sure to wake if the driver appeared. Cats are light sleepers, a cat hears every slightest sound, senses every movement. And, curling his front paws under him, Joe Grey dropped into sleep.

35

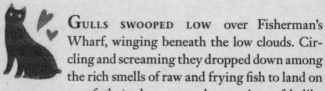 Gulls swooped low over Fisherman's Wharf, winging beneath the low clouds. Circling and screaming they dropped down among the rich smells of raw and frying fish to land on a restaurant roof; there they strutted, stomping softly like little thumping drumbeats, directly above Lindsey Wolf's head where she sat inside at a window table.

Having angled her chair behind a potted palm, she was out of sight from the hotel across the street. Distracted for a moment by the pitter-pat above her, she abandoned her surveillance, looking up—she looked back just in time to see Ray Gibbs pull aside the second-floor curtain, as he had done twice before.

Standing in plain view, he peered down at the narrow, crowded street, watching the wandering tourists, then looked across at the restaurant windows. She was sure he couldn't see her behind the palm and crammed among other diners. The interior of the restaurant, despite its big windows, was shadowy in contrast to the bright street.

He had the TV on, she could see its light flickering behind him through the thin curtain. She wondered, shivering, if the shooting was on the news yet, if that was what he was watching.

If she'd hesitated when he shot Ryder, she'd be dead, too. She was certain Ryder was dead, she couldn't have lived, the way she was shot. She grieved for Ryder, guilt had ridden with her as she hailed a cab, following Ray. Praying for Ryder, and riven with hate for Gibbs, she wanted to see him burn. Burn for Ryder, and for Carson, and for Nina Gibbs.

Why had he come *here* after he shot Ryder? Why not catch his flight, for which they must have had last-minute reservations? Or head up the coast among the small fishing and lumbering towns of northern California and southern Oregon, with all the open land and woods where he could disappear?

But maybe he thought, among the city's crowds of tourists, he wouldn't be noticed. The sidewalk below was jammed with gaudily dressed pedestrians moving back and forth across the narrow street, pushing around the fenders and bumpers of slow-moving cars, hungering to spend their money on little treats, or on useless wares to cart home as unique gifts for family and friends who would soon throw them away.

Gibbs moved again, letting the curtain fall back into place, and disappeared from view. *Had* he seen her, was that why he was staring across at the restaurant? She watched the street, praying to see Dallas's Blazer, praying they'd hurry. She was terrified Gibbs would come down, come across to the restaurant. Every time he left the window she drew farther back behind the palm, wanting to run.

When the waitress came to refill her glass of iced tea, she ordered a dessert that she didn't want, buying time. She couldn't sit there forever not ordering anything, the restaurant was too full. She had picked up her fork, was toying with the meringue when Gibbs stepped out the front door of the Argonaut. He stood a moment looking around, then headed across the street toward her, toward the door of the restaurant.

JOE GREY WOKE to the step of high-heeled cowboy boots, a distinctive sound one couldn't mistake. The next instant, the pickup bed shook as the cab door was flung open. He caught a whiff of male sweat, glimpsed the guy before he ducked back between the boxes—a squarely built man dressed in a faded western shirt and worn, western straw hat. There was a thud as he tossed something into the narrow space behind the driver's seat, maybe a suitcase or a duffel. Joe, snatching the phone in his teeth, leaped over the metal side of the truck bed just as the guy started the engine. Sailing to the roof of the next car, he leaped again to the top of a white Honda van, where he flattened himself against its roof, hiding the cell phone under him. The guy hadn't seen him, was busy backing out, looking over his shoulder, maneuvering the big pickup out of the tight space.

When the cowboy had gone, Joe rose up, hoping his weight hadn't punched any buttons on the phone that would send it into some incomprehensible mode that he couldn't figure out.

Should he call Clyde back, tell him he'd had to move? Or wait to see what happened? He hoped this van would stay in place for a while. It hadn't been there when he'd hopped into the truck. Hoped the driver wasn't just picking up a passenger. He must have been deep in sleep when it pulled into the parking space, he hadn't even heard a door slam.

He decided to stay where he was despite the fact that on the white van he was as visible as a dead rat on clean sheets. He was up high enough to see cars pulling in and out, to see the yellow roadster or Ryan's red pickup. He hadn't thought to ask what they were driving. He watched a beefy woman with three cranky, arguing kids approaching, heading straight for him, and he hunkered down again, praying the van wasn't theirs, trying to make both the phone and himself invisible.

And wouldn't you know it. Here they came, straight for him, the woman jingling her keys, the kids whining and arguing.

Maybe they were too busy arguing to notice him. He daren't move, they were feet from him. Frozen in place, he watched the flabby woman in her tight black pants and red T-shirt unlock the driver's door then slide the back door open. Crouched low, he was slowly backing away from that side when the tallest kid, a straggly girl of about ten, spotted him.

"There's a cat on top of the car! Ma, look! A cat!"

Hadn't she ever seen a cat before? What was it about innocent animals that made kids want to shout?

"Look, it's rearing up!" she screamed, running around the side of the van and jumping up, reaching. The kid was a good jumper, he hadn't thought she could reach that high. Her hand grazed him, and before he could stop himself, he'd slashed her a good one. She dropped to the concrete, screaming, "It scratched me! Maaaaa, the cat scratched me!"

He'd hardly touched her. Hardly drew blood. Well, only just a drop or two, glistening on her dirty little fingers. He wished he hadn't done it, that hadn't been a smart move.

But it was too late now, and the woman was furious. As she lunged up, reaching to grab him, he abandoned the cell phone, leaped to the roof of the next car. He couldn't drag the phone with him and let her see it, that would tear it. As he sailed away from one car to the next, the woman ran between cars chasing him, screaming, "Catch it! Catch that cat! It attacked my baby." Thudding and leaping across car tops, he glimpsed the flash of a red vehicle pulling in through the far gate.

Let it be them! He paused, rearing up, hissing at the woman to make her back off. Praying that was Ryan's red truck. *Let that be Ryan and Clyde. Please God—and get this woman off me!*

36

HAVING PRESSED her last twenty into the waitress's hand, Lindsey slipped out through the restaurant's kitchen. Behind her, the plump, motherly server told Gibbs there'd been no woman in there matching that description. She said a man had been sitting at the recently vacated window table, that she hadn't seen the woman he described. That maybe she'd gone into one of the other restaurants along the row. Pausing in the hot, steamy kitchen, Lindsey heard enough to know he was arguing, that he didn't believe her. She spotted the back door and fled among a half dozen busy cooks who turned to scowl at her, never breaking their rhythm of frying and slicing and dishing up. The place smelled of steaming crab and hot fries. And she was out the door, on the side street where she slipped into a group of tourists.

She moved away with them, and ducked into a curio shop, was mingling with the dawdling customers, looking out, when she saw him leave the restaurant.

He headed in her direction. Stepping behind a big, bald man in a pink T-shirt, she looked for another way out of the shop and saw none. She waited until the clerk at the cash register turned away, and slipped past her into a dark little storeroom.

The small, dim space smelled of cheap scented candles. It was crowded with cartons stacked on the floor. The shelves behind these were piled with T-shirts, cheap pottery, piñatas, folded Japanese kites, and Mexican baskets. There was no back door, there was only the one way out of the closetlike space. She turned at a scuffing sound.

Gibbs stood blocking the door. She backed away. He grabbed her, spun her around, and shoved the gun in her stomach.

He wouldn't shoot her here, she thought, encumbered by the crowd in the shop, he'd never escape.

But then she thought about news stories in which the shooter had killed in a crowd, and run, knocking people aside, and had gotten away, with no armed officer to stop him. Gibbs shoved her so hard she twisted, lost her balance, and fell. He jerked her up, gripped her against him as he faced the door, his gun drawn.

Two uniformed officers filled the doorway.

Lindsey didn't wait, she elbowed him as hard as she could in the groin, and ducked down behind a stack of cartons. He turned the gun on her. There was a shot, and another. Gibbs staggered, dropped the gun, fell nearly on top of her. She was grabbed from behind and pulled away.

"For God's sake, Lindsey." Mike held her close as an officer retrieved Gibbs's gun. Gibbs twisted, trying to get up. The other cop sent him sprawling again, and the two officers, snapping cuffs on him, jerked him up and duck-walked him out through the now deserted shop. She could see more uniforms outside herding the tourists away. Leaning against Mike, needing his warmth, she saw Dallas come in from the street.

"You okay?" Dallas asked her.

"I am now," she said shakily.

"You did good," Mike said, tenderly touching her face.

"Ryder's dead," she said woodenly.

Mike held her away, looked deep into her eyes, looked at the blood smeared across her tank top, Ryder's blood. She looked down at herself where she'd held her sister for an instant before Ryder went limp—before she turned and fled, to follow Gibbs, wanting to kill him.

What Ryder's life had been, and then her senseless death, only added to Lindsey's rage, to fury at herself that she'd done so little to change Ryder's life. Hiding her face against Mike's shoulder, she let him lead her out of the shop. She felt weak and hopeless, wanted only to be quiet, to be alone, just the two of them, Mike holding her close. Out on the street she stood within Mike's arms, oblivious to the cops and the staring tourists, stood in a world where there was no one else, where there was no cruelty, no murder, where there was only safety and love.

As Lindsey clung within Mike's embrace, some miles away the gray tomcat felt equally safe in the secure embrace of Mike's daughter. The feel of Ryan's shoulder against which he lay, the clean smell of her hair against his nose—and the fact that he was full of a burger and fries—filled Joe Grey with a deep sense of well-being. The team of Flannery and Damen was all right, the tomcat liked this new sense of belonging within a real family.

Where his relationship with Clyde had rocked along on good-natured male confrontation and wisecracking, Ryan added an amused tenderness that Joe hadn't known was missing, she added the gentle understanding that Clyde, too often, didn't like to exhibit.

Though back there in short-term parking, Clyde *had* stood up for him. Had laughed at the angry mother when she threatened to sue him, threatened to call the dog-catcher and have the cat quarantined—as if Joe had flayed that kid alive.

It was Ryan who'd retrieved the phone. Having double-parked her pickup behind the woman's white van, she'd glimpsed the phone on its roof and, hiding a grin, had put it in her pocket while Clyde fetched the first aid kit. And before Clyde fished out the bandages, she'd fetched her camera and taken pictures of Joe's minute claw marks in the kid's hand, and then of the pudgy mother doctoring the scratch and bandaging it. She made sure to photograph all aspects of both arms and hands, and of the child's face, to prove there were no other wounds.

"The cat didn't bite you?" Clyde asked the child as her mother bandaged the hand.

"I saw that cat—" the mother started to say, but the kid screamed, "It didn't *bite* me! It scratched me! Can't you see it scratched me!"

Taping the wound, the woman clutched her own cell phone, ready to call 911 and animal control. Until Clyde pointed out that if she did that, the authorities would take the cat away, and he, Clyde, wouldn't be able to give her the five hundred dollars he had intended, to cover her inconvenience. He told her Joe had had his rabies shots. He gave her their vet's name and address and, of course, his own address. When the woman stopped shouting, to accept the money and to sign a release that Clyde hastily wrote out on a scrap of paper, Ryan turned her attention to Joe, taking him in her arms.

"Does this mean a lawsuit?" Joe had asked her when they were alone, slipping into the passenger side of the truck.

"I doubt it. But between Dad, Max, and Dallas, we'll come up with an unbeatable lawyer if we need to. Personally," she said, grinning, "I think she'll drop it. Maybe try to hit us up for more money later." She looked deep into Joe's eyes. "Clyde and I aren't worried. Neither should you be."

Clyde slid into the driver's seat, cutting her a look, but said nothing. Heading home, Ryan kept telling Joe over and over, "It's all right." Holding him close, looking down into his worried face. "It's all right, Joe. You didn't hurt the little brat. We have pictures. Don't sweat it."

Joe had listened, hiding a smile, as Clyde explained to the woman the many steps she would have to go through if she sued him, the forms she would have to fill out, the time she would have to spend with an attorney, and in court, and the probable cost of an attorney. This, and the whining of her restless kids who were hungry and had to pee and wanted to go home, had at last induced her to accept the money, load up her unruly family, and leave the three of them in peace.

One thing for sure, Joe thought, purring against

Ryan. He never wanted to see the San Jose airport again. Not in all his nine lives. For a while there, he'd thought if he didn't starve in that oversize concrete crypt or get run over by some hurrying driver racing to catch a plane, he *would* be picked up by animal control, imprisoned behind bars for maybe the rest of a very short life.

Now, Ryan's concern went a long way toward dispelling that icy fear of abandonment. And as the three of them hit the freeway, heading home, he snuggled down in her lap, smugly comfortable, filled once more with macho confidence.

37

MUCH EARLIER that evening, Dulcie had stood on the roof of Clyde's house watching the red pickup pull out of the drive, watching Clyde and Ryan head for San Jose. *They didn't want me! Clyde and Ryan didn't want me.* She had been left behind. She was hurt, she was worried about Joe, and she was mad as hell. *Where else should I be when Joe's in danger?*

"Please, Dulcie," Ryan had said, "Rock's so upset and nervous. When I'm upset, he gets like this. I'll have to shut him in the house so he won't try to climb out of the patio and follow us, but . . . Please stay with him until he calms down. A Weimaraner can tear a whole house to pieces when he's frantic. Please, stay for a while. Later, when he settles down, if you go somewhere, please come back and check on him. Or call Charlie."

She knew they were trying to keep *her* out of trouble, that they didn't know what kind of danger they were heading into. But when Ryan asked like that, what else could she do? And Rock *was* upset, he was a basket case, pacing and panting and pawing at the doors.

Who would guess that a big strong dog like Rock could get so undone, could be so sensitive to Ryan's distress? Pacing nervously from room to room, he reared up to peer out the windows and to paw at them until Dulcie backed him away, hissing at him.

"Sit, Rock!" the tabby told him. "Sit, now!"

Rock sat, with that puzzled look he got when any of the three cats gave him a command. Dulcie kept talking and talking to him, to calm him. She'd seen him upset before, when Ryan was stressed over a job, but never this bad. The Weimaraner's sensitivity to human feelings showed his intelligence, but it made him a challenge to live with. Rock would never be a phlegmatic house dog who easily rolled with the punches.

But talking to him helped. He was always attentive when she or Joe or Kit spoke to him, he had never gotten over his amazement at the wonderful talking cats. At last she got him to lie down on the rug, and she stretched out close to him.

"They'll be back soon, Rock. It's all right, everything's all right."

He turned to nose at her; he was still shivering. Could he be upset not only because Ryan and Clyde were distressed, but because of some elusive canine sensitivity that told him Joe was in trouble? No human really knew the extent of an animal's perceptions. *She* could tell animal researchers a number of stories they'd find hard to believe.

Rock was still for a while, but then he rose nervously again, heading for the kitchen. He pushed and pawed at the locked doggy door, then looked at Dulcie angrily, as if she was the one who had locked it. She tried to get him to eat some kibble, but he turned his face away. At last he headed back to the living room, gave a sigh of deep resignation, climbed into Joe's ragged easy chair, and curled up tight, his nose hidden in his flank.

Dulcie didn't know whether to laugh at his dramatics or lick the big dog's face. Leaping into the chair beside him, she curled up in a little circle against his side, and began to purr to him; but worry about Joe ate at them both.

When at last Rock slept, snoring, worn out from his concern, she slipped down carefully, silently, and left him. *Just for half an hour*, she thought. *Just for a little while.*

Padding up the stairs, she sailed from the desktop to a rafter and quietly pushed out through Joe's cat door. And she headed over the rooftops, galloping across the village toward the Gibbs condo, her mind on a possible laptop and printer, on the source of that second anonymous note left at the back door of the station.

Landing on the roof of the complex, she dropped down to Gibbs's terrace, and peered in. Why waste the perfect time to toss the place, with Gibbs an hour's drive away, hopefully detained by the law.

Nothing moved in there. No lights. The TV dark and silent. She could hear no sound. She had the place to herself, and she had plenty of time for a thorough search. Sliding the screen back, she wondered if they'd been in too much of a hurry to secure the door.

No such luck. The glass slider was locked tight.

There were three windows facing the condo's terrace. Leaping up, clinging to the sills with stubborn claws, she found all three screens locked, and she could see that the locks on the windows were engaged. Going over the roof to the front door, near the stairs, she found that locked, too.

The kitchen had one window, which was on the outside wall, two stories above the street and with no roof access. A thorny bougainvillea vine clung to that two-story wall, but it was a five-foot leap from this landing onto the vine. If she missed, it would be a straight drop, two stories to the sidewalk.

She crouched, made the leap. Was scrambling through the bougainvillea toward the kitchen window, hoping they hadn't bothered to lock this one, when a squad car pulled to the curb two floors below.

Peering down through the leaves and red blossoms, she watched Juana Davis step out, tucking a folded paper into her uniform pocket. *Could that be a warrant?* Dulcie thought with excitement. *She's been to the judge already?* Well, Davis wasted no time. Maybe Ray and Ryder's hasty departure, plus the body at the ruins, had given her enough to request a search warrant.

Clawing her way back through the bougainvillea away from the window, Dulcie managed to leap back to the landing, where she crouched behind a small potted tree, waiting for Juana, waiting to slip inside behind her.

Coming up the stairs, Juana used a key with a large white tag that, Dulcie supposed, she'd gotten from the landlord. As she pushed the door open, Dulcie made a fast dash . . . She got only as far as Juana's heels when Juana turned, closed the door in her face, and stood looking down at her. Dulcie didn't know if she'd made some tiny sound or if Juana had felt a change in the air current behind her stockinged legs. The tabby stood frozen, staring up at her. Did Davis have to be so perceptive?

Juana looked at her for a long time, her dark brown eyes as unreadable as if she were studying the face of a shackled felon. Dulcie tried to look innocent. She tried her sweet cat smile, and knew she looked nervous and guilty.

But guilty of what? Juana didn't know why she was here. As good a detective as Juana Davis was, she didn't have a clue on this one. Boldly Dulcie rubbed against her ankles, purring as hard as she could manage.

"Dulcie, what are you doing here?"

Dulcie preened and purred.

"You were on the roofs, and you saw me?" Juana said quietly, the way she would talk to any animal. "Well, the roofs are a good place for cats. No cars, no dogs, nothing to bother you—but I don't want you following me inside. If you got lost among the furniture, and got locked in . . ." She looked deep into Dulcie's eyes. "I wish you could understand. You mustn't go into strange houses, you could starve to death before anyone knew you were there. You go on, now. Go chase a mouse." Turning, she slipped inside and closed the door.

So much for that, Dulcie thought, scrambling up the potted tree to the roof. She felt like a rookie who wanted to go on a case and instead was sent to direct traffic.

But if there was a computer in there, or any kind of evidence, Juana would find it. And instead of her planned break-and-enter, she headed back to Clyde's house to babysit a hundred-pound Weimaraner—and to worry about Joe. To wait nervously for a call from Clyde and Ryan to find out if they'd found him and if he was all right.

38

THE EVENING WAS pushing on toward nine when Charlie got home from Dr. Firetti's, the wind cold at her back as she hurried from her Blazer into the tiled mudroom that led to both the living room and the kitchen. Something smelled good, and when she stepped through into the big family kitchen Max was fixing a tray for their late supper. She could see through into the living room where he had set up the folding table before a welcoming fire.

Max had wanted to go down to Firetti's with her, but she'd begged him to stay home, to heat up something from the freezer and maybe make a salad—she couldn't talk to the doctor openly in front of him, and certainly the cat couldn't. She was just thankful that John Firetti was there for them, day and night. There was a clinic up the coast for after-hours emergencies, but Dr. Firetti took care of emergencies for a few of his long-standing clients, as had his father before him, getting out of bed at any hour, and he seemed content with the arrangement.

She and the two cats had told him every detail of their encounter with the coyotes. He'd asked how close they'd been to the animals, had asked the same questions Max asked. When Firetti was satisfied that no one had been bitten, he'd examined and X-rayed Sage's leg, put on a new splint, and rebandaged him. But he'd wanted to keep him overnight. Kit was unwilling to leave Sage, though they had spent most of the week battling and then making up. Maybe the tortoiseshell wanted to stay because they *had* battled, because she felt guilty that she'd made Sage so unhappy he'd run away and nearly been killed.

Dr. Firetti had fixed a warm bed for the two in his office and tossed a blanket and pillow on the couch for himself. Charlie left with hugs for both cats, hoping they'd sort out their differences; she left Kit snuggled as close to Sage as she could get without hurting his wounds, and before she turned away Kit had looked up at her with such confusion, with worry and hurt for Sage and yet with a clear uncertainty in her wide yellow eyes. Uncertainty about the state of her own heart? Torn between her fear for Sage, and her own needs? Charlie had felt tears start and had turned away quickly, leaving the clinic, worrying about where Kit's hotheaded young spirit would lead her.

Now, at home, Charlie washed her hands at the kitchen sink then followed Max into the living room, where she curled up in a big chair before the fire as he carried in their supper tray. She told herself that everything would be all right, that Kit would sort out her feelings, and as Max pulled his own chair near hers, she sipped her hot tea and reached hungrily for her grilled sandwich.

"Before we got married," she said, grinning at him, "you told me you couldn't cook."

"And you told me you didn't know how to fix a fence or shoot straight."

"This is the best supper I've ever had," she said, taking another huge bite.

"It's only a grilled-cheese sandwich."

"It's your famous grilled cream cheese and salami on rye, and it's delicious. Is there more?" she said, devouring her salad, too, and gulping the sweet, steaming tea.

"All you want, in the kitchen. Did you clean those scratches on your face? You're sure they're only from branches? The coyotes didn't get near you?"

"Not within yards, Max. Will you stop worrying?"

He took her hand. "Just glad you're safe—don't want you frothing at the mouth and biting people." He brought her another sandwich from the kitchen, and fresh, hot tea, then threw another log on the fire and settled down again to fill her in on the events of the evening. She had, while in Dr. Firetti's office, taken a call on her cell from Ryan.

"Joe's fine," Ryan had begun in a preamble to who-knew-what, then gave her such a brief sketch of where they were and why that Charlie had wanted to stop her, make her tell it slowly. "We're headed home now. Joe's asleep on my lap. He had a hamburger and then we stopped for dinner, smuggled him into a little steakhouse," she had said amused. "I can't believe how much this cat eats."

Ryan had had the speaker on, Charlie heard Clyde laugh.

Joe must have awakened; he had growled, "You'd be hungry, too, if you barely escaped being hauled off to the pound." And the tomcat's yowling harangue had assured her that he was just fine.

Now she waited for Max to give her the details of what had gone down at the airport and in the city. But by the time he'd finished with San Jose and the race to San Francisco, and was recounting how the San Francisco uniforms had decked Ray Gibbs, she was nodding and jerking awake.

"Bedtime," Max said, picking up her empty cup and plate. She rose, yawning hugely. "And Ryder Wolf is dead," she said quietly. She would have thought she'd feel no emotion for Ryder. She was surprised by how sad that death left her.

"What will happen now?" she said as they turned out the lights and headed down the hall.

"The usual," Max said. "SFPD will go over the stolen Audi, Santa Clara County sheriff's office will examine Lindsey's Mercedes and take evidence. Ditto with Gibbs's car. The sheriff will send a unit over to the city to transport Gibbs back to the Santa Clara County lockup."

"To be arraigned for murder," she said, crawling into bed. "What will happen to Lindsey? Is she under suspicion for Chappell's death?"

"Don't know yet," he said, slipping in beside her. "We've yet to identify the woman in the grave. Maybe that's Nina, maybe not. And we have to establish cause of death. Gibbs could be arraigned on that count, too." He looked over at her—and smiled. She was sound asleep.

Strange, Max thought, watching her. Although this case had endangered Mike and Dallas, it hadn't worried her nearly as much as had tonight's events involving the feral cat. The stress of forging back through that black tangle of woods to rescue the two cats—how many people would do that? The stress of having to shoot the coyotes. Her worry and fear for the cats always touched him. And she claimed she wasn't tenderhearted. Smiling down at his unpredictable redheaded wife, Max turned out the lamp and was soon asleep himself as the rising moon sent a first glimmer through the high windows.

BUT LATER, AS moonlight washed broadly through the windows of the Harper house, touching Charlie's face, she woke again to relive the scene in Dr. Firetti's examining room. As the doctor went to fetch some food for the cats, she had stepped out into the hall, leaving Sage and Kit alone, tucked up in the big basket he had fixed for them. But there, she had paused.

Behind her, she could hear them talking and she turned to listen; she was dismayed as Sage begged Kit to come back to the clowder, to join the clowder once more, to stay with him and be a pair.

She didn't want Kit to return to the wild, didn't want her to leave her life in the village, none of Kit's friends wanted that. Yet they all, cats and humans, wanted her to be happy. The question was, what did Kit want? Kit, herself, didn't seem to know. She made up to Sage one minute, snuggling and purring, and the next minute was fighting with him. Tonight she'd told him, "No, Sage. I won't come back."

"But we've always been best friends," he'd said. "You don't really want to stay here among humans, you can't really want to live as a captive, locked up in houses with humans."

"I *don't* live as a captive," Kit had hissed. "I come and go as I please, I do as I please. I'm not *locked up*! I belong here!"

"But what about us. If you love me . . ."

"We will always be loving friends," she'd said softly. "I . . . I don't know how I feel . . . Stone Eye is gone," she'd said, "but if another tyrant comes along, will you be obedient to him, too? So he'll protect you?"

Sage had said nothing. Only silence.

"Does being safe mean more to you than our freedom?" she'd snapped. There was a thump on the floor as she'd leaped out of the basket and come racing through the door—but Charlie had moved faster, catching her up and holding her close, Kit's heart pounding against her, a fast little trip-hammer.

"You can't run away, Kit. Just listen to him. Listen to his side, you owe him that."

Kit had turned her face away—but then in a moment she looked up at Charlie, and shame showed in her wide yellow eyes. As Charlie carried her back into the examining room, Sage had tried to rise, stumbling against the side of the basket, crouching as if to leap out. Charlie hurried to stop him, setting Kit down in the basket beside him, where the two hissed at each other. But then Sage had looked ashamedly down at his paws.

"I'm sorry," the pale cat had mumbled. "No one can force you to leave here, no one can force you to love me."

"*I'm* sorry," Kit had said contritely. "I guess . . . Maybe, sometimes, one doesn't have a choice in how one feels."

"I guess maybe sometimes," Sage had said, "one takes the easy way." He looked at Kit a long time, then lay down again. Tentatively Kit curled down beside him. Sage purred a little, and nuzzled Kit's whiskers—and Charlie turned and left them, slipping out of the room.

Two stubborn little individuals, she'd thought, feeling tears start. *So at cross purposes.* She'd hurt deeply for them, had headed home filled with concern for Sage and for the fiery young tortoiseshell.

39

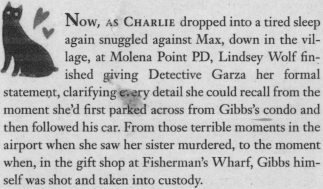Now, as Charlie dropped into a tired sleep again snuggled against Max, down in the village, at Molena Point PD, Lindsey Wolf finished giving Detective Garza her formal statement, clarifying every detail she could recall from the moment she'd first parked across from Gibbs's condo and then followed his car. From those terrible moments in the airport when she saw her sister murdered, to the moment when, in the gift shop at Fisherman's Wharf, Gibbs himself was shot and taken into custody.

In Dallas's office, against the faint sound of the dispatcher's voice from up the hall and the voices of various officers moving in and out through the building, she told Dallas everything she could remember. The long ride in the cab watching Gibbs's car moving in and out of traffic. Thinking her driver would have a cell phone, and he hadn't. Not wanting to relay her message through his dispatcher, not sure what the dispatcher would tell her superior and other drivers. Following Gibbs to the hotel, paying her cab fare, and slipping into the restaurant to use their phone, having to explain that it was an emergency. By the time they finished the interview, she felt wrung out.

"Come on," Dallas said. "Mike's waiting. You'll feel better with a drink and some dinner." And they headed for Mike's apartment, leaving the center of the village, its streets and shops bright and awash with moonlight, and heading up among the darker streets where the moon was hidden above pine and oak and cypress trees.

"Have you thought about what you'll do now?" Dallas said. "After all that's happened, will you find it too painful to stay here in the village?"

Lindsey looked at him for a long time. "You think I'll run away from ugliness again."

He glanced at her. "I don't know."

"That's not very flattering."

"I'm a cop. I don't specialize in flattery."

She smiled. "You don't use flattery in your work?"

He laughed, then was silent. Ahead, at the top of the hill, the over-the-garage duplex was dark on one side, but Mike's lights were bright and welcoming. She looked at Dallas as he pulled up the drive. "I don't think I'll run, this time."

From the living room above, Mike watched them pull in. He'd been standing at the windows nursing a drink, looking down across the moonlit village to the sea beyond.

He had stopped to pick up salad things and steaks, had put the potatoes in the oven to bake, washed and put together the salad. Turning to check the oven, he considered his new digs with satisfaction, the big, airy studio with its high, white-stained rafters, its tall windows looking down over the village. Ryan's roomy desk before the windows, offering a comfortable place to work—near the kitchen and coffeepot, he thought, amused.

At the back of the long room was a simple daybed, soft with throw pillows in the daytime, and two canvas camp chairs. With the dressing room and bath, he had the perfect bachelor pad.

Perfect, for now.

It would be pretty crowded for a couple.

But that was way down the line. He didn't know if Lindsey was ready for a real commitment. How tied was she, still, to what she'd had? What she'd thought she had with Chappell?

Turning as if to speak to Rock, he realized the big dog wasn't with him, that Rock was back with his mistress. *I don't suppose*, he thought, watching the Blazer pull in and stepping into the kitchen to mix Lindsey's drink, *don't suppose I'd ever find another dog like Rock.*

He thought about this morning, which seemed days ago, about Rock's exhibition of unerring tracking, and wondered what the real story was. Maybe Ryan would tell him, sometime. And maybe she wouldn't. And for a moment, again, he missed the youngster she had been, a handful of fire and stubbornness, as hardheaded as a young mule. Then he smiled. Was she so different now?

He put aside his fatherly sentiment as Lindsey and Dallas came up the stairs. Opening the door for them, he felt a stab of warmth at the sight of Lindsey—and, again, a sharp jolt of relief that she was safe. That she wasn't dead in that car, in place of her sister.

• • •

IT WAS NEARLY six the next morning when the Greenlaws woke and Lucinda reached down the bed feeling around her feet for Kit—then remembered that Kit was at the clinic with Sage, that Charlie had called from the clinic last night to tell her about the coyotes. Rising and pulling on her robe, thinking of Kit nearly killed by coyotes, Lucinda said a prayer of thanks that their beloved tortoiseshell was safe. And she prayed for Sage, too. What had possessed him to run off like that, into the wild, still encumbered by that awkward cast?

Love, she thought. Love and hurt and anger. She didn't want to think past that point, couldn't bear to think that Kit might love him in return, love him enough to leave them, to leave her home.

And how selfish was that!

Starting the coffee, pouring a cup before it finished brewing, she sat down at the dining table with the faded, handwritten letters taken from Olivia Pamillon's diary.

Though she and Pedric had read them at once, when Wilma brought them up last night, she wanted another look. The letters were addressed to only three people: two cousins, Annette Pamillon and Jeannine Pamillon Brink. And Jeannine's husband, Tom. That was the couple who had brought back the first speaking cats, secretly intending to breed and sell them. The messages were oblique in their wording. These seemed to be first drafts, with words crossed out or changed to make them less decipherable to the uninitiated. Surely Olivia had penned new copies from these, mailed them, and kept the originals; but why had she kept them? The replies were equally obscure.

Two implied that Olivia would take legal action to destroy Jeannine's title to her shares of the estate if she and Tom didn't abandon their commercialization of the cats and swear themselves to secrecy. A threat couched in obscurity but clear to someone who knew the truth.

But even Olivia's comments about the cats themselves, to Annette, whom she must have trusted, were oblique, phrases such as, *I love watching the wild animals around the estate. So many come to visit me, and seem to grow bolder each day.* And then there would be some innocuous and unrelated comment regarding clothes, or a recipe, and then—as if this was the pattern they'd worked out—the urgent part of the message: *John's houseguests are incredibly nosy, asking questions that are none of their affair.* Or, *I have asked Jeannine several times if I might stop by when I'm in the village. Every time they are busy, or are going out of town. My own cousin.* And then a few weeks later, again to Annette, *I think it's time we visited Jeannine together, a kind of surprise. What do you think?*

Lucinda laid the sheets aside. Strange that Olivia had kept these—maybe, as she'd gotten older, she'd held on to them and to the Bewick book as a link with her fading past. Lucinda hoped those who had known about the cats were all dead; she grew increasingly uneasy wondering who else might know, wondering how far the secret might have spread. To paraphrase one of her favorite authors—as secrets *will* do.

40

IN THE ALLEYWAY of the Harper stable, Kit and Sage sat side by side on a bale of hay watching Charlie saddle the buckskin gelding. It was two weeks since Sage had run away into the woods, more than three since Willow had first taken him to Charlie. His cast had been removed, and he sat up straight and alert. Dr. Firetti had told him he could go home, but must take it easy. He said Sage had healed quickly despite the trauma of his second accident. Almost, Charlie thought, smiling, as if his need to be away from closed rooms and humans had driven him to a fast recovery.

Though now, despite his eagerness for the open hills and freedom, the young tom looked up suspiciously at Bucky, understandably wary of making this journey on horseback. He had insisted he could go on his own, but Firetti disagreed.

Charlie was taking Bucky because he was reliable and steady. Her own sorrel mare was moodier, and liked to shy at the swift, small shadows they might encounter. Redwing was sure to snort and sidestep if the clowder cats came slipping around them through the woods.

Cinching up her western saddle, which she preferred when the cats rode with her, she looked over at Sage. "How will we find them, Sage? The clowder could be anywhere."

"They have favorite places," Sage said. "You can call out and if they see me, I think they'll come—Willow will come."

Charlie doubted that would have been true while Stone Eye was alive. She led Bucky forward to make him let out the air he always hoarded, tightened the cinch again, and tied her jacket across the saddle, snugged up against the horn to make a little pillow. Picking up Kit, she settled her there, then eased Sage down beside her.

Swinging up, she headed Bucky out behind the barn and into the woods. The last time she'd entered these woods, it had been black night. She thought of the coyotes, and shivered.

But this morning was bright and crisp, and the only movement ahead was shadows shifting from the blowing trees. Beneath Bucky's hooves, the earth smelled loamy and rich. Heading through the dense stands of oaks and pines, Charlie had no idea, when they found the clowder, what Kit would do. No idea whether the tortoiseshell would stay with Sage and become his mate, as he wanted, or would return to Lucinda and Pedric. Kit had told Charlie nothing. But if Kit remained in the wild, racing off with the clowder to vanish among the hills, she would break Lucinda's and Pedric's hearts.

Kit hadn't said good-bye to the Greenlaws. When Charlie asked her why, she wouldn't talk about it.

As they emerged from the woods onto the open hills that rose vast and green above them, Sage's small body went rigid with anticipation. Charlie held him securely as Bucky made his way up through the tall grass toward the high woods.

Within an hour they were on the little trail that led along the edge of the cliff between the pine woods and the sea. Far below, the sea crashed against the rocks, foaming and pounding, stirring the smell of iodine. Then, when at last they turned away from the sea into the woods, the smell of new spring grass came sharply again, crushed under Bucky's hooves. Nothing stirred among the woods; no bright eyes watching them, no shadow of a cat, not even a tail-flicking squirrel. She urged Bucky in deep among the trees, then pulled him up, letting him snatch at mouthfuls of grass though Max wouldn't have allowed him to do that. Around them the woods were silent. Snuggled before her in the saddle, the cats looked and looked, but they saw none of the clowder. Kit, leaping down into the carpet of leaves, began to search for scent. Sage crouched to follow, but Charlie held him back.

"You don't want to jump so far on that newly healed leg." She looked down at the pale-colored tom. "You'll be taking care of yourself now. You'd better do what the doctor said, Sage. If you give that leg time to heal fully, it will grow strong again. Otherwise, you'll cripple yourself. You don't want to live all your life lame, unable to run or hunt properly."

Sage scowled deeply at her. He'd had enough of being bossed by humans. But then, he'd had enough, too, of being crippled by the cast, and he remained obediently still.

They watched Kit circle where the clowder had often sheltered at night when she had run with them, the dense stand of blackberry brambles offering a safe haven from predators. Working in ever widening circles, Kit stopped suddenly and reared up, looking around her.

"They were here," she said. "Call them, Charlie. Call Willow."

Softly Charlie called. And warily she watched the woods, hoping some unseen hiker wouldn't emerge and wonder what she was doing. Again she called, and again.

"Louder," Kit told her. "Call louder."

She called, watching the dappled sun and shadows beneath the blowing pines. Every shape seemed to change and move in the shifting light, yet nothing really moved at all.

She called three times, then three times more. Bucky pulled at the reins, reaching to snatch at the sparse grass. Her voice, out of place in the silence, seemed to her a rude invasion of the wild woods. She was answered only by silence, and by the distant crash of water breaking against the cliff. Below her, Kit stood up on her hind legs again, like a little rabbit, watching the woods and listening. But when Kit looked up at her, Charlie couldn't read the expression in the tortoiseshell's yellow eyes. Agitated. Unsettled. A look that could mean anything.

When after a quarter of an hour there had been no response, no faint and distant mewl, no stealthy shadow approaching through the blowing-tree shadows, Charlie said, "I don't think they hear us. Can you track them away from the bramble?"

In her lap, Sage fidgeted, wanting down, wanting to

search, too, but still she held him. If they had to hurry away from some danger, Kit could leap to the saddle or could vanish as swiftly as a bird. But Sage's weaker leg would slow him, nor should he make a flying leap.

Kit, after a long search nosing into zigzags among the brambles, leaped to the top of an outcropping of granite boulders, a hill of tumbled stones that rose against an oak. There she reared up tall, staring into the treetops. Loudly she mewled, and mewled again. A strange, wild cry that made Charlie shiver; then Sage's voice joined her, their cries eerie in the empty woods.

And suddenly the woods weren't empty. Cats appeared all around them slipping out from among the far trees and from beyond the boulders and descending from the highest branches, down the rough trunks. They paused and stood looking, their ears forward, their tails twitching; none approached too close. Only Willow came to them, trotting up to Bucky.

Quietly Charlie dismounted, holding Sage against her. She knelt before the bleached calico lady, and put Sage down.

Willow licked the young tom's face, then turned to look at the clowder cats. And now all the cats came around them and rubbed against Sage and licked his ears and made over him. But all the while, ready to bolt, they watched Charlie and the big buckskin.

Then Willow's mate appeared, the white tom Cotton, racing out of the far woods, his friend Coyote beside him. The white tom and the dark tabby tom strode forward boldly to inspect Sage.

• • •

I T TOOK A while to tell Sage's story. Charlie, sitting on the grass among the cats, told the story alone; Sage and Kit had wandered away. Willow and the two toms sat close to her, listening, the shy clowder cats gathered behind them in a ragged half circle. Like children, Charlie thought, children gathered at story hour, their faces filled with wonder at Sage's ordeal, with amazement as Charlie described the hospital and how Sage had been helped by humans. And, like children, most of the cats believed her but a few did not. These five, their expressions skeptical, turned to look away toward the rock hill where Sage and Kit sat together.

Charlie could see that the two were arguing. She couldn't hear their voices—but with the sudden dropping of ears and lashing of tails, she could clearly read Sage's beseeching, and Kit's short, willful temper, and it was hard to keep her mind on the story. Then Sage reared up as if his patience was at an end, and smacked Kit hard in the face—a businesslike blow that made Charlie catch her breath.

All the cats were watching. Cotton growled, and Willow's surprised intake of breath was followed by her whispered, "Oh, my." And this was the moment of decision. Would Kit stay with him, now that he'd shown some tomcat macho? Was that what she'd been waiting for?

41

THE JOURNEY HOME was silent. Kit rode in Charlie's arms, her face hidden against Charlie's shoulder. She said nothing, she didn't look up at Charlie. She huddled deep in her own thoughts. Above them the sun pushed higher into the clear sky; the chill day grew warm despite the sea wind blowing up the cliff. Charlie didn't know all that had occurred between the two, she knew only that Kit was going home again, and that for Lucinda and Pedric and for all Kit's friends, that was the best news. But she grieved for Kit, and wished Kit would share with her what she was feeling.

RIDING CUDDLED AGAINST Charlie, leaving Sage behind, Kit was both sad and relieved. And was uncertain, too, wondering if her decision had been the right one and yet knowing, deep down, that it was right.

Lucinda had once told her that a person should not let pity shape their decisions, that pity seldom fostered clear thinking. Now, Kit clung to Lucinda's words, assuring herself she'd done what she must do.

She had, sitting with Sage atop the hill of boulders, looking down at Charlie with the clowder gathered around her, and then looking away deep into the woods and then out to the bright, wild sea, tried to think clearly. The trouble with clear thinking was that her feelings kept getting in the way.

She had looked at Sage and then looked away toward the village whose life was so far removed from the ways of the wild. She had looked back at Sage, looked deep into his eyes as he sat waiting for her decision, his patience at an end since he felt well and strong again. His sudden demanding attitude had pleased her, for Sage's sake. But then . . .

She'd thought about when they were small, how happy they had been in each other's company, just the two of them—except that Sage could never understand her dreams and yearnings. She had tried to tell him what she imagined and longed for, but he never seemed to care. But they'd been only kittens, and despite their bitter disagreements they had loved each other.

But now they were grown cats. What they believed had become more deeply a part of them and would shape them all their lives. And she thought that neither of them intended to change, certainly Sage didn't mean to examine what might be right or wrong or what had gone awry.

She thought about when the clowder had gone to hunt rabbits on Hellhag Hill, when she first saw Lucinda and

Pedric picnicking there. Sage and the rest of the clowder had crept away to escape the two humans, fearing and hating them, but she had hidden in the grass listening to the tales Pedric told and she'd been fascinated that humans were as hungry for those stories as she.

Later, Sage had been cross that she'd strayed so near to humans—and he'd said that humans had no right to any of those tales.

And then this morning, sitting with Sage on the mountain of boulders listening as *he* planned their life together, as *he* told *her* how it would be, she knew they were not the same. She knew that she could not do this, that she could not do as he wanted.

She had looked at Sage, whom she had known and loved forever, and wished she could be different. Or that he could. And she knew that wouldn't happen. Sitting close to Sage on the sun-warmed rocks, she had wept for them both.

Maybe her heart was like a bird fleeing among the clouds. And Sage's heart was like the steady robin, at one with the earth and the sheltering woods. She didn't know which was best. She felt ashamed of hurting him, but it was better to hurt him now than to hurt him more later.

Swallowing back her tears, she had told him goodbye . . .

And he had whacked her!

Surprised, she'd raised her paw to hit him back, but then she laughed. His blow freed her. She'd laughed and, despite his rumbling growl, she'd nuzzled him good-bye and she turned and ran, ran back to Charlie, ran away from him feeling free at last, so free, even if she was weeping.

• • •

THE CATS AND humans were gathered at the Damen house for potluck, an impromptu party that Ryan and Clyde said was to celebrate the sale of Charlie's new book, but in truth was in celebration of Kit's return home from the hills. For those humans who knew Kit's story, emotions were high. Max and Dallas, puzzled by the undercurrent of excitement, could only attribute it to the sale of Charlie's book. And Mike and Lindsey were too wrapped up in each other to notice anything out of the ordinary. Only Clyde was skeptical of Kit's resolve.

"I hope she doesn't change her mind, doesn't go through this again." He and Ryan were alone in the kitchen, setting out silverware and napkins.

Ryan set down a stack of plates, turning to look at him. "That's very cheerful. I didn't know I married Scrooge."

Joe sauntered in, leaped to the counter staring at Clyde. "What do you know about how Kit feels? Don't be such a sour face."

Ryan grinned, and winked at Joe. They heard the front door open as guests arrived, and they moved to the living room, where Kit was snuggling down before the fire beside Rock, looking as domestic as if she had never, ever considered running wild. Only the white cat moved away from the growing crowd. Snowball, though she had taken to joining the family since Ryan moved in, headed quickly for the laundry, wanting her own quiet space.

Drinks and beer were passed, and appetizers. Everyone toasted Charlie for signing her second book contract, then the conversation turned once again to the past few weeks, to the fate of Ray Gibbs, whose trial for the murder of Ryder Wolf was scheduled to begin in six weeks.

The night after Gibbs had been taken into custody in San Francisco, Dr. Emerson had called Dallas at the station to say he'd found Nina's dental records, that he'd called John Bern, and they had a match. So that *was* Nina in the Pamillon grave; they did not know yet whether that had been Nina in the tree house with Carson, they were waiting for a match on the DNA.

Lindsey said, "I know the lab's backed up, but what about the two bullets Dr. Bern found in Nina's grave? Do they have anything on that?"

"They do," Dallas said. "Those were .45 slugs." The bullets that had killed Ryder were .32 slugs and the rifling matched the revolver taken off Gibbs in San Francisco.

"But," Dallas told her, "OBI found the gun that killed Carson. Found it this morning, in the woods two miles from the tree house—they spent two weeks tramping the woods with metal detectors. This morning they dug up a .45 Colt with two smudged prints beneath the cylinder." He smiled. "Where Gibbs was careless wiping down the gun."

"Gibbs's prints," Lindsey said sadly, but not surprised.

"Ballistics matched it to the slugs in Chappell," Dallas said. "This will give their DA enough to indict Gibbs for Chappell's murder. With luck, he'll do time for that, as well as for Ryder's death.

"But as for the slugs in Nina's grave, they were so badly corroded it's not likely they'll ever get a match."

Lindsey sipped her drink. "I'll always believe that Gibbs killed Nina. I don't want to think that Ryder did that—I don't like to think Gibbs will never answer for that. But at least," she said, "if he's convicted for Carson's murder and for Ryder's, then he won't go free. I saw him shoot Ryder."

She frowned at Dallas. "I know I'm only one witness. I wish whoever else saw him shoot her, the man who called you from San Jose, would come forward. Why won't he? He was a witness, too! He was responsible enough to call you, so why won't he help us now? What's he afraid of suddenly? Ray's behind bars, Ray can't hurt him. But now he doesn't want to be involved anymore? Doesn't want to make sure the killer goes to prison?"

Across the room, the witness licked a white paw. He wanted very much to see Gibbs go to prison, but there was nothing he could do. He wished there were some way he *could* testify. Clyde and Ryan, and Charlie and Wilma, and the Greenlaws were all preoccupied, they daren't look at him.

Once again Mike toasted Lindsey for her quick, though foolhardy, action in following Ray Gibbs and cornering him. But no one toasted Joe Grey. No one rose to celebrate the tomcat's part in Gibbs's capture.

Those, however, who knew the truth gave Joe sly looks; Charlie winked at him and Ryan gave him a "thumbs-up" that no one else saw and that made the tomcat smile.

And as everyone toasted the newlyweds for the hundredth time, Kit watched Clyde and Ryan with interest.

What was it that made these two, in all the world, so happy and so right for each other? Why were they so perfect together?

And when she looked at Charlie and Max, she was aware of the same inner closeness.

She looked at her own dear Lucinda and Pedric, and then at Joe and Dulcie, and she knew that in all these couples, the same likeness of spirit had drawn them together and held them together, close and secure in their partnership.

But what, exactly, *was* that bond? Love, yes, but what *was* love? Where did it come from and what made it last? She didn't know what to call that mysterious oneness of spirit—she only knew she had not had that with Sage. She loved Sage, but not in the same way as this.

She thought about how Sage had suddenly turned so macho when he was well again and was back on his own ground, and she smiled, hoping that one of those pretty young queens in the clowder was the right one for him, that they would find, together, that same mysterious oneness.

MUCH LATER, when the party had ended and everyone had gone, when Clyde had put out the fire and Ryan turned out the lights, Joe and Rock and Snowball followed the couple up the stairs; soon they were all tucked up in the king-size bed, Ryan and Clyde sipping a nightcap as a fire burned on the hearth, its reflections dancing along the beams above them.

"Here's to Joe Grey," Ryan said, stroking the tomcat. "Gibbs is behind bars, where he belongs—you and Lindsey sure nailed him."

"And here's to Dulcie," Joe said. "If she hadn't alerted

you two, I'd be locked in some stinking cage about now—or smashed flat on the concrete, decorated with tire marks."

Ryan shivered, then laughed. "You're a disgusting tomcat." She picked him up and hugged him, deeply embarrassing him because she was wearing only a thin, low-cut nightie. His embarrassment made her laugh harder. She put him down, watched him curl up between Rock and Snowball. Clyde, finishing his drink, turned out the light and, for this one night, despite their newlywed status, he and Ryan settled down to sleep among the warm, bed-hogging menagerie.

Dozing off, Joe thought, *Sleep well, Dulcie. Sleep well, Kit*, and was glad to have the tortoiseshell settled in once more, hopefully content, again, with her adopted family.

BUT AT THE Greenlaw house Kit wasn't sleeping snuggled down with her humans. She sat wide awake in her tree house, alone in the moonlight, far too energized to sleep. She thought about joy. She thought about all the wonders in the world she hadn't yet seen and smelled and tasted and clawed and leaped over.

Lucinda said that joy was the deep-down power one was born with—that some folks nurtured joy and let it grow, and some folks crippled it. She thought about Sage and prayed for his happiness. And she thought that somewhere out there in the world was the right tomcat for her. Waiting for her?

She thought about that for a long time, wondering.

Then suddenly, filled right up to her ears with exciting thoughts, she raced out of her tree house along the oak branch, did a wild flip onto the windowsill nearly missing it, leaped inside onto the dining room table and off again to the rug, raced three times through the house as fast as a cat can run and landed on the bed, waking Lucinda and Pedric and making them laugh and hug her. And there she curled up between her two housemates. She slept at once, dreaming of so many wonders yet to see that in sleep her dark paws kicked and raced, her fluffy tail twitched, and she let out a little mewl of delight that made Lucinda and Pedric smile—made Lucinda think, as she so often did, *Joy is her nature, and that will never change. That will always be so.*

Author's Note

A Memoir of Thomas Bewick, Written by Himself, is a real book and does not mention speaking cats. It is quoted only in paragraph three of page 204. The "quoted" paragraphs that follow are fiction; these are what I think Bewick might have written if he had met talking cats in his travels.

The title mentioned on page 150, *Folktales of Speaking Cats and a History of Certain Rare Encounters,* is a fictional title and not a book that Bewick ever wrote (as far as anyone knows).

SHIRLEY ROUSSEAU MURPHY

CAT PLAYING CUPID

978-0-06-112398-6

Joe and his friends, Dulcie and Kit, will need to use their powers of feline perception to bring justice to the small town of Molena Point . . . and save Valentine's Day!

CAT DECK THE HALLS

978-0-06-112396-2

A stranger lies dead beneath the village Christmas tree. As they care for the child who may be the shooter's next target, Joe, Dulcie, and Kit realize they're facing their most heartbreaking case yet.

CAT PAY THE DEVIL

978-0-06-057813-8

When Dulcie's human companion, Wilma, disappears, Dulcie and Joe are on the case.

CAT BREAKING FREE

978-0-06-057812-1

When felonious strangers start trapping cats, Joe, Dulcie and Kit know they are the only hope for their imprisoned brothers—and perhaps their whole village.

Visit www.AuthorTracker.com for exclusive information on your favorite HarperCollins authors.

Available wherever books are sold or please call 1-800-331-3761 to order.

SRM1 1009